NATAKA
and the
BACKWARD GOD

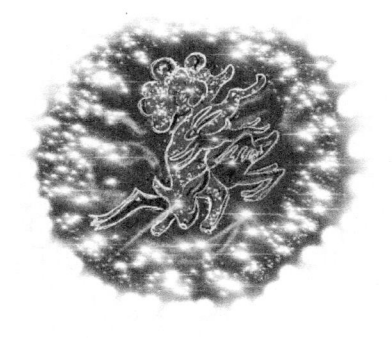

Leo K Daniel

Copyright © 2018 Dani F Kaye / Leo K Daniel
All Rights Reserved

TABLE OF CONTENTS

Note for the Reader	4
Dedication	5
Chapter 1. Sunny Shores	7
Interlude I	28
Chapter 2. The Windowsill Conference	30
Chapter 3. The Toffee Emperor	52
Chapter 4. Rescue Plan #1	64
Chapter 5. Skald's News	72
Chapter 6. Casing The Joint	92
Chapter 7. Rescue Plan #2	102
Interlude II	114
Chapter 8. Cat Therapy and Badger Potion	116
Chapter 9. Fagus	130
Interlude III	150
Chapter 10. Improvisation	152
Chapter 11. Escape	162
Chapter 12. Dance	177
Chapter 13. The Meeting	193
Chapter 14. The Howler Host... Hosti... Whatsit... That.	209
Interlude IV	228
Chapter 15. The Promise	233
Chapter 16. Catch Me If You Can	241
Chapter 17. The Big Question	253
Interlude V	263
Chapter 18. Roger Court – A Monograph	273
Chapter 19. "Am I Really *That* Repulsive?"	286
Chapter 20. The Wingco's Choice	297
Chapter 21. How To Woo A Pathway Tree	319
Chapter 22. The Cupid Missio4n	334
Chapter 23. Explosion	362
Chapter 24. Love And Its Consequences	381
Chapter 25. The Lesson	395
Chapter 26. Roger Makes Some Calls	410
Chapter 27. The Beast	421
Chapter 28. Thresholds	435
Chapter 29. Restoration	450
Chapter 30. And So It Goes	468
Chapter 31. Home at last	482

Epilogue	492
A Note from the Author	512
Appendix 1 – List of Characters	517
Appendix 2 – Alternative names for Howlers	520
Appendix 3 – Seasons and Times	522
Notes & References	523

*

Note for the Reader

*The **end-notes** and **appendices** contained in this book are intended to amuse and inform. Feel free to ignore them if you wish.*

LKD, DK

Dedicated to

My splendid husband, children
and brother
David, Gianna, Simon and John

Without whose encouragement and advice I would
have struggled to complete this tale,

And to

Leto and Chant

Our dearly cherished and mourned feline
companions,
who soothed, schmoozed, challenged and entertained
us, their Pets, for the best part of 2 decades,

Not to mention countless other Wanyama friends
I have loved and lost.

*May this serve as a memorial of
my love and gratitude.*

NATAKA AND THE BACKWARD GOD

A Fantasy

Leo K Daniel

With Contributions from Glose (the Raven) and
Tytus The Baron (the Owl)

Edited and Illustrated by

Dani F Kaye

"Of all the species that inhabit Dunia[i], none is so strange and perilous as the one we call the Howlers. Shun any you may encounter, for they alone are so demented as to despoil and destroy both themselves and all other life-forms, laying wanton waste to the air, soil and water on which all living things depend in their quest for personal gratification."
Tytus the Baron, 'Learning to Fly: A Fledgling's Guide to Survival'

"The darkest places in Hell are reserved for those who, in times of great moral crisis, maintain their neutrality."
Dante Alighieri, 'Inferno, The Divine Comedy'

"Do you see anything? It seems to me I am trying to tell you a dream – make a vain attempt, because no relation of a dream can convey the dream sensation, that commingling of absurdity, surprise, and bewilderment in a tremor of struggling revolt, that notion of being captured by the incredible which is of the very essence of dreams..."
Joseph Conrad, 'Heart of Darkness'

Chapter 1. Sunny Shores

*"What are the roots that clutch, what branches grow
Out of this stony rubbish?"* [ii]

It's like this: she got spotted.

I know, right? Unbelievable as it may sound, Nataka the Protean, an Immortal capable of Changing, Deceiving and Disappearing in a fraction of the time it takes a firefly to wink out its flame, actually allowed herself to get *spotted*. By a *Howler*. Just how careless was *that*?

I mean, ordinarily she would have twigged the approach of that Busybody in plenty of time to Disappear herself and her shelter, which sat in the corner of a bit of nondescript bramble-covered wasteland no passer-by ever noticed. Nowadays not even fly-tippers see it any longer, which is A Good Thing because, like all Immortals, Nataka despises littering but refuses to pick up after anybody else, on principle.

Nataka's always been big on principles. If any Howler were to drop so much as a chocolate wrapper over the rusty gate that punctuates the dishevelled hawthorn and yew hedge ringing her territory, in short order there would be a very bewildered cockroach, its mandibles clogged with chocolate, scuttling around inside one of a pair of still-warm Howler hoof-shields underneath a pile of collapsed Howler body-wrappings. That's how big she is on principles. So it's a good thing that she's ringed the site with a spell that stops most Howlers from noticing it (unless they're *very* nosy as well as observant, or very young and open to the world around them).

So anyway: back to our story.

The Howler Busybody whose interference kicked off the whole *matata* in the first place was a stringy specimen that regularly dragged his overweight, pink-dyed and pretentiously manicured poodle past Nataka's cottage on his daily strolls into the woodland behind her home. He had a long nose with damp flaring nostrils, perfect for poking into other people's affairs, and a scalp that showed pinkly in patches through his sparse, mousy, carefully combed-over top fur. He looked much like a particularly unattractive ferret. He also reeked of various obnoxious, eye-watering artificial stinks of the sort Howlers tend to spread on themselves to disguise their natural body odours. He also had an annoying habit of sucking his buckteeth and snorting when he spoke. And to cap it all, he was rarely silent but poured a non-stop commentary into his portable long-distance communication device[iii] while he dragged his pink dog along behind him. Presumably there was a very patient (or very deaf) fellow-Howler at the receiving end of all his chatter. Seriously, the creature was even more irritating than a dripping tap.

Yes, Nataka realised, she should have had plenty of time to Disappear so that he could have looked straight at her with that damp nose of his no further than a beetle's length from her own, and still failed to spot her. But just this once, probably because she'd been too busy cursing Glose under her breath as she pottered around in front of her home collecting the buds of early dog-violet and stitchwort for her potion (the very first to start unfurling their petals, as they always do at the turn of the seasons from the Roaring Wolf to the Dancing Hare,[iv] when green things start to push out of the ground and look around), her guard had been down.

The best she'd been able to do in the tiny instant after she noticed the Busybody's approach was to take a kind of magical short-cut and hurriedly Transform herself into a scrawny, poverty-stricken old female Howler in grubby, shapeless wrappings and tatty oversized footwear, and her home into a neglected two-up, two-down eyesore hanging off the end of a decaying terrace of three abandoned Howler dwellings they call *council houses* – in other words, the kind of individual and habitat most Howlers around those parts (a hamlet called Chissadove in the Addov'vai Valley, which lies within an easy crow's flight of Hereford and not far from the village of Chissaperchè[v] in the West Country - but don't take my word for it) were used to seeing, and therefore readily forgot.

But not *this* Busybody. *He*'d taken a long, hard look at Nataka with an expression of mixed affront and disgust on his ferrety features, peppered her with a barrage of intrusive personal questions (she'd turned her back on him and stumped off without saying a word), and then spoken to something called the *Social Services* on his mobile phone to report a vagrant and ask why the derelict old biddy wasn't being incarcerated and guarded as she (not to mention *he*, as a law-abiding ex-taxpayer) was entitled to expect.

Half of what he'd said into his mobile phone, in a voice that sounded more and more snide and sniffy as the conversation progressed, only made rudimentary sense to Nataka, who had determinedly refused to stay abreast of the latest doings of these Howlers beyond the absolute minimum she considered necessary to keep herself out of trouble. But as she watched the Busybody chattering into his mobile phone she began to wish that she'd spent a bit more of her time exploring the world of Modern Humans, as the last few scores of generations of Howlers had taken to calling themselves.

After all, over the past forty thousand Seasons or so these weird, semi-bald bipeds had begun popping up in increasing numbers wherever she went, which was disconcerting.[vi] And wherever members of the ugly, noisy species appeared they seemed determined to take over and interfere with everything and everybody they found [vii]. Furthermore - and most worryingly of all - since the last time she'd taken any interest in them, these Howlers had also developed an array of sophisticated tools and techniques to help them mess up everything from one another to their habitat at a genuinely alarming and accelerating rate.

Something was going to have to give soon, and Nataka was beginning to feel that when (not *if*) it did, not only would the Howlers scupper their own chances of survival, but they'd also manage to drag the whole planet and all its other inhabitants down the tubes with them.

And yet, and yet... she knew all too well how easy it was to get tangled up in this mad creature's complicated doings to such an extent that in the end you did something drastic, just to get some peace. Once burnt, twice shy. So for ages she'd held back, and held back, and held back, limiting her personal contacts and interactions to all the other life forms on the species-rich planet, apart from the Howlers.

Until then.

So, on balance, and taking everything else into consideration, perhaps boredom *had* played a part in events, leading her to let herself be caught by the Howlers and thus inevitably plunging back into close proximity with them. But other factors must have been at play too. Perhaps, after countless seasons of avoidance, the time had finally arrived when, like it or not, for better or for worse, Nataka simply had to dive back into the mêlée of Howler society.

Be that as it may, on this occasion there was no way she could simply have Disappeared *after* the Busybody had spotted her, not while he stood there outside her rusty gate, reeking of cheap and disgusting odour-disguisers and with his bulging eyes fixed on her every move while he hectored whoever was at the other end of the phone.

At length he said, "Good, that's more like it! ... I'll wait right here till you turn up, then... And mind you *do* turn up.

Soon, please. I haven't had my ... what? ... No, no; I'd better wait and keep an eye on her. I think she's not really *all there* any more, you know? ... Could easily wander off and disappear if I don't watch her... She's refusing to talk to me... Yes, at all, I tell you ... Yes. .... What? Oh, quite unreliable, I'm sure ... Yes, that's right ... I suppose you could even say..." (He dropped his voice) "... She's a bit what one might call *doo-lally* ... Yes, 'fraid so. ... It'll be a kindness to take her off the street ... Quite. A danger to herself, I should think ... No, no, no; never mind; no need to thank me" (he said this in a voice that suggested the opposite). "Just doing my civic duty..."

(Come to think of it, at any point while this was going on Nataka could just have sent a misty spell-chant into those damp, distended nostrils, one that made the Busybody forget all about her and allowed her to Disappear quietly, leaving him none the wiser... If she'd wanted to. But she hadn't done *that*, either. So she can't really have wanted to, can she? ... Odd, that. And telling.)

So she waited, annoyed and impatient, not attempting to Disappear or Transform herself, but instead maintaining the pretence of being an old, broken-down female Howler outside an old, broken-down Howler lair.

And the Busybody went on standing there on the stone river on the other side of the rusty iron gate, sucking his buckteeth and staring at her. Then he fiddled with his mobile phone and started to tell yet another Howler what he was up to.

And throughout this *palaver* the Busybody's fat pink dog lay at his feet, panting and looking dejected.

Nataka had immediately noticed the animal. You couldn't miss her, really. The ridiculously coiffed, shocking pink whisk of fur twitched on the tip of her close-clipped, docked tail. A pair of patiently suffering gold-brown eyes behind the long, sensitive muzzle locked onto hers, and the dog whimpered.

Then followed a silent conversation between them[viii] while the oblivious Busybody carried on chattering on his phone, his buckteeth clicking every so often.

Nataka: *What's with your Howler? He's starting to annoy me.*

Fat poodle: *I know. He always interferes. I hate him.*

Nataka: *Really?*

Fat poodle: *I know, I know. You're going to tell me I should love him because we're together, aren't you? Dogs are always supposed to love the Howlers they live with, aren't they? ... But I can't help it. I hate him. I feel very guilty about it because my instinct is to love him. But. Just look at what he and his mate did to my tail. Look at what they did to my fur. And they shampoo me. And they put ribbons on me ... I ask you.*

Nataka: *Crikey, bummer. What's your name?*

Fat poodle: *My - my name? ... Oh... oh no; no. You really don't want to know my name. It's horrible, believe me.*

Nataka: *Oh, go on; tell me.*

Fat poodle: *Well, all right... but don't say I didn't warn you. They call me Tarquiana Trichitina Tantamount III (*disgusted whimper*) ...and 'Trixie Snuffles' for short.*

Nataka: *Good grief.*

Fat poodle: *I mean, what kind of a name is that for a self-respecting Nyama [ix]? ... And that isn't all. I can't make puppies any more. It's all their fault. Not that I could keep any of the ones I did make – with another poodle I really didn't like. This Howler and his mate took away all my puppies as soon as the poor little things could walk and eat on their own. They did that over and over again. I don't think it even crossed their minds to ask whether I cared about what they were doing, let alone what the* puppies *wanted. ... I mean, what's the point? To them, I'm just some kind of living toy they can show off and use to make money – you know, that inedible stuff they're so addicted to.*

Nataka: *Howlers. Sheesh. I don't know how one can contemplate the tragedies they concoct for themselves and everybody else without laughing. It's either that or bite 'em.*

Fat poodle: *I take your point. But I'm just not the kind of dog that bites. And, worse still, I can't laugh any more. Not while my back legs don't work properly. It hurts to walk, let alone run. And what good's a dog that can't walk or run?*

Nataka: *What happened? How did you get this way?*

Fat poodle: *It happened some Moons ago at a dog show. The Howler and his mate made me do a double back flip off a table and catch a rubber ring in my mouth ^{x}. I slipped and fell onto my back. I should have landed on my legs. And on the way down I cracked my back on the edge of the table. They had to carry me out of there because I couldn't move. Then I was put through a whole lot of painful interference by another Howler that pretended to fix damaged Wanyama. Between you and me, I reckon they only do that kind of thing as an excuse to hurt you even more. I'm sure they enjoy it. Anyway, that's when I found out I couldn't make puppies any more.*

Actually, I think if I'd cost them less of that money stuff to start with, they'd probably have killed me then and there, you know? But, see, I used to win prizes for them, which is why they've kept me going. Hoping I'll get back to getting them more prizes and money. Now he's saying all I need is exercise and I'll be good enough to 'show' again [xi]*. You know, I've been getting fat from not exercising, which is hardly surprising. So now he drags me out for walks every Suntime. I used to love walking. But now... well, you can imagine. You know, I don't think he or his mate have even noticed that I'm constantly in pain, or if they have, they don't care. They just keep saying I need to get fit again, and snarling at me when I fall over. I mean, surely if they loved me they'd realise I'm in agony, my back legs aren't working properly, and what I really need is a long rest?*

Nataka: *No wonder you hate him.*

The fat poodle panted. Her rosy tongue came out and licked her nose. She struggled to stand up on her four paws. Her back legs trembled with the effort, but she made it. Then she stood swaying and trembling, and stared intently into Nataka's eyes.

Fat poodle: *I really need your help, Your Honour. I know you can help me.*

Nataka: *You do, huh? That's interesting.*

Fat poodle: *I've suspected it for some time. I catch your scent every time we go by, and now I'm certain. My nose never lies. I've got a great nose. It's pretty much the only part of me that still works properly, but it really* **works.**

So I'm right, aren't I? ... I mean, you can *help me; can't you, Your Honour?*

For an instant Nataka's wrinkled old-woman face looked both stern and beautiful. Her eyes glowed golden as a clear spring sky at Sunwake. She studied the bloated, ungainly, pink-dyed wreck tottering before her for a moment.

Nataka: *Why do you call me that, and what makes you think I can help you?*

Fat poodle: *I... I really didn't mean to offend you, Your Honour. But, begging your pardon, you* can *help me; I know it. I can smell it, and it's in your eyes. Ooh! I saw it again just now!*

The poodle's burgeoning excitement and urgency were disarming.

Nataka: *Hm. That's interesting, too.*

Fat poodle: *Seriously, Your Honour, I'm begging you. I need your help to die. I want to die so much. Please help me. I just want to die.*

Nataka: *Are you serious? I mean,* really *serious? Do you realise what you're asking? I...*

Fat poodle: *Oh, oh yes. I know. I've thought about it for ages. It's the only way I can ever escape from them. Oh, please, Your Honour,* please *help me!*

She paused for a moment, panting with the effort to stay on her wobbly paws.

Fat poodle: *Look; I'm sure you'll agree that this isn't a dog's life. I'd really much rather be dead. At least then I'd no longer be in pain. Please kill me. I know you can do it just like that. Please. I've tried to do it myself – you know, run under one of their stinking whizz-things or jump off a high place – but I just don't have the strength. And now he's got me tied or locked up all the time, ever since they caught me crawling out onto a busy stone river. I was hoping to get a stinky whizz-thing to squash me, you know, but I wasn't quick enough.*

15

Nataka: *Er... why* you*? Why not* him, *instead?*

Fat poodle: *What? You mean...*

Nataka: *Why not? I could do it just like* that (she snapped her bony fingers). *Nobody'd be any the wiser. I could stop his heart* now, *and you'd be free. Other Howlers would find him on the stone river and decide his heart had stopped, which would be true. Nice and simple. And then I'd take off that horrible collar you're wearing. You'd be free. You could do whatever you wanted. So why don't you ask me to kill* him, *instead?*

Fat poodle: *Er... but ... but... I don't have the right to ask for ... I mean, yes, I hate him, but I can't* kill *him!*

She shuddered.

Fat poodle: *N... no, I can't. How can I possibly decide whether he deserves to die, let alone choose* when *he dies? Surely nobody has the right to do that! But never mind. That's not a problem, d'you see, because I* can *choose it for myself. My life* is *mine to end whenever I want, isn't it? So... Oh*, please, *Your Honour, can't you just do that for me? Just release me. You know, stop my heart, like you said you could. Only, not his, mine. Please? All I want to do is end this... this... this pain ...this imprisonment ... this misery... I mean – yes, you're right: I know I'm weak and soppy, but I don't care. I'm in agony. I want to end it.*

Nataka's eyes darkened and widened. For some moments she studied the trembling animal before her. When she spoke again her voice was harsh.

Nataka: *But he's* tortured *you, Dog! He's cut bits off you and used you and pushed you around and imprisoned you and taken away your puppies and made you miserable in every way imaginable. Don't you think he deserves it, honestly? I would, if I were you!*

<u>Fat poodle</u>: *Sorry ... I'm so sorry to disappoint you, Your Honour. I'm sure you're right, but I just can't do it. Please forgive me. I don't have what it takes. I'm such a failure... I ... I just* can't...

The fat pink poodle hung her head and wept. Her rear paws collapsed, and her plump bottom thumped back down onto the stone river.

<u>Nataka</u>: *Forgive you? Oh, for Infinity's sake!* Forgive *you? I ...*

Just then, a vomit-with-mustard-coloured specimen of the noisy stinking whizz-things the Howlers call *cars* snorted up and came to a halt outside the rusty gate. Two Howler Do-Gooders got out of it, looked Nataka over and exchanged a brief "whys" and "wherefores" conversation with the Busybody. Then they turned and talked to Nataka, treacling their voices and using words that suggested they didn't believe her capable of logical thought.

In return she invited them to go for a walk up their own body cavities and leave her in peace. But instead of listening they just went "uh-huh; yes, dear" and "hmm-hmm", grabbed her by one arm each and herded her into the back seat of the car. They climbed back into the front and slammed its hard wings shut, trapping them all inside its body. One of the Howlers prodded and turned various knobs and a wheel. The car farted, groaned, and began to shuttle backwards and forwards on the stone river until it was facing back the way it had come.

The fat pink poodle cast a desolate look at the wrinkled figure in the back seat as the car door shut. She whimpered and flopped back down onto the stone river with her head on her forepaws.

The Busybody had stood and sucked his teeth, watching the car's manoeuvres with a smug expression on his face. Now he turned and prepared to resume his delayed walk. He gave a sharp tug to the lead attached to the half-dead dog's collar. It pulled up smartly, dragging Trixie Snuffles For Short's head up with it. Her tongue came out again and she struggled back up onto her paws, whimpering and panting.

Nataka thought of Trixie Snuffles For Short's plea. And she thought of the Busybody's voice, smell and nose. And then she thought of various itching and burning boils, rashes, and things of that sort.

Enough, she thought. And "*'Mammayo,*"[xii] she muttered, shut her eyes and concentrated.

A nondescript little ditty arose from her pursed lips, one that most people wouldn't even notice: a harmless little hum that sounded like bluebottles and wasps jostling around a carcass. She raised one arthritic forefinger and pointed it at the Busybody.

The tune continued for a moment. The two Howlers in the front seat twitched, scratched themselves and dug their fingers into their ears as if to dislodge something. An ugly green mist, with a dense black blot hovering in it like a nucleus, formed around the crooked finger and hung there, pulsating. Then, swift as thought, it slid through the windowpane - and it was done.

The song ended as abruptly as it had begun.

As the smelly, vomit-with-mustard-coloured car completed its turn outside Nataka's rusty gate, she looked back over her shoulder and watched her twin curses separate just before they hit their respective targets. The green mist slipped under the Busybody's wrappings and the pitch-black blot zipped into the poodle's head, directly above her snout and between her eyes.

The Busybody lurched to a halt after just a couple of steps. His face assumed the cross-eyed expression you see on Howlers when a particularly humourless hornet has found its way through their outer wrappings to the wobbly bits underneath. His mobile phone clattered down onto the stone river. His free hand dived under the wrappings and commenced an urgent fumble. It reminded Nataka of an octopus she had seen once that had been engulfed alive by a huge jellyfish. It hadn't gone quietly.

And – mark this: such timing isn't easy – at *precisely* that moment, the fat pink poodle whom the Busybody and his mate had burdened with the name of Tarquiana Trichitina Tantamount III ("Trixie Snuffles" For Short) emitted a funny little sigh, and sunk down onto the stone river like a deflating gasbag. A shudder rippled over the length of her obese pink body, the gentle, gold-brown eyes turned glassy, and she lay still.

"Trixie SNUFFLES!" snapped the Busybody, still scrabbling away at his wobbly bits. He jerked at the lead irritably. When she didn't respond, he bent over to look at her. "Trixie, up! Let's GO! … Trixie? … TRIX - … **NoooOOOOoooOOOO!**"

The Busybody clunked down onto his bony knees beside the deflated pink body, raised his damp muzzle, and howled.

A vindictive smile flitted across Nataka's wrinkled lips and a flash of poisonous yellow light sparkled in the eyes peering through the rear window of the car at the fast-receding *tableau* (but only for an instant; not long enough for either of the two Howlers occupying the front of the car to notice).

Mission Accomplished; she thought. *See how you like **them** apples.*

Nataka turned back to face the front of the snorting vomit-coloured car and began to consider what might happen if any Howler were ever to see her *real* home instead of a trio of abandoned Howler council houses. She concluded that most probably the sight would startle and outrage them so much they wouldn't even accept it was real. Which, of course, always makes it easier for us not to see stuff we're not meant to.

What was *really* there was Toki, Nataka's home. It could assume any appearance she – or it – wanted, but right now it was a cosily crooked witch's cottage of mossy stone and plaster, tucked up against a dark yew hedge at the foot of the forested hill that rose above the nearby village. Toki was the real deal as far as witch's cottages go, complete with deadly nightshade under the window; swallows nesting in the eaves (during the right seasons, of course; just then they hadn't yet returned from their regular journey to warmer climes); sparrows in the mossy thatch and a properly sinister twisted chimney, out of which smoke of various colours spun and pirouetted, turning into sparks or butterflies or dead leaves as it drifted away into the woodland and over the hill.

And that's not all.

Toki was the kind of cottage that could transform into gingerbread and chocolate during Hallowe'en or turn right round on its own axis so that the front door faced the forest when you didn't want to be disturbed by searching winds or if a spell required it - or if you wanted to bewilder unwanted visitors. You could also persuade it to stand up on its sturdy legs (right now they looked like massive oak trunks with splayed roots for toes); very useful whenever the river (which ran a good thousand strides of a running wolf to the south of the cottage) flooded all the way up the valley to the foot of the hill. And if you fancied a change of scene, Toki was quite happy to turn into a tree-house or cave or castle, or even to take you somewhere else entirely (at a slow but steady pace, mind you; it didn't like to be hurried, and generally refused to travel instantaneously from A to B. It was getting set in its ways, was Toki. So if you wanted to get somewhere fast it was much more practical, if a little labour-intensive, to woo a Pathway Tree). Toki was and is, in short, exactly the type of perfect magical home most Howlers don't believe in, which has always made it easy to hide.

Mind you, the Howler young amounted to a different nest of ants entirely. You had to watch out for them. Unlike most adult Howlers, they weren't so wrapped up in their own far-fetched fantasies that they stopped seeing what was really around them. Nataka had seen plenty of Howler young (called *children*) because there was a place they called a *school* (yes, like the fish) not too far from her cottage, where the Howlers sent their offspring to be looked after (and – presumably – taught something as well, as schools had done since Ancient Greek and Arab times), and it had long been obvious to her that on a purely biological level the Howlers made and reared their infants in much the same way as did other mammals.

But from her casual observations of the behaviour of these Howlers over the centuries, Nataka had also concluded that their children were rather different from those of the Wanyama in one respect: they seemed to start off their lives much brighter and more observant than the grown-ups of their species, only to progressively lose most of their intelligence and awareness as they grew older; whereas it was the other way round for the babies of other animals.

Of course there were exceptions. One of the fairly rare times Nataka had actually been close to a fully-grown Howler had been when she spent time discussing with a rather brilliant and funny specimen called Leo why, because of problems to do with their muscles and bones and the ratio between weight and power, he could never expect his own species to fly like birds by simply pasting feathers onto their bodies. If Leo wanted them to get off the ground (and he seemed determined to do this) he would have to think about finding them some additional power from somewhere. She'd enjoyed watching him tinker with the notion of flying machines and different artefacts for amplifying power. Some of his solutions had looked quite logical. Yes, Leo had been rather beguiling, calling her his Muse, painting her portrait[xiii], and generally making a fuss of her. She'd spent a long time with him, right up to the inevitable moment when he went through his final Change and she moved on.

Thinking about Leo, Nataka decided what made him so special was that all his life he had never really stopped being a Child in all the good ways (there are plenty of nasty ways one can be a Child, of course; but Leo didn't seem to have any of those). His mind had been wide open; he'd been full of curiosity and interest; and he hadn't stopped thinking. So he fully deserved to be called a Sap[xiv].

The fact was, she concluded, most Howler adults gave up more and more on thinking as they grew older, and as a natural consequence of their progressive laziness in thinking they tended to take increasingly illogical and bizarre short cuts in their decision-making, with the result that the older they got and the more powerful they became (Howlers tended to gain power as they aged, particularly if they wore funny head coverings and spoke gobbledygook), the more their decisions sucked and the more damage they caused.

Back in the mists of Time it had been this particular Howler paradox that finally decided Nataka to abandon her study of the species and concentrate on more sensible creatures. It was this inverse correlation between maturation and good thinking that rendered Howlers so dangerous and unpredictable, despite notable exceptions to the rule, like Leo. And Nataka hadn't wanted to be around them when it all ended in tears.

Yes. It was much trickier trying to fool young Howlers than fully grown ones. Nataka spent some moments imagining what might happen if she were ever to show herself and her home to a Howler Child. Probably nothing, come to think of it. Another thing children did particularly well, although their parents never understood this, was to hide the truth by telling it. Most Howler parents would dismiss as simple childish imagination or fibs the declaration "Mum, I saw a magic cottage with a real witch in it!"

But she wasn't sure she wanted to test her idea, at least not yet.

And in the meantime, here she was: trapped in a smelly car by two fully matured (and hence dangerously stupid) Howler Do-Gooders, being carted off to what they'd promised her would be a 'safe haven'. They called it a Nursing Home. They appeared determined to make her miserable in the name of Charity.

And all because Glose couldn't keep his noisy beak shut and out of her cooking.

Yes, that tiff she'd had with Glose was largely to blame for this *matata*, Nataka decided. Glose: *could* there be a more self-important, pretentious and infuriating raven than Glose? Certainly she'd never met one. Granted, he was full of entertaining lore and gossip, and could be very amusing (when he wasn't making snide remarks) because he was a passionate reader, which is always useful to have around. But he was also a *bona fide* pain in the neck, constantly pretending to be at the top of the pecking order around Nataka's home, trying to scare and impress the other Wanyama, and of course criticising her as well. What did *he* know about the correct formula for a potion to cure chilblains in badgers, anyway? He'd never made one. Full of scroll learning but not much more, was Glose. She snorted.

Words had become heated; old resentments had been unpacked and slung at one another. And that was not all. More than one spark had flown as well. Nataka snorted again in amusement as she remembered what Glose had looked like, flapping about and squawking, with a particularly well-aimed spark singeing his tail feathers. Pretty!

Yes. All in all, it had been a good argument. She'd forgotten how much she enjoyed them.

"Oh dear, that sniffle doesn't sound very good," said the female Howler Do-Gooder in the passenger seat of the vomit-coloured car, turning her plain, shiny face, patchily dyed hair and watery blue eyes to face the derelict figure in the back seat. "Are you getting a cold, dear? … Would you like a tissue? What's your name, dear?" She dug out a neatly folded, scented paper tissue from her large pretend-leather bag and handed it over the back of her seat to Nataka, who snatched it in her crooked fingers on the principle that you never refuse a freebie. As I said, Nataka was big on principles.

"Ah, you poor dear," said the DG, watching indulgently as Nataka stuffed the tissue into her threadbare sleeve, "living in that nasty old place all on your own - and without any heating either, I expect. Never mind, you're safe now. We'll soon have you nice and cosy with a hot water bottle and a cuppa when we get to your new home!"

"New *home*?" snapped Nataka, deciding to be cantankerous, "Nobody said anything about a *new home* to me. I've a good mind to report you for kidnap. I've already got a home, thank you very much. I'll have that tea and hot water bottle. But no home, thank you. ... And one of my names is Nataka, since you ask."

"That's lovely, dear. Natasha: a lovely name. We haven't had a Natasha in our home for years ... but you really can't go back to that nasty old place, dear. It'll be the death of you... I'm sure that row of houses must be condemned," replied the DG in a honeyed voice that Nataka didn't trust. "And if it isn't condemned, it *should* be. Anyway, let's just take this one step at a time, shall we? ... You can explore the pretty pink bedroom suite we're preparing for you, and then decide whether you would like to stay with us. I'd be surprised if your broken-down old house even had an inside loo!"

"Fat lot you know about Death, kapok-brain," snarled Nataka. "Even less than you know how to *listen*. You sound just like a collector from your nineteenth century. They used to go out to the rest of the world to kidnap other Howlers and bring them back to show off to people who called themselves 'Society' and ponced about in silly hats. You remind me of them, collecting people and stuffing them into your pretty pink bedrooms. Is there a good market hereabouts for showing off kidnapped old folk, then?"

The driver of the car had fleshy jug-ears and a receding ginger hairline. His fat mottled neck rolled over the collar of his shirt. He chuckled at Nataka's words and tapped the steering wheel with one large hand. Ginger hairs grew through the freckles on its back and fingers.

"Good one. Kapok-brain. Kidnapped. Sharp, she is," he said contentedly in a voice that had been pickled in a variety of alcoholic drinks. He shifted a stick and the vomit-coloured car's farts changed pitch. His humorous little boiled-sweet eyes stole a glance at Nataka in the mirror hanging over his head. *"Not all there*, my hat. That old codger can't have been looking. I bet this one's led her other half a gay dance in her time; haven't you, Pet? ... Look at those eyes!"

Nataka's eyes were the brightest green imaginable, full of laughter and spite. Except when they weren't. Sometimes they went dark, the shifting greys and browns of the sea under a snowstorm; at others they turned blue with laughter, purple or silvery with thought or interest... and when she was furious they could swirl so thickly with poisonous, lightning-stitched reds and yellows that even Glose clamped his beak shut and prayed for the volcano to stop erupting. In short, Nataka's eye colours were infinitely variable, charting and echoing her moods and Transformations. But whatever their colour, Nataka's eyes were never dull. The children that saw her always noticed them, whereas most grown-up Howlers tended not to. Nataka decided that maybe the Ginger Driver was more interesting than she'd first assumed.

"Oh, no," giggled the DG, "She's a gentle, sweet old soul, aren't you, Natasha dear? Wouldn't hurt a fly. But she will have her little joke. That's right. It's good to be cheerful."

"Gentle and sweet as ground glass; eh, Pet?" said the driver, winking at Nataka's reflection in the mirror over his head. He chuckled again and flipped a lever. A little light began to flash. Nataka decided that she might like this Howler.

She leaned back in her seat and reflected that, if nothing else, she was getting a pleasant little outing from this *matata*. She had plenty of time to try out the cuppa (whatever *that* was) and hot water bottle before returning to finish off the chilblain potion for Scrumpy the badger,[xv] who suffered hideously on cold nights. In any case, Nataka was satisfied that for now nothing pressed, and she could count on her friends to keep the cottage happy while she nosed around. She would have a bit of fun exploring and finding out more about the Modern Howlers than she had bothered to for a long time. And, she decided, she might even try out the pretty pink bedroom, which sounded hideous.

Fairly soon the stinking whizz-thing was crunching up a short gravelled drive that led to a Modern Monstrosity: a big, long, tastelessly designed white-and-yellow concrete box full of the windows and balconies of rooms and apartments that overlooked the distant river (if you were lucky) and the not-so-distant car park (if you weren't). The box had double swinging front doors and a ramp for wheelchairs and trollies that led to a hall with a reception counter barricaded behind artificial pot plants, through which a small army of harassed nurses and attendants scuttled and muttered. A pervasive smell of over-applied floor polish and detergent couldn't quite mask the general air of aimless dismay and fragmenting memories Nataka immediately detected as her small, shapeless, bow-legged figure entered the front door, hobbling between the humorous ginger driver and the wishy-washy DG.

And this is how Nataka first came to the Prison for Aged Howlers they called the Sunny Shores Nursing Home.

Interlude I

"Wheels have been set in motion, and they have their own pace, to which we are ... condemned." [xvi]

Behold: a patch of waste ground surrounding a row of derelict terraced houses, neglected for decades by the cash-strapped local council. A patch of waste ground floored with moss, ferns and clumps of nettles, and lying adjacent to an ancient forest on a gently sloping hill that descends to a broad river. In one corner, a weed-infested, oxygen-deprived pond of generous proportions, occasionally visited by itinerant frogs, newts and herons (they don't stay long).

A patch nodding with the translucent blades of Honesty and the butterfly-hues of St John's Wort, wild Cowslips and Forget-Me-Not in the Season of Dragonflies and Gnats, and pranked with Primroses, Daffodils and Bluebells under the Sun of the Dancing Hare.

A patch marred by discarded crisp packets and plastic refuse; rusting tins; piles of crumbling building bricks; bent bicycles and broken-backed sofas: all the rejects of Howler fly-tippers and casually littering passers-by.

One Suntime, like that. The next...

A shimmering ripple of Change, there-yet-not-there, noticed only by a lone, pale fallow deer nibbling the herbs, distorts the scene for an instant, passing over the dishevelled scene like an overlay, an intrusion into reality... or, who knows, possibly a reversion to Reality...

And now, in the neglected plot behind the lopsided, creaking gate and overgrown hedge a transformation has occurred the likes of which has not been seen in aeons. Now, here, a Presence is moving and reaching out in response to ... but to what, exactly?

Perhaps a plate on some ancient scales, freighted with century upon century of want and pain, has finally tipped in response to the ultimate feather-light increment that nudged it into dysbalance...

Perhaps a molecule of water vapour, condensed into dew, has *plinked* down onto the glassy surface of a bowl of water so full that only surface tension prevented it from overflowing before, generating ripples that propagated and spread until the fully-charged vessel brimmed over at last...

Or perhaps this is simply a response to the desperate, yearning prayers of one damaged, abused and suicidal little dog.

Who knows?

Be the reason what it may, the dishevelled plot has been transformed beyond recognition, although few mortal eyes can see it.

And the rusting tins, piles of rubble and sagging sofas no longer exist – unless, that is, you happen to be a Howler. In which case the illusion of their existence still presents to the eyes of passers by the familiar, cluttered, neglected site onto which they can conveniently dump their rubbish. If they can still see it, of course... and if they dare.

Chapter 2. *The Windowsill Conference*

"A Chinaman of the T'ang Dynasty – and, by that definition, a philosopher – dreamed he was a butterfly, and from that moment he was never quite sure that he was not a butterfly dreaming it was a Chinese philosopher. Envy him; in his two-fold security."[xvii]

Tarquiana Trichitina Tantamount III (Trixie Snuffles For Short) sat up, feeling a bit dizzy. She was in a wood-panelled room lined with dangling herbs, books and parchments, and containing a number of wooden tables and shelves covered in a clutter of dried mushrooms; cushions; cooking implements; astrolabes and orreries; bits of string; brass retorts and tubes (some full, some empty, many dirty); cobwebs and glassware of all descriptions.

In a huge stone inglenook, the flames of a chattering, popping fire caressed the rounded, smoke-blackened base of a cauldron suspended by three chains from a cast-iron arm that had been fixed to the side of the fireplace. A hinge mechanism enabled the whole contraption to be moved backwards and forwards over the flames by pulling on a chain with a wooden handle that dangled from the arm. Inside the cauldron, a potion bubbled busily, sending purplish and bluish smokes up the chimney and into the room, and misting it up with a comforting glow. To one side of the fireplace lay a well-stacked pile of dried logs, ready to feed the fire.

It took a little while before the poodle realised that all her garish pink, curled and cropped fur had disappeared along with half her body fat, and that she was again as she had once been: lithe, energetic and covered in a thick, soft pelt of curly fur of the palest cream that showed not the slightest trace of the frizzed and fluffed candy-floss parody the Busybody had made of it. Her gentle, chestnut and gold eyes gazed soulfully out at the world from between two floppy, fluffy, magically restored ears. The mutilated tail (which had quite involuntarily begun to wag) was back to its original length. But most wondrous of all was the discovery that she could again stand and walk without pain.

For a little while she stayed perfectly still, half-fearing that if she were to move, she would awaken from what was nothing more than an enchanting dream, and find all her sorrows still plaguing her. But when at length she dared to believe that she was indeed safe, she let down her guard and opened her senses to her surroundings.

The smells in the room enfolded her. A brisk, fresh and astringent mix of scents issuing from the cauldron evoked lemon groves and meadows full of wildflowers, strawberries, camphor and mint. It combined with a delightfully nostalgic reminder of the Season of Bird Flight wafting from a pile of wrinkled leatherjacket apples piled in a large, asymmetrically carved wooden bowl on one of the cluttered tables. The apples had spent the Seasons of the Sleeping Bear and Roaring Wolf wrapped in straw, and now they were doing a great impression of an apple orchard heavy with fruit. There were also the jolly mingled scents of ripe cedar, old books, worn leather, papers, parchments and well-used instruments; and the unique smell of hot resin and wood smoke rising from the logs in the inglenook fireplace wove intriguingly in and out of all the other scents, enhancing and enriching them. And, rising above all, Paa caught those most exciting smells of all to a dog's nose, the signature aromas of the many different Wanyama who regularly visited the room.

The trembling animal lifted her muzzle and breathed deeply and assiduously, finding each scent and wallowing in it, just as Saps luxuriate in a good book or seals in a warm sea-swell. As she did, she felt the tight knot of anxiety and trepidation that had lodged under her breastbone ever since she could remember gradually loosen and dissipate.

A large, sand coloured buck hare with russet-brown eyes was sitting on top of the stack of firewood. He seemed not in the least surprised at the poodle's appearance, but instead reared up on his hind paws, his nose snuffling, and waited for her to notice him. Then he spoke.

"Let's make something clear right away," he said pleasantly, "The Boss doesn't put up with blood sports inside this lair. Nor does the lair, for that matter. So there'll be none of the usual *me predator, you prey* nonsense around here. All right? ... Though to be honest, you look harmless enough.

"... *That's* Glose, by the way." He waved a negligent paw, indicating the opposite corner of the fireplace.

Trixie Snuffles For Short realised that the hare was referring to an enormous raven perching on the back of a rough-hewn wooden chair beside the cauldron. The bird had been so immobile that at first she had taken it for some kind of whimsical decoration. But now it leaned over, extended its neck, cocked its head, and examined the liquid seething in the cauldron with a critical, black and yellow eye.

"*Tsk, tsk, tsk. *Arkh*!* ...She's spoilt it. I *told* her she would;" The raven clicked its shiny beak, not deigning to notice the newcomer. "The colour's all wrong, and the steam ... well. Call that healthy-looking steam? *I* don't."

"Never mind him, then;" said the hare calmly, pulling down and grooming one long velvety ear with his front paws, "he likes to think he's in charge around here; it makes him self-important." He winked one butterscotch-coloured eye. "*And* he's just had a quarrel with the Boss. So he's even more grumpy than usual. My name's M'Kuu[xviii], by the way. What's yours?"

"My…? Er…" gulped the poodle, a bit overwhelmed, "You wouldn't – wouldn't want to know my name, believe me."

M'Kuu stared at her. "Ah," he said at last, "that bad; huh? … All right then; never mind. No doubt the Boss will know how to help you with that. Well, while we wait for her to return from wherever she's gone, you might as well relax and take a nap, and then we'll find you something to eat. You look all in.

"Don't worry, nothing will harm you in here, and it's nice and quiet right now, good for napping. It gets a bit noisy when everyone's around. The others are all out; they'll be drifting in sooner or later, no doubt. I always say, if you're not sure what to do next, sleep."

And with these words the hare lowered himself onto his forepaws, tucked up into a snug ball with his long ears laid down the length of his back, and shut his eyes.

This seemed like sensible advice, so the poodle followed it.

***

Glose couldn't believe his beady black eyes. *There* was the infuriating Immortal, sitting on a ledge of that horrible big lump of perforated rock, the kind of nest that Howlers actually chose to live in, instead of finding a good sturdy tree and building a proper nest of twigs, leaves and feathers. Glose had never completely understood the logic that motivated so many of the Howlers' weird choices, including this one of nesting inside artificially generated mountains of stone. And now (pluck his pinions and call him a turkey) Nataka was actually lying on a ledge of one of those grotesque trap-like monstrosities! What *was* she thinking, curled up like that, wearing her Maine Coon Cat – cum – Snow Leopard Transformation[xix] and blinking peacefully in the warm light of Sunsink[xx], on the edge of an appallingly ugly nest-opening more than the height of a tall elm above the ground? Couldn't she have chosen a less repulsive place to perch? ... *Really*!

It had taken a lot of flying to find her, and the raven was thoroughly disgruntled.

He landed next to her on the ledge (Howlers call it a *windowsill*) of the pink nesting hole into which Nataka had been put (and which was fully as hideous as she had expected). But despite his irritation, the raven was careful to stay out of swiping distance of her paws. You never knew with Nataka. When she was a cat she sometimes forgot herself and tried to hunt you. He preened his pinions for a second or two before going on the attack. Nataka pretended not to have seen him. Glose decided he'd wait her out and maintain a stony silence, determined to force her to speak first. But he hadn't figured with the fact that he wasn't at all good at silence. Ravens seldom are.

"So *there* you are!" he squawked at last, cracking. "Had us all worried when those Howlers came for you, and you didn't even put up a struggle. What were you thinking, riding off in their horrible big smelly noisy whizz-thing like that? Didn't you care that we'd all worry about you? Why didn't you fight back? You could have used some of those nasty sparks you shot at me for no good reason!"

"No good reason?" yawned the cat, stretching out one large paw, extending its claws and contemplating them through slitted eyes that shifted oddly between blue and amber, "You insulted me, you moth-eaten bunch of feathers. Remember? Know your place, Bird, if you don't want me to remind you of it."

Glose shuffled sideways along the sill until he was tucked into the corner of the window, as far away from the Maine Coon cat as he could get without flying, and cocked his shiny black head, eyeing her warily. Nataka in this kind of mood couldn't be trusted at all. "It's not *my* fault," he croaked. "You lose your temper too quickly. If you'd just *listen* instead of arguing, once in a while…"

"Oh yeah. I really want to listen to *you*, I don't think. When did *you* last mix a potion?"

"Well, when did *you* last bother to read a scroll? Culpeper clearly states that henbane …"

"Culpeper, *pshaw!*" snorted the cat. "I know him better than you do. I know all about his ludicrous, bumbling obsession with cramming the whole of Nature, including Howler illnesses, into the completely discredited notion of different *humours,* and relating them to the various planets and constellations he knew so little about.[xxi] A whole load of horse manure, *that* was. But would he be told? … Would he, my furry bum.

"And what's more, I've tested his ideas myself. Repeatedly. And most of them don't work. Besides, he was writing about treating Howlers - *and* getting it wrong, remember - so his ideas are even more wrong for everybody else … *And* - which makes your idea even more stupid -*he* was saying you have to burn henbane and make the sufferer inhale the smoke, whereas *you're* suggesting I cook that villainous poison into my potion and make Scrumpy *drink* it. Just you try doing that! Poor old Scrumpy isn't a Howler; he's a *badger*, in case you hadn't noticed, which makes him more susceptible to poisons than Howlers, just for a start. Drinking that mess would kill him in short order, because henbane that's added to potions is even more toxic than when it's burnt, although even *sniffing* it would do for Scrumpy. So only a smug, opinionated, half-educated featherbrain - "

"*Featherbrain?* … How *dare* - !" shrieked the raven.

"– *Featherbrain* thinks that *consuming* is the same as *inhaling!*" spat Nataka, sitting up sharply. "And what kind of a fool goes around believing that Howlers and other Wanyama are all so similar that you can give them all the same treatments, or that what you find when you fiddle with the anatomy or chemistry of one of them will be the same for the other? ... I'll *tell* you what kind of a fool: a great, black, noisy, horn-brained, rattle-beaked *raven* called *Glose*, that's what kind of a fool!"

"But – but – you're just *biased!*" squawked Glose, hopping up and down and flapping his wings, "You're - "

The fat spotted tail began to lash. "*Are* you going to start this useless fight all over again with an arbitrary, insulting *ad hominem* fallacy[xxii], you mangy bird? Why should I even listen to you? Why don't I just take a short cut to peace and turn you into my *dinner?*" interrupted Nataka with a bloodcurdling hiss.

"Dear, dear! What have we here?" came a peaceable voice from above. A particularly handsome barn owl flapped silently and elegantly down, and landed on the sill on the other side of the huge cat, where he folded his downy, gold-flecked wings and hunkered down on his claws. Glose couldn't help hopping. Tytus the Baron was so silent in flight that his arrivals always startled and unsettled the raven.

It isn't fair, thought Glose resentfully, not for the first time. *No bird should have that kind of advantage, going around like a ghost and appearing out of nowhere without making a sound to announce himself.* He re-settled his ruffled feathers with a disgusted squawk. The Baron blinked at him for a moment, then spoke again.

"Why are you good people still arguing? ... Nataka, I know how worried your raven -"

"I'm not her raven!"

"- *Your* raven was when you were taken away," resumed the owl, ignoring the interruption. "No doubt one of the reasons he's scolding you now is really because he's so relieved to find you safe and sound. And Glose, I'm sure our wise old friend has a perfectly good motive for being here, don't you, my dear?"

While he spoke, in a voice that always reminded listeners of dark chestnut honey trickling out of a comb, the Baron did that disconcerting owl thing of swivelling his head right round to check the pink room behind the window, before turning back again to stare at them both with his huge eyes. "Perhaps, Nataka dear, if you could just explain it all to us we might understand? This *does* seem an unusual – and unpleasant – place for you to perch."

"Thank goodness, a sensible bird at last. Welcome, Tytus," purred Nataka, leaning over to rub her broad muzzle against the luxurious feather ruff fringing the owl's face, and instantly forgetting the argument she'd been having with the raven. "To answer your question, I'm just having a bit of fun really, finding out a bit more about the current batch of Howlers; you know? This strange place is full of old ones sitting around ... unless other Howlers herd them about here and there, make them sit around tables or that box full of noise they call a *telly*, or eat, or go to sleep... Come to think of it, they're more like sheep than anything else, these Howlers."

"That's an interesting idea;" responded the Owl. "There certainly appears to be some strange magic at work that keeps Howlers doing things together, even if those things seem to make them miserable." He paused for thought.

"Why, for example, do they *all* have to get into those stinking, screaming whizz-things of theirs at the same time every Sunclimb and go off in the same directions on their stone rivers, getting all tangled up and making hideous noises? ... It's clear that they hate it; the stench and row they make leave me in no doubt about that. And then, what do they *do* all Suntime, grubbing around with their dead sticks and leaves in those odd huge stone nests, instead of sleeping or hunting or playing in the light, like all the other self-respecting Suntime-creatures?"

"Indeed. And - that old question again - why do they have to be so loud all the time?" agreed Nataka. "They just don't seem comfortable with silence. Everything they do has to be noisy. All the stuff they make and move around in roars and stinks, like those enormous hollow birds they use to get into the air, and those floating stones they get into to cross water. The only other Wanyama I met that were just as noisy as Howlers were baboons. But it's been a long time since I lived where they do."

"Ba-boons?" asked Glose, who had been following the conversation with such interest that he had forgotten to sulk, "I shall have to check my scrolls. What are these *ba-boons* you speak of?"

"Well, they're just like hairy Howlers, but with dogs' snouts, as I recall," answered Nataka. "They're full of screeching and restlessness like the Howlers, always running around in packs, squabbling and scrabbling over anything they find. But I think that even they must be a good deal more intelligent than Howlers. They've had the good sense to hang on to their tails and most of their fur, for a start."

"Yes; I've thought quite frequently and deeply upon such questions about the Howlers: what they are, why they exist – you know, what they're *good for*... but I've not really been able to work it out;" observed the Baron. "They have some amazing skills. I'm second to none in revering many of their writings, particularly the ancient ones. Ahh, the Sap Classics, wonderful! ... But then they also do totally illogical and odd things, like scraping off all their feathers – or is it fur? - And going around looking worse than skinned mice. I've actually seen them do that, believe it or not. I can't understand why they insist on keeping so little natural cover on their bodies. And *then* they have to find ways to protect themselves from the cold and wet by winding bits of wool or fibre around themselves - like the ones *you* wear when you Transform yourself to look like one of them, Nataka. I mean, how can a whole species be so brilliant in some respects and so idiotic in others? It's all very puzzling."

"Those bits of weaving are necessary, Tytus; Howlers really are mostly hairless, you know. They don't *usually* scrape themselves over their whole bodies. But for some reason they just don't have much fur," said Nataka. "I noticed that they started to lose it quite recently; I'd say – oh - some thirty or so million Moons ago[xxiii] ... and ever since then they've become progressively less and less furry. Odd, that. Just like this business of not having tails... although of course there are some other animals, mainly apes, that have given theirs up as well. I really can't understand why. Fashion, maybe? In any case, without fur one can get unbearably cold. That's why, whenever I Transform into a Howler, I make sure to add wrappings like theirs as well, just to keep warm."

"That's *very* interesting," answered the owl. "And I believe you must be right: perhaps Howlers *are* more like sheep than anything else, all going along with what everybody else is doing, rather than trying to think and act for themselves. I'd give a good few feathers to work out why. At any rate, we can be sure that they're not as clever as sheep. At least sheep stay out in the fields and fresh air during Suntime; *they* don't go dashing around in those stinking whizz-things, bashing into one another and killing anybody who can't get away quickly enough. I've lost far too many members of my own family on those stone rivers, eaten by the whizz-things." He half closed his eyes and clicked his beak sadly.

"Yes, there's definitely a lot of puzzling behaviour there;" replied the cat. She groomed her back for a moment before speaking again. "A lot to learn and work out.

"So anyway, the opportunity suddenly came up for me to get closer to these Howlers - quite without intending to, of course. And – well – I think it would be a pity not to stay a while, study them and – you know – play with them a bit. I really should try to understand them better, I think. Forewarned is forearmed. It's clear I've neglected them for too long. And the flock of Howlers in *this* lair doesn't seem to have anything more interesting to do with its time, so it might all just as well serve one useful purpose and entertain me for a bit while I study the species. As I say, I've begun to suspect it was a mistake to avoid them for so long.

"But honestly, you'd have done the same. The things they did to most of the few genuinely good Saps I made friends with in the past put me off them so thoroughly that I've steered clear of them for a long time. But even so, I do think now that I may have made the wrong decision."

"Things they did? … What things?" asked Glose.

"Oh, horrible stuff; practically anything nasty you can imagine. Cut them into pieces; impale them on trees; burn them; drown them; cut out their tongues and hearts; tear open their stomachs and pull out all their tubing; rip off their hides… you know, just generally torture one another. Lots of Howlers enjoy doing that to anybody who disagrees with them about the really *un*important questions in life, such as what they think about the movements of the sun and planets, or whether there is some kind of god and, if so, what its name is… as if such nonsense could possibly make any difference to what's *really* going on," she snorted.

"Goodness me, are you saying Howlers really did that kind of thing to one another?" responded the raven.

"They still do, believe me;" replied the cat. "All the time."

"But … do they eat the Howlers they kill, at least?" asked the owl, "Could it be some kind of dinner ritual or training to hunt, all this torture?"

"No. They don't eat each other after all that; in fact, with very few exceptions, most Howlers seem to think that eating one another is just about the very worst thing you could possibly do. They just seem to enjoy the actual hurting and killing. It beats me; always has.

"For instance, there was this one poor old man. He had to lie about some scientific discoveries he had worked out very carefully – very interesting information concerning the movements of the earth and the Sun, it was - to the people in charge of one of their nest colonies – you know, what they call *cities* – just to avoid being burnt alive for something they called *heresy*. His name was Gali - Something … hang on; it'll come back to me ... That's it. Galileo. Odd name. So anyway, you'll understand why I've steered clear of the species for such a long time," responded Nataka. "That kind of behaviour puts you off your fodder.

"And I remember another one – a true Sap, that – who lived even longer ago. He was good to be around because he gave you fish and he never shouted at you, and sensible Howlers – their kittens, you know – loved him. He always had time to play with them, too. Now, *he* told people that they should be kind to one another and treat everybody how they wanted to be treated themselves. Good sense, right? … Well, maybe not for what the Howlers call *profit* or *business*, I suppose; but then *he* wasn't interested in profit or business. He just wanted everybody to be peaceful. Well, they pinned him to a couple of crossed tree trunks for that, and let him die. Really slowly.

"Oh - And then – get this – *then,* for thousands and thousands of Moons since that happened, other Howlers have been calling themselves his followers, putting little images of the tree he was tortured on around their necks (idiotic, right?), and going around trying to make other Howlers think the same way they do … Except that, for Moons and Moons, they *and* the other Howlers who disagree with them have still gone on torturing and killing one another and anybody else they could find who disagreed with *their* ideas.

"I mean; imagine: Howlers actually go looking for other Howlers they can hurt for disagreeing with their ideas about the best ways of loving one another. And still they all shout that it's about Love. And nobody's spotted that this whole nonsense consists of an insane contradiction between their beliefs and their actions, quite illogical and hypocritical in every way. Bewildering, I call it."

She passed a huge paw over one ear.

"That's vile," said the owl.

"Yes; you can say that again," said Nataka, "No other animal I met before the Howlers came along – and that includes the dinosaurs, who had some weird habits too – has ever done that kind of thing. So why the Howlers?

"Then there was another old man – now what was his name? … Ah, yes: Socrates. He was a real Sap too; used his noddle, he did. He lived ages ago, by Howler standards, in a part of the world that they now call the *Cradle of Democracy,* whatever that's supposed to mean. Most

Howlers wouldn't recognise real Democracy if it got up and slapped them in the eye with a dead bullfrog. I expect you know a lot more about it than most other people, Tytus, because you're keen on the Sap Classics.

"So do I!" squawked the raven, "I've read my scrolls!"

"Yes, Glose, I'm sure you do. You're a well-read bird. Shut up. So anyway; he - Socrates, that is - liked to teach people by means of argument and discussion – you know, testing them with questions that showed them how to spot when they were talking nonsense. Very useful for Howlers to learn, I reckon. They talk plenty of nonsense, as a rule. So anyway, the leaders in his particular colony of Howler nests decided that he was corrupting their fledglings by teaching them to think critically, so they made him drink a poison called hemlock."

Nataka stopped again, drew a deep breath, stretched, and added in a matter-of-fact voice, "He also died horribly. Of course." She turned to Glose and added mischievously, "You sure you don't want me to put some of that stuff into Scrumpy's potion as well?"

The two birds were silent. Nataka had given them a lot to think about, and none of their thoughts was pleasant.

After a few moments she added, "But things seem to be a bit less ... *violent* ... in this particular nest of Howlers, so I think I'll have another look at them. Maybe they've become less idiotic over time; who knows? It's worth checking out. ... Besides, other bossy Howlers feed you in here.
Although the fodder is mostly disgusting it's still fodder, and it's free, what's more. And their tea is quite nice. So are the things they call crumpets. Hmm, yes; I like crumpets." She passed her rosy tongue over her muzzle. "Anyway, I never refuse a freebie, on principle. And," she concluded, lacing her voice with just the slightest touch of malice, "they don't

argue with you all the time. I'm sick of arguing with my inferiors." She shot a sharp golden look at the raven.

Glose squawked again. "Ah, not that again! ... Remember *why* we argued, Nataka," he complained, "I was just trying to help you!"

"Well, you didn't help, did you? ... Anyway, subject closed;" said Nataka, "I'm bored with it, and there's other mice to catch." Another thing that happened to Nataka when she was a cat was that, cat-like, she could very quickly and unexpectedly lose interest in a topic or issue. This was a mixed blessing.

"I've also been taking this opportunity to practise a new trick;" she said. "I decided that I simply must get it right because I don't want another annoying incident like the one with that Busybody today... Watch me closely, both of you, and tell me what you see."

"A sheep," said the Baron, and "A heron," said Glose at the same time. Then: "It's definitely a sheep!" and "What, are you blind? That's a heron; nothing like a sheep!" the two birds again exclaimed together, before stuttering into silence.

"You're both; aren't you?" ventured Glose after a few moments, "It's the only logical explanation. How d'you do that?"

"Good, isn't it;" answered Nataka.

"Well, I never;" said the Baron. "That's astonishing. How can you be two animals at the same time, Nataka?"

"I just have to work out what you each have in your head, so are more likely to see... and then I make sure that you see it;" answered Nataka. "You were still thinking about sheep, Tytus; and I caught a picture inside Glose of a heron he saw on the river today... And there you are. And now that you both perceive me as you do, it's easy to keep feeding and strengthening your first images so that you can see nothing else."

"Playing with our minds now, are you?" said Glose, wondering whether he should feel offended.

"Ha! You silly bird, I never stop playing with *your* mind," laughed the heron/sheep.

"Brilliant; quite brilliant... But can you please become something else now?" said the Baron, "the sight of a sheep on this cliff-edge is unsettling. I keep expecting you to slip and fall."

"Yes... and what if a Howler were to come into your ugly nest space (*Arkh*! So ugly! It looks like a trap to me) and see us here - an owl, a raven and a – a – herony-sheepy thing? ... What then?" fretted Glose.

"Oh, they wouldn't see us at all," said the heron/sheep, "I Disappeared us as soon as you arrived, or course. It's easy when Howlers don't expect to see you. Relax." But to the relief of both her companions she turned back into a cat as she spoke, and settled back down onto her haunches, tucking her tail neatly around her paws. "Well, this is nice," she remarked, and set to purring a rumbling, soporific song that encapsulated her memory of all the best Sunsinks and - sleeps she had seen over the seasons. The birds fell into a reverie as they listened.

"Well, I'd better get back to Toki before I nod off," the raven shook himself after a little while. Time seemed to have slipped away without a trace as they succumbed to Nataka's song and contemplated the light of Sunsink, which had a pleasing way of glinting off the distant river. He shuffled his wings, preparing to fly away. "So anyway,

Nataka, when are you coming home? Everybody in our nest's worried; and as for Toki, it's been thoroughly unsettled by all this *matata* and keeps shifting from foot to foot, rattling the china and furniture…

"And to cap it all, there's a daft new arrival in front of the fire – a fluffy dog that looks as if she's only got half a brain. She just stares and sniffs and stutters. Pluck my pinions, what's *she* doing in our cottage? … You wouldn't have anything to do with that, would you?"

"Toki'll settle down;" said Nataka, twitching her whiskers. "It knows I can look after myself. And that dog is to be treated with care and respect, mind. She's been traumatised for a long time. Besides, I have a feeling she's special. I'm going to need her. M'Kuu will know what to do for her."

"I can't see what's so special about her. Why in all that's feathered and furry would you need *her*, anyway?" grouched Glose.

"Because she asked me to kill her," replied Nataka, and a curious gleam lit her eyes for an instant. Then, before the raven or owl could comment on this puzzling assertion, she hurried on.

"As for the others, just use your common sense to keep them calm, all right? That shouldn't be beyond even your limited skills." She softened the insult by narrowing her eyes in a cat smile.

"So anyway, tell everybody I'll be back in good time to deal with anything that needs doing – in fact I'll probably pop in during Startime, as soon as I've explored this place a bit more;" she added. "That chilblain potion has a while to brew yet, and I'm not going to abandon it; am I? … And despite your annoying ideas you can help with that. You know the drill: don't let it boil over, but don't let it go cold either. And – yes - it needs another dozen or so dog-violet and stitchwort heads adding to it; that stupid Busybody made me drop the ones I was gathering. Their buds have to be barely open. But you'd better not ask Axl to help with gathering; he always eats what he picks." Axl was an almost-white fallow deer. He roamed Nataka's grounds, nibbling the sweet grasses and herbs.

Nataka paused for a moment, thinking.

"Dog violets and Stitchwort; yes," she said, "and it needs more fresh Liverwort – say, a handful - er - two beaks' worth - of each. There's a good batch of it growing in the damp spot underneath the hedge. Mind that you add it immediately after picking it: the fresher, the better; all right? ... And don't even *think* about arguing or substituting henbane, or fiddling with the recipe in any other way, again. Understood? I'll know if you have, and make you drink it; mark my words!"

The big black bird ruffled his wings but held his peace.

Nataka licked one forepaw for a moment, ruminating. "I think that's all; is it? Hang on: Dog Violets; Stitchwort; Liverwort ... Yes. So, if somebody could keep the fire burning nice and steadily and make sure the potion doesn't boil over until I can get back and sing over it, that'll be fine."

"Dog Violet and Stitchwort buds; Liverwort instead of Henbane; tend the fire... work, work, work;" cawed Glose sulkily. Then he perked up as a thought struck him. "I know; I'll get Pex to see to feeding the fire. He knows all the beavers hereabouts; they can help him with the timber."

Alopex, better known as Pex, was a fox whose brush Nataka had mended a couple of Seasons of the Sleeping Bear before, after a pack of overexcited hounds out on a so-called legal 'non-hunt' with their horse-borne Howlers had accidentally-on-purpose found his scent and done their level best to murder him. Despite all his tricks and dodges they'd got too close for comfort; in fact he'd only just escaped with his tail half torn off his rear-end by diving into a tributary of the great river and skulking around a beaver dam at a spot where the dogs and horses couldn't face the speed and depth of the water. Wurfl the beaver and his wife had rushed to the rescue, helping the struggling fox to keep his muzzle above water. And after the Howlers and hounds had left, they'd also helped him to scramble up the steep bank and accompanied him to Nataka's cottage.

Pex's experience was yet another example of the kind of Howler behaviour all Wanyama struggle to understand. Why kill anything, regardless of what it is, if you aren't in any danger from it, and don't intend to eat it? It just doesn't make any sense. The only justification for killing is survival, after all. But Howlers just don't seem capable of grasping that simple principle. Maybe Howlers really *are* crazy.

Anyway, Nataka had done a fine job on Pex, using a mixture of pain-killing and binding spells, spider thread and old cobwebs donated by Dora the huge and handsome Orb Web spider (her correct name was *Aryadnodondra;* another name that had a long and distinguished history, its roots going all the way back to the Ancient Greeks), and a soft poultice of pounded goose-grass. And now his brush was as good as it had ever been. But it had been touch-and-go there for a while whether it would come off, and no self-respecting fox can bear to lose his brush. Since then, Pex and his demure mate Ala had been eager to serve Nataka and Dora in any way they could, and they regularly brought their latest litter of cubs to visit the cottage. They also had a very affectionate and mutually supportive relationship with the beavers.

"Oh, there should be plenty of firewood, enough to last for some Suns," said Nataka, "but if Pex and Wurfl feel like bringing in more, just let them stack it outside, under Toki's eaves, to dry out."

Just before launching, Glose added "*Arkh*! I almost forgot. Dora wants to know whether she should put a web across the door."

Dora lives in the eaves of Nataka's cottage, and her orb webs are a very effective deterrent against Howlers, most of whom seem to be terrified of spiders, for some strange reason.

"Good idea," said Nataka; "Tell her to make it nice and big, thanks. Well; get home safe now, Bird. And don't forget the herbs."

The raven croaked a farewell, flapped off the sill, wheeled and disappeared around the corner of the Modern Monstrosity, heading towards Sunwake.

"He's a good bird, all in all;" mused the cat, watching him go. "Annoying but useful. Particularly for arguments."

There was a sudden clatter at the foot of the Modern Monstrosity below them. Nataka sat up and peered down in time to catch sight of a ragged, scrawny grey tomcat with a tattered ear, who had evidently just toppled a bin outside one of the ground-floor garden flats. He was slinking towards one of the hedges that formed neat little boundaries between the tiny lawns belonging to the flats.

"Oy! ... Noisy!" she called down, "What's your name, then?"

"'Oo's askin'?" replied the cat suspiciously, stopping dead in his tracks and peering up over his shoulder at Nataka, "An' what's it to yeh, anyways?"

"I'll give you my name if you'll give me yours," she said, rising to her full height. The alley cat's eyes widened.

"Nah then, 'old 'ard;" he meowed nervously; "No need to take on, mush ... just bein' careful..." as he spoke he edged away again, belly to the ground.

"All right, then; I'm Nataka," replied the Maine Coon cat, "You?"

"Name's Rav'n," the cat paused again.

"D'you come here often, then, Rav'n?"

"Wot's it to yeh if I does?" replied the grey cat, his eyes narrowing; "I s'pose a free cat can go where 'e pleases, then?"

"Yeah, I suppose so. Just being neighbourly, keep your fur on. Well, Rav'n, I expect I'll spot you around the bins sometime," said Nataka.

"Yeh; I s'pose so," the cat replied, "not that there's much good in 'em 'ere; grub's not exactly lah-di-dah. But yeh can try..." And with that, the tattered animal slipped away and disappeared under the hedge.

The big cat chuckled. "Some interesting characters around here;" she commented to the owl.

There was no reply. Tytus the Baron had fallen under the combined spells of Nataka's song and the lengthening light in a sky dotted with impossibly perfect pink little puffball clouds. He was fast asleep with his beak tucked into his soft, speckled bib. Nataka looked at him approvingly. Then she stretched out to her full length on the broad sill and shut her own eyes. Sleep was always good, in her opinion. In this she and M'Kuu the hare were of one mind. And with a warm sill under you and a snoozing owl beside you under such a golden Sunsink at the Turn of the Seasons, it was positively luxurious too.

Chapter 3. The Toffee Emperor

"All your life you live so close to the truth, it becomes a permanent blur in the corner of your eye..." xxiv

The sun had gone down, although a streak of pink still lingered in the sky. The brightest stars were putting in an appearance and very bright because the Moon, which was nearly full, had not yet risen. Nataka had passed a very pleasant Sunsink napping on the windowsill, listening to the pre-Sunsleep chorus (a single song-thrush had won it against stiff competition from a host of pigeons, a couple of blackbirds and one vociferous robin), and enjoying the distinctive aroma of approaching Wolflight. Then, Tytus had opened his great eyes and preened his pinions briefly before bidding her goodbye and sweeping away to hunt as silently as he had arrived.

Well, thought Nataka, contemplating Tytus's retreating figure, *time to get moving myself, I suppose.*

Transformed into a Vervet monkey, one of her favourite shapes, she checked out the water room in her ugly pink suite. The artificial waterfall was particularly interesting, and she played with it for a long while, turning the handles with all four limbs and experimenting with different water temperatures while dangling from the mechanism that spat out the water.

Then, turning back into an old Howler female, she made her way downstairs to the door of a chamber full of old Howlers (called a *lounge*), and peered in before entering. She was much cleaner than she had been in the camouflage she had adopted during that *matata* with the Busybody. On emerging from the water room she had found some fresh Howler clothes on her bed, left by some DG, no doubt (of her rags and tatters there was no sign; presumably they had been carried off for burning). The clothes were cosy, if a bit large: underwear; loose brown trousers that were too long in the legs so she rolled them up; a soft shirt, a long green sweater; slippers for her feet. *Good*, she thought. *Now I look just like all the other shapeless aged Howler around here. Nobody can possibly see what I really am, unless I get careless.*

All the old Howlers were sitting around in the large gathering space, doing things like playing with wool, dozing, or watching the noisy box in the corner called a *telly* while they waited for their last meal before going to their individual nest spaces to sleep.

As she watched the Howlers in the room pottering around, so many of them looking and smelling lost and bewildered, Nataka wondered whether it ever crossed the minds of any of them to groom one another as monkeys and apes did. Grooming was a great way to calm everybody down, and she was sure it would also help to get rid of the sour odour of aimless, muddled anxiety that filled the place.

One little old Howler in particular struck Nataka as pungent with emotion. She was sitting in a deep armchair in one corner, well away from everybody else, and she was rocking backwards and forwards with her arms crossed over her chest. A basket of wool containing an unfinished *something* on a pair of long needles lay neglected on the floor next to her feet. Nataka recognised her smell right away: the old Howler was mourning for something precious she had lost. Something no, some*one* – she had loved was no longer alive. She was grieving because she was thinking that he (it was definitely a *he*) had disappeared completely, and she couldn't bear that thought.

Ah, well; there was nothing Nataka could do about that. Some things, like Death, she really couldn't mend once they had occurred. It was a strange thing, this Death. It seemed to affect every species in this particular dimension, and all Nataka could do about it was watch, feel irked and harassed by the waves of unhappiness that washed over her from those who suffered its consequences – emotions that set her teeth on edge – and wish she could make people understand that it really only consisted of a series of Changes, even if some of the Changes were so sudden and extreme that for a while the individuals who experienced them struggled to cope.

The abrupt Change from so-called Life to Non-Life was arguably the most challenging. All the life forms subject to it perceived it as a complete ending, because it was so extreme. Other Changes were just as irreversible, of course, but they were often so gradual and subtle that nothing appeared to be happening even as they were actually occurring, like the growth of mountains and the shifting of the ocean beds … or the trenching of wrinkles in faces and bodies as they aged.

But in that case, she thought, *in that case perhaps, if this little old Howler could be made to understand that there never really **is** any ending to anything, it might calm her down?*

In any case, if nothing more, it would be an interesting exercise to see if a typical example of these unexceptional Howlers was capable of listening and thinking at all sensibly. Yes. It was worth a try.

Nataka strolled over to the old Howler woman and squatted down at her feet, next to the basket. Luckily nobody in the room seemed to register that she was really remarkably agile and supple for such a wreck of a Howler.

"Instead, of course, things go on," she observed, answering the most recent thought in the old woman's head. She extended a crooked finger and stirred the balls of wool in the basket. "Things go on, even after what you – er – *we* – call

Death. Nothing ever just stops and disappears completely. Stands to reason."

The aged Howler jumped, stopped rocking and turned her bony face, straggly grey hair and puffy eyes to stare at the oddly bright-eyed, wrinkled little figure that had seemingly popped up from nowhere and was now squatting next to her chair, playing with her wool in such a peculiar way – quite like a cat, in fact.

"What did you say?" she asked in a voice that had gone thready from too much crying.

"What has been Life and meant Everything to one small person or animal during the short period of time they spend in the single tiny dimension of what they can see - in other words, the thing they believe *is* Everything, even though it isn't, d'you see? - Really; vertebrate brains are so limited..." said Nataka, "Well, those Changed Lives just become Something Else in a different, greater or much shorter period of Time than the one we experience here. Right? ... And of course the Change is also to another dimension of Everything, a dimension you can't see here. And so it goes."

Nataka paused. Had she covered everything? ... Yes. Good. That made sense. That was it in a nutshell, as Brid the Squirrel would say. She resisted the temptation to pat a few balls of wool around (she was still a bit hung-over from her Maine Coon cat transformation), rocked back onto her heels and fixed her bright green eyes on the face of the old woman.

But her nose told her that instead of either disappearing or turning into relief or happiness, the sad old female's anxiety had merely changed into another kind of anxiety. This was strange; not the reaction Nataka had expected at all.

"My dear, are you feeling all right?" The old woman asked, her voice wavering. "You do talk funny ... are you quite well, dear?"

"Hmm." It was clear to Nataka that the anxious little woman had no clue. Perhaps she was like some blackbirds of Nataka's acquaintance, who simply needed something to fret about all the time. Here she was, now: worrying about Nataka's health instead of listening. Something about this old Howler reminded her of Glose: too wrapped up in one narrow way of seeing things to be open to alternative possibilities. But she wasn't going to give up on her experiment that quickly.

She rose to her feet and grabbed a nearby chair, pulled it close to the old woman and sat down on it.

"No. You don't understand," she said, leaning forward. "Listen. Nothing's ever destroyed or created. It's all just Transformations, nothing else."

She saw the look of bewilderment in the old woman's eyes and barely controlled the instinct to shout. Really! Didn't these people *learn* anything when they went to those schools of theirs? This was basic science, and an idea that had been widely available to Howlers since the time of Lavoisier![xxv] What could possibly be more simple or logical? ... *But*, she thought in exasperation, *shouting wouldn't help, anyway. It'd just freeze the few brain cells still functioning in that grief-addled old cranium.*

So instead Nataka drew in a deep breath and expelled it slowly. "Let me think for a minute," she ordered and sank back on her chair. Luckily the little old woman wasn't very observant, otherwise the sight of those wide, sharp eyes turning into two balls of silver would have terrified her.

After a few minutes' cogitation Nataka stirred, cleared her throat and tried again.

"Got it! ... Right. Now pay attention. See that doorway?" she asked her bemused companion, pointing to the door behind her, which led to the hallway of the prison for aged Howlers. "Yes? ... There it is, then. We agree it's there, because we can both *see* it: I can see it. You can see it. So you accept that it exists; don't you?" She paused until the little old woman nodded her head hesitantly, looking a bit scared.

"Good. *Now*, pretend that that very doorway is the end of Everything as you know it. ... Got that? ... And now, see this room? In that case, if we pretend that, you know, outside that doorway Everything you know disappears, then this room is all you can know or believe in, right? Because in that case, you've never left this room, so you've never seen what's outside it. Which is why you believe that this room is all there is. Agreed?

"So *in your heart*, no matter what anybody tells you about it, you just can't truly believe that there's anything else outside this room. Right? ... In fact, as far as you're concerned, this room is Life. And - hold on, stay with me, we're nearly there - for you this room, which is Life, is also Everything. Yes? Because that's all you know, right here and now. For you, Life *is* Everything. Yes? ... Good.

"Well, living creatures step through doorways like that - from the rooms they know into new rooms they don't know - all the time. That's what *you* call Death. But in actual fact, as I said, it's all really only Change, that's all."

Sometimes Nataka could see the creatures there after they Changed, and even follow them into their new situations for a while, particularly when she was travelling through a Pathway Tree[xxvi]. But she always returned because *she* didn't have the power to step permanently through any doorway. Something always held her back from achieving that final Change herself.

"So you see," she went on, "this is what living things fear: this stepping through a doorway and out of a room they can see - and know - into another room they can't yet see, and which they don't yet know. Right? ... So, naturally, they get to thinking that leaving the room they know means the End of Everything." She paused to let this insight sink in, then continued.

"But, you see, it isn't. It *isn't* the End of Everything. It's just a Change, like I said. That Change may involve something large breaking up into smaller bits, or small bits joining up to become something larger and different ... but it never involves a Total Disappearance. In other words, it's just normal.

"And the best thing about it is, you don't need to believe it, you only need to have a good brain to understand it, because it's logical. No matter what the Change may be, there is always still something left, and *at the same time* something new is always produced. Things go on."

A thought struck her, and she added, "Like you, for instance."

"*Me?*" squeaked the little old Howler, jumping a little.

"Yes; you. Everything that is now part of you was once part of a star before it exploded. So if that star hadn't exploded, you would never have come into existence. Exciting, isn't it?"

In many ways Nataka envied creatures that could die. It really wasn't fair that *she* couldn't step through the same

Changes as they did, but instead had to stick to this single Dimension all the time.

"Anyway, you see, it makes sense;" she continued, warming to her theme. "If you think about it, the reason you're so afraid of these Changes is that you have no proper idea of what's really going on, and no wonder. Ignorance is always frightening. But now you *know,* because I've explained it to you. So there's no need for you to be afraid or sad any more. Is there?"

"*Ohh...* I see; I understand now..." husked the little old Howler after a few minutes of silence, during which she had sat with knitted brows, twisting her hands together and peering at Nataka. She tried to smile. "You're trying to cheer me up, aren't you? ... that's very sweet of you, dear. But ... oh dear ... I'll just have to get on with it, I suppose ..." her lips trembled. She leaned over and patted Nataka's wrinkled little hand distractedly with her bony fingers. "Some things just have to be endured ... but oh, I do miss him so much, my poor little Toffee Emperor ..."

And suddenly Nataka could See the animal this little Howler was missing so much: a long-haired, toffee coloured Persian cat with an evil expression on his squashy face that had monopolised her lap; spread fur all over her furniture and clothes; taken the best bits of every meal off her plate; instilled holy terror in the birds, mice and other Wanyama in his neighbourhood; thrown up over her best antimacassars; and generally been a total menace. He'd died a few Suntimes before, from a nasty attack of indigestion caused by eating too many chocolates, which he'd stolen when the little old Howler (whose immediate memory was so-so) accidentally left a box of Quality Street open on her bedside table. She liked to suck a soft-centred chocolate or two before going to sleep at night (her false teeth would be out of her mouth and swimming in a glass of fizzy water next to her bed by then).

The Toffee Emperor had mastered the trick of unwrapping chocolates, and applied the skill far too often for his own safety. He'd ignored his own insides when they complained that they couldn't handle sugar. So they'd gone on strike by indigestion, an attack so severe that his heart had joined the picket line and stopped ticking. A stopped heart generally spells curtains for Mortals, unless there's somebody nearby with a bang box to shock the recalcitrant ticker back into action.

Anyway, long story short, the Toffee Emperor had had no such magician to hand when his ticker threw in the towel, so he had instantly and permanently departed this Dimension (having already squandered his previous eight lives in a very similar fashion). You might say that he was slow on the uptake.

*Well, at least this damp old Howler has the good sense to miss a **cat**,* thought Nataka. But the Howler's memories made it perfectly clear that the Toffee Emperor had been an out-and-out villain and that his passing had actually been a Good Thing for plenty of other life forms. Nataka wondered whether this insight might comfort the old biddy (whose incessant anxiety smells and noises were becoming more and more annoying), but after only a little thought she concluded that it would be better not to say anything that might upset her even more. Nobody likes to be told that somebody they loved was no good. Oddly enough, people prefer to stick to their illusions. And if Nataka were to begin her research into the Howlers by upsetting one of them, would anybody else let her near them? She doubted it.

"My poor, sweet, gentle Toffee Emperor was such a comfort to me; you can't imagine," whimpered the little old Howler. "I took my little ground-floor apartment here only because I was allowed to bring him with me when I left my home, you know? ... If I'd gone for the cheaper option of a bedroom I wouldn't have been allowed any pets. But the apartment has its own little garden, so I was allowed. And Toffee Emperor *loved* it here, bless him; he was so loving! He... he never hurt a fly..." She gulped, bent her head into her hands and started to rock again. A few tears squeezed through her fingers.

Good grief thought Nataka. *This isn't working at all.* The old Howler hadn't taken on board any of the wisdom the Immortal had so carefully decanted into her ears. The waves of misery she was transmitting still overpowered every other sensation; in fact, the anxiety coming from all the other old Howlers in the room was trivial, compared to it. Nataka felt as if she had accidentally flattened a nest of particularly tetchy safari ants: stung from all sides, distracted and exasperated. How could one ever *think* properly with all this negative emotion buzzing about? *Sheesh!* No wonder most of the Howlers in this place looked permanently stunned.

She sighed, sat back in her chair, curled her legs under her and studied the forlorn figure before her. There had to be a way to neutralise the safari ants' nest and make this old biddy feel more cheerful.

And then she had it, just as a bell rang and everybody started to shuffle out into the hall and towards the eating area. Of course! The only way to make this sad little Howler less sad was to distract her. She needed another cat to fuss over, to take her mind off the defunct Toffee Emperor. Simple. Nataka would have absolutely no difficulty organising *that*.

As she sat at one of a number of long tables along with the rest of the old Howlers and contemplated a plate of greasy mush containing a half-submerged dumpling that looked more suitable for knocking a wall out of a castle than for eating, she laid her plans.

"Who's your new friend, Gertrude dear?" asked a shapeless DG with lumps in odd places on her anatomy, leaning over the sad old Howler's chair some way down the table (*Aha,* thought Nataka. *This annoyingly grief-stricken old biddy's called Gertrude*). "I saw you having a nice little chat in the lounge just now. Isn't that *nice*?"

"Oh, this is Natasha!" sang out the saccharine voice of the wishy-washy DG who had helped to drag Nataka away from her home. The DG was carrying a jug of watery orange squash around the table and inflicting its contents on everybody. She had caught the lumpy DG's words in time to interfere. "Such a sweet lady, and only just joined us today. *Haven't* you, dear?" She added brightly, and then raised her voice. "Let's give a good, warm Sunny Shores welcome to Natasha, everybody!"

A sea (well, actually it was more like a swamp) of wrinkled faces turned towards Nataka. Some idiot began to clap.

Nataka jumped to her feet and pushed away from the table, scraping the chair on the floorboards and rocking the anaemic tinted water in her drinking glass. The last thing she wanted was to become the centre of attention. "'S'cuse me," she muttered acidly. "Tummy trouble -" and trotted out of the room before anybody else could react.

As soon as she was out of the room and well out of sight she sang a song of Forgetfulness, breathing a thin, opalescent mist across her fingers and through the doorway behind her. The Howlers inside the room briefly experienced a vague feeling of having missed something - a bit like what one feels on waking from a vanishing dream after nodding off for a micro-sleep - and then turned back to their greasy stews, lethal dumplings and tasteless blancmange puddings, unaware of the shadowy, furry, long-tailed and –fingered, child-sized creature with huge eyes and translucent bat ears (in appearance very like a giant bushbaby) that went bounding up from bannister to bannister to the ugly pink bedroom on the sixth floor, disdaining to set foot on the stairs.

Nataka carried on humming as she bounced along, delighted to have slipped out of her Howler disguise and into one of her favourite Transformations for a while. The song she hummed evoked sunlight and empty skies and beaches of clean sand. With the increasing distance from the dining area she gained with every step, it helped to dissipate the ant's nest effect caused by all the scattered, distressed and confused minds she had left behind her.

Chapter 4. Rescue Plan #1

"Fear is the mother of morality." [xxvii]

"So will you do it?"

Nataka was perching on one of the cars in the car park. Right then, the part of it that Howlers called a bonnet was a fine place because some Howler had recently got out of it, so it was good and warm under her tail and talons (next Sunwake the Howler would make a huge fuss about the scratches he found all over it). She was talking to Rav'n, the alley cat she'd spotted sniffing around the bins at the bottom of the Modern Monstrosity earlier that Suntime, and who had made an unsatisfactory meal from licking gravy off a pile of the mediaeval missiles masquerading as dumplings that had defeated the Howlers' dentures.

Rav'n (whose name was an abbreviation of what he called himself – *Rav'nous* – he wasn't very good at pronunciation and worse at spelling) was by nature uncouth and aggressive. But right now he was on his best behaviour because Nataka, who had been frightening in her Maine Coon cat guise, was terrifying as a Harpy Eagle. It doesn't do to alienate Harpy Eagles, particularly if they happen to be Nataka. Her appearance transfixed the alley cat and made him ponder a number of uncomfortable eternal verities he didn't usually confront, such as his own mortality and the damage a great hooked beak or humungous claw could wreak on a too-cheeky vagabond of his dimensions.

And indeed they were formidable weapons, those talons: capable of disembowelling small antelopes had Nataka wished. And the luminous yellow eyes in that dark-golden head with its handsome crown of tufted feathers - eyes that hung more than a rabbit's length above Rav'n – glared so fiercely into his own that he didn't have to be told their owner would tolerate neither insolence nor bad behaviour from *anybody*, including him.

So Rav'n was being very careful not to offend, despite his longing to explore an alluring fishy smell floating out of one of the bins.

"You'll get lots of pampering and food from that old Howler," pursued Nataka, "And I'll throw in a handsome new look, too. You know, fix that ear and make your coat shiny. If you do it. Interested?"

"So... run this by me agin?" meowed the disreputable animal, whose tattered ear was a legacy of a memorable rooftop battle with a squinting, long-nosed Oriental tom over a rather charming (if flea-bitten) queen, and whose coat at close quarters revealed the matting and bald patches that arise from a combination of hard fighting, irregular meals, worms and lice. "Yer wants me to be a *lap cat*? ... for an *'Owler*? ... *Har!* ..."

Rav'n's hoarse, derisory laugh suddenly cut off. He shook his head violently, doubled over and galvanised one back leg to scratch his ear. A flea had just nipped him at its base and, as every flea-bitten animal knows, it's mightily difficult to concentrate on anything else when that happens.

After a few moments of vigorous scratching during which he was lost to all other considerations, Rav'n dropped his back paw and added, "Bu'– 'old on; did yeh say yeh'll give me a new look? ... Fix me good? – As in, forever? Get shot of all them lice and fleas? ... And yeh reckon she'll feed me? Hmm... *yikes!*"

He flopped down, stuck a hind leg into the air in front of him to expose his dirty underside. His nose dived down into his belly fur and he worked his front teeth energetically in an attempt to neutralise the culprit that had just stung him in that tender part of his anatomy. That done, he went on to lick his secret parts, considering.

Nataka waited. There was clearly no point in hurrying the cat; let the idea sink in gradually.

"Gorra warn yeh, Nat," the alley cat said at last, looking up at her with his pink tongue still sticking out of his mouth, " It orl sahnds very tasty, but I'm not much good arahnd them 'Owlers, yeh know? ... Not much – er – wotsits - patience. I gets annoyed and then me claws comes out. I'm far better orf jus' grubbin' after the stuff they leaves behind... It's a livin'. Bu' granted, yer idea's temptin'; mighty temptin'..." His nose buried itself in his belly fur again.

"Your own dish," insinuated the Harpy Eagle; "and all the best bits from the old biddy Gertrude's table ... although I'd avoid the sweets and chocolates, if I were you. That's what killed off the Toffee Emperor."

"The Toffee Emperor? ... So 'e's gone, is 'e? ... I thort I 'adn't seen 'im arahnd recently. *That* was an evil animal, if yeh like;" said Rav'n, straightening up. "Kep' pretending like 'e wos in charge arahnd 'ere. Lef' a gap, 'as he? ... Well, well, well. If that ol' 'Owler could love the Toff Emp, I s'pose she should be able ter cope wiv me..."

"Exactly;" said the Harpy Eagle, and waited again.

"Hm... Me own dish... an' sleeping in comfort... *an*' a full belly ... Yes... temptin'. Ver*y* temptin'."

"And the new look; don't forget the new look," said the Harpy Eagle, "Although I'd want to make your fur rather longer – not too much longer, you know; just a bit... and, possibly, a fluffier tail and a flatter nose. As for your colour..."

"'Ere! 'old 'ard; *I* knows what yer up to!" hissed Rav'n, "I won't 'ave yeh turnin' me into another Toff Emp, Nat; that'd be unnach'ral."

"Oh, well; maybe you're right. Fair enough. I'll just do a straight refurb. I'll make you look great. You're a decent grey already, just a bit tatty and flea-bitten; nothing I can't sort out. A bit of spit and polish; some fat on your bones; get rid of your worms; and you'll be positively edible," said Nataka, winking one predatory eye and clicking her beak. The cat backed away from her by a paw's length. Nataka had begun to hum under her breath, and for some reason the sound made his fur stand on end.

"So when will yeh do this – this – refurb, then … an' will it 'urt?" he asked, teetering on the edge of the bonnet.

"What? – Oh, that. It's done already," replied the Harpy Eagle nonchalantly. And indeed, Rav'n the Alley cat was now a handsome feline: sleek; muscular; covered in soft, silky fur and sporting two perfect ears; with a warm, honeyed cry and fetching, plaintive gleam in his dark green eyes, bound to captivate a whole army of old biddies.

"Righto then, fair do's. Ah'm on. ... But I can't be spendin' all me time with that old bat;" meowed Rav'n, twisting round to admire his own tail and flanks. "Drive me barmy in short order, that would. I'll be needin' me time off, yeh know. What if she wants a cuddle when ah'm away on the tiles somewhere, tryin' out me new look on the talent?"

"Oh, I've thought of that already;" replied Nataka. The Harpy Eagle closed her eyes for a second, and when she opened them again the handsome grey cat nearly fell off the bonnet of the car. Nataka had Transformed into his exact replica. "The old biddy's used to dealing with cats; I'm sure she'll let you roam to your heart's content. But if you really need a break I'll be able to help. " She shimmered briefly, and the eagle was back.

"Gorra 'and it to yeh, Nat," said Rav'n a little nervously, "That's a neat trick. Nobbut wot yer magical; stan's to reason yeh can do them fings ... But don't do 'em too often, right? Unsettles a feller, does that sorta fing."

"Good; that's agreed, then." The Harpy Eagle settled her feathers. "Right, now let's make sure your lap skills are up to scratch. ...Weave."

"Weave?" answered the cat, looking puzzled. "Singe me whiskers if I knows what yer drivin' at, Nat, ole girl. What d'yeh mean, *weave*?"

"You know: arch your back; purr; lift and gently wave your tail in the air; make puddings with your paws; rub up against the Howler's legs; that kind of stuff. It wins them over and makes them want to care for you. So go on, then; show me what you've got."

"Oh, yeh mean the kind of daft exhibition wot the Toff Emp used ter lay on?" meowed Rav'n in disgust, "Nope, gorra draw the line there, Nat ole girl. 'S' beneaf me digni'y." He licked a forepaw with a virtuous expression on his newly minted muzzle.

"Did I say you had a choice, you miserable mammal?" snapped the Harpy Eagle, suddenly losing her patience, which had been wearing thin through the foregoing negotiations. She reared up, fanned her tail and spread her crest and wings. "*Beneath your dignity,* is it, you worm-eaten, flea-bitten, benighted gutter-crawler? ... I'll give you *beneath your dignity!* ... D'you really think all you have to do is stroll up to the old biddy, flop down on your fat bum and start licking your salty bits to make her fall for you? ... You've got to win her over, you lazy gutter-sniffer! Lap skills are *important*. Now snap to it and weave, or I'll have your tail off!"

Rav'n spat, jumped off the car and crouched on the ground with his fur on end and ears flat against his head. Nataka's earlier gentleness had lulled him into thinking he had some control over the situation, the poor dumb alley cat.

"'*Ere!* Calm dahn, calm dahn, Nat ole girl! I'll weave; I'll weave; orl right?" he said, fighting to keep a semblance of dignity. "But I'll be a kni'ed jumper if I knows 'ow! And besides, where's the Howler leg ter weave agin?"

"Oh, use your imagination;" replied Nataka, folding her wings and beginning to enjoy herself. "Pretend that round thing behind you is the old biddy. ... Now. *Weave*."

"I'm weavin'; I'm weavin', already," hissed the cat, arching his back, lifting his tail and rubbing up against the disc-like car paw (what Howlers call a *tyre*) specified by the eagle. "Yer a flippin' menace, 's' wha' y'are;" he muttered under his breath as he pretended to knead the tarmac with his front paws, "Pickin' on a feller when 'e's minding 'is own business, jes' because yer bigger ... an' stronger... an' – an' magical... an'..."

"What're you muttering about?" demanded Nataka, who had heard every word. "Now: walk up and down with your tail up, and rub yourself on that round thing... yes, like that; good... but more... *more*, I said. Go on; give it some welly! You've got to *feel* it... you've got to make *love* to that thing. That thing's going to *feed* you, you know. Good grief, you look more miserable than a camel sucking a lemon!"

"... Comes swannin' in, all beak and feavers, an' tells a feller 'e 'as ter *weave*..." muttered the alley cat, rubbing his flank against the tyre, but always with one eye on the Harpy Eagle. "... Ahh, *suck a toad!* Nah I've only gorn an' got muck all over me new coat..." He lifted his voice. "Yeh happy nah, yeh grea' bully? Look at me new coat! I'll 'ave ter wash for ages to get that lot aht! ... An' anyway, what's a *welly* when it's at 'ome? 'Ow can I give i' if I don' even know wha' i' is?"

"Keep strutting! Don't stop! ... On your toes, pudding, pudding, *pudding*! ... Purr, purr, *purr*! ... Tail *up*! ... *Don't* snarl! ... Better. ... Now: let's have a nice gentle *meow* mixed in with your purring – right now – on the turn – while you gaze soulfully into her eyes ... Look: pretend that thing – (she indicated the shiny object sticking out of the car the Howlers call a *wing mirror*) – *that's* her face. All right? Now give that thing a soft *meow* and gaze deeply into...

"*Ouch*! No! Not like that, that noise would wake the dead ... You're not in a catfight, you brainless bundle! Is that really the best you can do? ... It's got to be more of a *chirrup* than a *yowl,* you fool. You're not a flipping banshee, you know! Here..."

Nataka resumed her Rav'n appearance and jumped down to join him. "In Germany they have a word: *Fingerspitzengefuehl.* Means *feeling with the tips of your fingers* - in other words, sensitive awareness," she told the disgruntled cat beside her in her best pompous voice. "Well, you've got about as much of *that* as an elephant tromping over a clutch of eggs. Now, look here; watch. This is how it's done..."

"Don' 'ave fingers, smar'y – paws. So 'ow can I have that finger shpitting – what'ch'macallits – yeh said, anyways? ... And 'sides, I never signed up fer lessons in *sensitive dis-an'-dat* when we agreed to all this new look fing. Nobody told me ah'd be frog-marched up and dahn like this as part o' the packidge!" spat Rav'n as he copied Nataka. "An' what's an *elliphunt* when it's in its lair, now? Yeh keep comin' at a feller wiv new words wot don' make sense. Can I eat it? ... If I can't eat it I'm not interested, an' that's flat."

Had Tytus the Baron flown over the car park of the Modern Monstrosity at that moment he would have been both intrigued and puzzled by the sight of two identical grey cats romancing a car tyre, for all the world as if somebody had festooned it with catnip. But Tytus was far away, hovering over the moon-silvered reed beds around the river.

When Nataka at last flew away, Rav'n had satisfactorily mastered the art of making love to Howlers. They agreed to meet in the Old Biddy's garden next Sunclimb, after the Howlers' first feed. Then they went their own ways, each satisfied with the night's work: Nataka to pop back to Toki and check that everything was ship-shape, and Rav'n to knock the lid off the fishy bin. For him, as for every cat, being promised food tomorrow doesn't mean you should stop foraging around the bins today.

Chapter 5. Skald's News

"Men may dam it and say that they have made a lake, but it will still be a river. It will keep its nature and bide its time, like a caged animal..." [xxviii]

Toki's anxious shifting turned into a welcoming jig when Nataka the Harpy Eagle appeared through the window, Transformed into a giant bushbaby on the hearthrug and immediately went over to check the contents of the cauldron, which was now blowing bubbles of purple and silver around the cottage. The moon had been up for some time now, and many of the Protean's friends had gathered, as they usually did after Sunsleep, and were filling Toki with their chatter.

Glose the raven was perched on the mantelpiece, trying to edge in on a conversation between Miba the hedgehog and Brid the squirrel. Miba was complaining that nobody's life was safe from Howlers nowadays, and advising Brid that you had to keep your spines sharp and ready for any eventuality (a useless bit of advice to give to a squirrel, really; but Brid was a cheerful, good-natured animal who didn't let that kind of thing bother him. In any case, he was only half-listening to his friend while he amused himself, picturing Miba stuck all over with berries).

Wurfl the beaver, Pex and Ala the foxes and Fyrd the otter were huddled together under the pile of firewood (which had long served as M'Kuu's *de facto* form), indulging in a very satisfying moan about all the damage the Howlers had done to the woods and river recently. M'Kuu was sitting on top of the woodpile, staring down with his large eyes and listening to their conversation. Dora was the only person not taking part in the *powwow*. She was hanging under the ceiling from a thread, practising some new knots.

It was immediately clear to Nataka that something out of the ordinary had stirred everybody up. She spotted Trixie

Snuffles For Short sitting wide-eyed next to the hearth and watching the other animals. The newcomer looked rather overwhelmed.

"Great job with the potion so far," said Nataka after she had sniffed the cauldron and sung one or two chants over it. "It's coming on nicely. Colour's good; smell's fine; temperature's perfect. Well done, Glose. "So, what's up, people?" she added, picking up a black, long-handled iron ladle and giving the potion a last stir. She hooked the ladle over the rim of the pot, sat down next to the poodle, reached out and started to stroke the curly top of the newcomer's head.

"What's all this *matata*? Don't tell me that you've been worrying about me; that would be too ridiculous. Toki, if you don't keep yourself steady you'll spill the blasted potion." The cottage gave a happy little creak and stopped skipping. "Besides, everybody, where are your manners? You're unsettling our new friend with all your noise." She turned her luminous eyes and delicate ears to face the poodle. "What would you like us to call you, by the way?"

"*Me*? ... Call me? D'you mean a - a new name? ... May I really have one?" stammered the dog delightedly, her tail thumping on the hearth. "Oh, my!"

"Not too quick on the uptake," creaked the raven.

"Well?"

"Er... well, Your Honour..."

"Your *Honour*?" cackled Glose from his perch on the mantelpiece, "She called you *Your Honour*, Nataka. Hahahahaha! - **Aaaahk!** " Nataka's prehensile tail had reached for a lump of coal in the scuttle next to the woodpile, curled around it like a sling and knocked the raven's legs out from under him. Glose scrabbled and fluttered to regain his perch.

"Beak shut, Bird," instructed the Protean without turning her head. "You were saying?" she turned back to the poodle.

"Uh… well, Your Honour," said the dog timidly, hanging her head so that both her ears almost covered her eyes, "I've always loved the name *Paa,* although I can't explain why… maybe because it's simple and uncomplicated. It sounds… well, friendly. Something about it makes me feel kind of rounded, complete… I know it sounds silly…"

"Now *that* I can agree with;" muttered the raven into his breast feathers.

"Splendid name," declared Nataka, ruffling the poodle's head. "Nice and short and easy to remember. Paa it is, then." The poodle's nose lifted, and the curly tail began to wag again. "Welcome to your new home, Paa. Be at ease and let nobody distress you. They'll have me to deal with if they do. Have you had anything to eat since you arrived?"

"Oh yes!" said the poodle, "M'Kuu introduced me to your very handy meat store." Nataka's cottage had a cool cellar, perfect for storing perishable foods.

"Good," said Nataka. "And I take it everybody else has fed and watered as well? … Fine. I'll just have an apple… thanks, Wurfl." The beaver had used his tail to bat her an apple from the fruit bowl on the table behind him, and she fielded it with the long toes of one of her feet. She took a bite [xxix].

"Ahh. There's nothing better than an apple in one's own home; particularly when somebody's tried to feed you cannonballs in slime," she said, muddling her audience not a little. "So, then. To get back to the *matata:* what's up?"

M'Kuu the Hare said, "We've had some disturbing news, Boss; and in point of fact Tytus was on his way to call you..."

"... And is now back;" interrupted the barn owl, ghosting through the window and landing on the table top, which made Glose hop and squawk, as usual. "As soon as I saw your ghastly stone nest was empty I knew you were on your way home, Nataka. Happy to see you. We really do have some disturbing news..."

"Yes, indeed!" interrupted Glose raucously, "Terrible news! Life and death! A wolf's in trouble! We've had a message..."

"Skald the windhover brought it ..." interrupted Brid.

"...As I was saying, a message. That one of the wolves at an animal prison – a – what'd they call it? – *Zoo* – tried to escape and attacked a keeper!" snapped Glose, annoyed at the interruption.

"Quite. And they're talking about killing - " interjected Tytus the Baron.

"As I *was going to say* before I was interrupted *again* – really, some people are so rude – Killing ... " Glose squawked, hopping and flapping.

"... *Killing* him because they don't know how to calm him down!" barked and howled and yelped the beaver and foxes and otter all together at the top of their voices, while the raven squawked even louder in outrage and the other animals unanimously resumed their chatter. Toki jiggled and set all the bits and pieces on the shelves rattling.

"*Oy!*" squeaked a piercing little voice from the ceiling, "*How can I be expected to concentrate on my work with all this noise?*"

Dora reeled herself down on a piece of silk, glaring with all her eyes at the noisy gathering, and gesturing with one of her eight legs to a spot where she'd torn her ornamental web. "*I mean; really! … A bit of decorum, IF you please!*" All the animals fell silent and shuffled their various appendages, looking sheepish. Toki coughed quietly and stopped shaking.

"Dora's right, everybody;" said Nataka, "Cut the rumpus. Anyway, you're telling me this story back to front. What animal prison - er - zoo - are we talking about?"

"Er… What zoo, Glose?" asked M'Kuu, turning to the raven.

"Huh? – What? … What zoo? … I know that! … It's … uh … Curses, I *should* remember. Skald told me… I have it on the tip of my beak, but all this noise has made me forget … Er - uh …. Oh, pluck my pinions … Skald will have to remind us … now where is he?" fretted the raven.

"Went out to catch some dinner;" said the hare. "Should be back soon."

"So they've got a wolf and they want to kill it, you say?" prompted Nataka, looking at M'Kuu.

"Seems so, Boss;" he answered, "wolf ran amok, apparently. It's a bad show."

"A wolf;" mused Nataka, "I didn't know that any of the blasted prisons around here had wolves. But it's been ages since I looked. I wonder where it came from, and when. Anyway, it'll be a long way from home, wherever that is. Wolves stopped existing in the wild in *this* part of the world many hundreds of Moons ago. Killed off by Howlers. As usual."

Just then a skirling call outside the cottage heralded the approach of Skald the windhover. An instant later the bird swooped in through the open window and hung in the air for a moment, the firelight gilding his speckled breast, red-flushed upper wings and russet, bullet-shaped body. He sculled his great wings, rose till he was just beneath the eaves, and again hovered over the company (Toki accommodatingly raised its ceiling by a few metres). His pinions moved fractionally to keep him aloft and stable in the warm air rising from the fire. Improbably immobile, the beautiful bird turned his hooked beak and sharp great eyes, scanning and recording each of the room's occupants in turn.

And then, before anybody could speak, Skald abruptly tucked his wings tight against his body and stooped, plummeting vertically down in a dive that drew gasps from the Wanyama below, most of whom believed that it *must* end in his annihilation on the floor of the cottage ... except that, somehow, he again snapped his pinions and tail feathers wide at the last possible moment (a feat of which only another bird will ever fully appreciate the unimaginable strength and subtlety) to land light as a dandelion seed on Nataka's outstretched wrist; a virtuoso display of flying that drew a rare click of approval from Tytus the Baron.

"Very nice work;" said the owl; "couldn't have done it better myself." The windhover bowed wordlessly to him before turning his fierce golden eyes and razor-sharp hooked beak to face Nataka.

"You've heard, then?" he whistled. "It'll be death-row for the wolf if we don't look sharp. I don't usually fly at night, as you know; but this is urgent. Chant's all fluffed up and spitting; you know how she gets. She wouldn't let it wait till morning, so here I am. Quite a journey, I might add. I had to eat something right away, or flop. You know how it is. It's a good thing the Moon is bright, too. I'd have brained myself a few times on the flight here, otherwise. I'm not big on Batlight flying."

"Chant sent you?" said Nataka, "Ah. Well then, we're talking about that animal prison on the other side of the big water, in the direction of Sunwake. Right?"

Chant was a particularly intelligent, lithe and attractive amber-marmalade-white and charcoal - patterned calico cat with emerald eyes who kept the zoo's chief warden and his family as her own devoted Howler Pets. She had them firmly wrapped around her velvety paws: so much so that they obeyed her every whim, playing with her when she asked; brushing her; scratching her behind the ears; giving her treats and all the best cuts from their roasts, and letting her have the comfiest chair in their home. Chant was also a sly and subversive little beast. She patrolled the zoo daily, chatting and interfering with all the animals, and finding ways to make the job of every Howler working in the place as difficult as possible by encouraging the zoo's occupants to spill their drinking water, tear up and soil their bedding (a trick she enjoyed playing on *her* pets), throw up their food over visitors, sulk in corners when they were supposed to be cavorting outside, and so on.

Her littermate Leto (a beautiful, large, long-haired ginger-and-white tomcat with deep amber eyes who was gently drifting towards his next incarnation as illness hastened his current, highly revered life towards its end) was the philosopher of the ménage. He only raised his voice occasionally in plaintive song to demand food or affection from his Pets, and spent the rest of the time sleeping or gently patrolling his back garden, investigating the food on the bird table and contemplating the meaning of Feline Life. Occasionally he emerged from his long meditations to remind Chant that all her busy political scheming was a waste of precious effort and energy, for every cat with a modicum of genuine wisdom adheres to the three great Conditions of Successful Cat-hood, to wit ...

> *(1) The only things of true importance in life are: access to plentiful and wholesome food; peaceful days and spots to sleep in; and comforting cuddles and quarters on call. These constitute the indivisible magical Trinity that is the blessed philosophical and spiritual feline Condition of Fulfilment.*
>
> *(2) To achieve Condition One (Fulfilment) a Cat must own one or more reliable Howler Pet/s who will regularly and abundantly provide all its components. Therefore it behoves every Cat to labour well in order to capture and train such a Pet; and, having caught one, to prevent it from escaping again thereafter.*
>
> *(3) All else is Vanity.*[xxx]

Needless to say, Chant never paid attention to Leto's wisdom. She had her own ideas, founded on her conviction that she was the greatest Cat in existence, and that the Sun and Moon and all of Cat-kind revolved around her. She rather resented Leto his philosophical leanings and frequently hissed at him, accusing him of being a pompous old windbag. She would have been both furious and mortified if anybody had dared to tell her that her behaviour and beliefs were no different from those of any other average cat.

"Exactly right; *that* prison," said Skald. "It's a long flight, but it helped that I had a lot of water to fly over because the Moon was reflected in it, so I benefited from the light of *two* Moons. Good, that.

"Now, where was I? ... Oh, yes. The Howlers've been keeping a few wolves in the prison for some time now, actually; and things are pretty quiet and relaxed around their compound. But recently the Howlers brought in a new wolf, and he *really* doesn't want to be there. He's properly unbroken. He hasn't gone under to the whole prison system. To start with, he's not accepting the fact that the grub he gets must come at the cost of his freedom, as all the other wolves do. You know? ... He eats all right, but only when he can't bear to starve any longer. And he does it with a snarl, and doesn't let it relax him. He's also got that *look* in his eyes: still wild instead of half-asleep like all the rest of 'em. You know what I mean..."

There was a sudden loud whimper from Paa. "That was *me!*" she exclaimed, "*I* was half dead like that! ... I've only just woken up, thanks to you, Your Honour! ... Oh, that *poor* Nyama, he's fighting to stay awake!"

"Yes; you're right, Ma'am," said the windhover. He was a courteous bird. "Well. Mond (his real name's a regular tongue-twister, so that's what we're calling him)[xxxi]... *he's* going the wrong way about it, because he's been so barmy to get out of there he keeps trying to escape, and he refuses to let anybody else calm him down. Not even the other wolves have managed.

"He won't talk to anybody – or at least, not in any way *we* can understand. He chatters away nineteen to the dozen, but it's all rotten bone-pellets to us. We can't make any sense of it at all. And he just won't listen when they try to tell him that most probably he's not just a long way from his real home, but *such* a long way he'd be better off accepting that he won't be seeing his pack or cubs again. So, in short, he should try to make the best of it because at least he's got shelter and food; you know? ... Well, Mond's not having any of that. And he's unsettling everybody else because of it.

"And *now* the vole's well and truly scarpered, because a few Startimes ago Mond hurt himself when he attacked that horrible Howler barrier around the Wolf compound again – I can't tell you how often over the past Moon he's tried to escape that way, but he just doesn't seem to learn from it – and *this* time he was so violent that he got all tangled up in the wire and tore himself. Those Howlers have a kind of fizzy, webby barrier next to another one with thorns on it; you know?" Skald was doing his best to describe an electric chain link fence inside a barbed-wire barrier surrounding the wolf compound. He paused to draw a deep breath.

"Oh, no," whimpered Paa into the silence, where the only other sounds were the popping and crackling of the flames and the bubbling of the cauldron. The windhover was painting a vivid picture of the wolf's misery, and not even Glose had anything clever to say about it.

"'Fraid so, Ma'am;" said Skald. "The poor mad animal did his level best to *kill* himself against that fizzy thorny thing. And worse still, when the Howlers heard the rumpus – the screaming and calling and barking and whimpering from all directions in the Wanyama prison roused them, of course – *they* came running, found Mond tangled, and attacked him. Or perhaps they were just trying to get him out from all that stuff; who knows? Some people say this; some people say that. I wasn't there, so I can't say. But I *think* they were probably trying to get him out. After all, if they'd been attacking, why not kill him then and there, and be done with it? Stands to reason.

"So anyway, what does that crazy wolf do but fight them, just him against a good dozen of 'em, instead of letting them get on with freeing him? ... He even battled against that magic thorn thingy they shoot into Wanyama to send 'em to sleep... That's powerful magic, that. I've seen it down a fully-grown horse in a heartbeat. But Mond was snarling and thrashing long after he should have been asleep. I must say, that wolf's one strong animal, Nataka. Can you believe that he actually managed to stay awake for long enough to bite one of the keepers who thought he was out cold when he was just resting for a moment? A nasty bite, too, I hear. Took him in the chest and one of his featherless wings.

"Yeah, that's Mond: daft as a cabbage-bingeing caterpillar; totally careless of his own safety ... but amazing courage, genuinely amazing. I must admit that I've always wanted to tear a chunk out of a Howler. And Mond did it. Impressive."

"My word, that *is* impressive, particularly if he'd been stung by the magic thorn;" agreed the Protean, thinking how much she would have enjoyed biting the Busybody. "That thorn has a *very* strong potion in it. It can knock out any animal, and too much of it will even kill you. But I wish he hadn't hurt the Howler. No good can come of it." She shuddered.

"Yes, you're right. It's brought him nothing but trouble, because *now* those Howler keepers aren't at all impressed with him. Quite the opposite. If they felt sorry for him before, that's all gone. Now they're furious and upset. All those nice things you generally hear Howlers say about Wanyama – you know, about loving them and wanting to help and protect them, and so on and so forth; the things they always say to justify shoving everybody into a prison – *that* all seems to have gone. Now they're saying *mad wolf* and *menace to others,* and things like that. You know how it is.

"So anyway, to cut to the hunt, Mond did fall asleep in the end, and the Howlers finally managed to untangle him. And they also patched him up. So now he looks a right mess, with half his body all covered in those white wrappings they use to stop you leaking everywhere. So then, when he woke up, he started tearing at the wrappings, ripping them and making himself leak again. So they stung him *again* and put a big ... *something* ... round his neck to stop him getting at the wrappings with his fangs and hurting himself again. Which makes him look absurd, as though he's stuck his head through the top of an empty turtle-shell.

"And he still has to be tended, of course. And you can just imagine how much the Howler keepers are enjoying *that.* Nobody wants to do it. They keep pushing one another to look after him, and finding excuses not to go near him. Chant told me that her Pet was shouting at them about it just last Sunclimb, saying they all have to take it in turns.

"So that's the situation right now. They're keeping Mond in a tiny prison nest, away from the other wolves, and he's snarling and snapping at everybody who comes near him. Not really surprising, that; he's half out of his mind, what with all the pain, not to mention the fury and anxiety he must be feeling. And with the moon coming to the full I can't describe the noise he makes all through Startime. He sounds like a whole *pack* of wolves when he gets going with his gobbledygook, almost as bad as a flock of Howlers at one of their incomprehensible gatherings.

"And as if *that* weren't bad enough, to add to all the rumpus he's got all the other half-asleep lot of wolves waking up, deciding that they're miserable too, and joining in with his yelling. It's got so bad around there that I've had to move my nest to get away from it all. A bird can't be flying and hunting all Suntime if he hasn't got any sleep during Startime, and Nifl – that's my missus – well: *she* was getting positively hysterical about it all. Our eggs'll be hatching soon, and the chicks'll need peace and quiet to grow, as you know. So Nifl's kept yammering on about them spoiling because of the noise and the stress *she* was feeling, as well. So we moved. Pity we had to, though; I'd found us a particularly good site, overhanging a brook. Tall, sturdy tree; lots of hunting. It was perfect. Till all that *matata* at the prison for Wanyama started."

The windhover paused in his narrative. He ran his hooked beak over one pinion, ruffled all his feathers, looked up at Nataka and clicked his beak ruefully. "Not ideal, moving in the middle of a nest sitting, believe me," he said. "I'm never doing that again, no matter what. Quite apart from having to build the new nest – not to mention all the hoohhah that went with finding the place (you know how *that* goes: *this isn't a good area; there's dodgy neighbours in this tree; this branch is too wobbly; this one's too exposed, it isn't half as nice as our original nesting site ... nag, nag, nag*), transferring those eggs was a trial, I can tell you. Hanging on to each one for dear life and trying not to drop it, with Nifl flying along behind me screeching about them getting cold and *couldn't I fly any faster?* ... But if I'd dropped one of 'em, I swear she'd have torn me tail from wing in mid-air. *You* know how they get when they're brooding, Nataka; barmier than a thrush with a bellyful of fermented plums.

"But to get back to Mond: according to Chant, the keeper he bit had to go to one of those – whatsits – you know, those Howler nests where they cut one another up and so on ... I don't know what they call 'em..."

"A hospital?" said Nataka.

"Yeah, that's it. A host ... hosti ... whatsit ... that. He had to go there. And he's still in there. And to cap it all, tonight Chant heard her Howler Pet and the other Howlers having an *indaba* about killing Mond – now, what did they call it again? - Ah yes. *Putting him to sleep.* Chant says that most Howlers can't bear to call a killing a killing, so they dress it up in peacocks' plumage when they talk, just as they dress up and disguise their prey before they eat it. So Chant says now they're talking about killing Mond because they don't think he'll ever settle down. They've decided he's too wild; he's unsafe; he can't be tamed; and so on... Took 'em long enough to figure *that* out, didn't it? **Tsk**! ... In other words, *now* he's become a nuisance, so they want to get rid of him.

"So Chant's sent me double quick to ask you what can be done, because none of us wants to see the poor mad Nyama murdered, which is what it would amount to, seeing as those crazy Howlers in the prison never eat the animals they kill. Sheer waste of food, really. I could raise a whole season's worth of fledglings on one wolf, I could.[xxxii] ... But anyway, we should have come to find you a lot earlier than this, if you ask me."

Skald drew a deep breath and began to preen his pinions, clearly tired out by his long flight and account. Windhovers (also called kestrels) are not used to too much conversation. They fly, hunt, sleep, are devoted parents, and keep a very close eye on events in the world (preferably from a safe height) for the sake of their own families. But they don't generally like to participate too closely in the wider affairs of Wanyama, or indeed to spend too much time talking about them. Skald was exceptional because he cared for other creatures even while he was digesting them, and because he had managed to put together a very clear and coherent account for Nataka. Now that he had safely delivered his message, exhaustion overcame him. He shifted on Nataka's wrist, settled his pinions and let his hooked beak sink to meet his chest feathers.

But Nataka couldn't let him rest yet. "I'm sorry, Skald. I've got to ask you another question before you sleep," she said, stroking the windhover's back (this was unusual because, as you may have noticed, Nataka seldom apologised to anybody for anything). She had spotted the nictitating membranes under his outer lids begin to film over his great eyes from their inside corners, and she knew that when he finally slept he would not want to be disturbed again for the rest of Startime, and might even become violent if you tried to rouse him. "Did Chant mention *when* those Howlers are planning to kill Mond?" she asked, joggling her hand to keep him awake, "I need to know how much time we have."

"Eh? …What?" The bird jerked up his beak and snapped his fierce eyes wide. "Oh … Yes … sorry, Nataka. I'm all in. Should have told you, but I forgot. *You* know how it is. … Well, Chant said that the Howlers have to get a thing they call a *Special* - now what was it? – Oh yes, Permit - a Special Permit - before they can get on with murdering Mond; I think she said this means a particular Howler who patches up damaged animals has to come and look at him first. And then, if *that* Howler agrees that he can't be tamed, he'll be a goner. So anyway, Chant said they were talking about doing it in four Suns, if they can get that – er – Special whatsits – Permit."

"Thanks, Skald, that's very useful," said Nataka. "Sleep well; you've earned it." She raised the hand that held him towards the smoke-darkened beam Toki had obligingly lowered towards her. The windhover clicked his beak by way of thanks, hopped the short distance to the beam from her hand and hunkered down instantly, tucking his head under one wing. He was fast asleep before the cottage had stretched back up to its normal height, carrying the exhausted bird into the shadows.

"We'll have to speak softly now, everybody," said Nataka, settling back down on the hearthrug. "Skald mustn't be disturbed. Now; what are we to do?"

"We must rescue that poor wolf!" said Paa immediately.

"Yes, yes; of course; there's no question about that;" cawed Glose, hopping onto Nataka's shoulder; "I'm sure everybody here agrees that we have to stick together when the Howlers gang up on one of us. But how will we do it?"

"Hmm. Does anybody have any idea of the layout of that prison?" asked M'Kuu, "We really can't do much planning without knowing where everything is, can we?"

"Drat. We should have asked Skald before he went to sleep;" said Glose, "Shall I wake him and ask, Nataka?"

"No; better not. He's wiped out, and I wouldn't want to disturb him now for anything. Quite apart from the fact that he might shred you if you roused him again, he's got a long flight back after Sunwake - *and* a skittish mate sitting on eggs that are liable to hatch at any moment. She'll be all over him like a plague of gnats, demanding help and feeding, the minute he gets home. He needs all the rest he can get." Nataka stroked Glose's shiny black feathers. "Well, never mind. It really isn't that much of a problem. I'll just nip off and take a look at the place myself."

"Hold on," interrupted Tytus the Baron, "I can go. I've eaten well and had plenty of sleep last Suntime. I could do with some vigorous exercise to stretch my wings. What's to stop me casing the joint for you, Nataka?"

"*Do you know where this prison is, though?*" Dora had abandoned her weaving and lowered herself from the ceiling on one of her delicate threads to join the conversation. "*Not much good going, Tytus, if you've no idea* where *you're going, is it?*"

"Er ... good point, Dora; I hadn't thought of that," said the Owl, taken aback.

"Be a pity only to realise that when you're halfway there;" commented Brid the squirrel brightly, earning a sharp look from the owl. He stroked his gorgeous red tail and winked. Miba the hedgehog chuckled.

"Well spotted, Dora," said Nataka, "Yes, obviously I have to go because I know the way. But do come along if you want, Tytus. Two sets of eyes are better than one and it's always good to have somebody watching your back." She rose to her back paws.

"Good idea," said the owl and gave the squirrel another old-fashioned look. Brid responded by hopping around the room, flicking and flirting his tail at the large bird.

"Quit messing about, Brid," said Nataka, "if you don't, Toki and I might have to relax our *no hunting* rule and let the Baron teach you a lesson. That's better. Right, then. First things first. Tytus, you and I will look over that prison and have a chat with Chant, if we can get hold of her. You never know with Chant. One minute she's right there, the next she's liable to be some miles off, interfering with somebody or other. Well, we'll just have to take our chances on that.

"Hmm. I don't expect that we'll be back again much before Sunclimb, and I've got a special event organised then with an old Howler biddy and Rav'n the alley cat, so I'll have to go on to the horrible stone nest to look after that. We'll just have to delay our planning, I suppose.

"Never mind. Even if we wipe out next Sun, it still gives us another three Suns to get organised. Be here in time for next Sunsleep, everybody. In the meantime I want you all to think of ideas and suggestions for the rescue, so we can discuss them when we meet up. All right?

"M'Kuu and Glose, you're in charge till we return. Keep an eye on that potion. As soon as the steam turns bright green it'll be ready, so all you'll have to do then is swing it off the fire by pulling on this chain - like this – till I get back…" She demonstrated. "M'Kuu, will you see to that?"

"Sorry, Boss; *my* season's coming up and the Dancing Moon's nearly full already;" replied the Hare, sitting up and lifting his front paws to his chest. "I'll be out, dancing the first measures to greet it. And you know I can't be relied on for any duties while I'm doing *that*."

"Sheesh; I forgot. Of course. Your Season's here and that's just the way it is," said Nataka. "You have to be out there. And I expect all the rest of you will also be out and away next Suntime on your own affairs, as usual. Am I right?" The foxes, squirrel, hedgehog, beaver and otter all ducked their heads in agreement. She knew how it was. Life had to go on for each of them according to his or her own kind. There were nests to build; young to make and rear; any number of essential activities for each of them to attend to.

"Well, Glose, that leaves just you, then," Nataka turned to the raven. "You'll have to take charge again – that is, unless you've finally decided that this is the Season you change the habits of a lifetime, find a mate and build a nest of your own. … No? … Thought not." She laughed. The raven was perfectly comfortable in her company, assured of food whenever he needed it, rummaging around among the scrolls that crammed the cottage and quarrelling with her whenever the fancy took him. He wasn't at all interested in striking out and starting a family of his own.

"Well. Let's just see you move that cauldron, then. Grab the chain in your beak and pull it until the cauldron swings round off the fire, just like I did."

Glose hopped off his perch onto the floor and cocked his head first one way then the other as he eyed the cauldron. Then he waddled over to the chain, grabbed it in his horny beak, and heaved with all his might. But it wouldn't budge. All that happened was that his claws slipped and scrabbled on the floor.

"Nothing doing," he croaked at last. "It's too heavy." He didn't sound at all sorry as he hopped back onto his perch and started to preen a wing. "You can't expect me to do *everything* around here, you know;" he remarked to nobody in particular.

"But what about *me*?" interrupted Paa, "Why not *me*? ... *I* can do it! I'd *love* to do it, Your Honour!" She laid her forepaws flat along the floor, stuck her furry round bottom in the air and wagged her tail so vigorously that her whole body shook. Brid and Miba got the giggles and Glose muttered something unpleasant into his breast feathers.

"Look, watch me!" The poodle jumped up, grabbed the chain between her teeth, braced her paws, dropped her rear, and began to haul. "I **c'n** d't!" She mumbled through her teeth, her tail still wagging furiously, "'N' I p'm'se I w'n't s'p'll 'n'y'f'ng e'th' !..." [xxxiii]

The cast-iron arm bearing the cauldron joggled a bit, then began to move. It swung ponderously round as the poodle reversed, still tugging. At last it lumbered to a halt well away from the flames, and Paa let go of the chain. She plumped onto her haunches with her rosy tongue hanging and amber eyes fixed on Nataka. "Did I do good? ... Did I? ... Did I?" she panted.

Nataka chuckled. "You did fine. Not a drop spilt, either;" she said. The poodle bounced up, wriggling with delight. "Good work, Paa. You'll pull that chain as soon as Glose tells you to. Right? Not a moment before, mind! ... Glose, remember: get Paa to pull that potion off the flames as soon as you see it turn green. All right? ... Excellent. That's settled, then.

"Now: what else? ... Oh, yes. Don't forget, M'Kuu: if I'm not back before Skald wakes up, let him have anything he needs – food, drink, whatever – before he flies home. And

Dora, I trust to your good sense to keep everybody in line. Right, then: I think that's all. Ready, Tytus?"

And, while everybody else was still catching breath and digesting the whirlwind of instructions she had scattered about, Nataka whistled and spun herself into a Tawny Owl, and went bouncing out of the window, followed by Tytus the Baron. The two birds winged away towards the river, flying silently and swiftly by the light of the high and frosty not-quite-full Moon as they headed straight for the great water into which the river decanted itself, and which lay between their home and the animal prison – (er) – zoo. Toki puffed a fanfare of sparks into the air to speed them on their way.

Inside the cottage Paa turned to face the hare, her eyes bright with curiosity. "How *do* you dance, M'Kuu?" she asked. "Could I try?"

Chapter 6. Casing The Joint

"Howlers have perfected hypocrisy and self-deception to such a degree that when they cage another living creature they can delude themselves with the lie that they are doing it for love." [xxxiv]

"Let's keep this quiet," warned Nataka as the two birds approached the moonlit sprawl of compounds and cages that housed the zoo animals, "we don't want to alert anybody to…. Oh, er; maybe we won't have to be so quiet after all. Mond's *really* laying into it, isn't he? Skald wasn't exaggerating. Hark at him!"

The zoo was a cacophony of clamouring Wanyama with the lonely howls of the caged timber-wolf (a sound second to none for precipitating that prickly hair-rising-on-the-ruff sensation) overtopping all the calls and complaints issuing from the other cages and compounds of diurnal occupants determined to voice just how annoyed they were to be kept awake. To make matters worse, every so often the other wolves in the zoo, infected by Mond's cries, would join in with sad songs of their own, their cacophony compounding the melancholy effect of his laments. And in response, the hubbub of screeching and rattling by the zoo's other prisoners would also increase. Nobody could hope to get any rest in such a *matata*.

"Well, at least we can pinpoint where he is in all this mess of stone nests," said Tytus the Baron; "We just need to follow his voice. ... Ah. There he is. Look: it's that little trap nest, under those trees, near the fizzy prickly barrier thing Skald was describing..." As he spoke, the Baron dipped one wing and changed direction, heading down to hover over a small metal cage in which Mond the wolf had been isolated. Nataka followed him, and they both hung in the air, studying the cage from above.

Then Nataka tucked in her wings and swooped down to inspect the cage at closer quarters. She circled it twice slowly, flying just a few feet above the ground. She could make out the shadowy shape of the wolf in its dark interior, his head distorted by the lampshade collar that poked up behind his ruff and ears. The snarling and whimpering shadow was prowling restlessly around the tiny space inside the cage. Occasionally, as the wolf turned, one edge of his collar would catch and jerk against the bars of the cage, whereupon the wolf would stop dead, wrench his head free, collapse onto his haunches, lift his muzzle and emit a string of hoarse, plaintive howls. After a few moments his cries would subside into snarls and whimpers and the distraught Nyama once again lurch to his feet to resume his incessant, limping circling. He was clearly unable to rest, even though to Nataka he looked to be at the uttermost end of his endurance.

"He's trapped tight," she reported, rising to rejoin the barn owl. "The Howlers've locked him in with any number of those things they call *padlocks*. That's not good."

"Can't you just Transform those pad-thingies into something we could break, then?" asked the Baron.

"No, I can't. ... Or, better said, if I had the time I could *rust* them till they fell apart. But I couldn't do it quickly enough. That kind of Change takes a Moon or so for me to complete. It's annoying. I still haven't found a way to Change dead things, like those padlocks or that cage, quickly enough. They're made of something the Howlers call *metal*, which they harden in various ways. Mind you, I *have* managed to speed it up a bit over the past few thousand Moons ... but I still haven't got it fast enough to help here. Not in the time we've got."

She hovered, thinking. Her great owl eyes turned to the colour of lodestones.

"So what *can* we do?" prompted Tytus the Baron after a while.

"Nothing springs to mind," said the tawny owl. "I've been thinking about my powers, and it all seems a bit of a dead end. I can fool Howlers into thinking they or their things are different or not there, which is useful; but it doesn't mean those things *aren't* there; d'you see? The wolf would still be inside the trap. And I can make them believe they're seeing things that *aren't* there, which is also useful; but I'm not sure how that would help here, really.

"I can also Change living things, as you know. For instance, I *could* try to turn Mond into a small animal – say a beetle or a mouse – to help him escape. But I'd have to get his permission to do that, of course. And to be honest, after seeing the state he's in, I'm not sure that, even if he agreed, *this* wolf could handle the shock of such a Transformation without going completely mad, or worse. He's already in a dreadful state. No. I can't risk it.

"Curses. If that blasted trap were only wooden, I could Transform into a beaver and gnaw my way in or around those padlocks, or send a Green spell into it and turn it to grass or something else that's easily broken. Or if it were made of soil or rocks I would stand a chance of growing digging talons, like a mole or badger, or putting a freeze spell onto it to crack it, and get through that way. But *this*? ... No. I mean, even the *floor* of that horrible trap's made of metal. We'll just have to think of another way to break him out." She sank back into silence.

"Well, can't we at least try to calm the poor animal down a bit, first?" suggested Tytus after more time had gone by and his companion still hung in the air, silent and thoughtful. "He'll do himself serious harm, going on like that." He had a point. The wolf's cries had been growing ever more anguished.

Nataka shook herself out of her reverie. "Good thought, Tytus," she said, "First things first. Let's settle him down and make sure he survives to Sunwake, at least. Besides, this noise is worse than sticking one's head into a nest of hornets. Don't ask. Come along."

The two owls swooped down again, landing on the ground outside the cage.

"Listen, you!" barked Nataka (and a huge, handsome specimen her Wolf Transformation was, with a silver coat, ruff and tail that sparkled like ice in the moonlight, and eyes like molten lava). She stalked up to the grille at the front of the cage, planted her forepaws squarely under her, curled her lips back to reveal two rows of gleaming fangs, and uttered a volcano-rumble of a snarl from deep within her gullet. "Shut up! Quit wasting your energy and exhausting everybody, including yourself, with your row! ... Is this the way to behave just because you're in a trap, you moron?" Her deep voice throbbed with contempt.

The shadow inside the cage stopped dead in its tracks and the howling and snarling choked into silence. There was some snuffling and rustling, and a broad grey head emerged warily into the patch of moonlight pouring into the trap through the grille. A pair of distraught yellow eyes glared through the bars. The trapped wolf raised his snout and snuffed the air.

"Well?" demanded the silver wolf. She thrust her nose closer to the cage without breaking eye contact, keeping all her fangs on display, "What have you to say for yourself?"

"*Non… Comprends toujours rien, rien, rien, moi…*" The trapped animal's voice was hoarse and distracted, his pelt rough and shedding in patches, and his snout cracked and dry. An unhealthy, feverish glow flickered in his eyes. *"Hélas! Nom d'un nom ... Quel éspèce de loup est-ce, donc?"* As he muttered, he swung his hampered head from side to side, wincing and whimpering every time the large collar caught on the side of the cage.

"Non, non, non ... doit absolument être un autre cauchemar, ça... N'a pas l'air d'être normal, cet animal ... Est-ce possiblement un démon? ... Suis-je donc mort, et me trouve-je dans un éspèce d'enfer? ... C'est insupportable, ça..." [xxxv]

"Oh, for Infinity's sake!" snapped Nataka, sitting back on her haunches and barking a short, exasperated laugh, "This wolf's speaking *French*. I'll bet my claws he's a Canadian Timber Wolf. No wonder he's going mad. He won't have understood a thing anybody's said to him! Well, that at least I can change." She shut her eyes for a moment and hummed under her breath.

"Well, gild my eggs and call me Midas [xxxvi]," said Tytus the Baron, "that certainly explains a thing or two."

"Right then; this should make life easier for you," said Nataka to the wolf, "I've just Transformed your language skills so that you can understand everybody, regardless of where you are. Now, let's try again. ... Do you understand me?"

"You... you understand me?" the feverish, anguished eyes behind the metal grille snapped wide. "But... how is this possible? ... I am not dead? ... So I am – where? ... Explain, please?"

It didn't take long for Nataka and the Baron to explain the situation to Mond. And he in turn told them how one Suntime he had been hunting through his native forest for prey to feed his mate and her newly whelped litter of cubs, when he felt a sudden punching sting in his flank and then lost consciousness: *something* thorny had knocked him out. On reawakening he had found that he was being transported in the first of a series of a tiny angular things that he could only conceive of as traps, in which he was repeatedly jolted and bumped, heard unfamiliar noises and smelled appalling odours before finally being delivered to his present prison.

Mond had never met a Howler before he was captured, and quite understandably took them for monsters. It wasn't surprising either that he was desperate to return to his pack, his mate and his new litter of cubs. And to make matters worse, he didn't even know whether his family was still alive, and tortured himself with fears that his mate and cubs might be dead, or also prisoners and undergoing the same nightmare he was enduring. His bewilderment, homesickness and uncertainty made him frantic whenever he thought about it, which was all the time. So he screamed.

"So much is evident," commented Nataka dryly. "You're very good at screaming, better than the Howlers themselves. But, honestly, you're not really helping yourself with your behaviour, are you, Mond? ... Mind you, I don't blame you. All this time you've had no idea what was going on. *Sheesh*. What a nightmare for you. Well, anyway. As I said, we're here to work out a way to help you, if you'll give us a chance."

The great wolf shut his eyes, drooped his head to his forepaws (as far as he could - the collar was hampering his movements severely and the tight bandaging around his ribs wasn't helping either) and whimpered. He thrust one huge clawed forepaw out of the grille, towards Nataka.

"Here! ... Hold hard, old chap!" cried Tytus the Baron, rearing up and flapping his broad white wings, "You can't go trying to claw Nataka, that won't do at all!"

"Hush, Tytus," said Nataka, "He's not trying to claw me, you dodo; quite the opposite."

"I thank ... thank you... for the hope that you give me," whimpered the prisoner huskily. "Excuse please, my tears ... my lamentations ... it is for my kin that I weep ... and perhaps also for that I feel a bit of relief and hope at last. Alas! I shame myself ... Excuse, please..."

"A-*hem*..." The Baron shuffled from talon to talon, cleared his throat and pretended to have a sudden cold, for the wolf's words had moved him deeply, somersaulting his outrage into pity. "I say, chin up, old chap. They're perfectly understandable, your feelings; perfectly. I'd do the same myself, in your place. Absolutely. But... chin *up,* if you can manage it; all right? Stiff upper lip, eh? ... Show them all what you're made of; yes? I feel certain that our wise old friend will find a way to solve your predicament. So, bloodied but unbowed, that's the ticket, eh?"

"Oh, Tytus," exclaimed Nataka, laughing; "D'you realise that you're talking the way a whole pack of Howlers used to, before they swarmed off to maul other Howlers in their wars? ... *Stiff upper lip,* indeed! You're just one great big softie after all."

Tytus the Baron coughed again and fluttered up to perch on Nataka's broad silver neck. "It's quite understandable, you know;" he crooned, nibbling one of her ears, "Spend enough time with you, a bird begins to develop feelings that extend beyond his own nest. Stands to reason."

He raised his voice and spoke to Mond. "Listen, friend Wolf. Remember Ulysses, who didn't give up when he was trapped by the Cyclops, or by Circe the sorceress, *or* by the cannibals. He didn't let anything stand in his way. He fought his way past all his troubles, and got home in the end[xxxvii].

And what's more, he didn't have the benefit of our Nataka's help. I'd say you've got an advantage."

"Who is it, this ... *Ulysses*?" asked the wolf, his brow wrinkling. "Is it, perchance, another wolf whereof I know nothing?"

"Tytus, stop bewildering the poor animal," said Nataka, "he's got no idea what you're driving at, and now isn't the time to be filling his head with mythology." She turned back to the cage, lowered her muzzle and licked the paw that still lay on the moonlit grass outside the cage. Then she lifted her own forepaw and passed it through the grille under the timber wolf's nose. "See here," she said, "This is my vow that I shall not rest until you're safe. You have my tongue on it."

The timber wolf gulped, licked her silvery paw in turn, and then raised his head to gaze into her eyes. His tail wagged gently.

"Honoured I am to receive your taste and offer you mine, you who master the ways of my people. To you, also, I offer my pledge that I shall trust you. To you I give my confidence as I would to my pack," he said, "Although my nose informs me that you are not ... not *truly* of my kin. Yes? You are... *parbleu*,[xxxviii] how to say it? ... You are ... Otherwise. I mistake not?"

"You've got a good nose," approved Nataka, "Not many animals can tell the difference when I Transform. You're absolutely right, of course. I'm ... well; I'm what you call *Otherwise*, indeed. Right now I find it useful to be a wolf. But often I'm something else. None of me will harm you, whatever I am. Count on that.

"Right. Now we've a lot of planning to do if we're to break you out of this horrible trap in time, and for that I need to talk to Chant. And you have a task too, *mon ami*: you need to build up your strength for the escape. So to start with, I want you to sleep as much as possible, and consume everything they give you. I'll take away your fever, but you really *must* rest and eat. Everything depends on that."

The silver wolf shut her smouldering eyes for a moment. A thin, gold-tinged lace of light crossed the grille on a soft, barely audible version of the songs wolves sing to one another on frosty nights, and diffused into Mond's snout and mouth. The feverish glow faded from the trapped wolf's eyes and his nose began to bead with moisture.

Nataka grunted in satisfaction. "Good. That'll make you feel better. And if you have difficulty sleeping I can help you with that, too."

"*Merci,* Wise One," replied the wolf, "I beg that you will pardon me if I fail to eat more. Fear and sorrow have stolen my appetite, and the thought of food is nauseating to me. But yet I shall attempt to nourish myself, since you instruct me so. As for sleep, I assure you that I do not require your aid. I am very fatigued. Sleep will come now, for hope returns. I thank you."

He drew back from the grille and circled gingerly two or three times around a low straw-covered pallet that his Howler captors had laid at one end of the cage before lowering himself wincingly onto it. With some shuffling and groaning he finally settled into a relatively comfortable position, pillowing his hooded head on his forepaws and tucking his hind legs under his body. "I sleep now," he announced, gaped his jaws in a huge yawn that curled his tongue and exposed all his fangs, and shut his eyes.

"Oh, fidget and scratch;" muttered Nataka, "I could cure him of *all* his injuries right now. But it's just too risky. We don't want the Howlers' suspicions to be roused in any way, and a sudden comprehensive cure would certainly do that, even the most stupid ones would notice that. But it's frustrating. Ah well, it won't be for much longer." She turned away and loped off into the dark with the owl on her back.

Mond was not awake to see Tytus the Baron lift off Nataka's back and ghost away, to be joined a few moments later by the tawny owl that flapped silently off from where the running silver wolf had disappeared.

Chapter 7. Rescue Plan #2

"Naught in might exceedeth dread necessity." [xxxix]

"So where do you think we'll find Chant?" asked Tytus when they were aloft again.

"Um... Just a tick; I'll have to orientate myself ... Right, I know where her pets have their nest, and that's where we'll go to start with;" replied Nataka, "Follow me."

But they didn't have to look very far for the canny little cat. Her sharp ears had immediately detected the changes wrought by Nataka's ministrations, and sent her running out of her cat shelter (where her ailing brother Leto lay quietly meditating) with her thin, brindled tail curled like a question mark and her ears pricked forward. She wanted to find out why the wolf had finally stopped screaming and an unexpected silence fallen over the whole zoo as one after another of its exhausted inhabitants dropped gratefully off to sleep.

Nataka and Tytus spotted her as she sped along the roof-ridge of the Primate House, and swooped down to land next to her.

"Nataka!" Chant reared onto her hind-paws and batted the air playfully, pretending to swipe at the two owls as they descended, "So Skald reached you with my news, then? Excellent! I was a *tiny* bit worried about sending him off during Batlight, but ... well; this *is* an emergency, and I..."

"I'll say it's an emergency;" interrupted Nataka, Transforming into a black panther as she landed, and fixing her blazing yellow eyes on the cat, "I'm amazed you didn't send for me sooner, Chant. We've a ridiculously short time in which to help that wolf. What's all that about, anyway? What kept you from sending earlier?"

Chant sat back and washed her face, deciding that it didn't do to take offence at anything a panther said, even if the sun *did* revolve around one's own furry little bum.

"Yes. I should have sent for you sooner, I know. Skald said the same thing;" she admitted, making her voice soft. "But, you know, when they first arrive here, most newcomers fuss and barney to start with, but then they begin to enjoy being pampered. Because, let's face it, my Howler Pet really loves everybody and gives us a good life here; he's quite civilised for a Howler - thanks to *my* training, of course. And he's the chief Howler around here too; so all the others do the same. And so everybody considers this more of a holiday than a prison; you know? Food on tap; grooming and cuddles; treats; nice places to run and sleep and play…"

"What are you, a brochure?" snarled Nataka. "Quit selling the place to me and get to the point."

Tytus the Baron preened a feather, clicked his beak and chuckled to himself. "Brochure;" he murmured, "Selling. Most droll. Most apposite."

"Of course, of course;" chirruped Chant. *Honestly, Immortals are so touchy,* she thought. *And even more so if they're Nataka… Still, what a way to talk to me! … But – um – those fangs … and those claws … Nah. Just keep purring.*

"So anyway," she added hurriedly, "*Any*way, I suppose that, like everybody else, I was hoping the stupid animal would settle down and start to enjoy himself. Only of course he didn't. I've no idea how you've managed to settle him now. How did you do it, hit him over the head?"

A sudden commotion from the Primate House underneath them made them all jump. A pair of huge leathery hands

103

grasped the grille directly under the roof beam they were sitting on and rattled it violently.

"Oy! *Mush!* ... D'you *mind?* What does a chimp have to *do* around here to get some sleep at last?" yelled a furious voice directly beneath them. "No sooner does one rumpus end than another begins. Are you purple-bummed low-lifes going to sit up there yammering all night? ... Squashed bananas, I don't know *what* we're coming to ... Neighbourhood going all to pot... Noise, noise noise ... 'S'like trying to sleep in the middle of Lagos High Street ..." The voice trailed off in a string of simian mutterings.

"Oops," giggled Chant, who had turned into a ball of fur as soon the yelling began, "We've disturbed Kelele[xl]. Not a good idea; he's a grumpy old chimp at the best of times; and now, what with all this *matata*... well, I'd sooner play catch in a patch of stinging nettles than mess with *him*. He can be properly vicious. We'd better get off this roof and find a quiet place to talk. Follow me."

She led them off the building and down to a secluded corner beside a spacious compound surrounded by a fine-mesh fence full of rocks, tunnels, tree stumps, a small sandpit and swings. The enclosure housed a family of lively and inquisitive banded mongooses. Two brothers called Lerema and Tesho shared it very happily with three females called Wapi, Hapa and Twende, and their numerous kittens.[xli]

"We can talk here without disturbing anybody," said Chant, sharpening her claws on a corner post of the compound, against which there flourished a densely flowering hebe bush. "The whole mongoose family will be down at the sandpit, as usual..."

"Oh no, we're not!" interrupted a shrill voice from the depths of the hebe. A stub-eared, bright-eyed, inquisitive little furry wedge of a face popped out of the foliage, followed by the long-tailed body of a handsome male mongoose. The newcomer reared up onto his hind legs and sat with his forepaws dangling as he stared curiously at the Nataka the Panther and the Barn Owl. "So what's the *shauri* [xlii] then, Chant?" he asked, " I haven't seen your friends before, have I? ... Who are they? ... What're you all up to? ... Is it fun? ... Can I join in?"

"Tesho!" exclaimed the cat, "Show a bit of respect. This is Nataka, and this…"

"You're *kidding*! You can't be serious! ... Not *the* Nataka? ... Oh my tail and whiskers, you *are* serious! ... *Oitochoi!* [xliii] ... *The* Nataka!" shrilled Tesho. He bounded forward, reared up until he was teetering on the very tips of his hind-toes, and beamed into the gleaming eyes of the panther.

"Curl me up and call me a monkey's paw, I've heard *all* about you, Nataka! I've *always* wanted to meet you! ... Ooh, wait'll I tell Lerema, he'll be so jealous he'll eat his own tail!"

The little animal squeaked, dropped onto all fours and somersaulted around in the dust for a few seconds to relieve his excitement, and then bounced back onto his hind legs and shook himself. "Just *had* to do that, or burst," he announced cheerfully through the cloud of dust rising from his coat. "I mean, I really, truly *never*... Nataka herself, in the flesh!" Tesho burbled on before anybody else could say anything, "*Whoop*! This is more exciting than a nest full of scorpions… Oh hey, Nataka, do us a favour and show us some magic!"

And the irrepressible little creature hopped up and down on all fours with his tail in the air.

"HUSH! I'm talking here! ... This," spat Chant, "...*This* is Tytus the Baron, her friend. They're both here on *serious* business, all right? ... Do you understand, you dust-brain? ... So if you can't go away, at least settle down and keep quiet. They're not here to entertain *you,* you know!"

"Honoured and delighted to meet you both," chirruped the mongoose, quite unabashed, "We're going to have *such* fun together, I just know it! ... You must meet my family, they'll be chasing their own tails..."

"Ach, shred my bedding," snarled the little cat, fluffing up to her largest size, whipping her brindled tail and glaring at the mongoose, "I *said* we're not here for *fun,* you infuriating Nyama! Can't you just go away and leave us in peace?"

"Actually," said Tytus, who had been silent for some time, watching the mongoose's antics, "Actually, I wonder whether we might not find it helpful to include this excitable young Nyama[xliv] in our conversation. What do you think, Nataka?"

"You've got a point," replied the Panther, contemplating Tesho, "He might come in useful. Pleased to meet you, Tesho."

"Well, pluck my whiskers if I know what you both see in him," said Chant, sitting back and looking over the dusty little mongoose, who had now taken to simultaneously flicking his tail and washing his ears. "What's so special about him?"

"Well, for one thing, he must be very good at breaking out of prisons..." said the owl.

"Yes, exactly," said Nataka, "And if he can break *out* of prisons..."

"He can break *in*to them as well!" interrupted Tesho. "Yes! I *can* - and I *do*, regularly! *Oitochoi!* This'll be such fun... But I work better with my brother's help. Mind if he joins us?"

"Excellent. Fine. Why not?" said Chant. She was quick on the uptake. "Good idea, Nataka. Anything you say. The more the merrier. You'd better nip off and find him then, Tesho; off you go." She stretched luxuriously and rubbed her head against the post. "Either of you interested in stroking a cat while we wait? I'd properly enjoy a good scratch behind the ears right about now..."

So, while Tesho scampered off to summon his brother, Nataka assumed an orang-utan Transformation and stroked Chant thoroughly with all her digits, starting with the pretty brindled head and working down her back to the tip of her tail. The little cat lay purring in the dust, squirming and kneading the air with her forepaws. "Ohh, yes; that's good; that's *good;*" she chirrupped. "*There,* right there ...yesss ... perfect... perrrrfect... *frrrrr...*"

Then Tesho was back with his identical brother Lerema. After the newcomer had also bounced around a bit to dissipate *his* excitement, the group settled down to a serious discussion.

"To sum up," said Nataka after she and Tytus had explained the dilemma to their fascinated companions, "I need a way to get into Mond's cage, and I can't do that because the dratted contraption's made of that horrible stuff the Howlers call *metal*, which I can't Change quickly. And so far the only solution I can think of is that we find a way to lay our paws on those little things the Howlers use to get their ugly padlocks open – you know what I mean, Chant: they call 'em *keys*. Any ideas?"

107

"Oh yes, I know all about keys. They don't taste nice. Well, you could stay with me till Sunwake, Nataka, then pretend to *be* me while I make myself scarce, and nick the keys from my Pet before he picks them up during Sunclimb – you know, while he's washing and feeding his pooh to that big white water god he worships every morning;" suggested Chant. "Pluck my whiskers if I can understand why he doesn't just bury it, like normal folk…"

"Yes; I could do that;" interrupted Nataka, "except that I have to be somewhere else by Sunclimb to see to another *shauri*. I suppose at a pinch I could come back after that, though."

"But what about *us?*" squeaked Lerema, "we're really good at nicking things. So why don't *we* nick those shiny – er – keys – things for you?" His brother nodded vehemently, and they both wriggled the digits of their forepaws.

"Hold on, though;" interrupted Tytus, "How will you know *which* keys open Mond's cage?"

"Oh, that's not a problem," purred Chant, still very mellow from her massage. "My Pet keeps those key things on a lot of little twigs that stick out of the wall over a platform where he fiddles with dead stuff. [xlv] I don't know why he bothers to spend so much time doing that. He isn't grooming or de-lousing himself when he does it, and he definitely *isn't* killing and playing with those things before eating them, because they're totally inedible. So I'm not sure why he's wasting his time in such useless play when he could be worshipping me instead. … But that's Howlers for you …" Just then she spotted the warning red gleam in Nataka's eyes.

"… Well *any*way," she added hurriedly, "my Pet always takes the keys and gives them to whichever Howler has to look after Mond that Sunclimb – which they all hate, you know. They have to wash him, and change his bedding, and sometimes also see to his wounds..."

"Yes, yes, *yes*;" interrupted Nataka, "I know all that; Skald told me. So he hands the keys out to the Howler who has to see to Mond that day. I *get* it. Next?"

"Well, I *was* going to tell you, you know!" said Chant, stung. She wasn't used to being interrupted. "No need to rush a cat ... Anyway, when the job's done, the Howler comes back and drops the shiny key things onto my Pet's fiddling platform, and later my Pet hangs them up again when he comes in for his first feed. So anyway, I can watch him to see *which* keys he uses and *where* exactly he hangs them, you know ... and then point them out to Lerema and Tesho."

"That's right. And then, as soon as those key thingies come back and Chant's Pet puts them away, we can sneak in..." said Tesho.

"... And nick them!" added Lerema. The brothers slapped each other's front paws and chirruped "*Namna hioo, tu!*" and "*Bila shauri!*" [xlvi]

"Good... it sounds like we have a plan for *that* bit of the business, then;" said Nataka. "So now all I have to do is figure out what to do with Mond afterwards; how to get him away once he's out."

"One of your Transformations or Disappearings would manage that, I should have thought;" suggested Tytus.

"Yes. I *could* Disappear him and sneak him out," said Nataka, "But then I've got to get him away as far and as quickly as possible, too. Hm. There's bound to be a solution. I'll just have to work on it.

"But in any case, that's all got to wait for now. I've got another *indaba* ^{xlvii} back home at Sunsink tomorrow, and we should be able to thrash out a good plan for getting Mond well away once he's out."

She turned to Chant and the two mongooses, who were squirming with anticipation and excitement. "It'll be up to you three now;" she said, "Do you honestly feel up to your parts of the job?"

"Oh, don't worry; we can do this," / "*Sawa!* ^{xlviii} Just you watch us!" / "*Oitochoi!* Leave it to us!" said the three little animals at the same time.

After a little more *palaver* the conspirators agreed that Nataka, the Baron and a few other friends would meet at the same spot after Sunsink when two Startimes had passed. The idea was that Lerema and Tesho would have nicked the keys by then, and would hand them over. Then Nataka would release the wolf.

Timing was crucial. If the keys went missing for too long, Chant's Howler Pet would notice their absence, and they all wanted to avoid that. Chant and the two mongooses agreed to do some practice runs. And Chant said she would also pay Mond a visit during next Sunclimb to tell him what they were planning, so that he wouldn't be taken by surprise.

Then, much to Lerema and Tesho's delight, Nataka Transformed back into a tawny owl and took off into the slanting light of the gradually setting moon with Tytus the Baron at her side. The two birds sped away as the shrill voices of the cheering mongooses gradually faded away behind them.

"What a pair;" chuckled Tytus, "If their performance matches their enthusiasm this'll be easier than catching a lame vole."

As they approached the big water they had to cross again to get home [xlix], a dark cloud of barely visible bats whisked past them going full tilt the other way, their sonar signals like a bombardment of crystal-sharp noise-needles in the still night air.

"*Good hunting!*" squeaked numerous little voices, and "Good hunting!" hooted the two owls in return.

"*Rain coming! – Storm! – Imminent! – Fly to roost!*" shrilled the voices as the cloud whipped astern, driven by the wind.

"Thanks for the warning!" called Nataka.

"They're not mistaken;" commented the Baron, "Look at the moon."

The face of the sinking moon was visibly misting over, swallowed in a rapidly approaching, shapeless dark blot that had heaved up from the direction of Sunsleep. Soon enough the two owls were flying through a heavy, wind-driven squall of rain that became heavier and denser with every flap of their wings. And then the moon disappeared altogether, and Nataka found herself drawing on all her skills to steer a straight course for home through the pitchy darkness full of the buffeting wind and the crash of the waves below.

And then came the lightning and thunder, punctuated by sudden stinging spatters of hail.

"Hold *on*, Tytus!" called Nataka.

Her companion was already struggling to keep up. His rapidly flapping wings didn't seem to be driving him forward at all against the blast, and they felt more and more leaden as the heavy, driving rain interspersed with vicious, spattering particles of ice plastered the windward feathers against his body and stopped the breath in his nostrils and beak. He began to lose altitude as the rain and hailstones pummelled him closer and closer to the surface of the seething water beneath him. He had the nightmarish impression that some great monster was intent on plucking his feathers off him and leaving him defenceless, naked in the storm. Still he battled against the onslaught, even as he knew that he wouldn't be able to continue for much longer. Yet, owl-like, even in that extremity he uttered no word of complaint.

"Tuck yourself in under my leeward wing!" now yelled Nataka over the screaming wind.   "Come on! ... Here we go…"

"*Not* optimal flying conditions for a self-respecting owl;" grunted the Baron to himself. He thought wistfully of his cosy roost in the intact, ivy-festooned bell-tower of a derelict chapel. "I should have remembered that I'm no sea-bird, much less King Lear, to bide the pelting of this pitiless storm…" [1]

But Nataka's voice had revived his courage. Mustering one last surge of energy, he flapped and struggled till he gained the lee of the tawny owl's body, where he was relieved and grateful to complete his journey enclosed in the protective bubble of calm Nataka cast around them both. Inside her sheltering magic the storm was reduced to nothing more than an exciting spectacle. But even so, the Baron's energy had been so severely depleted that every thrust of his wings tested his rapidly flagging strength.

At last, after what felt like a lifetime of flying, Tytus realised that he was once again travelling over familiar terrain, approaching the wooded hillside on which Toki awaited them. The gentle rosy beacon Nataka's magical cottage projected into the sky to guide the travellers home was one of the most heartening sights the exhausted barn owl had ever seen.

That Startime he no longer hunted; he was far too tired. Besides, the storm lasted all night. Instead he slept, perching in Toki's eaves alongside the slumbering kestrel.

Interlude II

"Acceptance of what is. That is the shortest path to peace with yourself." [li]

Leto the Enlightened and Stoical roused himself from a sleep that had left him unrefreshed, and watched the storm through the glass of his Pet's sanctuary. He knew that he was experiencing his last Startime in his present incarnation, and he didn't want to miss a moment of it. And besides, he was now so weak from the disease that had grown inside him and robbed him of his energy and appetite that even sleep had become elusive. His legs trembled when he tried to stand, and he felt light-headed and insubstantial, liable to float away on a breath of air.

He watched a particularly spectacular lightning bolt flash across the sky, casting into sudden sharp relief the tossing branches of the trees in his Pets' back garden. A deep, rolling crash of thunder followed hard on the heels of the stab of light. It resonated through his bones. He had always feared thunder, but now he found the display exhilarating and wondrous. After all, he was dying: against the great Awe of that prospect, nothing could frighten him any longer.

"Fire, air and water;" he mused. "Soon I shall mingle with them again ... and then, once more onto the Great Wheel." He shut his beautiful eyes and sank into a reverie, contemplating the image of the great, inexorable spiral of Reality unrolling and curling back on itself through the many dimensions of Infinity it is granted to every cat to see just before it sheds a Life.

During the following Sunclimb, Leto's Pets held him in their arms, stroked him and wept as, soothed by a magical Howler potion to ease his pain, at last he slipped away, relieved and contented, from the exhausted, once beautiful gold-and white furred vessel that had borne him through more seasons than he could recall.

His litter-sister Chant had been tired out by the previous Startime's events. The storm did not disturb her, although she heard it tumble and cascade through her dreams. Oblivious of Leto's momentous fate, she snoozed on well past Sunclimb in her heated cot and dreamed of wolves, jailbreaks and twenty-fingered massages.

Chapter 8. *Cat Therapy and Badger Potion*

"Our gods are within us. We choose our own compulsions. Our souls are our own." [lii]

"So when's that there ole biddy s'posed ter turn up, then?" growled Rav'n. His large green eyes glared balefully at Nataka the leopard-spotted Maine Coon cat, who had just materialised in the neat little garden outside Gertrude's apartment.

Rav'n had hunkered down under the diminutive porch that jutted out over the apartment's diamond-clean French windows. He was trying unsuccessfully to shelter from the heavy slanting rain, the remnant of the previous night's storm. His sodden fur stuck to his body, making his head enormous and his body appear knobbly and undernourished. His drooping whiskers were strung with raindrops, which splattered off, hitting him in the eyes every time he moved. He hissed miserably, shaking his waterlogged ears.

"For 'arf a rat's tail I'd give up this whole flippin' lark," he grumbled, hunching his sodden shoulders against the wet, "Fool's game, s'wha' it is. I'm not a *frog*."

"Cheer up, Rav'n," said Nataka, "it's a bit bracing, but that can't be helped. I don't control the weather – or better said, I leave it well alone. But anyway, think of the advantage this gives you. You look regularly pitiful and half-starved like that. If I know the old biddy she won't be able to resist rescuing you."

"S'all very well for *yeh* ter say!" complained Rav'n, "*Yer* not 'arf drowned, like wot I am!"

The Maine Coon cat was sitting in the middle of the small lawn, dry and unruffled inside her protective shell.

"Yeh *could* do tha' fing – wha'ever yer doin' ter keep dry - fer *me* too, yeh know," yammered Rav'n. "Greedy cah," he added to himself under his whiskers, "Selfish, them magical folks is... Any more o' this, an' I'll..."

But Rav'n never completed his *sottovoce* threat (to which Nataka had been listening with great interest) because just then he heard a soft shriek through the opening French window behind him. Hackles rising, he whipped round. The little old biddy Gertrude was approaching him in tiny shuffling steps, half crouching over her hind paws. Her bony, hairless front paws were spread, reaching out to him.

"Why's she *doin'* tha'?" asked Rav'n anxiously, "Wha's wiv all tha' bendin' an' hobblin' ? .. She sick, or wha'?"

"Ha!" chortled Nataka (who was nowhere to be seen, having Disappeared herself the instant Gertrude opened the French window), "She's doing that to make herself look less threatening, you dumb mog. She must have heard you complaining just now, and come to check. Play along; she won't harm you."

"Ooohhh!" crooned Gertrude in a soft baby voice, "It's a *poor* ickle Kitty, and it's all *wet* and *cold* and *lonely, POOR* ickle fing! ... I saw you hiding in my porch, poor ickle Kitty! ... Ooh, is it all *wet* in this *miserable* weather, then? ... Is it a *sad* and *lonely* and *hungry* lickle *kitty*, then? ... Doesn't it have anywhere to *go* to stay out of this *howwid* rain, then? ... Does it want an ickle *cuddle*, then? ... Don't run away, kitty! Here, kitty, kitty, kitty..."

"Wha's *wiv* 'er? Is she *barmy?*" demanded Rav'n, backing away from the old woman's approach. His claws scrabbled on the slippery tiles. "Arskin' all them fool questions when she can *see* I'm 'arf drahned..."

"*Now's* your chance, you great fur-brain!" urged Nataka's voice, "No, don't back away, you fool! Use those skills I showed you. Go on ... Give her a sad little *meow* to start with..."

Rav'n pulled himself together. He gave up trying to escape (it was useless anyway; his paws couldn't find any purchase on those wet tiles), shook himself, sat up on his haunches, glared into the old biddy's eyes and let loose a plaintive yowl.

"*OooOOooh!* ... *POOR* kitty!" The old Howler sounded ecstatic. Her voice went up a notch. "I *knew* it! Poor ickle kitty wants Auntie Gertie to *care* for it, doesn't it? Oh yes, it *does!* ... Just a *teensy weensy* minute, darling, Auntie Gertie'll fetch a nice soft *towel* to dry you off; get rid of all that *naughty* wet, oh *yes,* she *will* ... Don't you run away, now; *pwomise?* Auntie Gertie'll be *right* back..." And the little old woman bustled back into her apartment, crooning as she went.

"Splendid work, cat," applauded Nataka, "She's hooked. Send a couple more of those calls after her, just to make sure. Make them as pathetic as you like. You're doing excellently, for a beginner."

Rav'n accordingly slunk on his soggy stomach towards the half-open French window, calling plaintively. He was rewarded by the voice of the Old Biddy cooing back at him from inside the apartment.

"Yes, yes, yesyesyes yes... *There's* a good kitty, *poor* ickle thing ... Here we go, then; *here* I am! ... *Look,* Kitty, look what *I've* got ... Yes! It's a nice soft *towel* to make you all *dry* and *warm* again, oh *yes,* it *is*..." The old Howler reappeared in the porch, made a sudden swooping pounce, and enveloped the sodden grey cat in a large purple towel. She straightened up, cradling him in her arms.

"*There*, now," she crowed, "*Now* I've got you safe! First we'll get you *all* nice and dry, and then let's see what I can feed you to make you *all* warm *inside* too, you poor ickle Kitty... You remind me of the Toffee Emperor," she added with a little catch in her voice, "*He* hated the rain too, and he *loved* to be dried and fed, my poor ... But never mind; what can't be cured must be endured; mustn't it, ickle kitty? ... Yes, it *must*. ... My, but you *are* a beautiful colour, aren't you? ... I wonder if you've got a name."

"*Oops*, careful, Rav'n! Keep those claws sheathed and don't struggle," warned Nataka sharply. The alley cat was instinctively tensing to struggle free of the old woman's hold. "You don't want to undo all the good work by losing your head *now*, do you? Sheath your claws. She won't hurt you. She's just going to carry you into her lair and make you comfortable, you lucky dope. Calm down.

"Well," she added, "I reckon you're home and dry now. This is the beginning of your life of luxury."

"Oy! ... 'Old 'ard ... don'cher abandon me, Nat, ole girl!" meowed the grey cat nervously over the old woman's shoulder as she bore him into her lair. "Don'cher go forgettin' ahr agreemen'!..." The wide green eyes that stared back at Nataka were dark with trepidation. "'S'all new to me, this is..."

"Oh, *relax,* cat;" called Nataka. "There's nothing to it, now you've won her over. Just remember all those lap skills we practised, and use them as necessary to keep her sweet ... Oh, and don't forget to go to the toilet *outside* her lair, somewhere in a hidden spot. OK? Old Howler biddies don't like to see your poo on their grass.

"Well, that's all, really... And of course, as we've agreed, I'll pop around occasionally, just in case. ... Well, I've got to scarper now. Other fish to catch, you know. Have fun!"

"Don't you *worry*, little kitty," crooned Gertrude, shutting the French window and bearing her soggy, meowing prize to her favourite armchair next to a glowing electric fire, "I won't hurt you ... Ooh, you're *such* a *talker*, aren't you? ... *Clever* kitty! Good kitty? ... *Here* we go, then..."

And before he knew it, Rav'n was receiving a comprehensive rubdown that made his fur fluff up like thistledown and his skin tingle in places he hadn't known he possessed. This was much more enjoyable than digging out fish-heads from waste bins in the pouring rain. He began to purr and knead the old biddy's lap in spite of himself, while Gertrude murmured contentedly over him, the ache in her breast steadily easing.

As she sped off, Nataka the Buzzard felt the turbulence of Gertrude's sorrow ease and disappear. She cheered "Mission Accomplished!" - and promptly forgot all about Rav'n and the Old Biddy.

***

The chilblain potion and its steam had turned green as fresh hazel leaves in the spring and begun to smell like fruit drops when Paa efficiently and neatly swung it off the flames, supervised by Glose. Nataka found the two animals side by side, admiring their handiwork. Paa was standing on the seat of the wooden chair with her paws resting on its back while Glose perched on the chair back next to her. They gazed into the depths of the cauldron with their heads together, sharing their impressions of the mesmerising fluid that swirled and curled inside it.

"It looks alive, doesn't it? Almost too good to waste on a badger," cawed Glose. "It's perfect. Of course, a lot of that was down to *me*, you know. I insisted on only the freshest ingredients..."

"Ooh, *look!* I'm sure I just saw a fish swimming around in there!" interrupted Paa, wagging her tail.

"A mere illusion, Paa, I assure you;" said the raven indulgently. "No fish could withstand the temperature. No, that's just an effect of the Magic. Look: now it's like a forest glade with butterflies and flowers. D'you see?"

"Oh, *yes!*" said the poodle. On an impulse she turned her muzzle and licked the startled raven on the side of his head. He squawked and reared away, almost falling off the back of the chair.

"What did you have to do *that* for, you uncontrolled canine?" he demanded indignantly, flapping his wings to keep his perch.

"You're so *clever,* Glose," said the dog, "and I've had so much *fun.* I just wanted to thank you..."

"Oh, well; since you put it like that," responded the bird, mollified. "Though I must say your thanks involve a lot of saliva. But on balance we worked together very well; didn't we? ... I never thought I'd say this to a dog, but you're really not too stupid, all things considered."

"Thanks, Glose," said the dog humbly.

At that moment Nataka the large-eyed and -eared Sprite, who had been sitting unnoticed on the windowsill throughout this exchange, bounced into the room.

"So, Glose, you pretentious, pompous old wind-bag," she laughed, "*You* insisted on only the freshest ingredients, did you? ... *Really*? ... And in your exalted opinion Paa isn't too stupid, all things considered, is she? ... Why, without her to help you, we'd all have been up an antipodean gum tree, and you know it!"

The raven squawked, ruffled his feathers and cleared his throat. "Where did you come from?" he demanded, "It just isn't *fair* to sneak up on people like that – it's bad enough that the Baron does it all the time..."

"Yes, you're right, of course;" said Nataka, winking at Paa, "Never sneak up on people, in case you hear something they don't want you to. That it, eh? Hahaha! ... C'mon, Bird; time to climb down off your perch and admit you're an old fraud."

"What's an anti-pod-Ian gum tree?" asked the dog interestedly, cocking her head to one side.

"Something you don't want to be *up*," replied the Protean, ruffling the fluffy bit between Paa's ears. "C'mon, let's have a look at this potion, then. ... Yes, that's fine. Well done, both of you. Now, all I need is to add one last ingredient..." she bustled off to a shelf stacked to groaning with vials and bottles, took down a little black glass flask that bore a label illustrated with wings and a halo, and uncorked it.

"Um, now; let's see. Ten drops should do it, I'd say; wouldn't you, Toki?" The cottage creaked. Nataka nodded and tilted the flask carefully over the cauldron, counting out the large, sparkling drops of jelly-like fluid that gradually collected and fell from it; "...Watch."

As the first drop of fluid fell into the potion there was a little flash of brightest pink that quickly turned to a blend of peach and greengage as the mixture sizzled and bubbled. The second drop, sparkling deep purple as it fell, turned the fluid an unexpected pitch black. Paa gasped at the alteration. Glose's beak flopped open. "Catching flies, that Bird?" teased the sprite. Her sharp green eyes glowed eerily in the darkness emerging from the cauldron.

The third drop of liquid dispelled the shadow and again caused the potion to boil furiously, but now the bubbles seething inside the cauldron were russet brown, while the fourth drop turned them as brightly red as fresh blood.

"What *is* this new thing?" whispered the poodle, mesmerised, "What makes it change like that?"

"A very complicated distillation of wild Angelica seeds, root, stems and leaves; [liii]" said Nataka, "mixed with one or two incantations and particularly clean spring water. Our potion's going to be what Saps used to call a *panacea*. That's well worth knowing about, by the way. Why don't you look it up and read it out, Glose?"

And while the enthusiastic raven scrabbled through various scroll chests, Nataka carried on adding drops. The fifth drop made the potion turn into streaky azure and denim blue with splashes of indigo in the mix; the sixth resulted in a whirlpool of mingled birch-leaf and sea-turtle green, in which flashes of silvery lightning surged about; the seventh drop turned the potion sunflower yellow shot with violet and mushroom tones; the eighth spawned a blob of orange in the heart of the brew that blossomed into all the vibrant, dancing colours of a driftwood fire; and the ninth drop roused a volcano of sparks and showers containing all the colours Paa had ever seen, as well as some she hadn't. "One more drop to go;" said Nataka, "You ready?"

"I can hardly *breathe*," whispered Paa, and turned her quivering nose backwards and forwards, peering intently at the bottle and cauldron in turn. "I can't *imagine* what's going to happen next … Oh, *my!* …"

As the last drop fell, the potion welcomed it with a glorious burst of gold that danced around the cauldron in wavelets - and then *suddenly* snapped into the brightest, most unblemished white imaginable, purer and cleaner than can ever be found on sharp, perfectly still mornings deep in the Seasons of the Sleeping Bear and Roaring Wolf, when the limpid blue sky arches over fields of untrodden, glittering virgin snow.

"Is it – is it *supposed* to look like that?" breathed Paa.

"Spot on," said Nataka. "Exactly what I wanted. The smells, too."

For of course each drop of the distilled liquid added by Nataka had also changed the scent of the mixture. In the right order they were: mixed apple, liquorice and tree bark; combined mud, cinnamon and cloves; raw meat with rosewater; forget-me-not and bluebells; sea-spray and lawn clippings; ripe wheat with a hint of yellow-flag iris and fungi; orange peel, wood-smoke and autumn leaves; the air, grass and earth after a storm, and … nothing.

The tenth drop had wiped out every scent, which came as a total surprise to the dog.

"We've made a liquid rainbow, more or less;" said the Protean contentedly, stirring the potion and lifting the ladle every so often to watch the drops of glistening white fluid drip back into the brew, which appeared lit from within and cast a delightful, pearly sheen over Toki's walls and beams. "And, as anybody can tell you who has ever studied Newton[liv] (not a very *nice* Sap, by all accounts; but a genius for all that), when you combine all the colours of the rainbow you get white. Good, huh? ... Glose, have you found that definition yet? ... Great. Read it out, would you?"

"*Ahem,* keep your tail feathers on; nearly ready ... " the raven cleared his throat importantly as he straddled a large and rather tatty vellum scroll he had hauled out of a chest. He was plonking various weights onto its corners to pin it down and stop it from curling back up into a tube. Eventually he bent over and began to trace its spidery script with his beak. "Here we are ... *Panacea.* ... Er ... You will appreciate that I'm leaving out various archaic descriptions ..."

"Yes, *yes;* understood. Get to it."

"... And also discounting ironic and sceptical comments," cawed Glose, raising his voice, "Which, of course, are not relevant to our ..."

"*Definition,* you feathered windbag!" interrupted the Protean. She pretended to rap the bird on the head with her ladle.

"Patience is a *virtue,*" intoned Glose sententiously, still scanning the scroll in a leisurely manner. He felt too self-satisfied to lose his temper. "Er... um... just a tick ... Hmm: oh – oh, no; *this* bit's irrelevant ... Ah... Here it is, then..."

He cleared his throat again, then read out: "The *panacea* is named after the Greek Goddess of Universal Remedy called *Panakeia,* and is also known in some circles as *Panchrest.* It is supposed to be a remedy that will cure all diseases and prolong life indefinitely. There. Satisfied?"

"Thanks, Glose. Got there in the end," said Nataka. "So, you two: you see before you a *bona fide* panacea, a cure for all illnesses, in other words. And I've added an additional

125

quality to it. It's also rather useful for introducing various changes to living things that *aren't* sick. Clever, huh?"

"*Brilliant*," Paa stared with shining eyes from the glowing contents of the cauldron to Nataka, "Just brilliant! ... So now you'll be able to help that poor badger Glose was telling me about ...er ..."

"Scrumpy," prompted the raven.

"Yes; yes, that's it! Scrumpy. ... Can we give it to him now?" Paa jumped off the chair and bounded excitedly around the cottage.

"*Careful*!" squawked Glose, jumping off the scroll and dragging it out of her path, "You'll tear the scroll, you uninhibited fur ball!"

Nataka took down a crystal bottle from a shelf full of different empty containers, which had just appeared on the wall (Toki was good at anticipating her requirements). She weighed it in her hand for a moment then shook her head and put it back. "Nope, that wouldn't last a minute with Scrumpy. He can be a bit rough-and-tumble. ... Ah. This'll do." She reached for a little leather-bound hardwood barrel with a good strong bung. "Perfect. Thanks, Toki."

Holding the miniature barrel over the cauldron, she ladled potion into it until it was full. Then she stoppered it tightly and secured a small leather thong around it, which she hung around Paa's neck, tying a bow that allowed the barrel to dangle under the poodle's chin. "Look, Glose," she instructed the raven, "You simply pull on *this* loose end and the whole thing comes away. Clear? ... Good. Tell Scrumpy to take a swig of it right away, and then to repeat the dose every Full Moon until the barrel's empty. That'll protect him from chilblains *and* keep his coat glossy, too.

… Mind you don't spill any of it when you get the stopper out, now.

"Off you both go, then. Remember: make sure to give Scrumpy plenty of time to recognise you when you find him; he's all bad temper, teeth and claws, and he can get a bit hasty if he's startled. Good hunting!"

Nataka stood in the doorway of her cottage and watched the two animals disappear into the forest on their mission of mercy. The rain had ended, and the skies were clearing behind the rain clouds that rolled away in the direction of Sunwake. Paa trotted away with her tail aloft like a pennant and the barrel swinging from her neck. She left little smudged paw prints behind her in the damp grass. Glose was riding on her back, squawking directions and flapping his wings occasionally to keep from falling off. "They're a right pair," Nataka commented to Axl, who had lifted his head from a patch of clover and strolled across the lawn to join her, "chalk and cheese."

"Caress?" whickered Axl in reply, nudging her gently with his velvety muzzle. "Scratch? Ears?" He was a deer of few words.

When Axl returned to his grazing after a thorough cosseting, Nataka re-entered the cottage and set to pouring the rest of the potion into the remaining containers on the shelf. Occasionally she added another ingredient or two: an incantation; a few grains of powder; some drops of liquid. Each addition again altered the appearance and scent of the potion. At last she pressed a finger onto the front of each sealed container to indicate what it was, before stacking each sealed phial, bottle, barrel and tub onto the new shelf.

When the cauldron was empty, the Protean inverted it carefully over the fire to cleanse it, whereupon the flames flared silvery-white and the whole cottage sparkled for an instant. Toki shivered and gave a sigh of pleasure. "You're welcome," said Nataka. She dragged the vessel off the flames to hang against one wall of the inglenook, and straightened up to admire her handiwork. "Done," she said, stretching, "that took longer than I expected." Toki creaked.

Everything done, she picked up the wooden bowl of fruit and a handful of nuts, and carried them to one corner of the inglenook. She tucked herself cosily against the cushions on the bench, wrapped her long furry tail around herself like a cat, and sat munching, thinking about Paa – there was a great deal to think about – and watching the fire. Then, dropping off as suddenly as a dormouse, she napped in the stillness of the cottage, lulled by the sound of the shifting logs and gently murmuring flames.

She dreamed that the poodle was standing before her, anxiously mounting guard over a dark doorway that had opened in the heart of the fire. The dog was again as she had been at their first meeting: crippled, obese, absurdly coiffed and ready to collapse from pain and exhaustion. And yet the absurd animal was quite clearly determined to prevent Nataka from approaching the doorway, or passing through it. Within that dark hole, Nataka could hear a voice at once seductive and terrible calling to her, and as she listened she began to long to enter and reap the rewards it promised.

But the ridiculous, fragile animal still steadfastly barred her way. Despite her evident agony, she resisted every attempt by Nataka to lift or move her, or even to squeeze past her and gain the doorway. The pink, trembling, suffering dog was as impassable as a shifting mountain of lead.

"Get out of my way, you idiot dog!" snapped Nataka at last, irritated and impatient. But the poodle only wept bitter tears and refused to budge.

"I said *get AWAY!*" Nataka shouted, and her own voice, crying the words out loud, jolted awake to find the fire reduced to a pile of glowing embers that shifted and creaked in the gathering gloom.

Chapter 9. Fagus

"The wiser men are, the less they talk about 'cannot'. That is a very rash, dangerous word, that 'cannot'." [iv]

Sunsink was giving way to Sunsleep and a strawberry pink Full Moon rising in the darkening sky. The cottage began to fill. M'Kuu arrived first, hopping onto his usual place on the woodpile with his eyes dreamily abstracted, full of the memory of his most recent dance. He settled with his ears laid along his back and stared deeply and silently into the glowing coals of the fire. He was followed by Pex and his good friends Fyrd and Wurfl (Ala was at home, making sure the cubs didn't get lured by the Moon to romp too far from their den). Then Tytus the Baron wafted in and settled on a beam. Miba and Brid came tumbling in together: Brid was giggling and running in circles around the hedgehog, who looked like a little walking shrub, having managed to spear numerous leaves and burrs on his prickles while rolling in the undergrowth.

Finally a scrabbling and squawking on the threshold announced the arrival of Paa, who bounded in with Glose teetering on her back. He was coming to the end of a long repetition of complaints about her unpredictability as a mount.

"Yes, Glose! Yes, Glose! *Yes,* Glose! … *Greetings,* Your Honour!" panted the poodle, romping up to Nataka with her pink tongue lolling and her tail working like a windmill. She seemed not in the least put out by the raven's scolding.

"Scrumpy took his first dose of the potion; didn't he, Glose?" she reported cheerfully, plumping her curly bottom onto the floor in front of the fire.

The raven squawked, tumbled backwards over his tail, and only just managed to recover and flap away to his normal perch. "*What* did I tell you about *warning* me before you *do* that?" he complained.

"Oh, sorry Glose! ... And Scrumpy sends his thanks ... He *does* smell strange, though; doesn't he?" said Paa. "And the wood was so lovely without a Howler dragging me about! I could stop and sniff things whenever I wanted ... *And* Glose fell off my back, twice! He looked so funny! ... Oh, hello Pex, hello Wurfl, hello Fyrd ... Hello, M'Kuu ... *Hello,* All!"

The whole company laughed. This joyous little dog was so different from the nervous, self-effacing animal they had met just one Suntime ago that they were all beguiled. The otter trotted over to rub muzzles with her, whistling a welcome. For his part, the raven preened his pinions in dignified silence, only clicking his beak once.

"Well, now that we're all together, let's start our *indaba,*" said Nataka. "Gather round, everybody."

I won't bother repeating what she and the owl reported to the gathering, because it's already on record. When they finished, Nataka opened the discussion about how they might be able to get the wolf away safely once he had been released from his metal trap. "Did anybody think about it at all?" she asked.

Wurfl spoke up, "Acsssually, Pex, Fyrd and I discusssssed thissss a lot after you left," he whistled through his long front teeth; "*We* think the *besssssst* way would be for Toki to go to that animal prisssson – er – *zssoo* , and wait till Mond'ssss releasssssed, then jussssst take him in and walk back again. You could Dissssssappear them both, you know, Nataka."

"Hm. It *would* be ideal, except that it would take too long for Toki to get there. Wouldn't it, Toki?" replied the imp.

131

"We just don't have the time." The cottage creaked. "We need a quicker solution. Any other ideas?"

Fyrd stroked his handsome whiskers and said, "We otters could guide him here through the woods and along the rivers. We know every twig of wood and trickle of water in this country, and how to dodge dangerous Howler holts, lairs and burrows. But of course the wolf would have to promise not to eat any of us on the way." Everybody laughed again, a bit nervously.

"Or – what about this – I could find and extend - or dig - a burrow near the prison for Mond to hide in till Toki got there;" volunteered Pex, "Although I'm concerned that if the Howlers start sending out hunting dogs, they might scent him and track him down…"

"I suppose you might Transform Mond into an owl or other bird, so he could fly here?" suggested Tytus, "However, it takes some practice, learning to fly."

"Hmm, yes, Tytus. I thought of that myself. It would be an ideal solution … but I really believe that the whole thing would be too much for him. Don't forget he's already traumatised. I just can't imagine Mond coping with the change *and* learning to fly quickly and competently enough for us to get him away without trouble," said Nataka. "Remember how long it took you to become a competent flyer when you were a fledgling?"

"***Pathway Tree,***" Dora had lowered herself to join in the discussion, and was now dangling tantalisingly close to the raven's beak as she spoke. Glose struggled not to snap at her. "***Stands to reason.***"

Having delivered her contribution, the spider quickly reeled herself back up to the ceiling.

"Of *course*, the Pathway Tree!" echoed Nataka, "Now why didn't I think of that myself? Thanks for the reminder, Dora. Yes, that's the best idea. I'll rouse Fagus. It isn't far from here. If I'd only thought of it last Sunsleep, you and I needn't have flown so long or got so wet, Tytus, old chum. In fact, we could've got there and back again in a jiffy. Well thought on, that spider."

"A *Pathway Tree*?" asked Paa, all eyes and lolling tongue, "What's that?"

"My beak and feathers, you haven't roused it for *ages*," said Glose, "Do you still remember how?"

"Well, let's see now… do you still remember how to fly, Glose?" laughed Nataka, "Come on, gang; no time like the present. We might as well rouse my old friend Fagus and get it ready for action as soon as we need it. ... I'll just want some of that panacea we made today, and a spot of wine for the libation."

"Sheesh; *I* should have thought of that," commented Brid, who had been too busy making patterns with the leaves stuck on Miba's prickles to concentrate fully, "I mean, Fagus is my home, after all."

A few hundred yards up the forested slope behind Nataka's home stood a large, low-branched, spreading beech tree of massive girth and height. It had grown in that spot for countless Seasons, watching many generations of other trees come and go in the woodland around it. It housed a wide variety of birds and animals, and was this season hosting a noisy rookery in its top branches, dozens of nests of assorted birds including robins, thrushes, sparrows, wrens and woodpeckers (who were under strict orders not to drill any holes into it without permission, if they knew what was good for them), and the cosy drey that Brid and his mate had assembled in a fork between the trunk and two branches about thirty feet above the woodland floor, where they were busy raising a very active nest of babies.[lvi]

Because Howlers aren't very observant *and* can't be bothered to check what they consider unimportant details, none of them had ever realised that Fagus was - *is* - identical to dozens of other spreading beech trees in numerous temperate forests around the world. All those identical trees are in actual fact *one* tree, being sprung from the original Fagus, which still grows deep in the Black Forest (where it has developed a taste for Riesling Sylvaner and Steins of blond Lager). Its roots have spread so far and deep through the soil in which it has grown, slept and dreamed over the centuries that offshoots have sprung up to flourish in many different temperate woods on the planet. In other words, like mushrooms, they are all parts of the single Fagus Super-Organism.

A very long time ago by Howler standards, while she was exploring every aspect of Life on the planet, Nataka befriended Fagus and discovered its true nature. She also found that with a bit of pampering and cosseting, Fagus and any of its offspring could be cajoled into opening identical temporary hollows inside their trunks through which she could pass into the tree's tissues (if she made herself small enough) and travel through its network of roots to pop out again in whatever location she chose. Oddly, each of the journeys took much less time than any journey over the surface of the planet. Even a very long journey between continents could be completed in a fraction of the time it would normally take if you were travelling over the surface of the planet. This is because the Fagus root network long ago discovered, and now occupies, an additional, *folded* dimension or hidden vector of the material world - a fifth dimension, if you like - that is beyond the senses and comprehension of non-plant creatures, and about which quite a few thoughtful Sap physicists have hypothesised for a long time [lvii].

What is really exciting about all this is that over time, Nataka has also worked out a way to make the Pathway Tree instantly self-replicate virtually anywhere she needs it to. The great Fagus super-organism enjoys this activity because it gets to see new places in the world. If you give it a gift (its favourite is a libation of *good* wine – none of your cheap plonk, thank you very much – sprinkled around the base of its trunk) and speak to it with the appropriate ceremony, it will let just about anybody travel through its network. However, it draws the line at beavers and termites, which is hardly surprising.

The collaborative deal Fagus and Nataka struck between them includes the protection of Permanent Invisibility and Repulsion for the tree in return for Nataka's Unlimited Travelling Rights. This means that for the past four thousand Seasons or so no Howler has been able to see the tree any longer; and if any of them walks in its direction, he or she will unconsciously draw away again without realising it. So no Howler ever bumps into it accidentally. And a good job too, because Howlers have this *really* annoying habit of damaging or destroying virtually every special and irreplaceable thing they find in Nature.[lviii]

The strawberry-pink Hare Dancing Moon was climbing in the sky as Nataka's little procession moved up the slope and headed for the trees that grew outside the hedge behind Toki, the animals casting inky moon-shadows on the silvery ground before them. As they approached the fringe of the forest, Axl the fallow deer emerged from the dark shelter of the yew hedge and joined them. The evening smelled sweetly of the departed rain, and the air was so still that a nightingale singing deep in the forest sounded close enough to touch. Paa felt her paws itch.

"I have the strangest feeling that I *have* to dance," she whispered to M'Kuu, who was loping beside her, his eyes still abstracted and dream-laden. "Why *is* that? I've never felt it before…"

"It's the Moon," replied the hare after a long pause during which his eyes gradually lost their dreamy look and focused on her instead. "You feel the spell of our Dancing Moon. During our Season it moves in the paws and limbs of every hare. It sets our blood singing and our paws itching, and it won't let us rest until we have paid it the tribute of a dance. I know *I* shall be dancing again tonight. Can't help it."

M'Kuu fell silent for a moment, thinking. Then he added, "You're a very unusual dog, you know. I've never heard that any of *your* kind felt the Call of the Dancing Moon, before. The call to howl, yes; that's really common among canines. Pity they can't all howl very tunefully, of course. But to dance? … No; I haven't come across that before. And now I remember: last Startime you asked me if you could try to dance, didn't you? Well, do you still want to?"

"Ooh! … Do you mean it? … Yes, *please!*" said the little dog.

"Then, given your itchy paws, I think you should try;" replied the hare, "You should. Not everybody feels the Call. … So yes. You should definitely try."

Paa bounced. "I'm going to dance with M'Kuu!" she yipped to Axl, who was walking close behind them.

"Sshhh - *Quiet!*" came the Protean's voice from up the slope before them, "Cut the chatter, Paa; we're getting close. And Wurfl, this is where you'll have to leave us."

"Oh, all right, if I *musssst;*" grunted the beaver, who had been waddling beside Nataka. He stopped and squatted down to watch the rest of the group file by. "Though it'ssssss hardly fair. One day Fagusssss will underssstand that not all of usssss beaverssssss vandalissssse treeesssss indisssscriminately," he added. "Ah, well ... can't be helped, I sssupposssse. Good hunting, Friendssss..." He touched muzzles with Pex and Fyrd as they passed, then turned and lumbered back down the slope.

Some dozen or so wolf-lengths [lix] further up the slope, Nataka and the rest of her friends passed through a thick hawthorn copse and emerged onto a gently hollowed green sward that stood open to the moonlit sky ... and there before them stood Fagus the Pathway Tree in the middle of the clearing. Its enormous, towering trunk was shadowed, partly obscured by the great umbrella of low-slung, widely spreading and thickly-leaved branches that showed fresh green growth alongside its as-yet-unshed older leaves, all gleaming faintly in the pink-and-silver light of the Moon and swaying infinitesimally to the deep rhythm of the great tree's slumber.

All trees breathe, of course; and if you stay still for long enough, fix your eyes and thoughts on one particular tree and don't let your mind wander or get distracted by the interference of the winds or birds or time, you *may* eventually make out the rhythm of its breaths, which are infinitely low and slow. But it takes a great deal of concentration and patience – and I mean a *great* deal.[lx]

"Best not to speak at all now, everybody," warned Nataka, whose eyes had begun to glow like the Moon, "Just wait here and let me approach Fagus on my own. We don't want to rouse it too suddenly."

So the animals stopped in the moonlight just inside the fringe of hawthorns while Nataka approached the tree, stopping when she was barely underneath its outermost branches. Tytus the Baron accompanied her and settled silently onto one of the low branches of the tree itself, but everybody else kept close to the hawthorn hedge and tried to breathe *very* quietly. Nataka lowered herself till she was sitting cross-legged in front of the huge plant, put down her flasks, and raised her hands. Then she started to hum a soft, silvery song, swaying her limbs and tail.

Paa caught her breath as the sprite's hair began to move like the leaves of a sapling and she herself appeared to be growing and glowing with a deepening golden light that spread from her body and arms towards the branches and twigs of the beech tree, gilding both the leaves and the sward around her.

As soon as the light had spread to touch the base of the giant trunk, Nataka lifted one of the flasks, rose to her rear legs and approached, still humming her song. She trickled the panacea onto the soil, circling the base of the beech as she did so. Then she stepped back again and resumed her cross-legged position.

… And then she was hovering in the air one wolf's length above the ground with her legs still crossed, while her tawny hair grew, spread out and intertwined with the branches and leaves of the giant plant.

Paa barely had time to blink before the moment passed and Nataka, dwindled back down to her normal size, was once more sitting cross-legged on the sward. She lifted her flask of wine and waited.

A shiver ran over the leaves of the tree, like the ripples a small breeze chases over the face of a pond. Then the long, low-spreading branches stretched and moved apart to reveal the huge trunk at their centre. Tytus the Baron spread his wings to keep his balance as the branch under his claws moved and settled again.

A pair of deeply recessed, opalescent moss-green eyes opened and a narrow crack some way up the trunk deepened, stretched and widened into a yawn. Then the tree spoke. Its voice was a treacle-thick, dreamy rumble, heard more in the stomach and legs than through the ears.

"Ahhh ... Aelfeynn Earda, is this indeed you?" whispered Fagus. Its voice was deep and soft and sleepy. It emerged like the sighing of the breeze through a distant forest, a long way off and a long time ago.

"Naturally, old Friend," replied the Protean, "don't you know me?"

"Well now; I can't be sure," sighed the deep voice. "I was dreaming of a great golden dragon-and-lion shaped beast in the desert ... a furious beast with your eyes. It threatened to devour the good soil and all the forest. *That* wasn't you, was it?"

"Certainly not," replied Nataka, "I haven't taken such a shape for millions of Moons, and I can assure you that I haven't been devouring anything. Nor do I plan to. Everything is as it should be."

She paused for a minute, thinking. Then she sighed, shook herself, and held up her flask of wine. "Will you accept a libation, old friend?" she said.

"*Not* you? ... But it had your voice and your eyes ... I *thought* it was you," replied the Pathway Tree, sounding a little fretful. "Yet who knows? If this image was not you, Aelfeynn Earda, then there may be another ... or it may *become* you ... who knows? ... Yes, this may yet come to pass."

The tree shivered. "A disturbing thought," it murmured.

Nataka's expression was grave. Fagus seldom dreamed, and it was unwise to take any of its rare dreams lightly. But there really wasn't anything sensible she could say. So she waited in silence to hear what else the ancient plant might tell her.

Who knows what goes on inside the mind of such a creature as this, and how or why its dreams are as they are? she thought. *Be patient. Wait.*

The tree again fell silent for a few minutes, apparently wool gathering, before it spoke again. "Did you say you have a libation? … I have become forgetful. Ah, yes. Good. For all its sweetness, deep water tastes all the better for the occasional change."

Nataka held up the flask before the deep eyes. "Good white grape wine, mixed with a few drops of meadow-flower honey, just as you like it," she said, approaching. The crack through which the tree had been speaking opened wide to accept her offering, and she poured it in, making sure to empty the container.

"Mmh," approved Fagus, then, "We must speak of this desert beast again, Aelfeynn Earda," it added, sighing gently and making comfortable tongue-smacking noises deep within. "The reason for my dream is hidden. And hidden things are … disturbing. They must be uncovered and understood. As you know, I do not dream lightly."

"I agree," replied the Protean, laying her hand on the silvery-green bark, "It'll be good to have a long conversation again. But right now, may I beg the favour of a Path? Our need is urgent."

"*Aelfeynn Earda?*" whispered Paa to M'Kuu, "Why does the tree call her *that*? I thought her name…"

"*Hush; not now!*" hissed the hare, his eyes wide and dark.

140

Oh, ticks and fleas, this is frustrating; thought the poodle, fidgeting. She hated to feel confused. *I wish somebody would explain.*

"Huh ... what? ... Not all creatures have just one name, Little Scrap of Animal Flesh. You yourself have already collected three in your tiny span of life," rumbled the great tree suddenly, fixing the startled dog with its mossy eyes, "And, as befits her age, Aelfeynn Earda possesses countless more names than the one you have heard. ... Yes. She has ... let us call it *lived*, for want of a better word... *Lived* longer than any Mortal can imagine. Even I, venerable as I am, cannot match her in this. Consequently, her names are also infinitely many. Yes. I doubt that even she remembers them all."

The mossy eyes shifted away from Paa and back to Nataka, who was standing quietly by, absorbing every word. "Not so?" said the tree, "If my memory serves me still, the first time you and I met you were feared and worshipped by the strange, uncouth Howlers that ranged the forests of my youth; were you not? Yes. Indeed. And you bore various names then, do you recall? Now let me think; I cannot remember them all ... *Nihtgenga* was one, was it not? ... And – and *Galdricge*. Yes; that was another. Oh, and *Aglaecwif*[lxi]...

"I recall even more names, but those suffice to make my point. Bark and root, but that *was* a long time ago. I was still quite a sapling in those days; a greenling sapling, swayed by the lightest breeze."

The beech tree chuckled and sighed, remembering.

This was all too much for Paa. She cowered down and covered her nose with her forepaws, trying to make herself as small as possible. That sinister great plant had spoken to *her* - and, more worryingly still, it had obviously read her

141

mind.

I shouldn't have said anything, she thought, *I should have stayed at home by the fire inside lovely, warm Toki ... What am I doing here, anyway? ...This is no place for a stupid dog!*

Beside her, M'Kuu reared back onto his hind paws and stared down at her cowering form with wide eyes. Through all the seasons of his friendship with Nataka he had never heard of the Pathway Tree addressing anybody apart from her; in fact, he doubted that Fagus had ever even *noticed* any of the creatures that accompanied the Protean on her rare visits to it.

"Who are you, *really?*" he hissed. "*What* are you?"

All this time Axl had been hanging back in the moon-cast shadow of the hawthorn hedge behind them. But now he stepped into the moonlight, approached Paa from the opposite side and planted his hooves to straddle her cowering form. He lowered his head and levelled his antlers in a wordless challenge, fixing the dumbfounded hare with his quiet stare.

In the stunned silence that followed, the soil beneath their paws began to tremble. Deep underground a distant rumbling noise awoke, grew and shivered through the limbs of the assembled animals and into their hearts and minds until all their senses were filled with its formless crushing roar.

As the crashing, roaring and rocking of the ground grew in violence for what felt like an eternity to the Wanyama, though in reality it only lasted a few moments, all of them apart from Axl and Nataka submitted to the bucking ground and deafening noise with their eyes shut tight, convinced that they would either be ripped apart or pulped into the soil.

But instead, the shaking and roaring gradually subsided and faded away, to be followed by a profound stillness. One by one the assembled animals raised their heads and peeped out again. In the end even Glose, who had been huddling behind Pex with his head tightly tucked under his wing and with all his feathers trembling, summoned the courage to raise his beak and gaze around him.

Nothing had changed: no trees had fallen, nor had cracks appeared in the earth. The sward on which they had cowered lay around them as before, smooth and undisturbed, and all around them, the life of the night creatures continued undisturbed. And as for Fagus, they realised with amazement that its moss-green eyes were glowing and the crack in the tree-trunk wide open and dancing, but not with anger. Fagus had been laughing. And so had Nataka, whose hand still rested on its great trunk. But most astonishingly of all to them all was the realisation that throughout the whole event the fallow deer had maintained his protective stance over the terrified poodle.

"Hahaha! *That*, Master Hare, is the most perceptive question I have heard in a long while!" said Fagus. "Yes, a very good question indeed. *Is* your new companion merely a dog? ... Or might she be – who knows – an elf, perhaps? ... Or is she merely some figment of Aelfeynn Earda's imagination, think you? ... Then again, she might be something else entirely. Yes, indeed! Why not?

"Clearly, the little creature summons loyalty and friendship with ease, *and* without asking for it, as we can see from the actions of this brave deer. So what might she *really* be? I confess I do not know. But her presence pleases me, Aelfeynn Earda; it pleases me well!"

Paa had never considered the possibility that she might appear to be anything other than a normal, fluffy, rather ignorant and over-emotional poodle. So, as far as she was concerned, Fagus's words amounted to incomprehensible gobbledygook. Might the old tree be cracking an odd, indecipherable plant-joke at her expense? … Or (she barely dared to think it) could it be going a bit dotty, being so old?

Whatever the answer, she dared not relax in its presence, despite its expressions of approval. And in any case, she didn't have the foggiest idea about how to respond to this situation, particularly as everybody else seemed to be taking all its gibberish seriously. So she kept her nose buried under her forepaws and her eyes tightly shut, and went on wishing she could be invisible.

The tree's eyes ranged over the strangely-matched trio: the startled hare, still reared up on his back legs; the thickly furred cream-coloured dog cowering on the ground and covering her muzzle with her paws; and the quiet deer protectively straddling her body, its antlers still on point. Amusement glittered in their mossy depths.

"A blessed innocence it is, that does not know itself;" it remarked. "Well, be that as it may, now you are three. A significant number, that. You will dance well together. Yes, very well."

Then, just as abruptly as it had spoken to Paa, Fagus snapped its attention back to Nataka.

"You need a Path, you say. So be it. Enter, Aelfeynn Earda," it said.

"Thank you, Old Friend. Tytus, join me, please. I need your help with direction-finding;" said Nataka.

The crack in the enormous trunk expanded into a round

doorway, and the Protean stepped over its sill. Tytus ghosted after her. As they disappeared from view, the deep eyes shut and the hole shrunk again. Fagus was focusing its thoughts inwards, tracking and shaping the travellers' journey through its roots.

Silence settled over the clearing. The animals sat up, stretched and shook themselves one by one. For a while nobody spoke.

"What… what was *that* about? … What did it mean? … And what's happening now?" whispered Paa at last, uncovering her muzzle and opening her eyes.

"Eh? … Ah. … Er. … Well, right now the Boss is Singing a Path inside Fagus – you know, through its roots," replied the hare, "And Tytus is helping her. And when she's done, there will be a new way through to the prison where Mond is trapped, and a new Fagus *there* just like this one *here,* through which they can come out again. So now we just have to wait."

"And how does she do *that?*" wondered Paa, her eyes wide.

"Ah. That I can't tell you. There you have me. All I know is, her singing helps Fagus to create the root passages and connections she needs to be able to get from *here* to *there,* and to sprout a new version of itself at the other end."

"Ohhhh!" Paa sat up, "Oh, that's *so* magical!"

"It is," agreed M'Kuu. Then he turned to the deer. "By the way, Axl, I really don't know why you felt that Paa needed protecting from me. I mean, *really*. I'm not a vicious animal, and she and I get on fine together, as you know. I'd raise my antlers away, if I were you; she's been in absolutely no danger from me all along. I was simply – you know – amazed when the tree spoke to her … not to mention to hear what it said about her."

The deer snuffled, grunted and stepped back, raising his antlers. "Little animal;" he said, "Alone. Afraid. Not fair."

"Oh, I *love* you!" Paa was enchanted by the words of the elegant creature standing over her. She reared onto her hind legs to lick Axl's muzzle, her tail wagging so furiously that it threatened to topple her over. "Thank you! Thank you! *Thank you!*" The deer dropped his head to receive her kisses.

"You're just lucky the tree found you amusing instead of annoying, Paa;" cawed Glose, "*I* found you annoying. That whole business could have gone terribly wrong. And then the whole mission might have been messed up - and all because you couldn't shut *up*. *Arkh*! Singe my pinions, but you really *must* try to keep your furry, slimy snub-beak quiet when important matters are …"

"Oh, give it a rest, Glose," piped Fyrd. "You're only jealous 'cause she got all the attention and *you* didn't." The otter rolled his sleek body on the moonlit grass and began whistling to himself, juggling a stray pebble and some empty beech mast shells on his belly.

Fyrd was right, of course. Glose's beak was thoroughly out of joint because the Pathway Tree had ignored him completely, which the raven considered unfair, given that in his opinion he was Nataka's most important companion. And to cap it all, Nataka had invited Tytus to help her sing the new Path. *Tytus*, instead of *him*. It was all too much, rubbing salt into his wounded pride. Scolding the poodle was a way of relieving his frustration and envy.

But he was the only one to feel that way, because all the other Wanyama were perfectly happy to have been overlooked. As far as they were concerned, the less something like Fagus noticed them, the better they liked it. There's great virtue in anonymity, particularly if you're a small animal in unfamiliar circumstances, and they knew it.

But Glose had one weakness: he couldn't abide a challenge to his dignity. And besides he was bursting to vent his spleen on *somebody*. So he lost his temper. He squawked, opened his beak wide, spread his wings, puffed out his feathers, bounced up and down a few times, and began a strutting advance on Fyrd, making himself look as big and threatening as he could.

The otter sat up on his hind paws, stroked his whiskers and watched the raven's approach with an expression of relaxed curiosity and amusement. His blunt muzzle twitched.

Whether Glose had ever intended to follow through with his challenge to Fyrd is difficult to determine. If he had, it didn't last. He quickly – and nervously – realised that the otter showed no sign of being intimidated. Besides, the animal had very nasty fangs and could also do severe damage to one's feathers with his front and hind claws. Even as he continued strutting forwards, Glose reflected with growing panic that he really didn't want to come to blows with such a powerful animal, no matter how angry he might be. He'd overreached himself badly this time.

I MUST pick my adversaries more carefully, he admonished himself as he caught a glimpse of one shiny fang; Fyrd was grinning in an intimidating, lopsided manner. *How do I get out of this and still save face? ... How? ... THINK!*

"**Arkh*!*" he cawed suddenly, trying not to sound relieved, "I just remembered. No hunting. Nataka's orders. And that means no fighting, either. Oh, *how* frustrating! I'd have pecked you to death, otherwise!"

"Nice try, but no fish," chortled Fyrd, "That rule only applies inside Toki. So. You coming, or what?" He stretched out one worryingly muscular forepaw and beckoned to the raven, his grin wider and more intimidating than ever.

For an instant the raven despaired. But to his immense relief, just before he was within pecking or clouting distance of the otter, Nataka stuck her head out of the crack in the Pathway Tree and whistled to get everybody's attention.

"Right, enough play, everybody," she called, "the Path is ready, and Fagus promises to keep it open for us for as long as we need; don't you, Fagus? … I'd like to skip along right away and have a quick look at what's going on at the other end. I've got a nasty hunch that something's amiss at the zoo, and the sooner I can find out what's going on, the better. Particularly if it involves Mond.

"Tytus, Glose, Pex and Paa, you're with me. We're off. Everybody else, expect us back very soon, if you want to wait."

"Yes. The path will remain open for as long as you need, Aelfeynn Earda," confirmed Fagus, "That was a sweet libation."

"You're just lucky Nataka interrupted us, fish-breath," Glose squawked at Fyrd as the animals assembled around Nataka, "Otherwise I'd have taught you a lesson!"

"Not a problem, bird-brain; we'll just postpone our scrap till after you get back. You're welcome to try your teaching skills on me then," retorted the otter. He scratched his own chest. The raven blinked nervously.

"But… but … but… what about our dance?" fretted Paa.

"Oh, don't worry, Paa. We'll get back in plenty of time for you to dance tonight," said Nataka. "… Oy! You two! Whatever you're wittering on about, now's not the time. Come along, Glose!"

Interlude III

"Time is a measure of space, just as a range-finder is a measure of space, but measuring locks us into the place we measure." lxii

Roots are routes. The pathways they trace through the deep soil - like the intricate network of veins and arteries that keeps Life flowing through an animal's body - know, invade and occupy places and spaces that we can only imagine vaguely, darkly.

A journey through these routing root systems traverses dimensions inaccessible to Thought or Imagination. Time and Space are enfolded in the network generated within their delicate, supremely intricate web of connections, a network that is the Cradle carrying each precious life through its allotted time in any specific Dimension.

Becoming liquid and air, and diffusing like molecules through the underground matrices of the Pathway Tree, Nataka and her companions sped on a journey that travelled through ages past, present and future inside the interconnected rooting Dimensions of the venerable vegetable, even as it spanned mere moments of Earth Time. And on this timelessly brief, multi-dimensional journey, they encountered songs yet to be written; lairs and nests and traps both created and long since lost in places no longer to be found or existing in Potential only; and myriads of faces alive but dreaming, as yet unborn, or recently perished.

One encounter in particular – with a softly furred, white-and-ginger cat bearing beautiful, wistful emerald-shot golden eyes – arrested Nataka on her journey. For a moment that felt like infinity in the distorted reality of that time/space, she paused in silent communion with the glowing apparition before her. Then she quickened her pace and swept on through the labyrinth, her companions hurrying behind her.

She knew, now, what had disturbed her. Chant's wise and stoical litter-mate Leto had Changed irrevocably just a short Sun- and Startime before, leaving the little calico cat bereft and grieving. For it was his fading presence she had encountered within one of Fagus's countless extra-realistic Dimensions between Lives.

Chapter 10. Improvisation

"Chance makes the casual momentous. It is the fulcrum upon which the levers of action rest." [lxiii]

"See? I *told* you Nataka would turn up and sort it all out!" chirped Tesho to Lerema, "I *told* you she'd know that everything's gone wrong and we need her! *Oitochoi!* She's not magical for *nothing!* ... I ..."

"*Hush!*" hissed Nataka. She had resumed her Maine Coon cat appearance after tumbling out of the giant beech tree that now stood within the fringe of forest adjoining the zoo, and immediately gone in search of Chant. Failing to find her, Nataka had led her companions to the hebe bush beside the mongoose compound, and found that the twins had been posting a look-out for her there since the previous Sunhigh.

Paa was still feeling queasy from shrinking to sub-molecular proportions and then being bounced back again to her normal composition and dimensions. It was also very difficult to grapple with the notion that she had come such a long way, and experienced so many sensations, in what had felt like a journey of a few minutes. So she sat on the moonlit sward outside the mongoose enclosure and panted quietly, waiting for her discomfort to pass and feeling embarrassed because none of the other animals appeared to have been at all affected by their experience.

"Tell me *exactly* what's happened, Lerema. You strike me as a bit more sensible than your annoying brother," said Nataka (Tesho was squeaking excitedly as he somersaulted around the visitors, chasing his own moon-cast shadow). "Keep it brief."

"Well," said the second mongoose, "You know Chant? ... Well, she's got a – she *had* a – *brother,* you see – a litter-mate... and *he* – "

"Yes. Leto. He died. Last Sunclimb. I already know that. So what's going on *now*? Where's Chant? What's happening with our plan? ... Get *on* with it!" interrupted the great cat.

"You already know about Leto?" squeaked Lerema, "*How?* ... I mean; how? ... *ume jua namnagani*?" [lxiv]

"*There are more things in heaven and on earth, Horatio…*" Tytus couldn't help himself; but one look from Nataka silenced him mid-quote, leaving the little mongoose entirely bewildered.[lxv]

"Never mind how I know. Let's just cut to the facts, all right?" snapped Nataka, her eyes beginning to go red round the rims.

"Yes – er …Well ... all right… It's just that Chant's *completely* floored by it;" gulped Lerema, while Tesho, who had finally caught on that the Protean was in no mood for celebration, stopped rolling about, shook the dust out of his fur and tail, and sat up beside his brother.

"She's refusing to think of anything else apart from Leto. She's crying that she never realised how much she loved and needed him till now, and she just wanders around from place to place or follows her pets…" said Lerema.

"…Yowling and crying…" Tesho took up the account, "you know – about how *bad* she feels because she always was so nasty to him when he was alive. Which she was. She used to hiss at him *all* the time…"

"… *And* her Howler pets aren't much better either. *They're* yowling and crying too…" interrupted Lerema. "I mean, they *doted* on that Leto…"

"... And since then we haven't been able to get hold of her to do our key thingy nicking plan *at all* ..." added Tesho, "and without her help we can't do anything..."

"... And *now* we've heard from the other wolves..." added Lerema.

"... Yeah, we've heard from the other wolves that Mond's to be murdered a lot sooner than they planned, because ..."

"... Because those idiotic Howlers've decided he's too dangerous after all... So *now* that weird special Howler who patches people up, you know? ... Yeah, that one. ... Well, the other wolves told me they'd heard that *now* the plan is for that Howler to turn up *this* Sunclimb to check Mond and - you know - murder him..."

"...Yeah! ... Like, *right away*! They're going to do it *right away,* the wolves said. ... Spiders, scorpions and snakes! – Just like *that* ... and *just* when we need her most, Chant's out of action. I mean, *completely* out of action. Useless. *Bure.* [lxvi] Totally." Tesho drew a deep breath and started to groom himself so fiercely that tufts of his fur flew around. Pex sneezed.

"But *why* have they decided to bring this murder forward?" demanded Nataka. "I mean, what's changed to make them hurry it all up? D'you have any idea?"

"*Oitochoi!* I'll be a moonstruck mamba if I know!" shrilled Tesho, "I dunno, these Howlers – proper *Waganda Tupu*[lxvii]. I mean, there's just no figuring them *out.* Just when you start to think you've got some idea of how they work, they go and do something so flipping *wazimu,* [lxviii] even a rabid hyena with sunstroke wouldn't dream of it. Sickens me. Totally." He bit the end of his own tail to relieve his frustration, yelped and sucked the spot he'd bitten.

"Maybe the Howlers just got bored?" hazarded Lerema, watching Tesho rock and suck his own tail, "you know? ... Bored with looking after Mond, I mean ... even though he's been a lot quieter since you visited him, Nataka. Really. I mean, he never yelled at all, last Sun- or Startime. First time that's happened since he arrived. So it just isn't fair.

"But then, what can you expect from a bunch of crazy Howlers? ... They're wailing and crying about poor old Leto – fair enough in itself; he *was* a very good Nyama, for a cat – but he was sick. Dying was kinda natural, in his case. Right? ... And yet while they cry about him, they're planning to murder another Nyama that's perfectly healthy, without even wanting him for food or anything. I mean, *that's* crazy, right? ... Yeah. *Kichaa* [lxix], I tell you. There's just no figuring them out at all ... D'you think that maybe Howlers just haven't got what it takes to think properly?"

"*Sawa*," agreed his twin gloomily, still sucking the tip of his own tail.

"Yes, well. Sitting here wondering what makes mad Howlers mad isn't going to help us," said Nataka sombrely. "We'll simply have to work with what we've got, which isn't much. Just a moment; I've got to think." She hunkered down, and her eyes turned silver. The mongoose twins watched her in awe.

"*Oitochoi,* but that's properly spooky," whispered Lerema to Tesho.

"Dear, oh dear, what a muddle," hooted Tytus softly to Pex and Paa, trying not to disturb the Maine Coon cat's reverie. "If Leto died last Sunclimb, it's highly likely that Chant never got round to telling Mond about our initial plans before she started grieving for him, don't you think? ... So maybe *he's* got no idea of what's going on, either. And in that case one of us should be getting over there and explaining things to him as quickly as possible. Perhaps we three could make ourselves useful, instead of sitting around, and go along there to have a chat with him – you know, get him up to date and prepare him - just for a start? I think the company of other animals might also comfort the poor animal a bit, don't you? …"

Nataka bounced abruptly upright, startling everybody. Her eyes snapped to bright blue. "Of course!" she exclaimed, "Well done, Tytus. First things first, again. We have to include Mond in our planning. Naturally. Let's get over there right away. You twins coming?"

"*Oitochoi!* Just you try and stop us," said Tesho, and the two mongooses dashed off with their brindled tails in the air, elated by her renewed energy.

"Be careful - don't let anybody see you!" called Paa after the scampering twins.

"It's all right, Paa; I've Disappeared us all. They're quite safe," said Nataka as they hurried along.

Mond was reclining in his cage with his face turned towards the grille and his forepaws crossed. As Nataka and her little group of companions materialised in front of the cage he raised himself stiffly to salute them, his tail waving gently and his ears pricked forwards. It was clear that he had benefited from a long rest; his eyes were calm and bright, and he no longer exuded the smell of bewildered anguish that had hung around him like a fog during their first meeting. But he still looked mournful and subdued.

"Greetings to you, Wise One - and to you too, bird most venerable. I rejoice to smell you again," he said. "But alas, I fear your arrival may be too late for our purpose. There is to come a … *they* called it an *inspection* … of my fitness to live. Yes. It appears that these same strangers that took from me my liberty now wish also to deprive of me my life, and very soon. Your friend the kestrel informed me. Is it not so?"

"Yes; I also have just heard that the Howlers have decided to ... inspect ... you during next Sunclimb, and that they have your murder in mind;" replied Nataka, who had resumed her wolf Transformation. "So, naturally, the plan we made for rescuing you won't work any longer. Worse still, we simply don't have the time to make another one. We've got to act *now* if you're to survive. We must do what we can to save you right away, however messy it may be. Do you agree to this? It may involve great risk, you know."

"Agreed. Of course. What awaits me, otherwise? Even great risk is preferable to certain death. ... But if we should fail, Wise One," said the timber wolf, "I would not wish you or your companions to mourn. You restored my hope for a short while, for which I thank you from my whole belly. And - and in truth, if it be my fate that even with your help I cannot escape, then I beg you to believe that for me death will be infinitely preferable to this life of captivity, deprivation and homesickness. I shall embrace it as a release."

Paa was overwhelmed to hear her recent feelings echoed so poignantly by the captive. But she didn't want to distract him or anybody else with her grief, so she turned her back and hung her head, burying her nose under her paws to stifle her whimpers.

For a few minutes they all sat in silence, contemplating their shadows in the moonlight. The situation seemed hopeless.

"*Arkh*! I've got an *idea*!" suddenly squawked Glose, lifting his beak and glaring around at his companions as if challenging them to contradict him, "If we can't do this secretly because we don't have the time, why bother with being quiet and sneaking around at all? Surely what we need to do is bother, distract, confuse and discombobulate the Howlers while we try to get Mond out of that horrible trap!"

"My brush and bristles; yes, why not? ... And in that case, what about stopping them from moving about altogether?" exclaimed Pex. "Now, *how* can we do that? ... What will keep all the Howlers around here inside their lairs and stop them from prowling around with those nasty sleepy thorny things, and - you know - interfering with us while we try to free Mond?"

"Oh! That *is* a good idea! We could take a leaf out of the legend of the Trojan Horse," Tytus flapped his downy wings, catching fire. "We need a disguise, but a *frightening* disguise. If we all looked and behaved like huge noisy animals - like lions or bears or suchlike – and roared about in the prison and near the Howlers' nests and lairs – *and* worked up all the other animals too – that should do it, don't you think?" He turned to the Protean. "Nataka, do you remember how you confused Glose and me on the ledge of that horrible Howler nest by adopting two Transformations at once? ... Well, could you Transform us like that, too?"

"Yes, exactly... And at the same time you could also Disappear Mond to make the trap look empty, to confuse any Howler who managed to get past us and see it, couldn't you? They might even open the trap to check inside it, and then Mond could – you know – charge out ... knock 'em over ... or -" cawed Glose, hopping up and down.

"Ooh! *I've* got an idea! *I've* got an idea!" Paa bounced up, forgetting her grief, "You can see the pictures in our minds, Your Honour, can't you? ... Well, could you do that with the Howlers, or with Mond? Because then you could find out what Chant's Pet looks like and Transform yourself or one of us to look like that Pet ... and then, and then, you see, that person could sneak into Chant's lair and nick the ... whatsits... the *keys* for this horrible trap, you know, while everybody else was doing the ... the roaring and running around ... and scaring Howlers away... And - and if anybody saw the nicking, they wouldn't think twice about it because they'd believe it was Chant's Pet ... and - and I think that would be a way to get Mond out, wouldn't it? "

"Look, you're missing the obvious problem with *that* plan, Paa. The problem *is* that we don't know which of those key thingies is the *right* one," interjected Glose, just like an exasperated teacher with a particularly dense student (he still hadn't forgiven her for the scene with Fagus, which was unfair; but anyway). "So which key would we nick? *That's* why Chant was so important to us; see? ... *That's* the problem."

Paa sat down, looking crestfallen.

"*Oitochoi!* Not if we nick *all* the key thingies, it isn't!" shrilled Lerema, bouncing into the air with his tail fluffed up, "If we nick 'em all, Nataka can try 'em all, you know, till she finds the right one. Why not?"

"*Sawa*! What's to stop us nicking them all? We're not trying to do anything clever like pinch only the right keys any longer, are we?" chimed in his brother. "So why *don't* we just Transform somebody and get them in there, like our *rafiki* [lxx] the fluffy dog says, and grab them all and scarper again?"

"Fluff my fur and call me a thistledown," said Pex, gazing admiringly at Paa and the twins, "That would do it, all right. Brilliant thinking, you three."

"But what if the Howlers try to stop you – you know – catch you at it?" asked Tytus suddenly.

"I can take care of that," said Nataka, who till then had sat and listened with a widening smile to all the ideas tumbling out of her enthusiastic companions, "with everybody's help I can certainly create such a confusing and distracting situation that any Howler who wakes up won't be able to spare any attention for somebody who sneaks in and scoops up all those dratted keys - particularly if that somebody's Invisible. In fact, I should think we could march a whole army of gorillas in there to nick the keys, and the Howlers wouldn't notice. But that really shouldn't be necessary.

"Also, come to think of it, with any luck we won't have to keep any other Howlers apart from Chant's Pet confused. Of course, if one or more further Howlers around this prison suddenly start to interfere we'll have to deal with them as well, and in that case we may have to rouse the other Wanyama to help us. But let's just keep it as small and simple as possible for now, take things as they come, and improvise as necessary. Agreed? ... So everybody, keep on your toes. Be prepared to adapt. All right? I want to make this rescue as sudden, quick and quiet as possible.

"And, you know, it'll probably be easier if I simply Disappear myself and do the actual nicking, instead of trying to make anybody else look like Chant's Pet - although that *was* a fine suggestion, Paa. Well done."

It was Glose's turn to fall silent.

"Anyway, Good work, everybody!" concluded the Protean. "The best thing about this plan is that we can get to work on it right away. We don't have to wait for other things to happen first. Now, before we do anything else, let's just work out what everybody's going to do, all right? ... and then make sure we all know our roles and signals.

"For a start, we'll need somebody to post a look-out over Mond's trap, so we can be warned if a Howler turns up at the wrong time. Next, we need a quick look at the enemy territory, so that everybody knows where it is. If everything goes wrong, we meet here, fight to the death, and rouse the rest of the prisoners. Agreed? ...

"Now: let's just work out the distraction. Gather round, then; let's plot!"

Mond licked his nose and his tail thumped the floor of his prison. "You lead a formidable pack, Wise One," he said. "I begin to hope again. I also shall do whatever you may command." He settled down on his haunches and pricked his ears.

Chapter 11. Escape

"In such cases as these, a good memory is unpardonable." [lxxi]

Leto's Pet Anthony was a conscientious, decent and caring Howler; not the kind to abandon his duties just because he was sad. Leto had been a wonderful companion for many years, more like a family member than a pet [lxxii]; but even though he was heartbroken by his loss, Anthony had worked hard all through that day, trying to find solutions to various problems and difficulties the zoo had been encountering recently. One of the main problems he was grappling with right now was that of the wounded Canadian timber wolf. It was getting more and more necessary to decide what to do with it.

Over the past several days he had reluctantly come to agree with the other wardens' repeated insistence that, no matter how hard they all tried, the wolf would never settle down and fit in with the rest of the wolf pack at the zoo. And the most recent transformation in its behaviour from all-out hostility and agitation to silence and passiveness was also very worrying. It raised the disturbing possibility that the animal's injuries might be undermining its health and weakening its will to live. Such a change of behaviour most often indicated one of three causes: a deep-rooted and potentially fatal infection, an undiscovered internal wound, or some exotic parasite. And given the unusual history of this particular acquisition none of those unpleasant possibilities could be ruled out. If any of them were the cause for the wolf's behaviour, the only humane course of action would be to put the animal to sleep and spare it unjustifiable further suffering.

Furthermore, as the Head of a zoo that had been badly disrupted for some time by the wolf's misery and violence, he fully understood why so many wardens were clamouring for it to be euthanised. They wanted to 'go back to normal', not least because, as was the case with all misfits of this sort, there was a danger that the wolf's behaviour might spread to the other animals in their small community. Quite understandably, also, ever since the unfortunate Sub-Warden Jim Bell had been mauled, calls from the remaining wardens and keepers for the frantic animal that had attacked him to be disposed of had increased in volume and frequency.

Anthony hated losing any animal. But at the same time he didn't feel it would be right to impose the care of a clearly dangerous, completely unmanageable - and now possibly also very sick - wolf on his workforce, either. There had already been arguments about the risks they all ran whenever they were changing its dressings and cleaning out its tiny cage; and at one point these had become so severe that he had been forced to lay down the law in no uncertain terms, insisting that *everybody* had to participate in the animal's care. For the sake of fairness nobody could be exempt. But not everybody cared for fairness so much as for his or her own skin. The meeting had been fractious, and Anthony had been obliged to raise his voice and insist on their obedience. He rarely swung his authority like that, and he had hated to do so in this case; but it really had become essential to keep everybody in line.

Since then, the mood among the personnel had become increasingly unpleasant and unstable. A number of keepers and wardens had taken to huddling in small groups and muttering among themselves; and whenever he approached them they'd go quiet and watch him with expressions that ranged from embarrassment to open hostility. He'd also received verbal warnings from two wardens that they would resign if the situation didn't improve, and he didn't doubt that more would follow unless he found a way to resolve the situation quickly and smoothly.

Clearly, it didn't help matters at all that Sub-Warden Jim Bell had been so badly mauled during the wolf's most recent disastrous attempt to break out that he was still in hospital.

One of the animal's huge canine teeth had pierced the young man's lung, and the wound had become infected, jeopardising his life. And that was not all. His left elbow had also been crushed, because somehow the animal had managed to clamp its powerful jaws over Jim's arm and torso, just when it really should have been unconscious from the effects of a strong sedative injection. At one point the doctors tending Jim had warned Anthony and the boy's family (who quite understandably were traumatised and outraged, and talking about suing the zoo) that if the infection could not be brought under control he might even lose his life. And if he survived he should expect life-changing health problems as a consequence of his injuries. That had been a dark moment.

There was to be an official inquiry to consider whether anything could or should have been done differently. And of course, Anthony's own competence would come under scrutiny in the process. Indeed, his future hung on the outcome of that inquiry. But Anthony hadn't had enough time to think properly about this, either. For now, he drew comfort from the most recent news that young Jim Bell's infection was gradually responding to treatment: he had finally been declared out of danger, although he really wasn't out of the woods yet. But this was the most important consideration, as far as Anthony was concerned; everything else paled by comparison with the young man's health. He had spent virtually every free moment at the unconscious boy's bedside, wishing he believed in a deity to whom he might pray.

Now, late in the evening of yet another long and traumatic day, Anthony was sitting at his desk, striving to come to terms with the reality of Leto's death on the one hand and the possibility of having to euthanise the wolf on the other. He had spoken on the phone with the zoo's contracted veterinary officer, and they had agreed to bring forward the vet's visit to assess the wolf's condition to the following morning, because the sooner they could reach a resolution, the better. If indeed the animal were sick - and the fact that it still wasn't eating properly suggested that it was - then it really would be morally unjustifiable to let the poor beast suffer for a moment longer than was absolutely unavoidable.

Anthony had already confided to the vet that he was sorry he had ever accepted the wolf in the first place. It was clearly quite wild, which suggested that it had been trapped as an adult animal. Such animals seldom settled down well to a life of captivity. And what made him feel even worse was that ever since the last break-out attempt, the poor creature had had to be confined in very cramped quarters for its own good, to prevent it from rampaging around and hurting itself even more. The miserable creature barely had the space to move around any longer, and although Anthony knew that it was in the animal's best interests to keep it strictly confined while its wounds healed, he still felt immensely unhappy about the need to trap it like that. What must it be feeling? No animal should ever have to suffer such unnatural conditions, in his opinion. The whole business was a total mess. But for once he really had no choice.

Thinking about all this, he dug out the paperwork that had accompanied the purchase of the wolf and pored over it again, feeling a headache start behind his eyes. He was tired out from work and grief and lack of sleep. But he reread the papers very carefully to make sure he hadn't missed anything.

The animal had been captured in Algonquin territory in French Canada. The company that had acquired and provided it, after approaching him about the sale with an unsolicited email, was obscure. He'd never heard of it before. Clearly, some unanswered questions surrounded the exact circumstances of the wolf's capture and transport, even though all the necessary immunisations and quarantines had been observed. Anthony had been uneasy about the transaction from the start, but money was always tight in a little zoo like this and he simply hadn't been able to resist buying the animal at the very reasonable price its vendors requested. He'd honestly believed he was getting a bargain. Now he wondered whether the cost hadn't in fact hidden shady goings-on. Wild animals were illegally captured and transported all the time, and he felt a flush rise up his neck and face as he admitted to himself that, before jumping at the offer, he should have checked the background of the organisation making it much more carefully to make sure that its *bona fides* and methods were all above-board.

Yes, he decided, there was no ducking it. He'd messed up royally. And the upshot of his messing up was a severely injured assistant warden and a dreadfully unhappy wolf.

He sighed, rubbed his hands over his already dishevelled hair, and carefully spread out the all the paperwork relating to the wolf – immunisation and importation certificates and transport details – on his desktop, ready for the next day. The vet would want to go over it when he arrived.

He raised his head and spotted Chant in the doorway. She'd been crying all day, following him and his wife all around the house and garden and zoo, begging for comfort and reassurance, for all the world as if she also were mourning for her littermate. But, he remembered, ever since they'd been kittens she'd always spat at Leto and they'd never seemed to get along … it was strange.

"Hey there, old girl," he said, "How are you? Still sad? … Horrible feeling, isn't it? I keep expecting to see the old boy dash in with his tail in the air." He reached down one hand and the little cat came over to have her ears scratched. Then she turned, stared at the door, and let out a mournful cry. Leto had always raced her into the office of an evening, competing for caresses; the tussle to be the first to be stroked and cuddled had settled into one of their numerous daily routines. And, Anthony thought, Chant had always appeared to resent Leto's presence when they did it... until now.

Tears rose in his eyes, brimmed over and trickled down his cheeks. He brushed them away angrily. "Grow up, you old fool," he said to himself, "He was *sick*, our poor old boy. Incurable. Would you really want him to continue suffering just so you could still have him? ... He's better off now. So. Get over it. Don't be so selfish. You're not a *kid*, dammit! ... And besides, you've got to stay focused. The poor mad animal out there needs you."

He turned back to the little calico cat, who again meowed plaintively. "Yes; you're right, Pest; time for bed," he said softly. "You can sleep in our room tonight, if you don't want to be alone. Come along then, old girl." He went out into the darkened front room, which doubled as a meeting room, to lock and bolt the front door. Then he returned, scooped the little cat up into his arms (she squeaked and wriggled, but didn't try to escape) and went out, switching off the office light as he passed through the door and trudged up the stairs to the flat he shared with his wife Fran.

The light of the full moon shone through the open curtains of the window in the wall opposite to the desk. It bathed the empty room in a silvery-pink glow, shedding enough light for Anthony to mount the stairs without throwing the switch for the light on the landing. Upstairs, after washing he changed rapidly into his pyjamas and climbed into bed next to his sleeping wife, Fran. Chant hopped up after him, chirruped and butted her head under his fingers for a final caress before settling onto the duvet between him and his wife.

The clock ticked in the office, and a barn owl hooted in the distance.

After a while the papers rustled on the moonlit desk. They straightened and arranged themselves into a neat pile, which rose into the air. The pile hovered there, folding itself sheet by sheet.

Then all the papers vanished at once.

After another pause, the rack of keys hanging on the wall over the desk began to clink and chime in turn. One by one, they rose off their pegs and gathered into a tight bunch in mid-air, clustering together so tightly that they made no sound at all. The tangled bunch flew out of the office towards the front door of the building, where it hovered briefly before flying back into the office through the darkened front room and crossing to the window in the wall facing the desk.

There followed a few furtive scrabbling noises. Somebody cursed softly. Then the window rose with a bit of a creak to start with … then …

A resounding *crash!!!!* rattled panes, furniture and cutlery, and rang through the quiet house like a clap of thunder on a still night. It was a sticky, old-fashioned sash window, and nobody had been able to open it quietly for decades.

"*Verdammt nomou!*" barked the keys.[lxxiii] They zoomed across the sill, dangled for a moment above the neatly clipped lawn outside, and then zipped off in mid-air, disappearing through the hazel and lavender hedge that separated the garden from the animal enclosures.

The light in Anthony's bedroom came on an instant after the crash. The window overlooking the garden shot up with a second bang. He leaned out of it and shouted.

"**STOP! … Who's there?**"

As if his words had been a signal, a bull elephant, a grizzly bear, a black-maned lion, a griffon vulture and the largest gorilla Anthony had ever laid his eyes on burst through the hedge onto the lawn beneath his window and rampaged around growling, whooping, roaring, shaking the bushes and clawing the walls of the house.

Chant had jumped onto the windowsill beside her Pet to see what the noise was about. Now she hissed, spat, flattened her ears and streaked for cover under the bed, where she lay and yammered imprecations in Cat [lxxiv]. Fran shrieked and jolted bolt upright in bed.

"A whole lot of animals have escaped into our garden!" snapped Anthony, pushing his feet into his shoes without bothering to change out of his pyjamas, and grabbing his mobile phone from the bedside table. "Must be some yobs from town, messing about again. I'll have their guts for garters, the idiots; get the police onto them; teach 'em a lesson once and for all!"

"Oh *no*;" groaned Fran, falling back and burying her face in her pillow. "It never rains but it... *Tony!* Don't forget to switch off the light... and *do* for heaven's sake put on your dressing gown, at least!"

Her husband grunted, snatched up his dressing gown, snapped off the bedroom light and went bounding down the stairs, cursing and muttering. Somebody was going to catch it... a gate or fence must have been left unsecured... why did people have to be such fools?

Halfway down the stairs he stopped dead in his tracks, remembering with a jolt that there *were* no gorillas, vultures, lions, bears or elephants at the zoo, which was too small to accommodate more than a handful of large animals.

"What the...?"

An opalescent mist, riding on a fragment of song no louder than the murmur of a moth, drifted up the stairs and into his open mouth. The rumpus in the garden stopped as if somebody had thrown a rock and squashed it.

Anthony shook himself. He gazed around him with his brow furrowed, wondering why on earth he was standing on the moonlit stairs in the middle of the night, with one arm in a sleeve of his dressing gown and shoes without socks on his feet.

He scratched his head, turned round and climbed back upstairs.

"That was quick," Fran raised her face as he entered. "Back already? What's happening with the animals?"

A plaintive *meow* from under the bed announced that Chant was wondering the same thing. Those animals had been big. And scary.

"What escaped animals?" said Anthony, "I've no idea what you're talking about, Love. Why did you send me downstairs, again?"

"*I,* send *you?*" retorted Fran, whose eyes were still red and puffy from all the weeping she had done over the previous day, "I did nothing of the sort! ... Look, *you* woke me, and said some animals were loose... you were calling the police..."

"I never did, did I?" Anthony frowned down at the shoes on his feet. "I wonder why. Hang on just a tick, Fran; let's listen. ... Can you hear anything? ... No, neither can I. ... There's nothing going on, nothing at all. It's all perfectly quiet. How can anything be on the loose? ... Where'd I get that daft idea from, anyway?"

He went back to the window and peered out. There was no trace of the beasts that had been racketing and roaring around on his moonlit lawn just a few minutes before. But this didn't bother him at all, obviously, because he retained no memory of them. Only Chant, still muttering quietly as she emerged from under the bed, jumped back onto it and curled up once more, had an idea about what had been going on. And she wasn't about to tell.

Still frowning, Anthony walked back, sat down on the side of the bed and prised off his shoes.

"And, you know, I really have no idea why I put these on ... Although ... I *thought* I ... No. It's nothing. Weird. ... Go back to sleep."

"Maybe you were dreaming - you know, sleepwalking?" suggested his wife, and turned over in bed. "By golly, you *were* noisy, though. Why d'you make that racket, anyway?"

"What racket? I don't remember making a racket," protested Anthony. "And I never sleepwalk..."

"There's always a first time. *I* think you were sleepwalking, anyway. Otherwise you'd remember, wouldn't you? ... Well, in any case, you'd better try to get some sleep. We're both going to have a tough day tomorrow. ... Night-night, darling. Try not to do it again."

"Do what again?" muttered her husband. "Well ... who knows? ... Yeah, probably I *was* sleepwalking. It's been a rough day. That might explain it. Goodnight, darling. Night-night, Chant."

Night-night, said Chant in Cat. *Try not to disturb me again.*

Cats are like that.

***

It hadn't taken Nataka long to find the key that opened Mond's trap, which she achieved by Transforming into the bright-eyed black female Howler. Those fingers were very useful for handling fiddly things like keys. The wolf limped out and crouched down, wincing, to lick her feet.

"No need for that," said the black girl gruffly. She stroked his head. "I promised. ... Besides, we can't hang about for this kind of thing. It's high time we were out of here. You never know: it would be just like some stray Howler to come checking what all the *matata*'s been about. Which gives me an idea. But hey, first things first. Can you run, Mond? ... Oh, *sheesh!* I forgot. You don't have to suffer like this any longer. Hold on..."

She closed her eyes for an instant and then passed her hands lightly over the wolf's bandaged back and sides. A tendril of gold laced around his body before disappearing into it.

"You'll be fine now; no need for all these wrappings," she said, tearing the bandages and collar off the huge animal as she spoke. "There. All gone. How d'you feel?"

"Behold!" said the vulture with the voice of Tytus the Baron as the delighted wolf rolled on the ground and gambolled around, revelling in his newly regained freedom, health and fitness, "Escape *and* a total cure. I told you she's the best ally anybody could want, didn't I? ... Er, Nataka, old friend, if you no longer require the services of this rather ugly (and evil-smelling) scavenger shape, might I be restored to my normal shape?"

"What? ... Oh! - Yes, of course ..." Nataka muttered a bird call and waved a couple of fingers. The huge vulture disappeared, leaving the barn owl behind. Tytus sighed and preened his downy pinions. "Fine birds, vultures; essential for keeping the savannah clean, of course. But how they can live with their own odour beats me," he observed.

Nataka turned to the elephant, lion, bear and gorilla. "Your turn," she said, and made a sound like the distant roar of a predator.

"*Oitochoi*!" complained Lerema, who enjoyed being a lion, "D'you *have* to? Can't I stay like this a bit longer?"

"I like being a bear, too;" growled his twin as both the mongooses reappeared.

"Look, there's no time for it. We've got to deal with any number of other details before we can be sure we're safe." As she spoke Nataka waved a finger at the gorilla and elephant, then sang a few notes that sounded like someone with a head cold humming to the rhythm of a muffled bongo. Both illusions vanished, leaving behind Pex and Paa.

"That was *fun!*" Paa rolled on the ground. "Did you see my tusks? Did you see what I did with my tusks? ... "

"It's what you did with your trunk I liked best, *Rafiki,*" said Lerema, "that noise: *wazimu*!"

Pex was gazing down at his forepaws. "Gorillas are terrific climbers, and *strong*," he said. "I could use that. Help no end against the hunters, it would."

"Speak for yourselves," cawed Glose. He alone had remained unaltered, perching on Mond's cage as Nataka's invisible lookout. "I don't want any part of *me* changing, thank you very much. You can't improve on perfection."

173

"Right, everybody!" Nataka called the group to order, "Time to get moving. Tytus and Glose, get Mond and the gang back to Fagus and wait for me there. I've got to return the keys before I can join you. Lerema and Tesho, you've been brilliant. I won't forget your help. I'm sure we'll meet again."

She jogged off without waiting for a reply and Vanished after a few strides. The gratified mongoose twins chattered, rolled on the ground and shrilled farewell greetings after her.

"Where's Her Honour gone?" asked Paa.

"You heard her; she's returning the key thingies, though I don't see why she should bother;" said Glose. "I'd just leave them right here, myself; let the Howlers find them and try to figure things out. *Arkh*, well, that's her business. Come along, then, everybody; let's go. Mond, follow me, please…"

The mongooses were too curious simply to go home right away without seeing the Pathway Tree, so they accompanied the departing animals to its foot. There they touched noses with Paa, Fyrd, the two birds and the wolf before racing each other, brindled tails erect, all the way back to their enclosure.

Within moments of Lerema and Tesho's departure, Nataka arrived to lead the way into the tree. But when it was the grey wolf's turn to enter he hung back and his ruff bristled. He felt a horror of that tiny space, having been stuck in one for so long.

"Don't worry, Mond," soothed Paa, licking his muzzle. "No wonder you hate tight places. I would too, after what you've been through. But you can trust Her Honour, you know. This isn't a trap, I promise. You'll be safe all the way through. Look, you go first, and I'll follow. Then I'll be right behind you ... No, we won't get lost, don't worry; not with Nataka to guide us. And if it helps, just pretend this is a game."

At last the great grey wolf ventured over the sill of the hole, sniffing suspiciously and whining deep in his throat. The cream poodle followed him, chatting as cheerfully and calmly as she could. No sooner had she entered the tree than the hole snapped shut behind her, leaving no sign of where it had been.

***

... And, after what had felt like an impossibly short but nightmarish journey to the awestricken, panicking wolf, the travellers were again tumbling out of the giant beech tree into the woodland clearing up the slope from Nataka's cottage. They were met by the rest of her patient (and surprised) companions, who pressed forward eagerly to make the wolf's acquaintance.

"I feel as if I have been struck by *un coup de tonnerre* [lxxv]. It feels like a dream! And that voyage was terrifying ... But ... now, this *must* be reality; yes? ... Is it not? ... If not, *nom d'un nom,* is it possible that I am still inside that trap, and quite mad?" he blurted, much to the amusement of Brid and Miba (the hedgehog even offered to prick the wolf's nose to convince him he really was awake).

And "You should acquaint yourself with the work of the Existentialists,[lxxvi] my friend," suggested Tytus. "To them, everything is an illusion."

"So what happened, Boss?" asked M'Kuu. The group was on the move again, everybody having been introduced to the wolf, fussed over him, and thanked Fagus for its help. "I thought you said you'd only be a short while, but we've all waited a lot longer than that. I couldn't bear to leave without knowing what had happened, and everybody felt the same. ... And now, bite off my ears and call me a mole, here's the wolf! I mean, I didn't have any idea that you were planning to break him out right away. Weren't we going to rescue him in another two Startimes?"

"You didn't have any idea because *I* didn't have any idea, M'Kuu," replied Nataka. "We had to wing it. It was either that, or let Mond die. ... Look, I'll tell you all about it when we're all back with Toki, all right? ... Now could you do me a favour and hold on to your questions? There's still a lot to sort out, and I've got to do some serious thinking."

Chapter 12. Dance

"Da trat hervor Einer, anzusehen wie die Sternen Nacht." lxxvii

"First things first," said Nataka. The tale of Mond's release had been told and everybody had finished commenting on what they'd heard as they sprawled, perched and curled around her in the sanctuary of the patient cottage. "I'll have to get back to that zoo before Sunwake tomorrow because there's a lot of tidying up to do – you know – loose ends to tie off, and so forth."

"*What* tidying up?" demanded Glose, for whom those two dreaded words usually presaged a lot of dust and annoyance and scrambling to get out of the way while Nataka and Toki turned his cosy, feathery, topsy-turvy nest upside down, "You didn't have a chance to make a mess, Nataka…"

"Well, listen. I got into the nest of Chant's Howler Pet a little bit before he left that space he works in. So I sat on the edge of his nest-hole, listened to his thoughts and watched the pictures in his mind. And, well, I found out that he's really not that bad, for a Howler. *He* thinks he's doing good things for all the Wanyama he's got trapped in that prison of his, and he really does care for them. In fact, I'll go so far as to say he loves them.

"Now, just hear me out for once, and don't interrupt," she raised a hand as Glose opened his beak to squawk his derision. "There *are* some decent Howlers around, and if you're very lucky you'll come across one of them every so often, as I have. This is one of them. Chant's lucky; I can understand why she keeps him, because he's an exceptional Pet. So anyway, what I found out was that he's been genuinely worried about Mond here, and furious with himself for not having been more careful about finding out where Mond had come from, before he got hold of him. And even though, obviously, he couldn't have prevented *that,* he still felt guilty about it. Which is actually quite admirable if irrational.

"And on top of that, he's tried very hard to care for everybody, including Mond, as well as he could, even now, while he's still very upset about losing Leto.

"So anyway, after Pex, Paa, Tytus, Lerema and Tesho staged that rampage around his nest to distract him from the noise I'd made opening the dratted nest-hole cover [lxxviii] (great timing, by the way, everybody; it worked excellently), I sneaked back inside just in time to see him coming down the steps from his sleeping space. So I puffed a Forgetfulness spell into him. So *now* he doesn't remember anything about Mond's capture or illness, *or* that rampage we staged to distract him - or anything else to do with Mond - at all. I've wiped it all clean out of his head. And his mate isn't taking anything that happened last Startime seriously either. *She* just thinks he had a bad dream. So that's all right too, as far as it goes. For now."

"*Yip*! You spoilsport! You mean the Howler won't remember our performance at all?" exclaimed Pex, "What a waste! It was *memorable.* I did a great bit of rampaging there, even if I say so myself. I wish you'd seen it, M'Kuu: regular gymnastics in all the trees and shrubs. Quite beautiful, even if I say so myself."

"It *was* fun," agreed Paa, "I specially liked how Tesho' bear clawed the house. And did anybody notice how I took the top off that cherry tree with my trunk? ... For the first time in my life I actually fancied leaves for dinner ... *Yuk.* I hope I won't get indigestion."

"Oh, so *now* you're getting all theatrical; are you, Pex?" laughed Nataka, "Look: Paa isn't complaining, so shut up for a moment and just think about what all this means. Chant's Pet doesn't even remember that Mond ever existed, as I said. That's right, Mond; he no longer has any memory of you at all, and his papers - you know, the bits of dead material they make their marks on to remind them of what they're doing – *they're* all … here…" She stretched out a hand and the papers off Anthony's desk materialised in it. "So they can't remind him about you either. In fact, as far as *he's* concerned, this whole miserable business since you arrived has never happened. So he won't be alerting other Howlers to go searching for you, which could have caused a whole lot of trouble for us. Yes? So that's a good thing.

"But now, consider what all this means for his mate and for the rest of the Howlers at that prison, everybody - *and* for the one that's due to turn up during this Sunclimb to check Mond over with a view to murdering him … not to mention the other young Howler you hurt when you bit him, Mond, of course. None of *them* has forgotten you, unlike Chant's pet. So *now* do you all see the problem?"

The wolf was lying before the fire, licking one of his huge forepaws while Brid sat on his ruff and played with his ears. He raised his head. "I understand now that the Howler did not deserve to be hurt, for he was only attempting to aid me. But – *parbleu!* – I was frantic, yes? And thus I became violent. Yet now I am truly sorry for what I have done, Magical One."

"Yes, well; seriously, nobody's blaming you, so don't worry about it," said Nataka, "You felt desperate and threatened. And to be honest I'd have done exactly the same in your place. *Sheesh.* I've wanted to bite plenty of Howlers in my time … *and* done worse than that, in fact.

"But look, everybody, let's get back to the main point. D'you get it yet? The point is that *now* we have a sick Howler who really didn't deserve to get hurt in a way that might make him *bure* for the rest of his life, and we have his Howler boss who's forgotten all about you, Mond, while all the other Howlers *and* all the other animals at that prison still remember you. Things could get really nasty for Chant's Pet. Howlers don't forgive that kind of forgetting, particularly on the part of somebody who's in charge. They'll think that he's pretending, and they'll punish him horribly for it. Howlers are really good at punishing one another. I should know. I've seen 'em at it. And I honestly don't think this one deserves it.

"So. All those Howlers have to be sorted out: I mean, their memories cleaned up so that Mond won't have existed for any of *them*, either. If we can pull it off, it'll be much better for us as well, because *then* we'll be able to work on a good way of sending him back home again without worrying that we might have a whole pack of Howler busybodies interfering with us at any moment."

"Right, Boss. I understand," said M'Kuu, who had been listening carefully. "Now we need to find a way to do that Forgetfulness thing to everybody who had anything to do with Mond. Crumple my ears, that won't be easy."

"You can say that again. I need to make sure nobody can upset the nest of eggs, and I've got to do it quickly; the sooner the better. They all have to Forget everything about Mond simultaneously – and I do mean *all* of them: the Howlers who've helped the damaged one in their Hospital; his nest-mates and friends; anybody else that may have heard about the whole *shauri* ... Good grief. The thing gets bigger and bigger the more I think about it." Nataka reached down as she spoke and absent-mindedly curled one of Paa's silky ears over her fingers.

"So there it is. There you have it. As you would say, Brid, *that's* my problem in a nutshell. I need a quick, foolproof method of delivering Forgetfulness to all those Howlers. I can't go from one to another of them doing the spell I did on Chant's pet, because it would take far too long. And

180

anyway, how could I be sure I'd got everybody? ... One good thing, at least, is that we can be sure the Wanyama don't need it, because no Howler ever bothers to understand - let alone listen to - *them*. And even if there is an exception out there among the Howlers (which I doubt), I know that none of the Wanyama would do or say anything to betray Mond. So that simplifies things a lot. It's just all the Howlers we need to sort out.

"... Oh, and of course the Forgetting must be very specific and targeted, too. Only memories to do with Mond must be Forgotten, nothing else. We don't want a whole stampede of Howlers staggering around wondering who they are, what they do, where they come from, and which way is up. That'd make a heck of a *matata*. So. That's the problem. Ideas, anybody?"

By now Miba was roaring, curled up and rocking on the rug. "I'd – *hic* – *love* to see all those Howlers - staggering around - *hic, snort* - wondering - who they are ... and which way is up..." gasped the hedgehog. "Couldn't you also - make them - *hic* - Forget - how to move - those nasty - *snuffle* - smelly - whizz things around - on their stone - rivers while - *grunt, sneeze*, hahaha! * *hic* - you're at it, Nataka? ... Oh, go on ... You *know* you hate them as much as I do ... *hic*!"

The hedgehog drew a deep breath, coughed, tried to sit up, failed and rolled back onto his prickles with his toes in the air. He dissolved in another spate of hilarity so infectious that everybody else was caught up in it. Within a heartbeat the whole cottage was roaring. Even Toki creaked and jiggled, rattling the vials and flasks on their shelves.

"*Argh!* ... In the name of Infinity, Miba, chomp down on an apple or something, but do *hush*!" scolded Nataka. "It sounds funny, but it really ain't. Come on, everybody; focus! I want to work out a solution quickly, so we can

181

finally go out and watch M'Kuu's Moon Dance before I return to the zoo!"

But the laughter did not abate. Mond joined in so vehemently that Nataka wondered how much of his behaviour was a hysterical response to the vast relief of his escape from imprisonment and danger. He barked, howled and whimpered in excitement, wriggling his body and wagging his huge grey tail in violent sweeps that threatened to knock M'Kuu off his woodpile. This in turn reignited the laughter, which swelled until it rattled Toki's rafters.

"Oy! ... *ENOUGH!* ... *Nyamaseni!* [lxxix] ... *Stop laughing!*" the Protean bellowed at last, "Axl's waiting! Paa's fidgeting with impatience to dance! ... Now don't you deny it, Paa; I can feel it. So let's get *on* with it, all right? ...Toki, I'm ashamed of you! You should know better! ... And until we can find a solution, we can't have the dance ... *HEY!* Listen! Can't *anybody* think of a solution?"

"That's exactly what you need, Boss – a solution..."

As she squeaked, Dora abseiled rapidly to dangle before Nataka's face.

"... In their water, you know. Everybody gets thirsty. Even Howlers," she added.

And just as rapidly as she had descended, the great spider reeled herself back up to her web.

"*Whoa* ... Dora!" called Nataka in the sudden silence that followed the spider's tiny, piercing voice. She held up one golden finger, "Come back, Dora."

The spider plummeted down again on her silk thread. She landed on Nataka's finger.

182

"*What* did you say?"

"**Well, it's true. Howlers do *get thirsty, just like us,***" insisted the spider a little defensively, rubbing four legs together.

"It certainly *is* true. Dora, you're a gem," Nataka stroked Dora's beautifully patterned thorax with a fingertip. "Every time you open your mandibles you come out with something helpful. Not like some other folk I could mention…" She cast a smouldering look at Miba, who was still rocking on his spiny back with his rear legs curled up and both his forepaws clamped over his nose. The dark eyes that twinkled back up at her didn't look in the least sorry.

"Again, thank you, Dora; that's a perfect idea; exactly what I was looking for," continued Nataka, "All I have to do is drop a bit of our freshly brewed panacea into the water those Howlers use. I can easily adjust it to induce Mond-related Forgetfulness. And all it'll do is make them feel healthy and mellow while they forget all about Mond, and – Oh! I've just had another thought – *And* if I make it so they don't even have to *drink* the water, we can be absolutely certain that nobody gets missed out. Yes; I'll make it so that just getting wet will do the trick."

Fyrd commented dryly, "Well, curl my whiskers; not only forgetful Howlers, but super-relaxed and fit ones, too. They'll think it's an epidemic."

Miba exploded into fresh guffaws, setting everybody else off again.

"*Now* look what you've done, Fyrd;" scolded Nataka, "You've got them all going again. We'll never get on at this rate. … OY! *Everybody hush!*

"Hmm, now let me think. First I'll do the animal prison – er – zoo. And then that hospital place. All the most important Howlers – the ones directly involved in this whole *shauri* with Mond, I mean – are bound to use the water at one or other of the two places, so that'll definitely do the trick as far as they're concerned. I mean, Howlers wash with water every time they go to relieve themselves, and they're constantly drinking it, too. So they're all bound to get wet and cop a dose of the potion very quickly after Sunwake.

"But just to make sure, I think I should also drop some of the potion into the Howlers' water supply for the whole area. That'll be safest. Fyrd, do you know where I can do that? ... Oh, *do* try to be serious!"

The otter sobered up, sat up on his hind paws, combed his whiskers and coughed. "*Ahem* ... er ... yes, Nataka; no problem. I know where the Howlers collect and store water for their lairs," he said, "And if you like I can put in the potion myself. I can get to that water from above, but that's all. During that long dry spell suffered over the last season of Dragonflies and Gnats – d'you remember? – Well, I tried to get at it then, and release it into our stream by burrowing *through* their dam from the side; you know? ... But even with Wurfl to help me (and *he's* a master builder), we found it impossible to break through that white stone stuff they use." [lxxx]

"Splendid. Thanks, Fyrd," said the sprite. "All we need is to pour one small flask of panacea into that water to account for any other Howler that may have heard about Mond, even if they weren't directly involved with him. And the best thing about it is I'll also be able to cure the wounded Howler at that hospital without anybody there getting worked up or suspicious, because nobody'll even remember why he was brought to them in the first place. Glose, remind me to destroy any notes about him they've got, too.

"Yes, the more I think about it, the better it gets. It's

perfect. Even preparing the potion is straightforward and won't take long at all. It simply couldn't be better. As I said, Dora, your idea is pure genius."

The spider climbed back up to her web, glowing with pleasure. "*I would say it's not such a big deal,*" she commented to herself, "*except of course The Boss thinks it* **is;** *and who am I to contradict her?*"

Then Nataka clapped her hands, turned to M'Kuu and Paa, who were gazing admiringly at the spider sitting insouciantly on her web, and said, "Well, you two, are we going to see that famous dance of yours, then?"

The fat Moon was losing its rosy tint and tilting away in the direction of Sunsleep, casting inky shadows under the shrubs and trees and gilding the lawn on which the tiny early blossoms – dog violet, cowslips and some impatient daisies – had curled up tight for Startime. M'Kuu led the poodle into the middle of the lawn, while the others gathered around to watch.

Nataka noticed that already Paa was absorbed in contemplating the moonlight, padding in a circle with her tail wagging gently as she gazed skywards, and occasionally rearing onto her hind-legs with her muzzle pointing towards the moon. M'Kuu began to hop and rear in a leisurely way, tracing his own circle and moving in the opposite direction to the poodle. The two animals' gentle movements formed a strangely symmetrical pattern, dreamlike and smooth. Then, as they circled, rose and fell, a pale shape emerged from behind Toki, and Axl picked his way across the lawn to join the hare and the poodle, who paused to greet him. For a few heartbeats the three animals stood immobile, muzzle to muzzle, engaged in silent communion. A strange thrumming tension and excitement seemed to build inside them, making them quiver.

The wolf took his place beside Nataka, moving as if he were

in a dream. He was clearly still in the process of absorbing all the changes of mood and circumstance he had experienced.

"Only last Sunsleep, Wise One," he rumbled, nuzzling Nataka's hand, "I was in pain, in prison and awaiting death without hope of release. And now…"

"I understand. You don't have to put it into words," interrupted the Protean, stroking his great muzzle. "Such reversals are very difficult to absorb. That's always the way with sudden changes, don't you think? … Well, if I were you, I'd just let things happen for now and not try to think too much. Your feelings have to catch up with your body, if you get my meaning. And a lot more yet – all of it involving Change – will have to take place, before you are home and safe once more. At least, now you can be certain that you *will* get home again. But first you need to rest and sleep for a while. You need time simply to *be* till you feel a bit more accustomed to everything that's been happening, and can face another journey. Yes, I'd just try to flow along with events for now, if you can… Look, the dance is about to begin."

The three incongruously matched dance partners on the lawn had begun to move again, weaving around and through one another's steps in an increasingly complex pattern. Although Paa had never danced before, it seemed to her that her paws already knew the steps to take and the patterns in which to move under the silvery moon, and that all she had to do was let them trace a path that didn't interfere with the patterns formed by her two companions, but instead complemented and enhanced them.

After a little while, as the weaving and braiding patterns of their dance became quicker and more intricate, the three animals reared up onto their hind legs: the hare boxing the air, the deer tossing his velvety antlers, and the little dog waving and shaking her ears, tail and forepaws...

And then they began to leap.

Glose, who was sitting alongside Pex, had been muttering rude comments about Paa's dancing into the fox's ear, unaware that his companion was so intent on the dance that he was quite deaf to everything else. But now the raven fell abruptly silent, mesmerised in spite of himself by the way the three dancers were leaping and bounding over, through and under one another's bodies and legs, their pelts gleaming in the moonlight and their movements so swift and graceful that they left trace-images of their passage behind them in silvery streaks, like the patterns created by those sparkling fires Howler infants wave and whirl around during some of their incomprehensible Startime celebrations.

Like short-lived fireflies in the air above the sward, the streaking after-images generated by the movements of the three animals coalesced into ephemeral, three-dimensional shapes that reminded the watchers of ethereal landscapes, caverns, ziggurats, trees and cloudscapes reminiscent of half-remembered dreams, experiences, fears and hopes, and evoked for each watcher a bouquet of sweet-and-bitter, half-forgotten pains, joys and longings...

And then – and nobody could say, later, how or whence it arose - weaving into and emerging from the patterns of the Dance Magic being created by the three animals as if the dancers were themselves being altered by their dance and metamorphosing into something new, *Something,* an ancient form, coalesced and emerged from the spectacle before them. Towering over the three dancers, cloudy and shimmering, it took substance above the sward, indistinct and elusive as a misty idea that can only be captured if you don't try to think about it too hard, or a shape that you may only see from the corner of an obliquely-cast eye, because it will vanish the instant you try to look at it directly…

… *Something* moved, proudly moved and inclined Its magnificent, star-limned, back-swept horns over a never-before-seen yet instantly recognisable, humorous, ancient, sharp-nosed visage with wise, laughing and perilous eyes and with a point of perfect light at the centre of its lofty brow… a figure that combined the sleekly muscled upper body, arms and hands of a Sapiens with the sturdy, thickly furred rump, legs and hooves of a mighty, rearing ram.

There it stood and swayed and breathed and danced before the mesmerised company, emerging from – yet still a part of – the three dancers, whose own forms were absorbed into it while still, somehow, remaining distinctly their own; each animal complete, yet fused with – and inside – the gigantic glowing Presence they had summoned with their Dance.

And for a moment that hung in each mind like Eternity it seemed to the awestricken watchers that an ancient breeze wafted its benison from a glowing, faraway country into the clearing before the cottage and that Pan Himself, the Legend-Become-Reality, a dream evoked and revered by every Nyama in need of haven and consolation, was dancing before them in the argent glow of the gradually settling Moon.

And perhaps it was an illusion or a trick of the moonlight that made the watchers imagine they saw a delicately twining, star-spangled, silken horn, glistening and translucent as rippling water, sprout and grow from the centre of Paa's softly curled brow, an ephemeral echo of the unearthly light cast by the vast figure dancing alongside her on the sward; who knows?

"Look at Paa!" breathed Tytus, "what's happening to *Paa*?"

And now the watchers heard, as from a long, long, dim distance within an echoing tunnel, the blood-quickening, soul-stirring, swirling skirl of a reed-pipe that called and sang a song so sweet, so plangent, so searingly and achingly beautiful, it felt to the listeners that their hearts must surely burst with the burden of it.

Beside Nataka the rescued wolf whimpered deep in his throat, dropped to the grass and bowed his head, followed by all the other animals. Time itself seemed to pause, and every living thing that moved under the stars to hold its breath, before the Apparition dancing on Nataka's lawn.

"Gilded beaks and claws," again whispered Tytus the Baron, "I see ... something ... And I hear... *Some*thing ... almost unbearable! ... What *is* this new magic?"

"They've opened a portal," Nataka's low voice sounded at once breathless and fearful, "their dance has opened a portal ... for something – no, Some*one* - to come through ... Do you see it – *Him* – too? ... There ... *there!* Do you see? .... Oh, I really had no idea just how magical this dance would be!

"Fagus was right. They do dance well together, so well that their dance is starting Something new ... and ... and it's doing something to me, too. I *feel* something – something I've never felt before... Ah! ... It's unbearable ..."

She clutched her hands at her breast and a strange look of agony, fear and ecstasy transformed her features for a moment.

Too soon the shadowy, starry figure before them faded once more, the wild sweet music dwindled, and the sublime moment came to an end, leaving the three dancers still dancing, but more slowly now, and alone again. But to the consternation of the owl and the raven, Nataka stood with her hands still clutched to her breast while tears flowed unchecked from her moonlit eyes.

On the tree-clad hillside behind them, the nightingale whose song had accompanied their earlier visit to Fagus burst into a fresh serenade, breaking the profound silence that had followed the disappearance of the Pan figure.

"What is it? What's wrong with you? Are you *sick?*" fretted Glose, flapping to Nataka's shoulder and laying his glossy black head against her cheek. In all his long seasons with her, the raven had never seen her weep.

"No ... yes ... *no* ... I can't tell! ...   I – I do believe that I'm feeling an emotion... I *think* it's joy ... it's like no other feeling I've ever had before," whispered the Protean, touching his head distractedly, "It's so frightening, because it's nothing like ... the usual things I feel... Amusement, or pleasure, or impatience ... Just joy – a joy that's so strong it hurts, you know? ... And... oh ... the strangest thing ... it's like homesickness, too ... A desire to return to ... *something* ... or *somewhere* ... though I don't know what ... and the dreadful fear that I may never work out what it is, ever, let alone get back to it again ... *Ahh!* It's unbearable! ... Can't you feel it?"

"I *think* I understand, old friend," murmured Tytus, landing on her other shoulder, "I also felt something like that when the music came. But it's fading now. Isn't it fading for you? ... I wonder, is *this* what the Sirens sounded like when they lured those poor sailors to their doom?[lxxxi]"

"Who knows? ... I do feel as if some kind of doom had been announced," whispered the golden Protean hesitantly, "*my* doom... or - or a Change I can't prevent... with this dance. And for the first time I've felt afraid... of *Him* ... and – and of myself too, somehow ... Oh, Tytus, what if I can't control these new feelings? ... What then?"

She turned abruptly, almost dislodging the birds on her shoulders. "What's *happening*, Toki?" she demanded, wiping her eyes, "What does this *mean*? Why do I feel like this, all of a sudden? Nothing is certain any longer!"

The cottage trembled and puffed a silvery mist from its chimney. Glose was sure it had spoken to his friend, although he didn't understand what it had said. Nataka drew a shuddering breath and sighed.

"Oh... Oh, all right, then; I'll be patient, if you insist. Although you know I hate having to wait, on principle," she said. "But yes. Of course I'll wait. ... But I'll hold you to your promise; mark my words ... I really *must* understand, and the sooner the better!"

The dance ended, leaving the three performers once again immobile and facing one another. They bowed their heads in unison, touched muzzles, and sank onto the grass. As they curled together on the lawn, Mond and Pex simultaneously lifted their muzzles and ululated at the Moon stooping ever further towards the Sunsleep horizon, offering it the ancient tribute of song given by every member of the Dog Kindred on such nights.

By the time their song ended, the very first streaks of False Sunwake had begun to gild the sky above the wooded horizon behind the cottage.

Following Nataka's lead, the Wanyama now turned and straggled back into the cottage, leaving the three dancers still asleep in the fading light of the setting Moon and the early glow of the False Sunwake.

Glose did not join the rest of the Wanyama immediately. Instead he fluttered up onto Toki's slanting roof and perched there, contemplating the slumbering trio on the lawn and trying to make sense of his own disquiet.

"I saw something ... and I heard something, most certainly ... although I'm already beginning to forget what it was," he cawed to himself, scratching his poll, "But what did Nataka mean with her talk, and why was she so upset? ... What was I supposed to feel? ... *Was* I even supposed to feel anything? ... That annoying owl said *he* felt something. Was he being honest, or only sucking up? I wouldn't put it past him.

"I must admit, though: the daft little dog can *dance*. Who'd have thought it? ... She's weird all right. And as for M'Kuu and Axl ... Well, I wouldn't have thought them capable of achieving that - whatever it was - any more than I'd expect them to lay eggs."

He sighed, clicked his beak and shuffled his wings to settle his feathers. "Ah, well," he concluded as he prepared to fly back indoors, "Look on the bright side. At least my fight with Fyrd's been forgotten in among all this *shauri!*"

On the lawn, the poodle snuggled closer to the slumbering hare and deer, and her paws paddled and twitched as she dreamed that she was still dancing in the moonlight while a silvery horn sprouted from her brow.

Chapter 13. *The Meeting*

"Steer not thy barque of life against the tide, since change must guide thy course." lxxxii

Anthony had informed everybody that the weekly Section Wardens' Meeting would focus exclusively on the problem of the troublesome wolf. But it got off to a slow start because, for the first time in his career at the zoo, he arrived late. And because this was so uncharacteristic of him, many of the other wardens (and especially the ones that tended to come late themselves) were inclined to be annoyed. We never forgive reliable people on the rare occasions when they fail to live up to their own high standards, whereas someone who's persistently late or messing up is both indulged and excused without a second thought - *and* lauded like a hero when or if he or she does occasionally do the right thing.

"He's taking the Mickey, 's'what he's doing;" grumbled Geoff Masters, the jowly, rumpled and unshaven warden who seemed unable to rid his grubby fingernails of the ripe odours of the Australian fauna in his care. Geoff didn't get on with anybody, which didn't bother him at all. Indeed, he seemed to thrive on a daily régime of complaints and multiple cups of free coffee. He also took particular exception to the fact that nobody else at the zoo gave two hoots about his numerous and ever-changing grievances, or (worse still, in his opinion) cared to indulge him when he tried to backbite the management or any other member of staff that happened to be out of earshot.

In other words - though without ever voicing their thoughts - his colleagues were convinced, not only that Geoff Masters enjoyed feeling aggrieved and resentful, but that it was the only thing that kept him going ... together with the free coffee, of course. Take away his sense of grievance and caffeine addiction, they reckoned, and he'd probably deflate like a punctured bladder. So when he arrived ten minutes late that morning and laid on a story about last-minute problems with a diarrhoetic wombat to excuse himself, it was all par for the course as far as his colleagues were concerned, and nobody even twitched an eyebrow.

There were ten section wardens at the zoo, each of them reporting directly to Anthony and themselves in charge of various assistant wardens and keepers, who didn't attend the weekly section meetings unless they were specifically summoned. The section wardens passed on any decisions and orders generated during these meetings to their teams, and it all worked very well. Most of the time.

This morning, they were finally all assembled and sitting around in groups, as usual. Most of the wardens were holding mugs of coffee they'd drawn from the dispenser that stood on a drinks table beside the chair reserved for Anthony. There was plenty of chatter while they waited for their drinks to cool.

There were several raised eyebrows at Anthony's uncharacteristic absence, particularly as this was to be such a critically important meeting, given that the only topics of universal interest were that troublesome wolf and the health of young Jim Bell (who still lay in hospital fighting the infection caused by his mauling, although his doctors were now satisfied that they were getting the better of it at last). Everybody present was impatient to get on with thrashing out the whole issue once and for all.

Predictably, Geoff had taken immediate offence on discovering that for once he wasn't the last to arrive at the meeting. "Not here yet? Typical! First he forces us to look after that mad wolf. And now he doesn't even bother to show up on time," he grouched. "Next he'll be telling us we've got to do overtime without compensation, or cutting our breaks, or some other such damn foolery. You mark my words. Ugh, *managers*."

He hitched up his dirty denim trousers and shambled straight over to the coffee dispenser, where he jabbed the little lever to pour the hot black liquid into his mug. His elbow jogged the large jar of drinking water that always stood next to it.

"'S'a flipping liberty, 'f'you ask *me*." He went on, and carried his mug to one of the empty chairs at the back of the room and sat down, placing the drink on the floor under his chair to cool. He crossed his arms and scowled around the room. Nobody had responded to his comments. His scowl deepened. "Miserable bastards," he muttered under his breath.

"The vet's due this morning;" fretted Marcie, the soulful, dumpy fifty-something ex-Hippy in charge of exotic birds, whose short strawberry-coloured hair clashed wonderfully with her tie-dye tops. Her hair had been coloured so often that now it had the consistency of straw and stood up off her head like a bottlebrush, lending her appearance a certain affinity with many of her crested avian charges. "Ooh, I *do* hope Tony gets here in time for *that,* at least." She fidgeted with a low-calorie breakfast bar, wondering vaguely whether to dunk and risk its disintegration in her muddy drink. She decided not to chance it. "He's probably still struggling with his bereavement," she added. "Don't forget his ginger moggie died yesterday. He *did* love him awfully. I -"

"Rubbish. Don't be *soft,* woman!" interrupted Geoff. "Cats die all the time, for Chrissake. Tony's not likely to go all soppy over an animal, like some female. Nah, I'll tell you what all this is *really* about. He's avoiding the wolf issue, *that's* what this is about. He doesn't want that bloody animal putting down, doesn't Tony. He'd much sooner we carry on breaking our arses caring for it … probably

195

wouldn't even give a damn if more of us went the same way as that daft bugger Jim ..."

"*Language*, Geoff!" snapped one or two voices. "Here! Ladies present!" yelped Alice of the Bugs department, and the zoo's resident herpetologist Malcolm Tripp added, "Nonsense! Of *course* Tony doesn't want anybody else hurt..."

"If you're sure he *isn't* soppy over animals, Geoff, how can you also claim that he cares more for the wolf than us? Doesn't compute for me, mate," added the humorous, sceptical voice of Bryony, the zoo's official fireball, who was in charge of Small Mammals. Recently she'd been rather more subdued than usual because of Jim Bell's injuries. In fact, she'd spent every off-duty moment at the hospital, keeping a vigil over his unconscious form and getting under the feet of the medical staff in her earnest attempts to help (Jim knew nothing about this, of course. He didn't even know *where* he was). Now that the young man had finally been pronounced out of danger, Bryony's cheerful disposition was reasserting itself with a vengeance. Incensed at Geoff's words, her voice was rather sharper than usual.

"I *tell* you, he thinks more of that bloody animal than us!" snapped Geoff, "I bet he reckons that by staying away and avoiding us - *or* the vet - he'll be able to put off getting the job done. That's what *I* think. He's probably upstairs right now, concocting some cock-and-bull story about being sick or something, just to put us all off. You mark my words! Well, I for one am *not* gonna stand for it any longer. That bloody animal's a menace. It should be knocked on the head. What the hell do we need more wolves for, anyway? We've got too bloody many of them already. Do we have any dingoes? Do we hell. And why not? I'll tell you..."

"A cock- and-bull story? You mean, something like *your* usual cock-and-bull stories for coming late, Geoff?" interrupted Bryony with a grin that showed all her teeth but didn't quite extend to her eyes.

"Look, Geoff; you don't *know* any of that. You're just speculating," insisted tall and lanky Malcolm, who was rather bookish and didn't much like Geoff. "Just because he's a bit late doesn't mean he'd deceive …"

"*Really?* ... How d'you know that, smart-arse?" interrupted Geoff, who didn't much like Malcolm either (not really surprising, given that he didn't much like anybody). "I *tell* you, he's making up an excuse right now; just you watch!"

Just then Anthony stepped in at the door. He looked rotten: dishevelled and heavy-eyed. His first proper night's rest without any worries about the wolf to keep him awake had not sufficed to refresh him. Instead it left him feeling as if somebody had taken a sandbag to his head. Unsurprisingly, he had overslept, and only managed to scramble into his clothes at the last moment, dashing downstairs without shaving or brushing his hair. Now he smiled ruefully at the assembled wardens and scratched his uncombed hair, making it stand on end.

"Really sorry I'm late, folks," he said, "I slept like a log, straight through the alarm clock. First time that's happened to me in ages. I must have been wiped out yesterday, more wiped out than I realised. Anyway, apologies. Won't happen again."

"G'day, Tone!" said Bryony, "No big deal, mate. How're you doing?"

"'Morning, Tony," said Marcie in the honeyed, unctuous voice do-gooders adopt when they're passing on bad news or condolences, "We were all *so* sorry to hear about your poor little pussycat…"

Anthony smiled at her, a lump forming in his throat. "That's very kind of you, Marcie," he replied, "Yes; we'll miss him, poor old boy … but … well, he *was* very sick … and … you know … it's better this way, because he isn't suffering any longer … and … er…"

He stammered to a halt, not sure how to continue, and then added, "Er well… we can't let my loss distract us from our work … Yes. … So, thanks anyway. … *Ahem*…" He sat down and looked round.

"Now, then. … Let's get down to business. First off, has anybody got anything special to report before we go on to today's work schedule?"

"Well … er … about that *wolf*, you know," said Malcolm, breaking the confused silence that had followed Anthony's words, "Only, I *thought* you said this meeting was going to focus on that before anything else - what we should do about it, you know – about where we go from here, whether to keep it, or … *ahem* … and about the vet's visit, of course…"

The other wardens nodded and made little noises of agreement. All apart from Geoff, who snorted.

Anthony smiled encouragingly. "Right. Thanks, Malcolm. … Er … OK. … Wolf. … Vet … Yes … Er - um … do us a favour and run all that past me again, would you? … Sorry, only, I've been a bit distracted lately, what with one thing and another, you know, and the details seem to have slipped my mind. … So. What wolf's that, then? … And why's the vet visiting, exactly?"

Ten jaws dropped, and ten pairs of wide eyes stared at him out of ten flabbergasted faces.

"Gor – don – *Bennett!*" exploded Geoff, "So *that's* your game, eh? Well, don't think you're gonna get away with it!"

"Sorry, what game's that, Geoff?" asked Anthony, turning to face the irate warden, "I really don't follow. … And, look, I assure you I'm not playing any games, whatever you mean by that…"

He cleared his throat and paused, staring round at all the other wardens, who were either still gazing at him incredulously or shuffling in embarrassment and failing to meet his eyes. He cleared his throat again. "Listen, everybody. I'm clearly missing something key here," he said at last. "I get the distinct impression that *something* big's been going down; something I'm not yet in on. Could somebody please explain – you know, give me the details - so we can all work on it together?"

"Something *big?* … Not *in* on it? … *Hah!* …" shouted Geoff, and rounded on his fellow wardens. "*Told* you lot, didn't I? *Told* you he was working on some bloody *trick*! Well, for once you lot can deal with it. I've had enough!*"* He half rose from his chair and glared around at his colleagues, who for a moment were too nonplussed to respond. "And I'll tell you something else for free. I'm not lifting another finger for that bloody animal. No matter *what*. So there!" He sat back down and groped under his seat for his mug, lifted it, slurped down a mouthful of coffee, swallowed and grimaced. "Coffee down to its usual crap standard, too. But at least it's wet…" he pulled a face and swallowed another mouthful.

"Why d'you drink it, then, if you hate it so much?" snapped Malcolm, losing patience. "You're constantly bending our ears about the damned coffee, but you carry on drinking it anyway. And besides, don't change the subject. What's the coffee got to do with that wolf, anyway?"

"I'd have to bring me own; wouldn't I?" snorted Geoff, "I give enough to this bloody place as it is, without having to pay for my own coffee as well." He tilted his mug and slurped again.

"Depends what you mean by *give,* I suppose;" commented Bryony. "I for one could use less of you giving us your opinion all the time." She grinned again. Bryony had freckles, a crown of naturally curly brown hair, a wide mouth, firm chin and cheeky hazel eyes. Her big hands were capable of remarkable gentleness, and every ounce of her rangy body radiated energy and optimism.

Even though he was irritated and bewildered by Geoff's complaints, Anthony couldn't help grinning at Bryony's words. He reminded himself that for some time he'd been thinking about appointing an Assistant Chief Warden to help with his workload. Perhaps she had the necessary cool and cheer for the job? Certainly she was efficient and ran a very happy department. And, most importantly of all, her animals adored her.

"Bryony's right, Geoff," he said, "It's time to stop moaning and come clean. You should either spit it out – and I don't mean the coffee – or stop complaining, all right? So. What is it this time? You still haven't told me what I'm supposed to have done to offend you so much. But something clearly *has* offended you, so out with it. .... C'mon, then. Let's get it sorted right away, and move on. What's your gripe?"

"Gripe? ... About *what*?" demanded Geoff, whose eyes had misted over and lost focus for a moment after the first mouthful of coffee. He blinked rapidly a few times, looking disoriented, but his expression quickly settled back into his usual belligerent scowl. "Dunno what you're on about," he went on, "what gripe? ... 'S'nothing to do with me, whatever it is, so don't pick on *me*. ... *Fft;* whatever. I'm getting another cup of this crap coffee. Damned mugs; all too small ..." he ran a calloused hand over his face, rose from his chair and shambled back to the drinks dispenser, muttering under his breath.

Marcie sighed, "It's about that poor *wolf*, you know, Tony;" she offered in her mellowest voice, "I really don't know *why* Geoff has to make *such* a fuss about it. Only ... well, to be honest – and I do believe in being honest, as you know – Geoff seems to think that you're planning something ... well ... something a bit *iffy* ... to get away from dealing with the wolf, you know; and ..."

She hesitated, sipped her coffee and nibbled her breakfast bar to gain a few moments in which to work out what to say next – and promptly drifted off into a misty-eyed limbo as her train of thought melted away.

"*Here*! ... I *never*! ... *What* wolf you wittering on about, anyway?" snapped Geoff, spinning round to glare at Marcie, " I don't handle *wolves*, in case you've forgotten, you daft mare! So don't you go putting words in my mouth ... I haven't got the first tossing *clue* what you're talking about!"

Marcie's eyes lost their blissful, stoned expression and snapped back into focus. She sat bolt upright, bewildered and upset by what she saw as Geoff's unwarranted attack.

"*You*? ... *I*? ... Honestly, I've got *no* idea what *you're* on about, Geoff! ... *You've* been complaining ever since you came in, as *usual*. You *know* you have! ... In fact, I stopped *listening* to your constant grouching *years* ago, you unreconstructed - square - male - chauvinist - *PIG*!"

Her voice went up a notch with each word she spat at him, until she was squealing, a bit like the pig she'd referred to.

"So why're you having a go at me? ... I *never* put words into your rotten mouth! ... *Did* I, everybody? ... I mean, *honestly!* ... Call me a *mare*, indeed! ... "

"'Bout a *wolf!*" bellowed Geoff, "Just now! You *said* –"

"I *never did*!" shrilled Marcie, "It wasn't *me,* it was *you!* ... *You* said –"

"Here – here, you two; calm down!" exclaimed Malcolm, jumping to his feet, "This doesn't have to get out of hand. There's no need to squabble… Let's all just settle down, shall we, and let Tony explain what *he* thinks we should do about the wolf, calmly and sanely. OK? ... *Geoff*! ... *Marcie*! ... Come on, you two…"

"Aw, *shut up,* you sodding great *toady*!" yelled Geoff, rounding on him, "I'm not going to stand here and be in*sul*ted – and – and – *accused* – by *that* dozy tw…"

"*Insulted?* ... *Accused?*" shrieked Marcie, now completely beside herself, "About *what?* ... You're just an ugly great *bully,* Geoff Masters, and everybody *knows* it! You – you've got a *dirty soul*!"

"Blimey. *That* bad, huh?" said Bryony happily.

"Toady, am I? Well I'm not some miserable *malcontent,* Geoff …" blustered Malcolm at the same time. Two bright red spots blossomed on his pale cheeks.

"You certainly did go on about that wolf, you know, Geoff," laughed Bryony. Anthony thought that if he promoted her they might have to have a chat about being just a little less up-beat in such situations.

The grumpy warden snapped. He snatched up the brimming water jug on the drinks table and threw its contents straight at Marcie. His movements were so wild that he managed to splash everybody else in the room as well. Then he whipped round and brandished the empty jug at Malcolm and Bryony. "You want some of *this?*" he yelled. "C'mon then! Come and get some of this, you bloody *****! ..." [lxxxiii]

The room erupted in shrieks, bellows and curses. The wardens sprang to their feet, scattering mugs and chairs. Anthony could have sworn that at one point in among the pandemonium he heard a raven caw, but he instantly forgot it again, distracted by the scene unfolding before him. He jumped to his feet but hesitated for a moment, struggling to make sense of what was happening, and wrong-footed by the speed with which the meeting had fallen apart.

But events didn't wait for him to catch up. Marcie had bounded to her feet, soaked and incandescent, and was charging towards Geoff, shrieking like a mynah bird and upsetting a couple of chairs standing in her way. Her strawberry hair bristled, her pink face blazed, and she brandished her crumbly breakfast bar, intent on ramming it up the grumpy warden's nostrils.

Geoff raised the empty water jug to shield himself, but the fury on the dumpy ex-hippy's face was so uncharacteristic that it startled him. He took a step backwards - and bumped into the coffee machine, which wobbled for a second or two as if considering its options and then toppled over with a loud ***CLANG*** and **whoosh*, taking everything else, including the table, with it. Scalding coffee, ground beans and water splattered on the floor, rapidly reducing the few remaining biscuits to mush (mainly rich tea biscuits, they were; nobody much liked those). The paper packets of sugar and sweetener dissolved, and their contents melted and mingled with the mushy biscuits and soggy teabags that lay spread around the upturned basket that usually held them.

China cups and mugs bounced and shattered; plastic teaspoons littered the floor and skittered under the chairs. And to cap it all, the drinks table slithered sideways across the width of the room, collided with a stack of spare chairs in the corner and knocked them over, too.

The curses and shouts crescendoed. Wardens scrambled to stand on chairs or snatched up their feet to avoid the scalding mess on the floor. Bryony seemed to be the only one having fun. She whooped and laughed as she wiped the freshly spattered drops of water off her face, wearing the kind of expression you see on kids who've just heard the tinny music of an approaching ice-cream van.

Anthony had jumped onto his chair too, and now he stood on it, wobbling and staring in amazement. This was chaos. He could hear his wife calling from upstairs, demanding to know what the hell was going on. He *had* to take charge before things got even worse. Now was no time for sensitivity. He filled his lungs and roared over the hubbub.

QUIET!"

Again he could have sworn he heard the harsh cry of a raven. But, like the first time, it stopped again so abruptly that he couldn't be sure.

In the startled silence that followed his uncharacteristic outburst, he snapped, "Geoff, that's *your* mess. Clean it up right now! And consider yourself formally warned. I want to see you in my office at the beginning of lunch break, at twelve sharp. Understood? ... No; *no* discussion. Be there!

"Right, then. Marcie and Malcolm, I also want *your* written reports on what's just happened in here. Make sure I get them by noon, too. Anybody else who cares to act as a witness, same drill for you. ... That clear? ... All right.

"Now, as Malcolm said, everybody settle down and let's talk this whole nonsense through, properly and calmly, once and for all."

"*Did* I say that? ... How clever of me," murmured Malcolm dreamily, running a sleeve over his dripping chin.

When the wardens were again seated (all except Geoff, who was picking up the toppled coffee machine and mopping up the spillage with paper towels), "Now then," Anthony said, "and don't all talk at once, please. *Will* somebody finally explain to me what's going on? ... I mean, what*'s* all this about a blessed wolf you're all going on about, and just *what* appears to be the problem with it, anyway?"

Nobody could tell him.

The wardens sat dabbing themselves with sleeves, tissues and paper towels, stared at one another with blank faces and wondered why their boss seemed to be fixated on discussing some animal about which none of them could summon the first clue.

And if a few of them were beginning to suspect that The Boss might be losing the plot and needing a long rest, they weren't about to voice it. No, Sir. This new, authoritative and unapologetic Anthony was clearly nobody to trifle with.

Geoff Masters worked away at the mess on the floor, head down and ears burning. For the first time in his life he was feeling increasingly sheepish and anxious. He hardly dared raise his eyes to Marcie, who crouched on her chair, smouldering and glaring venomously at him while she mentally composed the blistering complaint she would hand in to Anthony.

Several more minutes went by in an increasingly fidgety silence, broken only by the sounds of Geoff's mopping, an occasional cough and the rumbling stomachs of wardens that hadn't had time for breakfast before the meeting. In the end, Anthony scratched his head again and concluded that everybody must have been labouring under some thoroughly incomprehensible misunderstanding, because, despite that fuss, it seemed there really wasn't anything especially urgent to discuss after all. For that matter, nobody could even suggest a sensible explanation to account for why the vet had been summoned.

Anthony decided that the main problem must have been Geoff's constant complaints, and the fact that everybody else was heartily sick of hearing him grouch all the time. That would have to be dealt with. He wondered whether, perhaps, Geoff might be better off working somewhere else entirely. Of course this wasn't entirely fair on the grumpy warden, despite the fact that he really was a pain in the neck.

Then Anthony began to think that he could be spending his time much more productively giving himself a quick shave and wash instead of sitting around waiting for somebody – *anybody* – to cast some kind of light on a topic they all seemed to have completely forgotten; a topic that felt more and more irrelevant and fragmentary with every second that ticked by on the suddenly loud wall clock behind him.

So in the end he moved on to the next item on the agenda, which was the usual round-up of each department's weekly report and plans for the coming days, reminded Geoff of his appointment, and brought the meeting to an end.

Some time later, when Anthony was again downstairs and at his desk after a good wash and brush up, a van drew up outside and in bustled the dapper little vet who served as their first port of call whenever a zoo animal fell ill.

"This is all such a sad business; such a pity," he said, shaking his head. "Ah well, best get it over with; eh? …

I've brought everything with me, just in case. But to start with I'll have a wee peek at the paperwork, if that's all right with you. And – ah – er … d'you mind if I just nip into your bathroom first – you know, before we get down to business?"

"Certainly, Doc, help yourself; you know the way," replied Anthony. He still had no idea why the vet had turned up in the first place, and was hoping to get a clue from their conversation. "Actually, to tell the truth I'm running a bit late this morning; haven't even eaten yet. I was about to make myself a coffee and toast, and boil a couple of eggs," he said, thinking to gain a bit of time and more opportunities to work out what was going on. "Care to join me?"

Some forty minutes later, Darren, a burly assistant keeper, knocked on the door to find Anthony and the little vet sitting at Anthony's desk, sharing a cuppa over the plundered remains of two egg breakfasts, and grumbling comfortably about the cost of various vaccines, the rising prices of permits and leases, and government regulations in general. Darren wanted to get rid of an empty metal holding cage lying just inside the wolf compound. There didn't seem any good reason for it to be there. Did Tony have any plans for it? Nobody else seemed to know why it had been dragged out and put there in the first place; it was quite empty and a bit of an eyesore, really. Anthony readily agreed that it should be carted away and put back into storage.

"Jolly good," commented the little vet, his voice a bit plummy from consuming quantities of Fran's home-made marmalade and plum jam. "Keep the place ship-shape and attractive. Excellent."

Chant the calico cat sat in a patch of sunlight on the windowsill, soaking in the warmth with her eyes half-shut and her tail wrapped neatly around her paws while she waited for an opportunity to complain to her Pet about how much she was missing Leto. There was an off chance that she might wangle a treat or two out of him. She also wondered how long it would take for her Pet to notice the patterns of scratches on the side of the house. They looked for all the world as though a very large animal – like a bear or a lion – had repeatedly attacked the wall with its claws, gouging the stucco and brickwork. But the zoo didn't house bears or lions.

It was a puzzle she could have answered, had her Pet asked. She washed her neat little brindled face, thinking about it.

Nataka turned to Glose, who was perching on her Invisible shoulder. *So far, so good, thanks to Fyrd.*

Glose didn't reply. During the meeting she had clamped her fingers over his Invisible beak more than once to muffle his squawks of amusement, and he was sulking.

Well, let's just hope all the rest goes as smoothly as this, she added, unperturbed. *The mellow mood didn't last very long, though; did it? Most Howlers really are a miserable bunch of fusspots. But I like the look of that curled spotted female. She's sharp, that one.*

Right; well. Now to deal with the wounded Howler...

Chapter 14. *The Howler Host- ... Hosti- ... That.*

"Beauty, woman's curse..." [lxxxiv]

Gasping for air, Jim Bell awoke from a nightmare in which he was fighting a losing battle against a pack of slavering wolves intent on excavating him for his internal organs. He had tossed and turned as the nightmare progressed, and somehow twisted over onto his broken ribs and arm, which throbbed and stabbed him with shooting pains with every breath he drew. Some invisible maniac was using his head for drumming practice, and his parched tongue felt rough enough to file his teeth.

"*Not my giblets!*" He croaked.

A throaty chuckle answered him.

The befuddled young man winced and forced his gummy eyelids to open, wondering what anybody could find to laugh at. A cough forced itself out through his throat and he gasped as a bolt of pain lanced through his chest.

He had barely managed to discern the presence of a tall figure silhouetted against the light of the window next to his bed when a cool, astringent and fluid sensation enveloped his wounded side. It burrowed into his arm and torso like a soothing, healing breeze, erasing the tearing, stabbing discomfort that had been his constant companion for days.

With the pain, the feverish light-headedness caused by his infection melted away like a low-lying morning mist dissipating in the warmth of the rising sun. For the first time since receiving his injuries, Jim felt perfectly lucid, casting off the momentary disorientation and bewilderment he had felt on awakening. Fearing that they might return at any moment, he drew a tentative breath ... and was instantly flooded with so much energy, optimism and restlessness that he might have been a child again, bounding awake on the first day of the school holidays.

He lay still for a moment, marvelling at the miracle of simple breathing, but still hardly daring to move lest the pain should return.

But that feeling didn't last either, because in the midst of his light-headed gratitude and relief, his cognitions executed a vertiginous, swooping tumble-turn...

... And now he was simply bewildered, wondering why he was lying in a hospital bed, and what all those bandages on his arm and torso might signify. And what or who was that shadowy figure beside his bed?

"What? ... Who?" stuttered the young man, staring up at the figure, "*Why*? ..."

"All very good questions," responded a rich contralto voice. The figure bent over him, revealing a young black face surrounded by a halo of raven-coloured curls. The large, black-lashed eyes, iridescent and variable, reminded Jim of Tiger's Eyes. A mobile, full-lipped, sardonic mouth curved over a dimpled, rounded chin of what Jim instantly decided was the most perfect face he had ever seen.

The loose white lab coat that hung open over a pair of casually rumpled jeans and T-shirt informed him that the young woman was a medical practitioner. A hospital badge and a large-faced, upside-down medical watch hung from the lapels of the coat. The coat pockets were stuffed full of pens and implements for pinning down tongues and peering into ears, and a stethoscope was casually draped around the young woman's slim neck.

Jim Bell's mouth dropped open.

"'Morning, Mr Bell. I'm happy to tell you that your tests are all uniformly satisfactory. You're quite well," said the woman as she briskly removed the drip from his arm. "So we needn't detain you any longer. Here -" She turned to his bedside locker and took out a suit of clothes, which she laid on his bed, "your family left these for you. I'll go out and let you dress. All right? ... Do you need anything else before I go?"

Arkh! *Nice. Tests. Good ploy. But it doesn't explain all those wrappings.* Glose had stopped sulking. Nataka was relieved that she'd ensured the bird still clinging to her shoulder was inaudible as well as invisible. She didn't want a repeat of the noise he'd made during the meeting at the zoo.

Oh, shut up, Bird. I can't think of everything all the time. "You had a bit of a tumble at work, Mr Bell. We've had you in overnight for observation, just to make sure you were all right. Turns out you didn't need all these bandages after all. But better safe than sorry, eh?"

She chuckled again and bent to remove the dressings. "Just a few bruises; nothing to worry about."

"I ... tests? ... Home? ... Oh ... I had such a dream..." Jim's eyes remained fixed on Nataka's face. "... A nightmare ... pain... wolves ... fangs ... Oh, my God, those *fangs*... But then I woke up ... and you ... who *are* you? I've never seen you before..."

"Ah. Um. A nightmare, eh? ... Don't worry; it's only a dream; shouldn't trouble you again;" said the young woman. She touched his forehead with one cool forefinger.

Sheesh; I should have Seen that dream and made sure he Forgot it before waking up.

Yes, you should. *Arkh*! ... What's the matter with this Howler, anyway? ... Have you seen the way he's looking at you?

The boy was staring at her in a most peculiar way. He looked fascinated, mesmerised and – it came to Nataka in a flash – smitten.

Oh-oh... she thought.

Oh-oh, indeed. I'll be a coddled egg, but I think he's...

Don't say it!

"Well, goodbye then, Mr Bell," said Nataka, turning to leave.

Last thing I need, an enamoured Howler.

Your own fault. You just had *to assume a pretty female Transformation, didn't you? Why couldn't you have chosen that ugly old vulture with all the wrinkles and warts, instead? ... I'll tell you why. Vanity.*

"No! – Wait ... Please - don't – don't go..." exclaimed the young man, struggling upright in his bed, "I've never seen anyone like you before..."

*Arkh! *You've no idea how right you are, poor fool.

"... I ... I'd really like to see – see you ... again ... please?"

Too late, sniggered the raven. *He's snared.*

I swear I'll glue that beak of yours shut if you don't keep quiet.

Arkh! Temper, temper.

The expression of irritation and impatience that fled momentarily over the young woman's face startled Jim, who paused to consider his own words.

"Oh ... Oh, I see ... I'm sorry... Was that ... unacceptable? ... I mean, inappropriate ... because you're a – you're a doctor?" he blurted, "It's only ... I can't help it ... I've never felt like this before ... I can't bear the thought of not ... of not being able to see you ... again – er – socially ... you know..."

He blushed as he spoke, but even so, his wide eyes never left hers for a moment. And now he reached out and managed to capture one of her hands in both his own. "You're... you're so ... beautiful... and kind... and – and your eyes ... Oh, my God, your eyes ... please say I can see you again; please!"

Good grief. The idiot's experienced a coup de foudre[lxxxv]. *I really don't need this. I'd better wipe it out of his head, pronto. Twit that I am, why couldn't I have made sure I was ugly instead of tarting myself up?*

Told you.

As she raised her hand and touched the young man's brow to erase his infatuation, Nataka was taken aback to realise that she would be sorry to see the look of naked admiration and amazement disappear from his eyes. A pearly bluish mist diffused from her fingertips into his forehead on a tune she hummed so softly only she could hear it, and she drew a deep breath of mingled regret and relief, knowing it was over.

Except that it wasn't.

The boy was still holding onto her hand and his eyes glowed as they gazed into her face, their unselfconscious devotion reminding Nataka of Paa. For the first time in aeons one of her spells hadn't worked. For a moment she stood still, at a loss for what to do next.

Pluck my pinions, what have you done now? ... You must have got it wrong. Concentrate. Try again.

Jim Bell leaned forward. "Are you ... are you worried – you know? – Because ... because we're so ... different from one another?" he ventured at last in a low, tentative voice, "I know we look ... I mean you... you're ... you're - black - and I'm... well, I'm not... " he smiled self-deprecatingly, and drew a deep breath, "But ... I mean, honestly, that's really – really not an issue, is it? ... At least, not for me ... unless it bothers *you*, of course ... I mean, I just think you're the most beautiful, magical..."

This has gone far enough, fretted the bird. *Don't just stand there,* do *something!*

"That'll do, young man," snapped Nataka, pulling her hand away, "quite apart from being entirely unprofessional and bang out of order, I'm not interested in you. You're not my type. And besides, seriously, you must be kidding, right? ... You've no idea *who* I am, what I'm like ... heck, you don't know the first thing about me!"

You can say that again, snickered Glose. Nataka tossed her head. *Don't distract me, Bird,* she snarled.

"Believe me, this is simply ridiculous," she went on, glaring at the young man, "So do us both a favour and pull yourself together. Take my word for it, it's the best thing to do. Go back to your life and forget all this nonsense. ... In fact, I suspect you may still have a touch of fever, because your behaviour isn't normal at all. ... Here, drink this."

As she spoke she decanted some drops of a sparkling substance in what looked like a crystal phial into a half-full glass of water standing on the bedside cabinet, swirled the mixture and then held out the glass to him. "Drink this down. All of it. It'll deal with your temperature – I'm sure you still have a temperature, otherwise you wouldn't be behaving so irrationally," she said. "This'll make you feel a lot more like yourself, believe me. And then you can go home."

The last thing Jim Bell wanted was to feel different, but if the enchanting creature before him had asked him to walk out of a third-floor window he'd have done his level best to obey her, so certain was he that she could do no wrong. Such beauty could not be anything but good, in his eyes.[lxxxvi] So he obediently drained the glass, his eyes never leaving her face.

Nataka could instantly tell that the potion was having no effect whatsoever, because his expression didn't change. Something was at work here against which even the highly magical panacea was impotent.

It hasn't worked, fretted Glose, ruffling his invisible wings. *The fool's still looking at you like Paa ogling a pile of chopped liver.*

No, really? ... You think?

The furious Protean turned on her heel, slapped the door open with the palm of one hand and strode out of the room, her white coat flapping and her medical clogs slapping on the non-slip, easy-wash floor tiles.

'Bout time, said Glose. Nataka swatted at him.

"*Oh!* – Oh, *no!* ... *Please* don't go! ... Are you offended? ... Have I offended you? ... I'm sorry! ... I didn't mean to!

... You can't leave me – not when I've only just found you!" called Jim Bell after her retreating figure, hastily putting down the empty glass, "I've been waiting so long to find you," he added forlornly as the door slammed shut.

And then he was out of bed and scrambling into his clothes. Not bothering to check himself in the mirror, he ran his fingers through his unruly sandy hair and stared just once around the little hospital room, still wondering vaguely why he'd been there in the first place, before dashing out through the door in search of the spectacular young woman that had so swiftly and comprehensively stolen his heart.

He's coming after you! Glose was hopping and flapping to keep his perch on the black girl's shoulder as she strode at a mighty pace down the corridor.

Oh great, thanks for that. I would never have guessed, otherwise. A new line for you, is it, stating the obvious?

Nataka flung open the next door she found and ducked through it into a small waiting room. In it, a male Howler kitten and his parents, who had clearly been arguing, fell abruptly silent at her entrance. The female had been crying. Their kitten looked to be close to tears but fighting to contain them. The adult male Howler's face was dark, and his heavy brows knitted. He glared at Nataka, resenting her intrusion.

Nataka twitched an impersonal smile in their direction, not wanting to know what they had been arguing about. She had enough on her plate as it was.

Curses, now I can't Disappear; not with that lot watching me. Should have done it outside.

You're just full of brilliant choices today, aren't you?

She turned her back on the Howlers and stood at the door, listening and slowing her breath. She wondered why she should feel so stirred up by the behaviour of that daft young Howler.

It's his eyes, she decided at last. T*hey look just like Paa's: guileless; brimming with uncomplaining, no-holds-barred devotion. Sheesh. It beats me. How can anybody – particularly a Howler – grow up in* this *Reality, surrounded by all the nonsense that Howlers concoct, and still be so thoroughly innocent and vulnerable? Incredible. ... And why, in the name of all that's rational, didn't my spell work? ... What in the name of Infinity went wrong?*

Whichever way she turned it, she could think of no good answer.

In my opinion...

Shut up, Bird. I'm sick of your opinions.

I know, Nataka. But just listen *for a moment, can't you? ... I think the reason your spell didn't work is because...*

Glose hesitated.

Well, why? What's your exalted opinion, then? Spit it out, and let's get it over with.

Promise you won't lose your temper, or hit me, or – or ...

All right, all right, I promise. Let's have your blasted opinion, then.

All right ... but remember, you've promised. ... I think it didn't work because ... you ... didn't ... really ... want it to work.

217

What?

You promised! Remember you promised! Glose jumped off her shoulder and flapped off to the furthest corner of the room, just in case. He examined Nataka's face carefully and, when she showed no sign of wanting to pursue him, returned to her shoulder.

Look. It's nice to be loved, great for one's self-esteem; a kind of emotional panacea, I reckon. And it hardly ever happens – I mean, to be loved like that, at first sight - you know, without question or judgement - or even knowledge. So, you see, I think you felt quite sad at having to kill whatever it was that made the daft Howler look at you like that ... and ... well, I reckon the magic felt it - I mean you *felt it – so it didn't work. ... Well, anyway. That's what I think.*

The raven cleared his throat.

And now you can peck holes in my hypothesis to your heart's content. I've had my say, he concluded.

Good grief.

Nataka fell silent, chewing the idea over. She furrowed her forehead.

I hate to admit it, Glose, but I really think you may have put your finger – er – claw on it. I did *regret having to kill that emotion. I must have stymied my own efforts to get rid of it. Well, I never.*

Glose preened.

Caw No charge to you. All part of the service. I'll be here all Moon. Hehehe.

218

Infinity, this is a bind. How'm I going to fix it? ... If you're right, and I suspect that you are - oh, stop gloating, you infuriating feather duster! - Well, what this means is that I've got to want *to kill the love in that boy's heart before the magic can work. And I really don't know how I'm going to be able to do that – or whether I even have the right to do it. ... I mean, it would be like wanting to slap a puppy, just to make life convenient for oneself, not because the puppy deserved it, and then actually doing it. ... Curses.*

Not that *extreme, surely? He's only a* Howler, *after all. Not really one of* us.

Rubbish! That's just prejudiced nonsense. Regardless of who's involved, genuine innocence and love are rare and precious – heck, you said so yourself just now, didn't you? ... And for some reason I have a serious problem with the idea of simply killing such a feeling stone dead for my own convenience. Sheesh. Who cares where the feelings come from, anyway, provided they're genuine? ... Howlers have just as much right to their emotions as we have, and just because we don't like 'em, that doesn't make them less entitled to their feelings, does it? ... And – you realise, don't you? - This kind of event also explodes the idea spread by so many of you Wanyama that Howlers aren't capable of experiencing emotions as deep as yours.

Anyway. My main point is that, like it or not, Howlers have rights too, whatever we may think of them. So don't you dare hit me with your species bias!

Or maybe you don't really mean all this worthy stuff and just enjoy being adored, insinuated Glose. *All this cackle and coo about the rights of Howlers never bothered you before, did it? You've got a taste for it from the way that daft dog worships you, I reckon.* He tensed as he spoke, poised to take flight again, if necessary. But Nataka only sighed.

Ach, who cares? Whatever, Bird. I don't give a rotting worm-cast for your opinion of my motives. So you just go right ahead and think your worst.

She opened the door a crack to listen to the sounds in the corridor.

Now *look what you've done with your blether. You've distracted me from listening out for that poor idiot outside,* she added, not entirely fairly.

Well, if you're going to get all huffy, said Glose, *I'll just go away and do something else.*

Ah. Now that is *a good idea. You can make yourself useful. Get out there and recce the place, Bird. Check where the Howler's gone, and then come back and report to me. After all, you're Invisible. ... If I hadn't been so taken aback by all this we could've done it right away. The sooner we can get out of here without being spotted by that boy, the better. Off you go, then.*

On my way, answered the bird. *But you may want to think about this while I'm gone: you don't go on about Howlers having a right to their feelings when you don't* like *the feelings they're having, do you... so why not?*

With that parting shot, the Invisible raven flew out of the door Nataka had eased open for him. Nataka turned her back on it, breathed out, and aimed another vague smile at the trio of Howlers sitting on the chairs furthest from the door, who had dropped their voices and returned to their argument. Resisting the impulse to peek into their thoughts, she sat down in an armchair at the furthest end of the room from them, took out a note-pad and began to write on it to signal that she was absorbed in her own affairs and uninterested in anything they might be saying.

But she glanced up after a few moments when she realised that the Howlers had fallen silent again. Not only were they silent, they were staring at her wearing the kind of expression you see on animals that are hoping you'll feed them some of your dinner.

Sheesh, what now?

"Don't mind me," she said, hoping to nip any incipient conversation in the bud. "I'll be off again in a moment. Waiting to be called." She turned back to her notes.

"Well, *actually*..." said the female, forcing Nataka to raise her head again. The female hesitated and glanced nervously at the male beside her, as if she wanted his approval before going on. When he didn't respond she took a deep breath and said, "Actually, Doctor, we were just disc - ... I was just wondering... perhaps you could give us some advice?"

"Advice?" echoed the Protean, collecting her thoughts. ***Potz Donner!*** [lxxxvii] *I keep forgetting just how easily Howlers let appearances influence them. One glance at my camouflage, and I bet this lot would be willing to jump into boiling oil if I told them it was a cure for haemorrhoids.*
"Er, well. If it's about somebody who's already being looked after in the hospital – a relative of yours?" The small Howler nodded. The two adults looked at him, then nodded too.

"Aha, right. Well, if you want a second opinion about a diagnosis or treatment - or anything in that line - the hospital has procedures and rules about that. You'll have to go through the proper channels. You know, ask the person who's already dealing with the case to refer you on for a second opinion. ... I mean, you've a perfect right to ask, of course, but it's not really done just to talk to a random staff member, like me..."

"For *Chrissake*!" interrupted the man, "Red tape, we'll drown in the bloody stuff! ... Look. My wife only wants you to recommend a good nursing home for -"

"But…" interrupted the little Howler, turning pink.

"Hold your *tongue*, Boy!" snapped the man without looking at the child. He glared at Nataka. "Well?" he demanded, "… *Do* you have a recommendation? We need a nursing home that'll take care of an elderly gentleman until he feels better, that's all. Or …" he made his voice heavily sarcastic, "… do we have to ask somebody to refer us to you first?"

Not at all perturbed, Nataka put away her notebook, sat back in her chair, crossed her arms and studied the Howler. He had stocky legs, a thick-set, muscular body that 'worked out'[lxxxviii] and broad, carefully preserved hands with stubby fingers; hands that would have looked appropriate on a builder or ditch digger. But judging from their softness, they had never been employed for anything more strenuous than holding parchments or phones. A short, thick neck jutted forward from the Howler's bunched shoulders and deep chest, thrusting his low-browed face at the world chin-first. Under the small, deeply sunken eyes swelled heavy pouches and cheeks that looked slightly mottled and spongy (*Aha: so the gym sessions aren't quite overcoming the bottle),* a thick nose with broad flaring nostrils (ditto in the sponginess department), and a square blue chin under a mouth that drooped at the corners. Topping it off, a neatly coifed and gelled mop of brown hair looked as incongruous on his bullet head as a toupée on a Cape Buffalo.

Nataka decided that the Howler's features must once have been conventionally handsome; indeed, she thought dispassionately, even now he might be quite engaging if he tried. But he wasn't trying; far from it. Combined with the coarsening effects of self-indulgence and an evidently volatile temper, his present impatience and hostility merely served to render him thoroughly repulsive. Nataka's lips twitched as she imagined clouds of cartoon steam whistling out of his nose and ears, an iron ring threaded through his nose, and his limbs translated into cloven hooves. *Should I play with him - turn him into a bull and put him into a ring with a bloodthirsty toreador - see how he likes it? ...Tempting ... be a laugh...*

But then she took in the drawn faces of his two companions.

No; better not. They're stressed enough as it is. Pity, though.

She observed with interest how his face darkened and his thick brows knit together even more heavily than before under her calm scrutiny. Beside him, the male Howler kitten sat scarlet-faced, staring at his own feet. The pale female held her breath and wrung her hands, not daring to speak.

"*Well?*" the Howler hitched forwards on his chair and clicked his fingers under her nose. "Come on, out with it. *Chop-chop!*"

"Hm. Yes. I do have a recommendation, since you ask," replied the black girl evenly, after another long silence during which she had again surveyed the Howler's face and body with an expression of such serene, leisurely contempt on her face that the veins in his forehead swelled and his cheeks darkened. "To begin with, you'd be well advised to mend your manners. It's far better to remain silent and only *seem* like an arrogant swine, than to speak and remove all doubt.

"Furthermore, quite apart from the fact that your behaviour is inexcusable, clinically speaking you'd also be well advised to consider the effects of your clearly habitual hostility and impatience on your own health," she went on.

"No amount of bullying and hectoring can delay or reverse the effects of a heart attack, you know. Which is where you're heading if you continue to behave as you do. Remember, the concept of *mens sana in corpore sano* [lxxxix] cuts both ways. In other words, a healthy mind also contributes to a healthy body.[xc] So I suggest you take yourself in hand, grow up and get a grip on your temper. It's high time for that anyway, judging from your apparent age, which I'm confident is on the wrong side of forty."

Before the furious Howler could respond, a single hissed sibillant and one slim finger twitched in his direction secured his silence and immobility. Nataka's luminous eyes turned to the pale female sitting beside him. She had covered her mouth with one hand and was staring over it at the male with eyes that were wide and dark with shock and trepidation. It was obvious that few people ever had the courage to speak to him like that, let alone emerged unscathed from the encounter if they did. Now the female Howler sat hunched and tense, dreading the explosion that never came.

"*Was* that what you were going to ask me, then – about a nursing home, I mean?" Nataka asked her.

"Er... Y – yes... it was... yes..." came the whispered reply. The female looked thoroughly bewildered that the male still wasn't doing or saying anything but instead stayed on his chair, silent and immobile. But only a blind person would have failed to notice that his face was turning puce, his eyes bulging and his whole body shaking like an overheated pressure cooker.

On the other hand, the Howler kitten didn't appear at all intimidated. He leaned back in his chair and stared up at the man with such an expression of combined satisfaction, curiosity and loathing in his eyes that Nataka didn't even need to peep into his thoughts to know that the two males despised and resented one another, and that they weren't biologically related.

The young Howler turned to look at Nataka, as if sensing that she was studying him. His deep blue eyes were still brimming with resentment, tension and misery, despite the gloating satisfaction they had borne as he stared at the adult male beside him. But she also saw something else in them, a quality rarely found in such a young specimen: grim, iron determination.

Interesting, she mused. *Unlike that old biddy Gertrude, this Howler Kitten isn't wallowing in his misery, even though he's struggling with something he obviously finds pretty much unbearable and that could easily overwhelm him, if he gave in to it. Some important duty or task, something he's absolutely determined to achieve, is keeping him from breaking down. And so he's refusing to give in to his feelings. Yes. Admirable. As usual, that cub is by far the best of them.*

"Well, I'm sorry, I can't really help you. I don't know anything about support facilities outside the hospital. But perhaps you and your ... let me see: mate? ... Husband? ... Yes? ... Ah. A pity..."

The male Howler's chair began to rattle.

"Anyway, I'd ask the hospital's reception staff, if I were you," Nataka went on, "I'm sure they'll be able to suggest a suitable place. They might even help you to book something convenient. I mean, if you're looking on behalf of somebody close to you, surely where *you* live is important – you know, for visiting. So..."

"Yes ... yes, of course ... I should have thought of that myself," interrupted the woman nervously, still eyeing the male Howler like a novice sapper confronting her first landmine. "Of *course*... Reception ... Yes, you're right. We *will* need somewhere close to home. You're quite right. ... It should be where we live, north of the estuary. Of course ... So that'll be nice for you, dear," she added, leaning over to speak to the little Howler, "you'll be able to see him a lot, that way; won't you? ... That'll be nice... Yes. That *does* make sense... Don't you agree, Roger?" She appealed to the male Howler beside her, whose colour now gave him the appearance of a gigantic, over-ripe black plum. The trembling black plum rolled his bulging eyes at her but still didn't move or utter a sound.

His appearance worried the female so much that she swayed and looked ready to faint from sheer stress, so Nataka hastily twitched a couple of fingers and hummed a ditty that eased her previous enchantment, and instead cast a subtle Moderation spell on the man and Calm enchantment over the woman and child. As the male felt his tongue loosen, the plum hue gradually faded from his face, but his eyes still blazed with outrage at his own silencing. He was even more incensed when he found that his tongue was still refusing to utter even a mild complaint, let alone the torrent of abuse he was longing to unleash on the obnoxious creature sitting before him. Instead, he was mortified to hear himself say "Yes, dear; of course," so meekly that the female nearly fell off her chair and a savage, gloating grin briefly transformed the features of the small Howler.

And when the man turned to Nataka with an agonised expression on his heavy features and added, "sorry... I ... was... rude..." the words forced themselves out through clenched teeth and his eyes crossed with his futile struggle not to speak them. Nataka had to grin at the gleeful expression that again sped across the little Howler's face. *The cub's enjoying this. He* is *canny,* she thought.

"Apology accepted. The first of many, I trust;" she replied, rising briskly and going to the door. "Well, I must be off.

Good luck to *you*," she added, looking into the little Howler's eyes.

She had decided not to wait for Glose any longer, because it had suddenly occurred to her that of course she herself could simply go out into the passage and Transform into somebody unrecognisable, or even Disappear entirely, provided that no Howler spotted her doing it. So there was no reason for her to lurk about in hiding, after all.

Now why *didn't I think of that before?* She chid herself as the waiting room door shut behind her. *I've been making daft choices all this Suntime. Ah, well. At least I gave that obnoxious Howler something to think about.*

Creak *...so you clicked the solution too, did you?*

Glose thumped down onto her shoulder.

I was just coming back to point it out. But never mind. That annoying moon-struck Howler flapped and fussed all around this nest of horrible smells, hunting for you and bleating like a motherless calf. He got all worked up because nobody he asked about you had any idea what he was going on about. Naturally. Anyway, he gave up at last, and took himself off down the stone river in one of their smelly whizz-things.

Let's go home. I need a good feed and roost.

Interlude IV

"Ere Babylon was dust
The magus Zoroaster, my dead child,
Met his own image, walking in the garden."[xci]

Three Startimes after Leto the Enlightened had shed his most recent incarnation, his stricken littermate Chant and Howler Pets Anthony and Fran all dreamed one dream. In it they were sitting on the bench in their back garden that had been Leto's favourite basking spot on sunny afternoons, grieving and trying to comfort each other.

And then Leto was strolling towards them over the green grass, under the hoverflies and bees that wove and darted through the dappled sunlight under the trees. He looked sleek, lithe and young with his splendid tail erect and weaving, just as he had looked in his finest seasons, before the dark disease hollowed him into a shadow of his former glory and left only his magnificent, thick marmalade-and-white tail intact to remind all who saw him of his erstwhile beauty and grace.

And he spoke to them, purring.

"Why do you continue to grieve for me?" he asked, sounding genuinely puzzled.

"We... we saw you ... leave!" sobbed his female Pet, who had held him in her arms and stroked him as he died (and who, let it be noted, was much too damp at that moment for anybody to wish to stroke her). "You stopped breathing ... and I can't stop crying!"

"What's the matter with you, anyway? D'you think I'm grieving because I've got a bellyache, you idiot? Split my whiskers, you're stupid enough to be a dog. I miss you, you great dumb fur-ball!" hissed Chant, who was mad at Leto and didn't care who knew it. "I miss you, and I hate feeling like this! I didn't want you around before you went away, and now I feel lonely. And I wish I hadn't spat at you so often. I've never felt like this before, and it's all your fault! I had no idea how it would be. I've been prowling around everywhere, calling for you, ever since you left. It just isn't fair! Why should I feel like this? How could you do that to me? How could you just up and die on me like that?"

Leto looked at her. "Dude," he said mildly.

Chant stared back at him, wide-eyed. She had nothing to say to that. So, cat-like, she stopped thinking about it.

"Was that you under the walnut tree this morning?" She asked. "Did you come back? I felt something there when I called, but I couldn't see anything. It made my fur stand on end. Was that you?"

"What do you think?" Leto had always been a cryptic cat in life and didn't seem to have lost the habit outside it.

"So what's going on, anyway, Leto? Why are you here?" asked Anthony. He'd always been the Pet most likely to cut to the heart of a question, and at the moment he was also the only one still able to think properly.

"I've only returned to remind you that you don't have to be sad. I'm not dead, you know; just Changed," said the amber tom, still weaving his splendid tail in the air. "You all struck me as being much too upset. I couldn't ignore it. So I got Nataka and Dux to help. And here I am."

"But – but we cremated you after you... left!" wailed the Damp Pet.

"Yes. I did notice that. I was there, after all. Couldn't exactly have missed it, could I? ... And, yes, in that respect I've certainly Changed completely, and rather more quickly than usual. Well done, you, for finding that short cut," he teased. "But nothing of me has disappeared. What you once saw and touched is now air and water and ashes, all converted by the magical application of fire, and all ready for further miraculous transformations in Nature. But I - the entity you called Leto, I mean - well, somewhere, even if in a distributed manner, something of what I was will always persist."

"*You see? I* told *you!*" said Anthony to his damp wife (who also suffered from chronic scepticism). "He still exists, even though his body doesn't. He's just moved on."

"*Exactly. So. Be of good cheer,*" Leto sat back on his haunches and ran a paw over his white and pink nose. "*It's nothing drastic, you know. Only Change. The next kitten you meet will look at you with my eyes. And anyway, none of you will ever be alone while someone like me loves you. That's just the way it is.*"

He stopped and looked them over. Chant was calm now, but the Pets still looked confused and sad.

"*Think about it,*" prompted Leto. *He was very patient, because he knew that Howlers were generally obtuse when it came to the simple ideas. They needed time to understand.* "*Do you still remember the first time we met? I'd spent a Moon or so in my new Life. Your Kitten picked me up and held me in his paws. We looked into one another's eyes, and right away I knew without any doubt that this one –* this *one – was special to me and would belong to me forever. He was my first and only True Pet.*

"*That kind of thing doesn't often happen to a Cat, you know. Or, better said, it's never happened to* me *before. But when it does - well, it alters everything. Mere Change, like being apart or even going through the big Change you call Death, can never destroy that bond. Your Kitten will always be much more than just a Pet to me. And, of course, so will you. By extension. Because he's* your *Kitten. ... D'you see?*"

Leto purred, licked one snowy paw and passed it behind his right ear. "*It's going to rain later,*" *he observed.* "*Well, I've got to go. Dux has promised to show me my new hunting grounds. Be of good cheer, my Pets. Don't overdo the* grieving. Sooner or later we all pass through the same cat-flap, and then... well, there's no need to worry about that, either. Where we end up depends on what each of us is looking for, and nothing else. It's a great adventure."

He narrowed his gold-and-emerald eyes in a cat smile. Then he rose, opened his pink mouth in a mighty yawn, stretched himself front and back cat-style, and turned away.

"Remember me next time you light the fire in the Season of Bird Flight, my Pets," he said by way of goodbye. "I liked sitting with you while you lit the fire. That was fun."

"What else can you tell us before you go, dearest Leto?" called Anthony to the retreating cat, who was beginning to fade into the soft air underneath the plum and apple trees. "What other words of wisdom, comfort and guidance can you leave us?"

"Ah. Good question. I want a nice-smelling flower over my ashes. I enjoyed smelling the flowers with my Pet," came the reply. "And - oh, yes - next time let's have more fish..."

Leto's voice was fading with his body, which was so transparent by now that they could see right through it to the fronds and stems of a fern in the shrubbery behind him. "Much more fish... it's good eating, is fish..."

And then he was gone, having strangely comforted his grieving sister and Pets, who went out and found a sweet-scented camellia for him.

And in a newly birthed litter Somewhere, Sometime in the eternal Present that is also the Past and the Future, a kitten with delicate pink paws and nose, its milky eyes still tightly shut against the blinding light that had guided its journey into Life, stirred and wriggled against the warm, purring softness of its mother's fur.

Huh? It thought.

And then ... Ah.

And **Here we go again.**

Chapter 15. The Promise

"The high and mighty cannot brook refuting arguments from their inferiors." [xcii]

The little boy called Terence (well, actually he was eleven years old, so he wasn't *that* little, except that he was a bit plump, so he looked shorter than he was) wandered disconsolately into the deserted lounge of Sunny Shores Nursing Home. He had been battling not to burst into tears (like all eleven-year-olds he dreaded nothing more than making a fool of himself in front of other people), but it had become more and more difficult to keep calm as the whole distressing day went on. And now this particular room, which resonated with the feelings of desolation that accumulate in any space which is repeatedly filled with the aching hearts of a succession of deserted, aimless people; this stage for pain, empty but for a few dozens of sagging, overstuffed, fading sofas and chairs redolent with the smells of camphor, mothballs, disinfectant, stale air-freshener, lavender and mint ... in short (because it's high time to bring this ridiculously long sentence to an end), this room finally proved too much for him. Despite all his efforts to suppress them, the tears finally surged over the dam of his eyelids and chased one another down his cheeks and chin.

A cat the size of a small leopard was lying on one of the room's deep windowsills, with its paws tucked under and fat tail neatly wrapped around its body. It looked uncannily like a furry sphinx, except that it didn't have a human face. As Terence entered the room it turned its head and stared at him. He caught his breath at its size. Then he noticed the large eyes, which were mesmerically variable, like tigers' eye gemstones. A vague memory stirred; he wondered where he'd seen them before.

Under normal circumstances Terence would instantly have approached the animal and tried to make friends with it because he loved animals of all descriptions and took every opportunity to befriend them. But at that moment, with his mind full of fear and heartache, he felt more uncomfortable than curious under the animal's sharp, indifferent scrutiny. Somehow the beast looked disconcertingly aware – indeed, intelligent. But, he reminded himself, it *was* only a cat, despite being so big. There was no need to worry about what a cat might think of him. And yet, as its tail began to twitch and it narrowed its eyes, for all the world as if it were sizing him up, Terence had the most irrational impression that his presence in the room was annoying it.

"Daft," he muttered to himself, half turning away to wipe his nose on his sleeve. "'S'only a stupid cat, you great wooss. Get a grip." He parked his backside on the arm of an overstuffed armchair and began to scuff the slightly grubby, flower patterned wall-to-wall carpet with his trainers.

The boy had just gone through yet another futile argument with his parents and aunt about his grandfather the Wingco,[xciii] who was lying entangled in a web of tubes, needles and beeping monitors inside a manure-green bedroom four floors above the public lounge into which the boy had wandered. The old man's bright blue, long-lashed eyes (eyes his grandson had inherited) were at that moment ranging intently over the faces clustering around him, searching for his grandson.

The Wingco's daughter, stepson and stepdaughter were chattering over one another, at the old man and at the medical staff in charge of settling him in, peppering them with questions, comments and demands, and doing a great job, overall, of getting in the way of every useful person there.

The whole scene reminded Terence of vultures flapping and screaming around a dying lion. And there was nothing he could do about it.

"It isn't *fair;"* he muttered to himself, his tears flowing again despite all his nose-blowing and scrubbing, which only served to make his nose and eyes look red and swollen. "They – they just aren't *listening* to the Wingco, or me. I *told* him what it'd be like. ... They don't care about what *he* wants at all ... and they're ignoring him, just like I said. ... It isn't ... right..." He hiccoughed and used his other sleeve to mop at his eyes.

It just not cricket, old chap, the Wingco would have said, laying on a poncey accent to make his grandson laugh.

And cricket it certainly wasn't. The Wingco had told all his family often enough and clearly enough that he hated the idea of "being a vegetable". He'd told Terence even more often than the others, because the two of them had a very special friendship, more special than any of the others in the family.

"Ter, old chap," the Wingco had said, tapping his grandson on the shoulder with his reading glasses, "I know that they're your parents and that you love 'em ... well, at least your mum. *I* love her too; she's all right. ... But, for Pete's sake, don't let 'em keep me going when it's high time I was pushing up the daisies; all right? I know your step-dad; he's quite apt to bulldoze the lot of you in the direction he wants to go, and there's a little matter of a life insurance policy that's not quite matured yet, and he'll do his damnedest – oops, language; beg pardon – *utmost* to keep me ticking on till that happens. But it won't be right - at least, not for me. That blessed policy won't mature for a good wee while yet, and if I go the way both my brothers and old man did - bless 'em - and have a stroke, he's bound to try to keep me alive for however long it'll take to cash in on that insurance with its gold-plated bonus. But don't you let him do it, Ter, my lad. Promise?"

Terence (who preferred to be called Ter, so that's the name we'll use from now on) had no idea what an insurance policy was, and didn't for an instant stop to think about the heavy burden the old man was laying on him with this request. Instead he contracted his eyebrows and screwed up his eyes, trying very hard to make sense of what the Wingco had just said.

"What's a gold-plated bonus, Wingco?" he asked. "Some sort of trophy? ... Couldn't we maybe nick it, you know, and hide it to stop him getting hold of it?"

The Wingco laughed out loud. "No – hah! – Sorry, old chap, I shouldn't be laying all this confusing stuff on you; but I just can't think of anybody I trust more, even though you're a kid…"

"Not such a kid, Wingco!" interjected Ter, "'sides, what does age matter? You're the one who told me about Mickey Free, and *he* was only twelve years old when he started scouting, remember? Just one year older than me [xciv]…"

"Haha! Right you are again, Ter, as usual," the old man laughed again, his eyes sparkling with amusement and affection. "Right you are. Anyway, I do feel you can be trusted, and not only because you don't know what a gold-plated bonus is, eh? ... Anyway, don't worry about that; it's just a boring detail to do with money.

"But, look," The Wingco stopped smiling and leaned forward, "What I'm asking you to do for me is this. Are you with me? This is serious, OK? ... All right. Here we go. If I get so ill that I can't move or talk properly any longer, and the doctors say that I won't get better – you know? It happens. Well, if *that* happens, I want you to remember and remind your mum and stepfather that I really don't want anybody to force me to stay alive. Which they will, my boy; take my word for it."

"But - Wingco - you don't really want to die, do you?" asked Ter, his eyes wide and his lower lip in danger of trembling, "you don't, really, *do* you?"

"Ter, old chap, think about it carefully," urged his grandfather. "Imagine not being able to move or make sense any longer, to have to be like ... well, like some dummy that people dress up and clean and feed on baby food and talk *over* and *about,* instead of *to* ... imagine not being able to do all the things we do together now, but just be there, useless. Would *you* want that for yourself, especially if you knew you could never get better? ... Wouldn't you just rather slide away quietly and see if there's a better adventure to be had on the other side?"

"N – no; I'd hate that;" admitted Ter, "I'd want to have a go at the other side."

"Exactly. 'Course you would. I knew you'd see it my way. I mean, I've been lucky so far. None of the aches and pains that other old codgers get, so I can mess around and get into all sorts of adventures with you, no problem at all. But I do have a family that tends to suddenly drop dead or half-dead from a thing called a stroke, and when *that* happens ... well, it's usually time to bring down the curtain, because people hardly ever get better from it.

"Now, then. I'd like you to imagine how *you* would feel about me, if I hung on, unable to talk or move or feed myself – let alone clean myself and so forth – for ages, getting more and more useless and helpless and doo-lally, you know? ... Till *you* also forgot how I'd been – you know – *before,* and about all the good times we've had together... and, let's face it, till you ended up seeing me as some kind of vegetable that needed constant attention. Ugh, that would be thoroughly horrible for both of us, *compadre,* wouldn't it?"

"I ... you're right. I couldn't bear it, Wingco," Ter took hold of the old man's work-hardened hands as he spoke.

Ter and the Wingco knew all about adventures. They were very good at them. In fact, it's fair to say that they were best friends. And their adventures reflected the absolute trust that only best friends have in one another. Something inside the Wingco had *Never Really Grown Up*, as Ter's stepfather (SF for short) would complain whenever the two of them came in from some mad-cap event that left them laughing like drains in a storm (little did the SF know that the Wingco took all his criticisms as compliments). Their escapades were many and varied, and frequently resulted in some hilarious accident. Just the other week they'd dripped river water all over the landing after falling off their home-made raft into the river, and not so long before that, they'd both found themselves in the dog-house after a woad-making experiment had turned them both blue for more than a week and left stains all over the upholstery.

Perhaps the Wingco's experience of being near death over and over again during the Falklands War and again in the Gulf War had made him what he was: determined to grasp every moment of his life and *live* it, savouring it with all his senses and faculties 'wide open and receiving', as he put it. So he was the best companion a boy could want for doing wonderful things: building tree houses; re-enacting the river adventures of Tom Sawyer and Huck Finn; going out at night with torches to track the night creatures in the woods; pretending to be Picts and Scots on border raids into Roman Britain; spending long, laughter-filled hours building a transistor radio from scratch and then fiddling with it, which had the added bonus of making noises that drove the SF batty.

The Wingco had taught Ter to spot and identify different animal footprints and track them through the undergrowth; to identify wild mushrooms and various rock types; to rig up light-traps and lure night insects in for identification with a hand lens; to guddle the shining, dancing trout out of the becks that bounded down the fells above their home; to crouch motionless for hours in the twilight till they saw the badgers waddle and grunt out of a sett in the deep woodland to roll in the dew-starred grasses, or the otters emerge from their holts onto the banks of the river and slide, slick as furry quicksilver, into the water. And on one memorable spring evening they had even witnessed the first emergence of that season's young beavers under the vigilant eyes of their parents to scramble, plop and doggy-paddle around their untidy timber lodge in the river, begging for help, sneezing and squeaking like an army of rubber bands when the water got up their noses. Ter had never realised before that these amazingly adept water-mammals had to learn how to swim, as he had – and that they, too, puffed and wittered through their lessons.

"Life's for *living*, Ter, my boy;" said the Wingco, "And by Jove, we've certainly lived it together; haven't we? ... Well, when we can't do that anymore, when the time comes to leave it all behind, I want to do so properly and *quickly,* once and for all, instead of hanging around cluttering up the place like a broken toy, while all the fun we had together fades into the distance in your memories, and you only visit me because you feel sorry for me. Good Lord, I couldn't bear that. I couldn't bear that at all. You do understand, don't you?"

"Yes ... Yes, I do, Wingco. ... But, Wingco, they won't listen to me, anyway, you know – Mum and *him* - the SF - I mean. You know they won't," said Ter, "I'm just a kid. They never take me seriously. They'll just ignore me, whatever I say, even if I tell them that it's what you want."

"Good point, Ter," said the Wingco, "Of course you're right." He fell silent for a few minutes, thinking. Then said, "But ... let's see. If I write a letter and seal it, and you look after it till the time comes, they'll just *have* to believe you, won't they? ... Hold hard. I'll do it right away."

The Wingco went to his desk and wrote a note. Then he signed it.

"Here we are," he said, "This makes it quite clear that I want to be allowed to slip away good and quickly if I get so sick that I can't move. I've told them that I categorically refuse to be artificially kept alive. That should do the trick, don't you think? ... Now all you have to do is hang onto it and produce it when you need to."

The Wingco had slipped the paper into an envelope and handed it over to Ter. And then he'd suggested they go out and see whether a clutch of blackbirds' eggs in their neat, woven cup-nest resting in the privet hedge at the back of the house had hatched yet.

Chapter 16. *Catch Me If You Can*

"No battle plan survives contact with the enemy." [xcv]

... And the row had erupted a few months later, just a few days before the Easter Holidays. The Wingco had been rushed into hospital in an ambulance, having toppled sideways off his restaurant chair during a visit to Ter's sour-faced step-aunt Ida, who lived south of the estuary, not far from the zoo. ("If I'd known *this* was going to happen, I could have been prepared," said Ter's aunt resentfully).

Ter had always disliked those trips to his aunt, and when the Wingco suddenly fell ill, his face contorted and his arms and legs unable to move, the boy had been devastated and half-inclined to blame the miserable company of his aunt and the SF for the incident.

While his mum cried and the SF gabbled into a phone, nobody apart from Ter noticed that the Wingco had a little slick trickle of saliva coming out of the corner of his mouth, or thought that this would be driving him crazy. So he sidled up and mopped the spit away with one of the restaurant's paper table napkins (it was one of those tacky-posh places, which served sides in oddly shaped buckets and jars, but whose pretensions didn't quite extend to providing cloth napkins), and then carefully scanned the old face. The bright blue eyes gazed into his own, alert, intelligent and urgent in the sagging facial tissue that surrounded them.

"It's OK, Wingco. I remember;" he whispered, "I've got it safe. I'll show it to them. I'll tell them. But listen, I want to be sure you haven't changed your mind. OK? Blink once if you understand and ... and if you still want me to use it."

The eyelids sagged, curtaining the Wingco's eyes for an instant. Then they rose again. Ter's heart lurched, but he bit down on his emotions. He could see that now the Wingco's eyes were calm. The urgency had gone out of them. This was what the Wingco wanted, and what *he* wanted, Ter wanted too, for his sake.

"All right. I promise I'll tell them," repeated the boy, and lifted his hand to touch the old man's cheek.

And then it was ambulances and grown-up talk and being shoved aside and the flurry of getting to the hospital, where after a series of tests and scans and long hours kicking his heels in various uncomfortable waiting-room chairs, the emergency medical staff confirmed what everybody had suspected: the Wingco had suffered a massive stroke, leaving him without speech or movement. A succession of doctors warned Ter and his family that the old man was unlikely to recover, although they would operate urgently to ease the pressure on his brain arising from the haemorrhage that had caused the stroke. After that, if the operation was successful, he might linger for weeks, months or even years, provided that they kept his vital functions going. On the other hand, they said, the family might wish to consider allowing him to slip away… organ donation…

And just as the Wingco had predicted, Ter's parents (well, actually the SF,) had insisted that the Wingco be treated, supported, resuscitated if he should falter and kept from dying at all costs, even if this entailed the prolonged use of a life-support machine.

That was when Ter had mentioned the letter, keeping his promise to the tough old man he loved so much.

"The Wingco just wants to die," he appealed to the startled adults around him. "He doesn't want to carry on living like this, just because of the gold-plated bonus you're so keen on … *Please*. Just let him die. Please. … I've got his letter at home and I'll show it to you. But I learnt it off by heart ages ago, to make sure. This is what it says..."

And he'd recited it, his child's tongue stumbling on some of the more difficult words. *Resuscist – Resusci-tation. Categori-cally refuse. Artificial. Dignity. Final wish.*

But Ter might as well have been talking to a tub of goldfish. Even after they were all back home again on that horrible first day (with his aunt Ida tagging along like a bad smell) after the Wingco had been operated on and was being tended in the Intensive Care Unit of the hospital, and even when Ter produced the letter to prove what he had said was true - even then, they refused to listen.

And after a week or so, when the doctors declared that they couldn't do any more for the Wingco and finally transferred him to the Sunny Shores Nursing Home (recommended to the family by the Reception staff at the hospital because it was close to their home and had a good reputation for terminal care) they *still* refused to listen.

His aunt Ida (who had come along for the ride yet again - mainly, Ter suspected, because she enjoyed getting in the way as much as possible) pretended to weep and exclaimed that she was shocked Ter could play such a mean trick on them; she'd though he loved his old 'Grandpa'! And the SF was furious. As usual. "You've disgraced yourself!" he yelled, "Just when we all need your support more than ever, you go and pull this nonsense! How dare you? ..." Etcetera. While his mother just wrung her hands and wept and begged Ter not to complicate matters or make the SF angry.

How *did* grown-ups manage to twist things round to make you feel guilty?

"*Look!* Look at his eyes!" he screamed. "The Wingco wrote this letter himself! ... If you don't believe me, ask him yourself! ... Ask him to blink *once* if he wants to die and *twice* if he wants to stay alive ... He understands what you're saying, you know! He knows everything that's going on! ... And he *can* answer! ... Go on! ... He'll tell you himself!"

In short, Ter had fought for the Wingco as hard as he could, but all he'd managed to do was earn the acid promise of severe punishment when they got home. And the SF had tried to snatch that pesky letter out of his hand, as well. But Ter had been on the watch for such a move. He'd run off with it, careful not to burst into tears in the presence of his relatives.

And this is why now he found himself in a strange room, facing a huge cat, having wandered blindly around the horrible nursing home, and only vaguely noticing the room's clutter of ill-matched chairs, run-down and faded chintz curtains, antimacassars and cheap vases on spindly side-tables, stuffed with badly arranged artificial flowers and dusty *pot-pourri*... And, of course, that cat.

The huge, richly furred, leopard-spotted, round-eared animal with those extraordinary eyes, paws almost as thick as Ter's arms and the fat, furry, incessantly twitching tail-tip was still sitting on top of the windowsill and watching his every move. It didn't blink. It didn't purr. It didn't hiss or *meow*. All it did was sit on the windowsill and watch him. And twitch its tail.

Ter reflected that the SF was nothing more than a great bully. And it was a bitter thing to realise that there was nothing he could do about it. He wished he could sort out the bully good and proper. Because Mum never would; she was too scared: scared of the SF and of his sour-faced sister, the hatchet job Aunt Ida. Ter couldn't wait to grow up and be big enough to take apart the SF, who'd always ridiculed and resented the Wingco, and who now wouldn't even grant him his last wish for a decent, dignified death. But he also knew that he'd just have to cope and fight, even though he had so little power at his disposal, because now that the Wingco was sick there was nobody left to stand up to the SF any longer. The Wingco had never been intimidated by the SF and had kept him more or less in control, particularly when it came to the way Ter was treated. But ever since he had fallen ill, that bully had begun to rule the roost, and nobody'd even tried to resist him...

Nobody, that was, apart from that incredible black doctor who'd totally impressed and even cheered Ter at the hospital that first day, long after the Hatchet Job Aunt Ida had finally left them alone and gone off to one of her prayer meetings. The SF had properly got it in the neck from *her,* and he hadn't even yelled or rampaged about as he usually did. That had been good. The young doctor'd chewed the overbearing bully over good and proper, as the Wingco would have said. Yes. That had been something else. The Wingco would've enjoyed seeing *that.*

And suddenly Ter remembered where he'd seen the strange cat's eyes before, even as he started to cry again because he realised that the Wingco was past ever enjoying anything like that ever again.

Life sucked.

"If there's one thing I can't abide, it's a person who clutters up the space I'm trying to relax in with his misery," said the cat. Then it yawned, stretched, and jumped off the windowsill. "Pluck my whiskers and claws, call that courage? ... If I were you, I'd pull myself together, stop feeling sorry for myself, and *do* something instead."

It yawned, stretched, lofted its nose and tail, and strolled towards the open door through which Ter had entered the room.

"Well?" it added, pausing and staring over its spotted shoulder at the flabbergasted child, "Are you going to stand around with your mouth open and catching flies, all day? ... Cat got your tongue? ... Hah! I like that; did you see what I did there? ... I *said* ... Oh, never mind.

"So. *Are* you going to stand around with your mouth open like a hungry carp, feeling sorry for yourself, or are you actually going to *do* something about the Wingco instead?"

Ter staggered. He was being talked to by a cat. A *cat*.

Granted, it was an unusually large cat with the weirdest eyes ... but ... and ... hold on ... how did it know about the Wingco, anyway?

"What ... what ... you ... The Wingco? Did you say *Wingco?* ... How d'you *know*...?" he stammered.

"Well," purred the splendid animal archly, "To find *that* out you'll have to catch me first. C'mon then, catch me if you can!"

Just then (at the precise moment when the extraordinary beast was crouching down and working its elegant shoulders and haunches, preparatory to bounding out through the doorway) a spitting, hissing grey streak darted into the room through the open door in the opposite wall, which led to the nursing home's garden apartments. The grey streak screeched to a halt opposite the large spotted cat and paused long enough for Ter to make out that it was a handsome, green-eyed grey tomcat with all its fur standing on end.

"Tha' ... Tha' bloomin' – *Howler*! Tha' ... crazy ... ole ... *biddy*!" it yowled in fifty unattractive combinations of cat-song as it dived out of sight behind Ter's overstuffed armchair.

246

"Nat, yeh mangy fiend, wot 'ave yeh *done*? Nah she only wants to shove me into a cauldron of wa'er an' *bile* me! Split my whiskers, bu' she's a flippin' monster, s'welp me if she ain't!"

Before the astounded boy could move, a bony little old woman, clad in slippers and a floral housecoat that billowed like the square-rigged sail on a river barge, came hobbling energetically into the room through the same door. Her frizzy grey hair was awry and her flushed, wrinkled little face wreathed in smiles. She was preceded by her voice.

"Yoohoo! ... *Here,* Misty, Misty, Misty! ... Puss! ... Puss! ... pusspusspuss-poooss! ... *Here*, kitty! ... Here, Misty! ... Bathy-wathy tiiime! ... Now, *where* have you got to?"

The old woman caught sight of the large spotted cat, which had jumped onto a convenient chair opposite Ter and was sitting, blinking impassively at the new arrival.

"Oh, *good* ... Natasha, dear! You're just the person I wanted!" exclaimed the pink-faced woman, heaving- to and dropping anchor alongside the spotted cat. Ter was sure she hadn't even seen him. "*You* haven't by chance seen Misty, have you? Only the naughty little darling's run off, just as I was about to give him a bath. Ooh, but he's such a naughty, *naughty* moggy!" she crooned. "Not but what my poor darling Toffee Emperor was *just* the same; always a bit of a challenge, was bath time. Dear things! They really are like babies, aren't they? Bless them! ... Here, Misty, Misty, *Misteee!*..."

The spotted cat appeared quite unconcerned by the fact that the old woman was talking to her. It stretched and yawned. "I suppose you're referring to that grey cat you've been petting recently," it said. "So you call him Misty, do you? Well. I'm sure it's a perfect name for him."

Ter's chair hissed.

"Hm. Now let me think;" the large cat went on. "Oh, yes ... unless I'm much mistaken I saw him run through here a few minutes ago, heading *that* way - towards the lobby, you know. He did seem to be in a bit of a hurry."

Ter's chair snarled softly.

"Ooh, that *naughty* Misty!" the old woman hoisted anchor and sail, then hobbled ecstatically towards the door. "Trying to make a run for it, is he? My, such naughtiness - *and* after all that cod liver oil, too," she added inconsequentially. "Misty *loves* his cod liver oil. Thanks so much, Natasha! ... *Here,* Misty! *Here,* puss! ..."

Her voice wavered out of the door and down the corridor towards the lobby, leaving Ter to assimilate the fact that the little old woman seemed to have thought nothing of having a conversation with a cat big enough to be a leopard. Perhaps the little old woman was mad? ... But then, if *she* was mad, what about *him?* He pinched himself to make sure that he wasn't dreaming.

"Ouch," he said quietly.

"Well, that's got rid of *her* for a while," said the cat, and raised its voice to talk to the chair. "You can come out now, Rav'n. Heat's off. ... And just so you know, she's not trying to boil you, you dozy great hairball. She just wants to wash you."

The handsome grey cat poked his head around the side of the chair, his fur gradually settling.

"Dratted Howlers," he yammered disgustedly. "Suck a toad! Since when does a cat need ter wash wiv water, anyway?

What're our tongues for then, I arsk yeh? ... An' didja clock the daft name she's callin' me, Nat? Flippin' insult, 'f'y'arsk me. *Misty*, my furry boll..."

The grey cat interrupted himself, suddenly registering that he and the large cat weren't alone. He crouched down, puffed up his pelt, flattened his ears and glared at Ter.

"'Ere, Nat; there's one of 'em Howlers 'ere right nah, in case yer 'aven't noticed..." he hissed out of the side of his mouth. His tail began to lash.

"Never mind him, Rav'n; he's all right. He's really quite decent, for a Howler;" replied the large cat, jumping back down onto the floor. "I've been watching him. Actually, we were just about to play a game of *Catch Me If You Can With Twenty Questions* when you interrupted us. You might as well join us. Right then, Kitten; let's do this. Ready? ... Here I go –"

"So wha's in i' fer *me*?" demanded the grey cat as he crouched down and began working his hind legs.

"Well, for one thing you'll be getting away from your bath," said the spotted cat, "And for another it'll stop you getting too fat. Cod liver oil, indeed. If you don't watch out, you'll turn into a second Toffee Emperor. Ready, Kitten? Here we go!"

And, without really knowing why, Ter found himself chasing the large spotty cat and the grey tom through the door and up the first two flights of stairs in the large hallway outside it, which both the cats zipped up effortlessly, but he could only ascend by leaping two stairs at a time, struggling to keep his quarry in sight. On the second landing, the spotted cat suddenly stopped short and began to groom the base of its back, so Ter managed – *just* – to touch the fat tail before it whisked out of reach of his hand.

"Caught me once! ... You get your first question," said the big cat, which wasn't even out of breath.

"What – er – *who* are you? ... And why can you speak ... and why can I understand you?" asked Ter immediately.

"That's three questions, not one," said the cat. "You're cheating."

"Aw, go on, answer them, Nat, old girl; uvverwise we'll be 'ere all flippin' *Sun*," urged the grey cat, who had stopped on the carpet beside them and was working his legs and tail impatiently, "I wanner get away from 'ere; somewhere the ole biddy can't find me."

"Oh, all right then. One: Nataka. Two: I'm magical, so I can speak everything. Three: I'm allowing you to;" said the spotted cat, leaving Ter to work out exactly what he'd asked, and launched herself up the next two flights of stairs, closely followed by the grey cat.

The boy scampered after the two animals, now using the bannister with both hands to help him jump three steps at a time. He copped an earful when he rounded a curve in the stairs and almost collided with an octogenarian sporting a plantation of warts and liver spots, who was grimly wavering down the stairs, one hand clutching the bannister, the other leaning on one of those walking sticks with four feet to keep them from toppling over, and whiffling as he went. "Do you *mind?*" yelped the old man in a reedy voice, "This isn't Le Mans[xcvi], you know! ... Young hooligan ... no respect ... in my day..."

Ter was in too much of a hurry to stop. "Sorry! Sorry! Sorry!" he called as he swerved and bounded around the old man, who continued to witter on for some time, anyway.

Ter again came face to face with the cat calling herself Nataka when he nearly bumped noses with her. She was perching on the newel post at the top of the fourth flight of stairs, peacefully washing her ears.

"Took your time. I thought you'd never catch up," she yawned. "So I gave myself a handicap. Next question?"

"How come that old woman talked to you? ... And why wasn't she surprised when you answered her? ... *I* was surprised!" asked Ter.

"Aha. Good questions. See, Rav'n? This kitten really is quite bright, for a Howler," said Nataka to the grey cat, who had flopped down in a spot of sunlight on the landing. "Well, Kitten, *she* saw an old woman. *You're* seeing a cat. Simple, really. I'm magical, remember. I can do that kind of thing. ... Off again!" And she took half the next flight of stairs in one breath-taking bound.

"... An' 'ere we go agin," commented the grey cat, streaking after her. He seemed to be enjoying himself now, because he was purring. "She's a caution, is Nat. Bu' a bit smug wiv all her magic, too; in'she?" he added, and disappeared up the stairs.

But Ter didn't move right away. He was thinking hard, putting two and two together.

If she isn't a cat or an old woman, what does she really *look like? ... Ohhh... Hang on... remember her* eyes...

"I know who you are! ... You're that doctor!" he called out as he galloped up the stairs, "You *are,* aren't you?"

There was nobody on the fifth landing, so after a brief scan of the corridors branching off it, Ter dashed on, up the next flight. By now he was thoroughly out of breath, but also excited, and even a bit elated.[xcvii]

As he reached the top of the sixth flight of stairs he caught a glimpse of Rav'n's tail vanishing through a door some way down the left-hand corridor leading off the stairs. He hurried after it, coming to a halt outside the half-open door. There he hesitated for the first time and asked himself, rather belatedly, whether it was a good idea to go into a room he didn't know with strange cats – or whatever they were – he hadn't properly met, let alone understood, when a long-fingered black hand shot out, grabbed his shirt-front and yanked him into a hideous pink bedroom, slamming the door behind him.

Chapter 17. The Big Question

"I was standing suddenly, it seemed, on the brink of a whole new concept of the world, where everything was upside-down and rearranged..." [xcviii]

And, sure enough, there was the same young woman Ter had seen at the hospital, grinning at him from where she sat, cross-legged and barefoot, on a gaudy pink bed in the middle of a hideous pink room. She wasn't wearing a medic's coat now, just a pair of faded jeans and a T-shirt. Her tigerish blue-green-and-gold eyes sparkled with mischief and good humour.

"Cracked it," she said. "Didn't take you long at all, really. I thought you'd take ages. Now let's talk about the Wingco. It's best we do that without being disturbed, which is why I shut the door."

"So. Welcome to my horrible bedroom. Isn't it disgusting? Everybody in this place thinks I'm a derelict old biddy, which is why they carted me in here. They think they're rescuing me. Hah! ... Still, it *is* rather handy.

"Make yourself comfortable, if you can. That chair isn't too bad. ... And, Rav'n, you can keep half an eye out for snoopers, if you like."

"Orl right, then, Nat, seein' it's you wot's askin';" the grey cat jumped onto the broad windowsill. "Blimey. Never thort I'd be lookin' through this winder from the inside, I didn't ... Yer goin' up in the worl', Rav'n;" he purred to himself, and craned his neck to take in the view. "See me bins from up 'ere, I can."

Ter advanced into the room and perched on the edge of a pink armchair that stood facing the bed. He gazed at the young woman before him.

"Well now. What's on your mind?" asked Nataka when it seemed that he would never stop staring at her. "Spit it out, then."

"I – I was just wondering," he replied, plucking up his courage, "I was just wondering, you know... what you really look like. ... I mean – is this really *you*? ... Only, just now you were that cat... so is that the way you really look? ... And you also said earlier that the old woman who was chasing – Rav'n? ... Yes, Rav'n – that *she* saw an old woman when she looked at you, which is why she talked to you like that – you know, without freaking out. Which is also weird, you know, because *I* was seeing a huge cat at the same time.

"But ... So ... Or – I mean - are you something else, really? Like ... some kind of – of monster or something? ... I mean, when you're being ... really *yourself*? ... Sorry, I don't mean to be rude ... but ... I'm just wondering... what you really look like..."

Nataka grinned and the grey cat chortled from the windowsill. "'Ang onto yer fur, Howler Kitten," he said, "Yeh never know wha' she'll be like when yeh see 'er."

"Rav'n's right," said Nataka, "I don't really have a real Self – I mean, bodily. I just use whatever Transformation works best for the situation I'm in, if you get my drift.

"In the Dimension I come from, I belong to a group of entities I suppose you Howlers – I mean, you *Humans* – would call Proteans. Or I suppose you could call me a shape shifter, sort of. Except that I don't really have a shape at all. I don't turn into ...oh, I don't know ... a blob or a snake, or – or anything else at all, when I'm not wearing a Transformation. I just borrow some of the energy in this Dimension to assume a body you can see and touch. So ... well, I suppose you *could* say that what you're seeing right now is as much *me* as anything else I might look like. The cat, for instance ... yes, I like my cat Transformation a lot."

"*Whoa*," breathed the boy, "cool..."

"G'won then, Nat ole girl; show 'im that bloomin' giant bird fing yer used ter frighten me, tha' other Startime," urged Rav'n from the windowsill.

"Forget it, Rav'n," said Nataka, "I'm not here to entertain you. So, young Howler, what else d'you want to know, then?"

Ter hesitated then asked, "All right ... er... could you show me how to do that thing you did at the hospital – you know – when you shut my step-dad up? ... I know you must have done something special to shut him up, because, well, he never holds his tongue or apologises to anyone; you know? Not even the Wingco. That just *never* happens. So when you shut him up like that, I reckoned you must have hypnotised him or something. And... and well, I wanted to know if I could learn to do that, too. ... I mean, could you teach me how to do that? ... Please? ... Er – and you can call me Ter, if you like... unless you prefer Kitten, of course."

The black girl threw back her head and laughed. "Brilliant! Well, Kitten – oops – Ter – I'll have to disappoint you. I didn't hypnotise your step-dad; I only Froze him – you know, made it impossible for him to move or talk. And no, I can't show you how to do that, because you aren't a sprite or imp or Protean or shape shifter, or whatever else you want to call me. Pity, really. Anyway, never mind. Moving on. Tell me about The Wingco."

So Ter sat there and told Nataka all about his grandfather and the illness and the old man's wish and the letter. And then he found himself spilling information he hadn't shared

with anybody before: about how his proper dad had died
when he was six (killed by a sniper in Afghanistan while he
was on a tour of duty with the Marines); and how his mum
had got together with the loathsome SF whose name was
Roger Court, who never used Ter's name but just called him
'Boy' and clicked his fingers at him, and who despised both
Ter's dead father and the Wingco because they'd been in the
military ("where you never make money unless you're
prepared to be *really* creative with the rules, Boy") when, in
his opinion, anybody with any sense would go into
something like real-estate or any of a large number of
entrepreneurial activities that "make *real* money, Boy. And
I'm not talking about your piddling thousands or even tens
of thousands. Only losers work for that kind of money, not
to mention for other people, particularly when it involves
personal danger. I mean, imagine: your father never even
had an offshore account when he died! And the best car he
ever owned was an ancient Rover 216, which he kept for
more than ten years! … Seriously now, Boy, *how* lame is
that? …" etc.)

And then Ter told Nataka about his equally vile step-aunt
Ida, the SF's older sister, who couldn't abide boys and hated
his mum for having 'snared' her brother, who sniffed
whenever she saw him, as if she had a bad smell under her
nose, who went on and on about how all boys were dirty and
grubby and unhygienic, and who spread sheets of plastic on
her chairs and newspapers on her floors whenever he visited
her ridiculously tidy flat, to save those precious surfaces
from contact with his unhygienic body.

Aunt Ida was so hysterical and fastidious about cleanliness
and propriety that she'd driven away every male Howler
who'd ever shown any interest in her (even though she'd
been quite attractive in a pointy-nosed kind of way, and had
fancied the idea of having her very own personal Howler to
order about). Anyway, she was still a spinster at the age of
fifty, and grimly obsessive about her church gatherings and

her charitable works, where she enjoyed alternately bullying, boring and terrifying everybody from the vicar to her fellow-churchgoers with long drones, interspersed with sharp rants, about their sins, incompetence, untidiness and anything else she decided they were getting wrong with their lives. Given half a chance, and had the church rules let her, she'd have clambered up onto the pulpit and delivered the Sunday sermons herself, because she considered the ones by the vicar tame affairs without enough in them about Hell and brimstone and weeping and gnashing of teeth and rending of robes, all part of the destinyin store for people who didn't wash properly. [xcix]

And for the first time it didn't matter to Ter that the tears rolled down his cheeks as he spoke, because he didn't feel embarrassed about telling the quiet black woman who listened to him so intently and whose shining, calm eyes never left his face, how much he loved the Wingco, hated his SF and aunt, and resented the fact that his mum had allowed that bully and his hatchet-job of a sister to take over their lives after his father's death; so much so that he and his mum would have been utterly miserable for years if the Wingco hadn't been there to support and protect them from the worst of it … until now…

At which point he could no longer speak.

Nataka spread her arms and gathered the distraught child into them, cradling and rocking him while he wept himself out. Over his tousled dark head she met the gaze of the grey cat with eyes that were suddenly fierce and bright as forge-heated iron stabbed through by sharp spikes of lightning. Rav'n shuddered and crouched down, looking out of the window to avoid the gaze of those terrible eyes.

Somewun's goin' ter cop it proper, he thought. *Bu' it won' be me. Not if I can 'elp it.*

"Ole biddy's back in 'er own gardin agin'," he observed softly. "Looks like she's given up huntin' fer me. Heh! ... So much for 'er bahf. ... An' look 'ere, if it ain't yer noisy bird, Nat."

Glose clattered in through the window, landed on the bed, folded his wings and shook himself. Ter stopped crying and bolted upright to stare open-mouthed at the huge raven.

"*Arkh*! So what's going on, Nataka? What's keeping you from coming home now? ... You *know* we still have to work out how to get Mond away..." The bird sounded peevish.

"Hush! Glose, meet Ter ... Ter, this is Glose. Take everything that comes out of that ugly great beak of his with a pinch of salt," interrupted Nataka.

Before the raven could croak his annoyance, she went on, "Look, Glose; think. We can't do anything about Mond right now because he's still got a horror of travelling through Fagus. You know that. He needs a bit of time to get used to the idea. So I'm focusing on Ter right now, because he's got a serious problem." Without waiting for a reply she began to summarise Ter's situation.

Glose forgot to be grumpy. He hopped onto a bedpost and listened with his head cocked, looking Ter over and cawing the occasional question.

"So now you know all about it;" concluded the black girl, "What's happening is just *wrong*. So wrong that I can't simply leave it alone. Just like Mond's situation, in fact. I couldn't have left that, either."

Ter hadn't a clue what she was talking about.

"Hold on! ... Mond's one of *us*," cawed the raven, "*This* one isn't. So why ..."

"Because, you gnat-brain, as I've told you before, we can't justify ignoring an injustice and letting it continue, simply because we don't like the species it's happening to!" snapped Nataka. "Look. We've had this out before, and I don't propose to go over it all again. I don't generally like Howlers any more than you do; but *this* one..."

"And that's how it all starts, every time;" interrupted the raven. "You get involved with one of them ... They annoy you - or you pity them ... you can't leave it alone ... they take a feather, then they take a claw, then a wing ... And before you know it, you're trapped and they're plucking you. *And* you know what Toki would say, too. Getting Involved means Trouble. Because you get carried away. That's how you get hurt. That's how *everybody* gets hurt. Howlers *always* upset you. You know that. ... Though I must admit, this fledgling seems all right..."

"I – I'm sorry, but I'm not sure what you're talking about, exactly, Mr Bird – er – Glose," stammered Ter. "I mean, I don't understand half the things you've said... and I don't know who Toki is, – or M-Mond, or that other person you mentioned. But if you're afraid that I'm likely to hurt anybody, I give you my word that I've never trapped or chased or hunted any birds - or anything else. And the Wingco's the same. In fact he taught me to respect other animals. I mean, even when we guddled trout we always put them back in the water afterwards and let them swim away, you know? ... Uh, well – sorry – that is, unless we were *really* hungry and had to eat them - which happened once or twice, when we ran out of food after a long day on the fells..." c

"See? Not all Howlers kill and maim people for fun," interrupted Nataka, wagging her forefinger at the raven,

"Some are decent. And this one is. I'd stake my Skills on it. Anyway, whatever. I've made up my mind. I'm not going to let that Howler get away with his *fitina* ^ci without trying to help the fledgling, and that's that. End of discussion."

She turned back to Ter.

"Now then," she said, "I've got just one question for you. Be careful with your reply. Do you want the Wingco to die?"

"What?"

Ter struggled to breathe. Life without the Wingco was inconceivable to him, and yet...

He stopped and thought carefully. Then he said, picking his words, "Of course I don't want him to die; 'course not! I... well ... I love him..." he turned pink. "But ... but I don't want to see him like *this* either, you know? ... If he's going to be like this, then it's better he goes. You know? ... For him, I mean. For his own – his own peace of mind, just like he said."

Ter put his hand into his pocket and took out the (by now very crumpled) sheet of paper on which the Wingco had written his wishes. He unfolded and handed it to Nataka, looking at the raven and black girl in turn while she scanned it. His eyes filled with tears again, but this time he clenched his jaw and managed to fight them down.

Nataka spread the sheet of paper on the bed, and Glose hopped over to read it at her elbow. By this time Ter was getting used to such surprises, so he only blinked a few times at the sight of the bird reading.

"The best thing for me – I mean the *very* best - would be to have him back again; you know?" he added, as they read.

"I mean, healthy and happy and - and *full of vim,* as he says ... as he used to say. Just like before ... B-but I don't know if that's possible? If I could have my wish. But they – the doctors – say it can't happen..."

"Well, they would;" observed Nataka, "They're only doctors, and a seriously outdated and mediaeval lot too, most of them. I, on the other hand, can do either. I can help the Wingco to enter his Death Change and leave this Dimension whenever he wants, if he wants. Or I can make him better and bring him back, if *that's* what he wants. The only time I wouldn't be able to do anything would be if he'd already died. I don't have the power to reverse *that* Change. My Skills have never worked across that particular barrier. But the Wingco's still here, isn't he? So that isn't an issue anyway - yet.

"Right, then. All we have to do now is make sure we know exactly what he wants. Agreed? ... So let's go and have a chat with him."

She jumped off the bed, grabbed the paper and handed it back to Ter, who folded it and stowed it back inside his pocket. "You coming then, Glose? ... Rav'n?"

"Nah. I'll stay put a bit, make sure the ole biddy forgets orl abaht that bahf," meowed the handsome grey cat, jumping off the windowsill and weaving around Ter's legs by way of farewell. "See yah arahnd, Kitten. Yer orl righ', fer a Howler. So long." And he jumped onto the warm spot Nataka had left on the bed, curled up nose to tail, and shut his eyes.

"*Creak*, modest soul; isn't she?" commented the raven, fluttering up to perch on the boy's shoulder. He seemed to have decided that Ter could be trusted. "That's our Nataka for you. Don't worry, young Howler, I don't plop on people - unless they startle me, that is," he added, chuckling

261

hoarsely. "Come along then, let's be looking at that Wingco of yours."

He cocked his head at the black girl, who had gone to the door and opened it. "Just remember what I said, Nataka. You're getting tangled up with Howlers again," he rasped. "Keep your head. ... Never mind me, Fledgling; I'm only reminding her, you know. She tends to get carried away when she's around your lot."

He gripped the boy's shoulder firmly with his leathery claws. "Let me know if I'm holding on too hard ... and I *may* just grab your ear with my beak if you joggle too much."

"Shut up, Bird," said Nataka as she went out.

"But – hang on – you can't chat with the Wingco," said Ter, hurrying down the corridor with the raven on his shoulder, and skipping to keep up with Nataka's long-legged stride, "He can't talk."

"Wait and see;" said the black girl as she raced down the stairs three at a time, "I won't have to get him to blink; you can be sure of that. Oops, watch out - Codger alert, next landing."

And the bemused and enchanted boy found himself rushing back downstairs, past a dreamy pensioner descending on the stair lift. The old man never saw the incongruous group dash by because Nataka had Disappeared them all, but he shivered in the brief draught raised by their passage, and superstitiously concluded that somebody must have stepped on his grave [cii].

Interlude V

"Courage was mine, and I had mystery; wisdom was mine, and I had mastery" [ciii]

Sunclimb! Improbably perfect little puffball clouds began chasing one another across the periwinkle blue sky as soon as Sunwake burst upon the world and started warming away the jewelled dew. Delicate white buds unfurled on the hawthorns and wild cherries; meadow blossoms, birds and insects swarmed out all together as if a starter whistle had sounded, and crowded the sea of tender, fresh greens in woodland and field with their array of hues and noises. Has there ever been anything more wonderful than the bustling working song of the bees and birds? There is no sound like it for engendering sheer contentment. No wonder the Dancing Hare is beloved of all Wanyama and enlightened Howlers.

Robins, sparrows, blackbirds, thrushes and starlings vied with one another in song; wood-pigeons and ring-necked doves crooned their love chants and strutted their flushed legs in a mating ritual as old as bird-kind itself; while infant rabbits, hares, lambs and squirrels bounced around making plaintive baby noises that reverberated in the balmy air. In the calm patches under the banks of the river, glittering trout snapped at early mayflies, leaving swift, expanding ripple-rings on the surface of the water, while the sinuous shadows of hunting otters slipped through the green depths after them.

The Season of the Dancing Hare had come into its Glory.

Paa burst out of Toki's door, barking and cavorting for no other reason than that the air demanded it. She raced over the sparkling grasses with her paws barely touching the ground and her tail wagging so quickly that it was a blur.

Of her moonlit dance she remembered little, apart from a legacy of boundless awe and exuberation.

Axl the deer emerged from the shade of the trees to see what all the noise was about, and the furry dog bounded up to him, slalomed joyously around, under and between his legs, veering off again at an angle to intercept Pex, who had come running around the corner of the cottage. Then began a game of chase, with the poodle attempting to catch the fox's beautiful brush while he danced teasingly ahead of her. Catching their mood, Axl bucked and gambolled after them like a fawn.

At length Paa fell to chasing her own tail round and round in ever-decreasing circles, until she overbalanced and toppled onto the grass. She lay on her back and wriggled ecstatically with her paws in the air and long pink tongue lolling. Then she lay and panted, relishing the feel of the sunlight on her belly.

Pex trotted up to the little dog and cocked his head, gazing at her. "You've got something shiny on your head," he observed, "I haven't seen it before. What've you done to yourself?"

"Eh? ... What? ... Shiny? ... Me? What're you talking about?" Paa was only half-listening.

"Your forehead, Paa," said Pex, peering more closely, "You know, that bit above your snout and between your ears. The bit reserved for storing brains. Well, you've got something that looks like a - a patch ... or a shiny tear - something like that - on it. ... Have you been messing with one of Nataka's potions? ... Axl, do you see it?" he added as the deer joined them.

"Rubbish;" yawned the poodle, sitting up and scratching her ear, "I haven't touched anything. I leave Her Honour's

things alone. They're magical and scary. Anyway, I can't feel anything. I expect you're just seeing things. Must be the Sun in your eyes."

"Axl sees it too, don't you, Axl?" insisted the fox. "It's a kind of shiny, ragged – thing, I tell you, just sitting there on your head. You sure you can't feel it? Doesn't it hurt or anything? ... Here, let's get you to the pond so you can see for yourself. Come on."

"Do I have to?" complained the dog, "I just want to stay here and sniff the air and listen to the birds, and stuff." She ran a paw over her ears and head. "I can't feel anything. Who cares?"

Just then a low exclamation from outside the garden gate brought the three animals' heads swivelling round together. An old, bowed and stringy Howler was standing on the stone river a few wolf-lengths away. He was staring at Paa with his mouth and eyes wide open. He had a long, poky nose and teeth that stuck out of his flabby mouth, and he was leaning heavily on two sticks. His Howler wrappings hung loosely off his body as if he had shrunk inside them, and there was a look of exhaustion and suffering on his pasty face. He seemed to be in pain, because he kept shuffling from one hind paw to the other as he stood, never taking his eyes off Paa.

Paa scrambled up and whipped around to stand at bay, facing the Howler. Her eyes widened and darkened, her ears flattened against her skull, her fluffy tail whipped under her hind legs, and her hackles rose. Her lips curled back to expose needle-sharp fangs, and she unrolled a string of guttural snarls from deep inside her throat.

Pex and Axl stared at their companion, amazed. The transformation of their friend from cheery indolence to bristling hostility was so sudden, not to mention

265

uncharacteristic, that it almost floored them. They'd never seen her like this, not even when Glose was being particularly obnoxious towards her.

"What is it, Paa? What's the matter?" demanded Pex. His hackles rose in sympathy. "Why're you snarling?"

"Howler. Danger," grunted the deer, planting his hooves alongside the poodle and lowering his antlers, "Frightening."

"Ah. Well, look, Paa; I don't think you need to worry," said the fox reassuringly, "No Howler can come into Nataka's space unless she allows them, and she never allows them. You're perfectly safe. Relax. ... But who is that Howler, anyway?"

"That was my Howler," snarled the poodle between her teeth, "That was my Howler, who tortured me and tortured me ... before Nataka. I hate him."

"I see. Well, he looks – and smells - pretty useless now," said the fox, snuffing the air. "Can't you smell him? ... That's a broken Howler, if you ask me. I don't think that Howler's functioning properly. I bet he couldn't torture a frog now, if he tried."

"Trixie Snuffles!" moaned the Howler suddenly, "Trixie Snuffles, can it be you?"

Paa glared at the Howler and stopped growling only long enough to let loose a volley of sharp, vicious barks. Then she went back to snarling even more vehemently, backing away as she did so.

"Oh, Trixie Snuffles," whimpered the Howler (who was the Busybody, of course; but a shrunken, sad, sickly and distracted shadow of his former self), "Oh ... oh, I'm sorry," he added, looking stricken, "Of course I know you can't really be Trixie Snuffles ... only, you remind me so much of my poor pet ... who died right here, in front of this gate, not very long ago..."

He paused and looked the poodle over, then said, "Of course, she ... she was rather more – groomed – than you ... but you have her eyes – and her nose... and – and for a moment I forgot..." The Howler gulped, dug out a scrap of material from a hole in his wrappings, folded it around his snout, and honked.

"Yup. He seems very out of sorts, from what I can judge of Howlers. Not that I know much about them;" Pex was interested. "Look at all the water coming out of his eyes. That's usually a sign that they're not functioning properly, isn't it?"

"I don't care if he is out of sorts;" muttered the poodle through clenched fangs, "I hate him."

"I know you can't be Trixie Snuffles, of course," repeated the Busybody, wiping his leaky eyes as he spoke, "I saw her die. I – I carried her home, my poor little girl, and – and buried her... But you look just like her, you could almost be her twin..." he gulped once or twice.

"And – and you looked so happy just now - that you ... you made me wonder ... if ... if maybe I didn't allow Trixie Snuffles to be – you know – herself, enough? ... Because she never behaved like you – I mean ... so happy and – oh, I don't know – relaxed...

"But I was so proud of her! ... I dressed her up, and I trimmed, her ears and tail, and dyed and fluffed her fur, to make her look even prettier... and I showed her off, you know? She had a marvellous pedigree[civ], oh, marvellous! And she was so clever ... I taught her to do all sorts of *wonderful tricks ... I mean, she won prizes! ... I loved her so much ... but maybe I should have – I should have cared less about the prizes, and more about making her happy?*

"It's just that... looking at you has made me wonder, was she happy, at least sometimes? ... I was sure she must be... but now – now *– I'm wondering if she* was *happy, ... or if she was miserable instead?*

"Oh dear! I can't help thinking she must actually have been dreadfully sad ... and I can't help remembering how she cried when we took away her puppies and sold them ... I lie awake at night, remembering how she used to cry ... And she was in so much pain, towards the end, too ... I knew she was in pain - her legs, you know - only I didn't want to believe it, because I couldn't bear to ... Oh, what did I do to her?"

Paa's snarls had risen in pitch and volume at every mention of her loathed former nickname. She trembled with disgust and outrage as the Busybody repeated all the different things he had made her suffer. But her open hostility didn't seem to be putting him off; he was clearly too busy unburdening himself of all his sorrows to care. Typical, *she thought.*

Gradually the poodle fell silent. Now she had to fight the urge to whimper out loud as the memory of all the pain she had endured at his hands came flooding back with every word he spoke. Curse him! He was spoiling her perfect Sunclimb, forcing her to remember like this, making all her memories raw and painful again. Why couldn't he just go away and leave her in peace?

But he just kept on chuntering.

"Oh, Trixie Snuffles! – Oh, sorry – I beg your pardon – I mean... little dog, beautiful little dog ... I'm not even sure you have a name? ... Oh, well... not that it matters, I

268

suppose ..." (he made a big sighing noise), "If anybody else could see me talking to you, they'd think I was crazy. But I don't care.

"I just want to tell you that when I saw you looking so happy as you rolled in the sunlight just now, I couldn't help feeling ashamed and sorry for not having allowed my darling Trixie Snuffles to be as happy as you. And – and I wish so much that I could tell her that, you know? ... But she's gone, my poor little girl ... and I'll never be able to tell her anything, ever again ... I'll never be able to make it up to her..."

The Busybody's quivering wet snout dived into the (by now sodden) bit of material again, and the next words that came out were muffled. He seemed unable to stop leaking.
"I – I've been quite – quite – unwell," he forced out between the deep, wracking sobs shaking his whole frame, "I don't know – why ... but – ever since – the day – Trixie Snuffles – died – I've had – a terrible infection – At least – they – the doctors – think it is – and I can't sleep – I can't eat – I can't think – properly – any more ... And the doc – the doctors – don't know – what it is...

"It's almost like – some terrible – puh – punishment ... It feels – like sitting in – a horn – a hornets' – nest – all the time ... Ohhh ... it's dreadful ... I just had – to tell – some – somebody ... you ... who – won't – judge – me ...

"And my – my – wuh – wife's – so – sick – of – my – muh – muh – moaning ... I cah – can't...tell her..."

The Busybody's sticks clattered down onto the stone river. He folded his stringy forepaws on top of the rusty gate, slumped his ferrety snout onto them, and fell to grunting and heaving so hard that Paa and her companions couldn't make out his last words at all. It all came out as a mix of noises that sounded a bit like "mmmf – mfblbmngf –snarrffffglugh – hiccup – argh".

"Grotty things, Howlers," observed Pex. "Cop a load of that smell. It's like meat that's gone so off not even Glose would touch it. Tweak my brush and whiskers, though; he is properly snout-by-tail, isn't he?"

Paa didn't reply. She sat back on her haunches and contemplated the figure slumped, weeping, on the gate. And it came to her as she stared at it that her own happiness could only be marred by the sorrow of another creature, even if it was that appalling Howler.

"I don't want any more suffering," she said under her breath.

And, without thinking about what she was doing, she trotted up to the gate, rose up onto her hind legs and snuffed at the stringy paw dangling over it.

Pex was right. The whole of the Busybody smelled of decay and neglect, as if his body had begun to decompose from the inside. He also smelled sour-and-salty from the tears that had come out of his eyes. The smells were tangled up with the more familiar, hated odours of the cloying potions he had always used to wash and colour her fur.

For a moment the little dog recoiled again, remembering those dreadful baths and colourings.

Then she swallowed the bile rising in her throat, drew a deep breath and reared back up onto her hind-paws, bracing her forepaws on the gate. She could just reach the bony fingers that dangled above her head with her warm, soft, rose-coloured tongue. So she licked them. They tasted as foul as they smelled.

The Busybody's head snapped up. He stared down at the little cream-coloured dog, whose tongue had felt so comforting on his fingers.

"You... you! ... Did you just lick *me, little doggie?" he breathed, his voice thick. "It ... It's almost as if you understood everything I've said ... you're amazing ... Thank you, little doggie ... thank you..."*

Paa lowered herself back down onto her haunches. Her mouth stretched in a smile, her pink tongue emerged, and she panted gently, gazing into the red-rimmed eyes of her old enemy. He was just another poor creature after all, trapped in a world he could barely understand. Not worth hating.

The strange fuzzy patch of brightness Pex had noticed on her forehead sparkled for an instant.

Then the poodle rose, shook herself from head to toe, and trotted off without a backward glance. As she passed them, the deer and fox wheeled round and followed. The three animals disappeared behind the litter and nettles and weeds growing around the corner of the derelict semi-detached council house (which, you will recall, is all that most Howlers will ever see of Toki).

The Busybody gazed after them. And then his eyes widened, and he blinked. The itching, scalding pain that had been torturing him ever since the death of his poodle seemed to have disappeared. Hardly daring to breathe, he ran a hand under his wrappings and carefully, gingerly felt himself.

The boils were no longer there.

"No!" he gasped, and hurriedly un-tucked his upper wrappings from his baggy under-wrappings to peek down at

his lower belly, which had been particularly badly infested with running, weeping sores and lumps.

All he could see was his own pale, baggy skin. There wasn't a blemish on it, apart from the usual wrinkles, liverish spots and warts of old age.

"Good gracious…" he caught at the gate to steady himself, and raised his eyes worshipfully to the corner of the derelict building around which the dog had vanished.

It was some time before the Busybody finally left off gazing open-mouthed at the nettles and litter. But in the end he retrieved his sticks and began to hobble homewards, feeling at once exalted and diminished, wishing rather irrationally that he had kissed the stone river in front of the rusty gate, and murmuring words like "miracle" and "angel" [cv] *as he went.*

Nataka was bounding downstairs in the prison for aged Howlers with the boy and the raven when she felt the surge of energy that streamed out of Paa as she forgave – and cured – her former torturer. She hesitated for an instant, not long enough for her companions to notice, and her eyes widened and flashed gold as a broad smile spread across her dark face. Then she bounded on.

Toki gave a tiny jig of joy as Paa's energy rippled through its fabric, generating a rainbow of light that bounced and danced off every shiny surface inside it. But the cottage was careful not to disturb the exhausted wolf lying asleep before the glowing coals of its fire.

And in the Sun-drenched woodland clearing, Fagus the Pathway Tree, roused from a daydream, blinked, ruminated for a moment, and then whispered contentedly.

"Ah. Aha. That, then. Good!"

Chapter 18. Roger Court – a monograph by Glose the Raven, in his own words

"What, then, is to be done? Are we to be kept forever in the mud by these hogs to whom the universe is nothing but a machine for greasing their bristles and filling their snouts?"[cvi]

I, Glose the Raven, having collated all the information passed on to me by my Master Nataka the Extraordinary (and frequently Inscrutable), have been tasked by her with producing this record of the profound Howler paradox that was Roger Court, capturing for posterity the insights we have gained into his bewildering life and behaviour. The reasons for so doing are as follows.

First, this particular Howler's choices and actions catalysed such profound changes in the destinies of Nataka, her associates and the Howlers most nearly involved in all his doings, that they may safely be described as critical to the genuinely earth-shaking events that followed them; events previously unforeseeable to all those involved, including Nataka herself. Indeed, the very fact that such a deeply flawed and self-absorbed Howler should have exerted the influence on the course of Nataka's own behaviours and development it did is itself amazing and noteworthy. So much so, that it constitutes more than sufficient justification for preserving an account of his behaviour and nature for the benefit of posterity.

Second, this compilation of the motives, attitudes and actions taken by Roger Court is confidently expected to provide students of Howler society and *mores* with many important insights into the characteristic behaviours of the species; insights that cannot fail to be valuable both to them and to every Nyama that is obliged to share Dunia with them.

I shall commence my account by stating a conclusion and then explaining it. The conclusion is that Roger Court was a

product of the way his parents had raised him from when he was an egg, together with his own tendencies and instincts[cvii].
 In other words, he couldn't have avoided turning out as he did, given his parents and personality. I'm not *sure* about this, of course; but it's useful to keep the idea in mind (particularly if you're as interested as I am in trying to understand what makes most Howlers so brain-addled), and perhaps we should also try to feel some compassion for his situation. I mean, it can't be pleasant to be as nutty as one of Brid's winter troves if you can't even understand *why* you're like that, not to mention constantly feeling miserable because you're hankering after something elusive, something that you can't even name most of the time and that is probably best expressed as *Contentment* [cviii]. Indeed, for most Howlers, Contentment seems to be a condition more difficult to capture than a Halcyon's feather.[cix] Roger Court was desperate to catch Contentment, but the problem was that his parents had taught him to look for it in all sorts of wrong places, and he just didn't know better.

Let me explain. It's easy for us Wanyama to forget that Howlers have developed an all-encompassing and absorbing mythology – indeed, a religion - around the fantasy that only *money* and *property* can provide happiness. And they've developed such a complex and insane network of ideas around this fantasy (giving them fancy names like *profit margins*, *equity*, *liquidity*, *consumption*, *affluence*, *material goods*, *luxuries*, and other suchlike gobbledygook) that most of the species genuinely believe this is the only route to Contentment.

Such deluded Howlers – that is, most of them – also harbour a dangerous fantasy that *not having* lots of things they don't really need (and, worse still, not *wanting* to have them) must be a sign of either mental illness or stupidity, both of which they equate with *failure*. And *failure* is something that simply terrifies them. So, for them, life revolves around the concept of *getting things*. Virtually any behaviour in the pursuit of this *getting* is generally approved and admired, even if it's officially condemned by many of them.

Most Howlers will slave from Sunwake to Sunsleep in cramped lairs and nests inside their vast, stuffy, ugly and noisy stone rookeries and den complexes: writing on parchments or other bits of dead material; shuffling them around; arguing with one another through their speaking devices (their *telephones* and *mobile phones*) ... and all in order to amass a strange thing they worship – usually represented through the dead material they call *money* – by means of all this useless activity [cx].

Take my word for it. Difficult to believe though it may be, I can assure you that the majority of Howlers really do love and value this ugly, inedible thing called *money* more than all the other real, natural and magical things that keep them alive on their planet. They'll lie awake through whole Startimes, worrying, if they've messed up some of their dead materials and lost money by mistake, or if they think that other Howlers have more money than they do. They work this out in a variety of ways. One of their favourites consists of checking one another's possessions, such as: the kinds of nests other Howlers occupy; the quality of their wrappings; the size, noise and smells of other Howlers' cars (you know: those stinking whizz things in which they scurry around on their stone rivers, killing innocent Wanyama without a second thought), compared to theirs; and so on. And in the meantime they won't think twice about poisoning and killing off all the truly precious things around them, the ones they *really* need to survive: the water; the soil; the plants; us Wanyama; even the air we all breathe. From such behaviour we can safely conclude that they really are as w*azimu* as a caterpillar taking on a blackbird.

So, by and large, Howlers are an anxious and obsessive species, given to snarling and attacking one another in many different ways, including sneakily with words and frontally with sharp tools or banging tools. And all this, purely because of their endless quest for money.

And plenty of very confusing rules and ceremonies surround this thing *money:* what's allowed, what isn't allowed; what's admirable, what isn't admirable. Mind you, this whole topic is stiff with contradictions. I'll give you an example. The worst crime of all, in the minds of Howlers, involves trying to get hold of money in ways that aren't officially allowed. But – the first big paradox – it's also quite clear to anybody observing them that the condemnation Howler Society heaps on one of its members for doing *really bad* things (they call this *committing crimes*) to get money isn't really because they're angry about the crime itself. They're much more angry with the Howler who did it for having been stupid or careless enough to *get caught committing it.*

In fact, provided that the crimes are big enough and successful enough, Howlers can even avoid getting punished *after* they're caught, especially if the crimes they've committed have made them very, very *rich.* Yes, believe it or not, sometimes even getting caught doesn't ruin a Howler who is *very* rich. What happens is that other Howlers find some way to twist their own thinking about it, 'reasoning' that in fact the crimes involved were acceptable *because* they've made the Howler involved very, very rich. At this point they may begin to call such crooked Howlers *heroes* or *public servants,* reward them for the crimes they've committed, copy their behaviour instead of punishing it, and, *kichaa* as it is, even appoint them to powerful positions within their communities. Such 'heroic' criminals are called *celebrities.*

And finally, if anybody *is* caught committing a very serious crime *and* is in danger of getting punished for it, there's a special magic the Howler can use to avoid being punished. This magic immediately makes Howlers who have been caught (and who now have to face other Howlers and answer for the crimes) appear so sick and disabled that they can no longer be properly held to account for what they've done. The magic makes it so that they are no longer able to walk, talk or think. When that happens they're considered incapable of defending themselves for their crime, and so the crime is forgotten. This forgetting is called *acquittal*. It's very useful magic for dodgy Howlers, this sudden sickness. They call it *dementia*. You or I would call it *malingering* or *lying doggo*. You can easily tell when the disease really is malingering or lying doggo, because it always disappears again as soon as the Howler involved is no longer in danger of punishment. It's very strong magic, is that.

So anyway, now that I've presented my conclusions, back to the topic of Roger Court. He strikes me as a typical product of his time and upbringing, because he was raised by parents who both fervently worshipped money, and whose every thought was about how to get more of it than all the other Howlers they knew. The lessons that the chick Roger learned from the moment he broke out of his egg[cxi] all revolved around the notion that the world was made up of 'winners' and 'losers' in money terms. 'Winners' made their own 'packet' of money one way or another, so that everybody else ended up respecting and envying them. It didn't much matter *how* they did this; it was the winning that mattered. 'Losers' weren't even to be pitied because they only had themselves to blame for not having - or getting - money. Roger's parents preached that poor people weren't tough enough or sly enough or quick enough to make money; they were 'soft', or 'slow off the mark', or 'soppy', or too 'liberal'... and so on. In other words, they *deserved* to suffer. *Wazimu*.

Roger's elder nest-mate, Ida (a genuinely scary female Howler with more angles than curves that I had the mixed privilege of studying at close quarters) reacted to this parental doctrine by adopting a combined Do-Gooder and Busybody attitude. She pretended to despise money, but actually worshipped it just as much as her brother Roger, although *she* always justified having so much of it, and hanging onto it more tightly than Miba protecting his own belly against a badger, by saying that her *god* had decided she should have it, because that way she could (and sometimes did) make use of bits of it to stick her damp pink beak into everybody else's business in the name of Charity.

But Roger wasn't so sly or independent in his thinking. He spent his fledgling season pitifully struggling to gain the approval and love of his *wazimu* parents, which meant he *had* to show them how well he could 'make his packet'[cxii]. The only praise he ever received from his money-obsessed mother and father related to his achievements or failures with regard to money.

When Roger's parents finally dropped off their perches, he was proud of the fact that he could use money to organise the most expensive funerals [cxiii] available for them, with no expense spared to show the world how well *he* was doing in his life, because (like the stinking whizz-things he drove too fast down their stone rivers and changed every few Seasons, or the ugly stone nests he was constantly taking over and then getting rid of again, or the female Howlers he'd brought into his nest and then thrown out again when he decided they were no longer worth keeping because they'd begun sagging in various parts of their anatomies), *how* he finally disposed of his dead parents was a way he could show off his 'success' or 'manhood' to the rest of the Howler community.

In fact, just to show other Howlers how successful he was, he was also quite willing to do all sorts of increasingly shady and criminal things, because not only did he want to continue showing off his 'manhood'[cxiv] to everybody else, but also to make them see it getting bigger and bigger, by hoarding more and more things he didn't need. Odd, really. After all, as the old saying goes, a bird can only ever roost in one nest at a time. Why then go pecking and scratching after more?

And yet another paradox about Roger Court: it's clear that all the time he was behaving in that feather-brained manner he was struggling with a gaping void in his life, just like a crow that's taken over a tatty rookery instead of going to the trouble to build one himself, and then struggling to keep his eggs from dropping out through the holes in it. An emotional hole, that is; a hole that the *unconditional* love of his parents could have plugged, but didn't, because of course they'd never given him any of it.[cxv] So, clearly, meeting the fledgling Ter's quiet and gentle mother Maddie Bourne (whose mate had been killed in one of their never-ending Howler wars) briefly filled that hole for him. It made him feel quite hopeful for a while, because she was so different from anybody else he had known.[cxvi] She actually loved *him* - that is, she did to start with, although his constant obsession with money quickly plucked the feathers off *that* illusion. She didn't care whether he was rich or not, which was a good thing for him, because just then he was recovering from a bruising experience involving a shady arms deal[cxvii] in which he had been properly messed up by his so-called *trading partners*, and about which he couldn't do anything because the whole project had broken a whole lot of different Howler rules, so if he'd tried to do anything he'd have ended up in worse trouble than the Howlers that had clipped his wings.[cxviii]

And now we come to the main paradox about this Howler. Roger still longed to be loved for his own sake, *but* at the same time despised anybody (and this included Maddie) who didn't put a price on his or her own love, as his *wazimu* parents had done. When he realised that nobody – not Maddie, nor that fledgling of hers who made such an impression on Nataka, and least of all Maddie's father, the highly admired Wing Commander Bourne (the Wingco) – cared less than two hoots of a hunting owl[cxix] about his material interests and possessions but were much more interested in invisible and intangible things like decency, honesty, compassion, joy and laughter (all of which he *really* didn't understand because he couldn't buy them), the early flush of excitement and hope Roger had felt on discovering Maddie quickly turned into frustration and resentment. No matter what he did, he couldn't get his new family to show what he considered a 'proper' appreciation of his money skills and interests, which he himself was quite excited about. He had launched himself on a new shady deal in the arms trade and was beginning to fix his *packet* again. In fact he was sure he'd be successful this time round [cxx].

And because, unlike either the Wingco or the dead warrior he had replaced, Roger had never risked his own life for anyone else or done anything other than gathering and losing money, he felt particularly jealous and resentful of both Maddie's dead nest-mate and her father. Now: I've often observed that when we envy and resent somebody, we tend to find reasons to despise that person. And this is precisely what Roger did. He despised Maddie and the Wingco. He also utterly and wholeheartedly loathed the look of resentment and contempt – yes, and even of pity – he saw on his step-chick's face whenever it looked at him. So he became more and more sarcastic and rude when he spoke to his new nest-mates (that is, when he wasn't sulking or throwing tantrums), and practically all his talk was about how useless and unsuccessful they all were, compared to him.

And so Maddie became more and more silent and sad and withdrawn, which is hardly surprising. She wasn't a fool. She realised her mistake and regretted that she had inflicted this money-mad stranger on her grieving chick. And of course her chick avoided Roger like avian fleas, which meant that he also spent less and less time with her and instead stuck to playing with his school friends and grandfather.

To begin with, I struggled to work out how and why the mating between Roger and Maddie could have managed to flap on like a pigeon with a broken wing for a further twenty seasons or so - I mean, without one of them chucking the other out of the nest. Howlers have a strange reverse-mating ritual they call *divorce*, which allows them to get rid of a nest-mate they can't stand without killing them. But for some reason neither Maddie nor Roger ever took that step. I wondered why. After all, they had got to the point where they were barely able to communicate with one another anymore. And Howlers aren't swans or pigeons or penguins, or any other Wanyama that mate for life. I mean to say, Howlers frequently break their mating ties. So why didn't *they*?

I couldn't work this out at all, so I asked Nataka for insights (she's useful that way). And she told me that, even though Maddie had quickly lost any interest in her new nest-mate, for a long time she had been very worried about how she and her chick might survive without the money Roger was bringing into the nest. And she kept on worrying, despite the fact that her former mate's father had reassured her about it. So she decided to keep her mate in the nest. Yes; regrettably enough, she wasn't immune to the Howler money fantasy. And for a long time she kept on believing and hoping that Roger would turn out to be a safe and stable – and rich – partner. How mistaken she was!

As for Roger, *he* didn't abandon the nest because he wasn't sure he'd find any other Howler who'd be prepared to stay with him, and who was so quiet and accepting. He'd found and discarded plenty of Howler females before Maddie, but he'd got to the point where *they* had begun to discard *him*, and he didn't like that feeling, or the feeling of being alone, at all. And then there was his sister Ida, who was constantly predicting that his nesting arrangements would fail. He didn't want to give her the satisfaction of squawking "I told you so!" if his mating with Maddie fell apart like a rotten egg. I watched those two siblings quite a lot, and if they liked one another they certainly never showed it. But they *did* spend a lot of time talking on their noisy Howler mobile phones, pecking and scratching through all the money discussions Roger couldn't have in his own nest because Maddie and her family simply weren't interested. Just like a pair of hysterical chickens plundering an ants' nest, those two.[cxxi]

And then something happened that changed everything for Roger, and made the chance of a split between him and Maddie even more unlikely. He found out that the Wingco had an excellent life insurance policy[cxxii], which he'd begun many seasons before. He'd been through a number of Howler wars – doing what they call *active service* - and always managed to come back from them without getting *nyoroshered* [cxxiii], but while he was out there and in danger, he wanted to protect his nestmates, so he'd taken out an insurance policy that would provide for them if he got killed or injured. Over many, many Seasons this policy had matured [cxxiv] to the point where it was enormous. The Wingco had told Maddie in confidence that if he managed to stay alive for at least another dozen Moons or so, he would win what they call a *gold-plated bonus* [cxxv] for having stuck with the policy for such a long time. He also told her that he'd arranged for her to get every bit of that money when he died, so that she could use it to raise their chick. In fact, she would have plenty of money anyway, because he planned to cash in [cxxvi] his insurance the minute that special bonus became available. And she would get it all. So all *he* had to do was stay alive for a few more seasons for the amount of money she'd get to be gigantic.

I'm not sure how Roger found out about all this. Maybe Maddie was stupid and flapped her beak about it to him one Suntime when he was moaning about how he had to spend money on her and her family all the time (which wasn't true at all, as far as I could make out; but still) ... or maybe he went poking his beak into the Wingco's affairs. I wouldn't put it past him. But in any case, that's really not the point. What *is* the point is that Roger immediately thought of what he could do with all that money when the special bonus finally came along in just a few more seasons. He'd been asked to spend a lot more money on a very big shady deal to send arms to one of the places where other Howlers were ripping seven different kinds of giblets out of one another in yet another disagreement about one of their gods or nesting rights or some other equally idiotic issue. And he calculated that if he could persuade somebody to give him enough money early, against the promise of paying it back later (using that insurance and bonus the Wingco was growing[cxxvii]) , he could become very, *very* rich very, *very* quickly.

So now it became important for Roger (a) to make sure the Wingco stayed alive till the insurance policy was old enough for that gold-plated bonus to become available, all the time knowing that this guarantee was sufficient to keep him supplied with arms for trading on at great profit, and (b) to find ways to get his own claws onto the money as soon as possible after the bonus matured (which he calculated would be easy enough, because he could persuade or frighten Maddie into giving it to him once she had it).

But there was a problem. At about the age that the Wingco had reached not long before, the males in his family had a habit of dropping like snake-bitten turkeys from something that made their brains bleed. Howlers call this thing a *stroke*. The Wingco's father had died that way, and so had his grandfather and his elder brother. It didn't seem to matter how carefully they lived and how fit they were, this stroke thing seemed to be something that happened to them, regardless... and, by the gum that clogged my beak when I tried to eat some of Nataka's eucalyptus resin the other day (well, it smelled so tasty!), the Wingco was as fit as a super-energetic dung beetle *and* had some nasty combat tricks tucked away, too. He could have flattened Roger Court with one of his hairless wings pinned behind his back if he'd wanted, even though he was an old Howler.

In other words, if the Wingco was destined to have one of those strokes nothing would prevent it. Very worrying, these strokes are, because Howlers don't really know how to cure them, particularly the big ones (strokes, I mean; not Howlers. *Do* try to keep up). Howlers who have big strokes generally die or end up passing their final few Sun- and Startimes being not much more active or useful than a broken tail feather. In that case, Roger would have to keep the Wingco alive for as long as it took, and persuade everybody that the quality of his life wasn't as important as keeping him alive – at least, till the gold-plated bonus came along.

Sure enough, the Wingco suffered a stroke. Whereupon Roger immediately took charge and insisted that the old man be stuck all over with weird snaky and bleeping and ticking Howler magics that forced his body to keep breathing and his heart to keep pumping, even though he could no longer move or speak. Just to make sure that his insurance bonus would grow as fat as possible before he died.

But the Wingco was a canny old bird. He'd suspected all along that Roger would pull some trick like that. So he wrote a letter, which he gave to the fledgling Ter...

... Which brings us to things you already know. So I don't have to tell you again, and I don't have to write any more. Good. And if you want me to write anything else, forget it. I'd sooner go and whisker-tweak Scrumpy inside his sett.

GloSe RavENn, fAitHfuLL ComPAnyon And sCryBe to NatAkA yE Proteann, His Mark. [cxxviii]

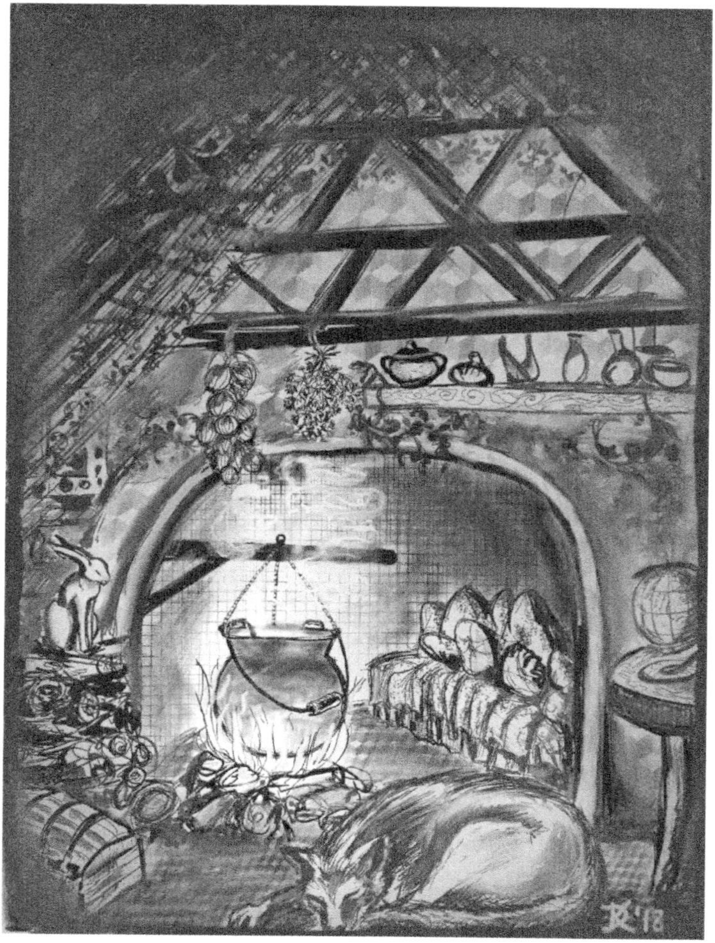

Chapter 19. *"Am I Really* That *Repulsive?"*

*"The range of what we see and do
Is limited by what we fail to notice."*[cxxix]

Bryony emerged from the mongoose compound, where she'd found all the food gone – as usual – and all of the Mongooses gone too – also as usual. She whistled tunelessly between her teeth, as she always did when she was thinking, and circled the perimeter of the compound for the umpteenth time, examining its strong wire mesh for holes or tears, and the soil underneath it for signs of burrowing, as she had done over and over again.

And – also as usual – she completed her inspection without finding anything wrong anywhere. Every inch of the fence looked intact and secure. But there it was: despite the entirely sound condition of the enclosure, yet again those elusive little creatures were nowhere to be found.

"Beats me;" she said to herself at last. She sighed and sat down on the ground just a few feet away from a dense little hebe bush that grew at the corner of the mongoose compound, many of its tangled branches and twigs interwoven with the mesh of the perimeter fence so that the bush was half inside and half outside the compound. She leaned her back against the nearby post, stretched her safari-booted legs out in front of her, and set to tapping the toes of her boots together, keeping time with her whistling, as she pondered the puzzle of the disappearing mongooses all over again.

She'd lost count of the number of times she and Anthony had been over the problem, trying to work out how on earth the furry little escapologists might be managing to get out of their enclosure time and time again, only to pop up again inside it at odd moments, as fresh as dew-washed daisies, full of squeaks and caresses, and clamouring for attention and food. Their bizarre disappearing act had everyone stumped. How *were* they getting out?

If Bryony had taken a much closer look at the bit of mesh under the densely branching, blue-flowered tangle of hebe a few feet from where she was sitting, she might have spotted the place where, under some particularly low-lying and entangled twigs, busy and dexterous little mongoose paws had excavated a subtly graded, shallow tunnel into the soil beneath the fence, back-filling both ends with pebbles and loose soil to make the surface of the ground appear solid and unmarked, and disguising every trace of their passage by sweeping their tails over the soil behind them as they slipped away. It was masterfully done.

But even though she was a very good sort for a Howler and all the animals in her care loved her dearly, Bryony still didn't credit her little African charges with enough intelligence or resourcefulness to disguise their bolt-hole so subtly. So Lerema, Tesho, Wapi, Hapa and Twende's escape route remained undiscovered.

"Four-legged, brindle-tailed Houdinis, the lot of 'em," muttered Bryony. She picked up a loose twig and began digging it into the ground beside her, her brow furrowed.

Just then she caught sight of Jim Bell walking towards the Raptors' enclosure. The torch Bryony had long carried for Jim Bell had troubled her sleep for some time, but she disguised it so well that nobody, least of all Jim, had any idea about it. And from the way he treated her, it was obvious that the thought that she might care for him more than for anybody else had never crossed his mind. When they were together he behaved towards her as he might towards a tomboy sister or any of his other buddies, which demonstrated that he saw her as somebody to share a pint and a joke with at the end of a day's work; somebody, even, in whom to confide a personal worry or sorrow, feeling assured that she could be trusted to listen sympathetically and offer sound advice, but nothing more.

This situation probably also had a lot to do with the fact that Jim had too often seen her elbows-deep in manure and mud, a rake or shovel in hand, straw sticking out of her hair and smudges on her nose. He had seldom seen her look feminine (not to mention *clean*) in what she called 'girly' clothes and make-up. Zoo work didn't leave much room for dressing up (quite apart from the fact that Bryony had little time for it), and was highly unlikely to generate romantic thoughts or ideas in a man. Not surprising, really. Maybe she should try harder to be feminine, once in a while?

Anyway, there was Jim, slouching past and looking down in the dumps.

"Ahoy, there, amigo! Wherefore the miserable mug?" she called as he trundled by with his hands thrust deep into the pockets of his work trouser and his face half-hidden by the hunch of his shoulders, "Park yourself for a sec and tell us all about it."

One thing you had to give Bryony, she never let a sore heart undermine her cheerfulness and kindness. Which made her a woman in a billion.

Jim's head lifted, and he turned towards her. "Oh; hello, Bry," he said, "I didn't see you." He approached and stood over her for a moment, and rocked from foot to foot with his hands deep in his pockets. Then he uttered a hollow sigh and crumpled down to squat beside her, folding his long legs like the poles of a collapsed tent.

"So," said Bryony, "What's up? ... You look as miserable as a shark on a cabbage diet. Care to talk about it?"

Jim stared into the middle distance for a moment. Then he sighed again, and said in a hollow voice, "I met someone…"

Oh, shit.

"Oh? … Sounds good. Is she nice?" Bryony didn't let her voice betray the fact that a cold hand had clutched her guts and was now slowly twisting them.

"Nice? … *Nice?*" echoed Jim, staring at her, "My God, Bry, she isn't *nice;* she's *amazing.* She's everything I've ever dreamed of! … But…"

"But? …"

Oho. There's a but*. Keep breathing.*

"But she doesn't give a damn about me," added the young man, and dropped his face into his hands.

Hallelujah!

"Oh … Oh, that's too bad. I'm sorry," she said, trying not to sound relieved, "I wonder why…"

That was all it took. Jim raised his head from his hands and poured out his sorrows, telling her all about how he'd met a captivating young medic at the hospital, how he'd tried to secure a second meeting with her but failed, and how she'd then seemingly vanished into thin air, because nobody at the hospital – and he assured her that he'd searched and asked high and low – *nobody* could tell him anything about any young black medic of her description. It was almost as if she hadn't existed at all, though of course she had.

But the worst thing of all had been how she'd responded to him.

"She just wasn't interested at all ... I mean, *not at all,* Bry! ... I mean, *I* knew *right away* that she's the only one for me. I really did. I still do. Just one look was all it took, I swear. I've never felt like this before... she's my – my soul mate – don't laugh! I know it sounds corny ... but... she really *is* ...

"But she just ridiculed and scolded me, Bry ... said she wasn't interested and that I must be sick, gave me some medicine to drink, and marched off. Just like that. I mean, she wouldn't even *listen!* And now I can't get her out of my head... that face... those eyes ... that voice ... that laugh ... the way she *moved*..."

Jim's voice broke. He groaned and glared into the distance. But then, suddenly, he turned and took Bryony's face in his hands, whereupon her knees felt as if she'd downed too many neat gins on an empty stomach and her heart began to rattle.

"*Listen,* Bry. You're a mate. Be honest, OK?" His voice was urgent, "Tell me truthfully. I'll know if you're kidding. ... Am I really *that* repulsive? ... I mean, what's the matter with me, that I can't seem to get women to like me?"

The matter *with you? You're a blind fool, Jim Bell.* That's *what's the matter with you, mate. ... Repulsive? Good grief, what an idiot you are. I've fallen for a flipping idiot.*

Bryony took a couple of deep breaths and cleared her throat noisily before she felt safe to speak.

"You're not at all repulsive, Jim - quite ... quite the contrary," she said, reaching up and lifting his hands away from around her face (it would have been impossible to leave them there and not make a fool of herself).

"Look, Jim; listen. That's just how it goes, you know? ... I mean, sometimes it works; sometimes it doesn't. Don't you think? ... I can't guess how often one person falls – in love, I mean – while the other one doesn't ... but it must happen a lot. And ... well, I suppose this young medic – she sounds incredible, by the way – well, *she* just didn't have the same reaction as you, you know? ... But, hey, that doesn't have to mean there's anything wrong with *you,* does it? It just means that the chem – the chemistry didn't work the same way for her, though goodness knows why ..."

She hesitated and then added a little shyly, "Jim, I've got a suggestion. Look around you. Carefully. All right? ... Check out the people around you. *Really carefully*, I mean ... I know you'll find at least one person, not a million miles away from you *right now*, who's crazy about you. Literally – you know – losing sleep over you ... except that you haven't noticed her..."

"No, don't laugh! I'm not joking... I *know* it's true! ... Jim..."

But he'd pulled away from her with a derisory bark, and now he stood up. "Nah, that's just nonsense," he snapped. His face flushed. "Honestly, Bry, you don't have to say that kind of thing to make me feel better, you know. I'm not a kid. I'd much rather you were honest and spelled it out. This ... this consolation - or whatever you think it is – doesn't help. If anything, it's making me feel worse, because I know you're just pretending, to make me feel better..."

"I'm *not* pretending, Jim! I mean..." interjected Bryony, her face bright red.

But he interrupted again, brushing the dust off his trouser legs and avoiding her eyes while he spoke. If he'd bothered to look at *her* instead of at his own feet, he might have

291

noticed that Bryony's eyes were bright with unshed tears and that she was trembling. And then he might have clicked. But he didn't. For all his good sense, Jim Bell could be remarkably obtuse, and although he generally noticed details exceptionally well, he could also be totally blind to what was right in front of him. A pretty normal Howler, all things considered.

"Ah, *c'mon,* Bry; cut the crap, all right? We're old mates, for Pete's sake! You, of all people, don't have to tiptoe around me … I mean, you don't have to sweeten the pill, not with me. All right? … I *know* if something's true or not.

"Look, the fact is, all the women worth anything are way out of my league, that's all. That doctor was. She was – just *perfect.* What could somebody like her see in somebody like me? What could I offer her, anyway? … Dirty fingernails? … No. Way out of my league.

"So why can't you be honest and just say that, instead? … *You're* a woman: you know it's true; you only have to look at me to know it's true!

"But … um … er …" Suddenly he caught himself and flushed, realising that he'd raised his voice and shown very little graciousness or gratitude in response to her kind and supportive words.

"Er – look, Bry … I'm sorry for being a bit emotional … and rude … just now. Honestly. I – uh – really appreciate what you were trying to do … and I shouldn't've raised my voice. Actually I shouldn't even have laid all this nonsense on you in the first place… and… and…

"Well, anyway … Look, thanks for listening, OK? … And sorry again. … Er - gotta go now, … I'll see you around."

And he left, without waiting for a reply.

Bryony watched him retreat. She didn't try to call him back. She pulled up her legs, wrapped her arms around her knees, and lowered her face onto them.

Brilliantly handled, you stupid, stupid, stupid ... Full marks for making a complete pig's ear of that.

Hell. Why didn't I just tell him how I feel?

No. that'd do no good at all. He's totally lost to that other woman. Damn her, why did she have to turn his head? She sounds like one of those sickeningly ideal types: gorgeous, flawless complexion, not a hair out of place, all snooty and superior and – and – irresistible ...

Shit! I hate her!

But even if she hadn't turned up, what difference would it have made, really? I'm just not his type. He's obviously into mysterious women with glowing eyes and sexy voices, not freckled and crusty workhorses like me. If I tried to tell him how I feel, I'd just end up embarrassing us both.

No. Might as well give it up. Better get used to it; that's all.

Deep in the hebe bush, three pairs of wide eyes in furry, wedge-shaped faces peered through the twigs at the forlorn figure of their warden. Lerema, Twende and Wapi had left the rest of their family in the sunny hideaway by the river while they slipped back to the zoo to collect any goodies that might have been put out for them, and they had arrived early enough during the conversation to grasp what was going on.

"*Oitochoi!*" whispered Lerema, turning to his companions, "I didn't know Howlers could feel that kind of thing, just like us; did you? ... Did *you* know Howlers could feel upset like that? ... *I* didn't. I thought they were more like safari ants instead of real people - you know, dashing around non-stop in long columns, rampaging and hurting and killing people randomly ... messing up everything... *Kweli,* [cxxx] this a real eye-opener!"

The mongoose cocked his little head and watched Bryony in silence for a little while.

"Ahh, look at her. She's miserable," he added. "That's real feeling, all right. I don't care what anybody says; there's no mistaking it. Reminds me of that day I thought we'd lost Kidole[cxxxi]; d'you remember? ... Properly heartbroken, I was, before we found him snoozing under that rock."

"Yeah, I remember; you curled up just like that Howler;" said Twende. "I also remember you were so pleased when we found Kidole safe and sound, you tried to bite him. *Fft.* Men."

Lerema ignored her last comment, straightened up and whispered, "Well, that's it. Our Howler's in trouble. When you're in that kind of trouble you stop eating. I stopped eating for ages - most of a Suntime, in fact... I was starving."

"*Men*;" muttered Twende again, under her whiskers.

"And if she doesn't eat she may die. We can't have that," insisted her Lord and Master, again carefully ignoring her muttered interruption. "I know I thought *I'd* die. ... No, we can't have that. I'm going have a chat with Chant."

"What good'll that do?" demanded Twende, "What can Chant do? This isn't even *her* Howler."

"Chant knows how to get hold of Nataka, stupid. And Nataka can fix anything," whispered Lerema, "She can fix

294

our Howler. ... No, listen, Twende; don't interrupt. We've got to do *something*. Even if our Howler doesn't die, if she gets too upset she may forget to feed us. Have you thought of that? ... No. Exactly. That's why I'm the boss around here."

Twende snorted. She sounded a lot like Geoff Masters when she did that.

"We obviously can't risk that," continued Lerema. "Besides, I'm fond of our Howler. She knows just how to scratch my ears."

"You're assuming Nataka'll want to help. I'm not sure she'll be bothered;" said Twende doubtfully, "Why should she care about any Howler *shauri,* anyway?"

"I don't think there's any harm in trying Lerema's idea," said Wapi, who usually listened and thought carefully before opening her mouth. "Lerema's right. We don't want to risk our food supply getting cut off, which could happen if our Howler gets sick. And she isn't as bad as most of the others. I reckon she's worth rescuing. You never know what *kichaa ganda tupu*[cxxxii] might take her place if she dies. Better a Howler we know than one we don't.

"So I agree, Lerema: why don't you slip along and find Chant? Twende and I can go back to tell the rest of our clan what's going on, after we've checked the provisions. *Sawa?*"

"*Sawa,*" agreed her two companions. The little animals exchanged nose kisses and then parted, slipping away as noiselessly as smoke.

A little later Bryony sniffed, scrubbed her nose and eyes, thumped her own knees with her fists a couple of times, and rose to her feet. There was work to be done, regardless of the state of her heart, and this was just another private sorrow to be borne with gritted teeth. Like many genuine tomboys, Bryony didn't have any female confidantes, and her parents, to whom she might have spoken about her troubles, lived a long way away in New Zealand. As for all her male buddies, there was no way on the green earth she would have dreamed of opening up to any of them about such a personal matter. It just didn't go with the tomboy job description.

Being a genuine tomboy can be a very lonely business.

Chapter 20. The Wingco's Choice

"To die, to sleep no more..." cxxxiii

Reality had shrunk to the confines of his bed and to the pain and heaviness he felt throughout his inert body, a coffin of flesh, inside which the machines ticking, whirring and beeping around his bed held him captive. His thoughts raced round and round and round in a never-ending cycle of frustration and passionate, impotent anger, the desperate, fruitless pacing of a tiger in a cage.

Where's Ter? ... How can I get out of this? ... How can I make them listen? ... I should have involved my lawyer ... why didn't I involve my lawyer? ... I should have helped Ter ... they'll never listen to him ... we need help ... How can we get help? ... I want to die ... Where's Ter? ... Surely he hasn't abandoned me ... how can I get out of this? ... How can I make them listen? ... I should have involved my lawyer... Where's Ter? ...

The machines hissed. His body felt like a lump of aching lead suspended from a brain incongruously light and active and whirling with activity; his eyes ranged incessantly, searching for one understanding expression among the professional, frustrated, tearful, determined and stubborn faces around him.

His eyelids could blink, and his eyes move. His thoughts were crystalline in their clarity, but he could feel his sanity threatening to go off-beam out of sheer misery and frustration.

Much more of this and I'll go bonkers. I can't even scream. For pity's sake let me die, you sadistic maniacs! What use is being able to think when all my other functions are lost forever? ... Where's Ter?

His ears were working perfectly - too perfectly, if anything. They transmitted to his intact cognitions every word spoken by the son-in-law he had always found obnoxious, and whose newfound power he now also resented and feared.

As for the daughter he had gained by her marriage to his dead son and whom he had loved as a true daughter, thankful for her life and for the life of his grandson, *now* he both pitied her in her sorrow and bewilderment, and despised her for being so weak in the face of her husband's demands.

After all, this was *his* life; nobody else's. This damaged body was *his* body. And *his* wishes had been very clearly expressed by that wonderful child, as well as in his letter. How, in all conscience, could they ignore such very clear wishes? ... Did they have any idea how appalling such an imprisonment must be to a person who had always been active? ... Good grief, he couldn't even *talk* any longer, let alone lift a finger. What was the point of being in life, if one couldn't participate in it? ... This was nothing short of torture.

I should have involved my lawyer ... Why didn't I involve my lawyer? ... I should have helped Ter ... they'll never listen to him ... He did warn me...

And the voices went on and on and on, and the faces came and went: the obnoxious son-in-law; the repulsive sister of his son-in-law; the tearful, trembling face of his grandson's mother. All faces that approached too close to his for him to be able to focus on them without discomfort; all either talking too loudly or whispering too softly; all annoying him with their baby talk, their stupid questions to the doctors and nurses, their demands and intrusive comments *about* him instead of *to* him, as if he were a helpless infant again and unable to think for himself, simply because he no longer had command of his own movements or facial expression or speech ...

... Where *was* Ter? ...

And the voices kept on. Even after all the doctors had left and there was just a nurse left.

Roger: "He's tired, that's all; he's only tired. He'll feel a lot better soon. That's right, isn't it, Dad? Of course it is. I'm sure it is. You're *tired,* aren't you, Dad? ... I'm right. He's just tired."

Don't call me Dad, you bastard. I'm not your dad. You've trapped me like a slave in a cage at the bottom of a pit, although you know what I want. And now you're talking at me and daring to call me Dad.

He closed his eyes to shut out the face of the man who was torturing him.

Ida: "He'll feel much better once he's had a chance to rest. This is the best solution for him ... for us all. Honestly, Maddie. ... Oh, *do* stop crying! ... Listen. He can't have been thinking when he wrote that letter... I'm sure he's sorry that he ever wrote it and made us all worry like this. *Aren't* you, Uncle Carl? .... Yes, I'm sure he is. He'll feel much better soon. Won't you, Uncle Carl? ... Of course you will. And then everything will get better.

"Besides, if we were to obey that silly letter we'd be committing murder, a *mortal sin*, condemning all our souls to Eternal Hell ... had you thought of that? .... No. Of course not. But *I* think about it all the time ... And he may still get better, you know ... The Lord giveth and the Lord taketh away ... Oh, for Heaven's sake, Maddie, stop *crying...*"

And so on; non-stop.

Shut your trap ... voice like a band saw, face like a vulture. Except that vultures are honest, at least. Using your religion like a weapon. You know I'm never getting better, you voracious, hypocritical harpy. You know why your repulsive brother's forcing me to stay alive. As soon as he doesn't need me alive any longer he'll pull the plug on me in a heartbeat. But it'll be too late by then. I'll have gone totally mad by then.

Oh, Maddie; you must have told him about my nest-egg. Why? Why did you do that? ... I should have been more careful... Aah; it's all my own fault...

He closed his eyes against Ida's sharp face and greedy eyes too.

... Where is Ter? ... This has all been too much for him, poor lad. No wonder he's cut and run. I'm a fool. I asked too much of him. ... Damn! I should have involved my lawyer...

There was a moment of silence while they all looked at his shut eyes. Ida and Roger seemed to think he'd gone to sleep. They edged away from the bed, speaking together in undertones.

He opened his eyes because Ida's voice had blessedly stopped rattling. Maddie's blurred face was filling his field of vision.

Too close for me to see you, dammit! ... Pull back, I can't focus on you...

Something in his eyes seemed to trigger understanding; she drew back to arm's length, where he could view her without straining. Her face was tear-streaked, woebegone. As she whispered, she reached out trembling fingers to stroke his flaccid, immobile cheeks and hands.

Maddie: "I'm sorry, I'm sorry; oh God, I'm *so* sorry, Wingco ... I'm sorry ... I don't know what to do... They insist that you have to live ... and Ter's insisting you want to – to – leave us ... and I can't bear it, I can't bear it ...

"What can I do? How can I be sure what you want? ... And now he's disappeared, he's run away... I don't know where he is... poor boy, he's so upset..."

You can fight.

Roger: "Now you're woken him up again. *Honestly*, woman! ..."

Ida: "You're spoiling that boy, Maddie. That's the trouble. You and his Granddad. He runs wild like a..."

Roger: "No wonder he's run away. He's ashamed of the fuss he's kicked up, and so he should be. Should have been taken in hand years ago...Well, from now on, I'm -"

Maddie (suddenly fierce, with a snap in her voice): "No, you won't, Roger! Ter's *my* son, mine and poor John's. And you *promised* never to interfere with how I raised him. You did, faithfully. You know you did!

"Look, listen. He's dreadfully upset because the Wingco's so sick, and why not? Why shouldn't he be? ... He doesn't want to – to – lose him. That's why he ran off. That, and because everybody was shouting at him ... No, not everybody: *You.* You two were shouting at him.

"He adores the Wingco. You know he does. And he's only doing what he believes the Wingco wants. D'you think he'd make it up? He's doing what the Wingco told him to do,

301

and it's tearing him up ... He had a letter, and he *had* to tell us about it. And *you* bit his head off and refused even to listen to him. He's a good boy!"

At last! Well said. It's been a long time coming, but here it is at last. Keep showing them your teeth, girl. Go on. More of that! You and Ter will be total victims, otherwise ... I wish I could speak and back you up ... Oh, my heart ...

Ida: "There's no such thing as a good boy, Maddie. They're all..."

Maddie: "Nonsense! You've never had kids. What do you know? Stay out of ..."

Roger: "Don't you raise your voice to my sister!"

Maddie: "Don't *you* raise your voice to me! I'm your *wife*. ... You should be supporting *me*, not -"

Ida: "Oh, that's nice. That's kind. After all that I've done for you. Maybe I should just leave, seeing as I'm not welcome here..."

Maddie: "Good idea."

Roger: "No, Ida, don't go; you've got as much right to be here as -"

Maddie: "No, she hasn't. She hasn't *any* business here. She should go. The only good idea she's had all day. Good-bye, Ida. ... And *you* can go with her too if you want, Roger. Don't let me keep you, if you prefer to be with your sister. Or you can stay and support me. But I mean *support*, not bully..."

Roger: "*What?* ... How dare you? -"

Nurse (entering): "Now then, that's enough! You're disturbing the patient. He needs peace and quiet. So please, either stop arguing, or leave the…"

Maddie (interrupting): "I'm not scared of you, Roger. I'm never going to be scared of you again. That's done. You can glare all you like; it won't make any difference. Go on, have another tantrum. Do. Start yelling and threatening and bullying again. Show the Nurse here what you're *really* made of, shouting over the sickbed of the only genuine man in this room…"

Good one. I didn't know you had it in you, Maddie. Keep fighting them, girl. I'm proud of you. Keep it up. No, don't cry; fight! You've got a son to care for.

Chaos. Raised voices. Maddie yelling, with tears pouring down her face. Ida screeching a malediction before storming off without buttoning her coat. The nurse insisting more and more loudly that they should all leave the room, but being ignored. Roger suddenly trying to moderate his tone as he realised that he couldn't afford to destroy his relations with Maddie; not right then; not when so much was at stake. Trying to calm her down, making his voice reasonable …

He closed his eyes again.

Ahh… If there is a god, I want it to let me go to sleep now *and never wake up again. I'm done. I'm not strong enough to bear this. … No? … Damn. No god, then. Thought not. I want my money back.*

… And saw a golden glow and heard a mellow voice that reminded him of the taste of chestnut honey; a voice that sounded inside his head, not outside it (while at the same time he could still hear Maddie at the foot of his bed, complaining to the nurse about her husband while Roger interrupted her with embarrassed and impatient "It's-not-that-bad-really-she's-just-stressed" platitudes, trying to get the nurse on side.)

Wingco. That's what they call you, isn't it? The *Wingco. Are you – now, how d'you lot in that odd little Air Force put it - Are you on my wavelength? ... Yeah. That's it. Wavelength. Are you on it? ... Or, hang on: do you read me? – Ter, should I say 'over'?*

A contralto chuckle.

Good grief; this is it. It's happened. Didn't take long. I'm already hearing things that aren't there. Isn't that supposed to be one of the symptoms of psychosis, hearing voices talking to you that aren't there? ... Yeah, it is. My mind's definitely going. They've finally done for me with their...

Oy! *Listen up, Wingco. Snap out of that useless* palaver *and pay attention. Ter has something to tell you.*

The voice had taken on a peremptory, impatient tone.

Ter? ... Where is Ter? ... How can this be happening?

Wingco ... I'm here, Wingco. Can you hear me? ... Please say something ... She says you only need to think what you want to say, and we'll hear you. It's true, too. I heard your thoughts just now. It really works. So can you try? ... Please answer me, Wingco ... Please? ... Can you hear me?

So I'm not hallucinating? ... Is this really you, Ter? ... Who's she, anyway?

Another rich, throaty chuckle, and the sudden hopeful giggle of a young voice. Yes. That sounded like Ter. But how could this even be happening?

How can I be sure it's really Ter I'm hearing, and not some wish-fulfilment – you know – some fantasy?

Another throaty chuckle.

How d'you know anything *isn't fantasy?* said the contralto voice.

Then Ter's voice again, proud and hopeful.

That's my Wingco all over. ... See, Nataka? I told you. ... That's him. He never takes things on trust without testing them.

A pause. Then:

All right, Wingco. I've thought of something. ... D'you remember what I said about Mickey Free the day you wrote that letter? You and I are the only people who know that; right? ... I said that his age didn't stop him being a scout, didn't I? And you laughed and agreed. ... Wingco?

You are Ter. You really are. *Oh, my boy...*

A wave of grief and gratitude forced a lump into his throat and for the first time since he had collapsed, tears rose into his eyes and tracked down his cheeks.

Don't cry, Wingco, please *don't cry, or I'll start again too... Listen,* she's *going to help you, she really is ...*

She? ... Who? ... Why? ... How?

I found her, Wingco. We're so lucky ... She says she can help you to do whatever you want. I know what I *want, but you have to choose. ... OK? ... Wingco? ... Can you still hear me?*

Another voice: harsh, for all the world like the cawing of a crow or raven...

Arkh! *Give your aged Howler a chance to think, Fledgling. Don't rush him. This is quite a beak-full of worms to swallow all in one go, you know.*

What? ...Who said that?

The warm chuckle again.

Actually, I think we can safely call this one a Sapiens instead of a Howler, Glose. And it'll be a lot easier if we just show him, don't you think?. Hold on, this is a bit tricky. ... All right, Wingco, ready. Open your eyes. Here we are.

But - how can you do that? Won't the others see you as well? Ter sounded anxious.

You still underestimate me, Infant Sap. Only your Wingco will see us. We're Invisible to everyone else, naturally.

A brief pause.

Go on, Wingco, open your eyes. Don't be afraid.

So he opened his eyes.

A huge raven was perching on his chest, filling most of his field of vision as it contemplated him with its head cocked to one side. Behind the bird was his grandson, leaning forward over the foot of the bed and gazing at him with an eager and anxious expression on his pale face.

Beside Ter stood the most beautiful young woman the Wingco had ever seen. Large, iridescent eyes, glowing in her serenely smiling dark face, reminded him of sunlit water dancing over opalescent pebbles in a mountain stream.

More captivating than the glitter of a handful of diamonds by candlelight and so strange as to seem impossible, the eyes gazed into his own while the fingers of one mahogany-coloured hand danced lightly on the boy's shoulder, as if they were fingering an invisible keyboard.

The nurse (a stocky, efficient Asian woman who looked capable of flooring you) had finally lost patience with Ter's bickering mother and stepfather. She was herding them out of the sickroom, snapping and snarling like a short-tempered border collie. As soon as they stepped through the door she followed them out, shutting the door behind her with a snick. Her voice could be heard, shrilly admonishing the couple outside the room.

But the Wingco had no attention to spare for them. He was intent on the three figures before him.

How...?

Relax. Let's start at the beginning and do this properly, responded the black woman's voice in his head. *We have to make sure you can make a rational, fully informed choice.*

A choice? ... What choice?

Why, between life and death, of course. What else is there?

Oh ... so nothing too serious, then.

The raven chuckled and clicked its beak. *I'm beginning to like this Howler – er – Sap, despite myself,* it creaked.

Wingco, listen. You've got to be careful now. Ter sounded anxious again. *She* will *give you whatever you want, you know... and you won't be able to change your mind afterwards. All right? You only get to choose once. ... So* please *choose carefully.*

... I mean, if you decide to – to die... the boy faltered on the word and his lips trembled, *of course I'll understand. ... But if you want to come back I'll be so grateful and happy ... and so will Mum... You know we will.*

Er – hold hard, my boy... One question for the lady, if I may. Madam, if I choose life, will I be disabled? Call me a coward, but I don't think I could bear that.

The lady arched her eyebrows.

I don't do half-jobs, Wingco. On principle. As you'll discover. If you decide to stay, I'll make you as fit as you were before your illness. Play your cards right, and I might even sort out that dodgy knee (forced landing onto an unstable deck with engine gone, wasn't it? ... Thought so).

But all that said, don't expect to stay here forever. That can't be part of the deal. At some point further down the line you'll have to go through your final Change, just like every other Mortal.

She paused and contemplated the Wingco for a moment, cocking her head to one side, just like the raven.

Hmm... from the look of you, I reckon that change shouldn't happen for some considerable time. You'll have plenty of Seasons to enjoy yourself, play with your infant; watch him grow up... all that. If you want to, that is. ... And, of course, it'll also give you a chance to put that life insurance nonsense right too. You do *need to fix it urgently, you know.*

Hmph. So you know about the insurance.

Of course. So does Glose.

Pleased to meet you, I'm sure; cawed the raven, half-spreading its wings and ducking its shiny black head. *Glose the Raven, at your service - within reason. Oh, I say, is that...?*

The bird cocked its head to examine the Wingco's left arm. It hopped sideways, ducked, and pecked at the cannula snaking out of it.

Arkh! Yuk ... Not a worm. Quite inedible, despite appearances.

Ter giggled.

I'm hungry, added Glose plaintively. *So come on, then, Aged Sapiens. Have you decided yet?*

He gazed at them, thinking. The boy's eyes, still wide, trusting and fearful, were fixed on his. The raven, combing a pinion with his beak and muttering about food, wasn't even thinking about him any longer. The remarkable young woman stood immobile, watching him with an expression that reminded him of a number of statues of the Buddha he had encountered in the Far East.

The great burden of responsibility and trepidation he had felt ever since the tragic loss of his son six years earlier lifted from his heart and mind. He knew that he would never have to worry about the well-being of his grandson again, not now that the child had managed to gain such a powerful and affectionate ally.

Yes. Even if he chose to die immediately, jettisoning his useless body, Ter would be well supported and perfectly safe. For a while the child would grieve bitterly, of course. However, he would recover from his sorrow and become stronger for it. Death was part of every human's lot, and the boy would encounter and cope with it, just as he had with the loss of his father. And, even more importantly, all through that trial his grandson would be well protected by the amazing young woman he had befriended. The Wingco knew this with absolute certainty, without stopping to work out where the feeling came from.

And in that case, of course, Ter's mother would also be safe. The Wingco was no longer plagued by the desperate fear that his death would abandon a weak mother and her vulnerable son to the vagaries of ruthless and selfish individuals like the SF.

The thought comforted him immeasurably. And for a moment, knowing this, the temptation simply to let go and rest forever from his struggles became almost irresistible. His body felt exhausted and heavy, a burden he would feel relieved to lay down at last. He had fought so hard to keep himself going through the long years, battling his own grief and frustration for the sake of the remaining two creatures on this planet dearer to him than himself. Why not just let go now, slide away, let slip the dead weight of his exhausted flesh, and be free of it all, at last?

And all he had to do to achieve that longed-for peace was choose it; *she* had said so. He didn't doubt for an instant that she would instantly do his bidding. The thought was intensely seductive.

But ... but...

Life! Who, even feeling as drained as he did, could possibly resist the opportunity to explore it even more, particularly now that he knew there were such amazing, unexpected creatures in it as this young woman and her bird?

And Ter. How could he possibly turn his back on the joy of more time with his beloved grandchild?

In the end, he realised, the decision had been made for him all along.

Good choice, said the young woman.

Wingco! I love you! Ter was jubilant.

Good, cawed Glose. *High time.* Now *can we eat? My stomach never signed up for starvation duty, you know. It wants something in it. Now.*

Roger, Maddie and the nurse were still squabbling in the passageway when they were silenced by the blinding light that streamed out around the doorframe and through the keyhole of the sickroom door for a split second, drenching them in rainbow-hues.

An instant later, two familiar voices inside the room erupted in whoops, laughter and whistling.

After an initial moment of frozen disbelief, Roger shouldered the two women aside, slapped the door open and barged into the sickroom, only to stop again so abruptly that Maddie and the nurse cannoned into him from behind.

The Wingco was sitting on the side of his bed, his bare feet on the floor. His grey hair was tousled at the back from having lain so long on the pillow, but his eyes were bright and his skin glowing with health. He was whistling the theme song from *The Bridge on the River Kwai* while he wrestled with the wires, tubes and needles that connected him to the various drips, drains and monitors clustered around the bed.

Ter was kneeling on the bed, facing his grandfather. Watching the animation in his face and voice, Maddie's heart squeezed as she realised just how crushed her son had been feeling since the old man's illness. But Ter was unaware of his parents' entrance and oblivious of his mother's scrutiny, so absorbed was he in the old man's every word and act.

Every so often the Wingco would interrupt his song to make a comment or issue an instruction, which Ter hastened to fulfil, practically falling over himself and as enthusiastic and clumsy as a puppy.

"Here we are, then. Ready, that man? ... *Out* it comes, then ... **phew*!* - Watch out, here comes the blood. ... Cotton wool pads to the fore, staunching, for the use of. There's a whole mountain of them over there ... Thanks, son. Those damned needles, eh? ... Look here ... *ouch,* no! – No, my boy; don't do that! Just press *this* pad thingy onto the hole for me; right, ... And I'll unstick the plasters..."

"Good man, *that's* the ticket. ... *Oops* – whoa there, Pilgrim, not so fast ... Hang on, just a tick ... more pads, that man? ... Ta. That's fetched her. ... Now then; there's also all this blasted sticky stuff to get off my arm. Bloody itchy. You've got to hand it to those nurses, they're a whizz with knots and plasters. Truss you up like a turkey, they will, given half a chance ..." And the old man rendered such a good imitation of a turkey gobbling that the boy toppled over, helplessly giggling, onto the bedclothes.

Glose had flown off in search of food, but Nataka was still in the room. Invisible to Roger, Maddie and the nurse, she perched on the windowsill and smiled as she watched the old man and his grandson at work.

"Ahoy there!" called the Wingco, noticing the intruders at last. "So there you are. Catching flies, are we?

"I must say, I wasn't at all happy when you ignored my final wishes and insisted on keeping me going like that, Roger. Shabby behaviour. Yes, definitely shabby. Not cricket at all.

In fact I could cheerfully strangle you for it. But all's well that ends well; huh? If you hadn't refused to send me to my final rest, none of this would be happening. So instead of chewing you out, I suppose I'd better thank you, eh?

"I say, Maddie, my girl, you're just the person I wanted. I could use your fingernails to get under some of this damned tape stuff on my arms and head. My nails just don't seem…"

His daughter-in-law uttered a muffled *scream-squeak-sob* and squeezed past her husband, who was still standing in the doorway with his mouth wide open and his face the colour of stale wallpaper paste. She flew across the room, flung her arms around the old man's shoulders, buried her face in his neck and burst into tears.

"There, there, lass. It's over;" he murmured, patting her on the back, "There, there. All better now, my poor girl … Um, darling … about these plasters, you know?"

"But *Wingco*! … I thought you'd never… Oh, my God, they told me you were … how? … *How*? … I mean, what *happened*?" sobbed Maddie, laughing and crying at the same time. She drew back, her hands still grasping the old man's shoulders, and turned her wet face and shining wide eyes backwards and forwards between her beaming son and the old man.

"I mean, how? … *How*? … Really, *how*? … And – and where did *you* come from, Ter? … You weren't here just now! … And now, seriously, you only want to talk about the plasters, Wingco? I mean, *honestly*? … How? … What happened?"

As she spoke, she stroked and patted her father-in-law's face, hands and arms as if checking for tricks or flaws, or searching for some strange mechanism that might be making him work.

"All in good time, my girl. Let's just take one step at a time, all right?" replied her father-in-law, grinning widely. He kissed Maddie on her cheeks and brow. Then he again took her hands in his and guided them to where he wanted her help with the bits of elastoplast still festooning his head, chest and arms.

"There'll be plenty of time for explanations later, I promise," he said, "but, you know, right now these plasters are important; they're *so* ... *Ahh*, that's better ... The ones they used to stick the ECG pads onto my chest and legs were driving me batty. ... Thanks, darling. Itched like jam, they did. Mind helping with the ones on my head, as well?"

His strong, hearty voice seemed to reassure and calm his daughter-in-law.

"Now then," he went on as Ter and Maddie continued to prise him free of tubes and tapes, "Nurse – may I call you Nurse? ... Splendid. Could you possibly find somebody in this place to rustle up some grub for me before I go home? I know it's not strictly your job, but you'll be doing me a favour. I'll be forever grateful. I swear I'm so hungry I could eat the carpet. Those IV drips are all very well when you're not doing much more than lying about trying to die – hah! – But to a healthy body they're worse than starvation rations. I'm ravenous. Is that all right?

"... Actually, on second thoughts you'd better make that at least two portions of whatever's going, if you don't mind. Ter's hungry too; aren't you, my lad? ... You haven't eaten properly since all this business began, I'll be bound. Tum probably thinking your throat's been cut, eh? ...

"Oh – and Roger, be so good as to skip off and see what's happened to my clothes and other things, would you? I particularly want my mobile phone and wallet. ... Now let me think: they were in my jacket pocket last time I looked – you know, in that horrible restaurant where it all went pear-shaped.

"Incidentally, just so you know, Roger: you're never getting me into that bloody restaurant again. Never. Call me irrational if you will, but from now on your sister'll just have to find another pretentious, overpriced hole for us all to languish in when we visit her. *If* we visit her, hah! ... You know, on reflection, I wouldn't be surprised if that execrable cabbage and stale cheese-flavoured excuse for a quiche we ate in the place had something to do with my stroke. Now *there's* a thought. What d'you think, Ter, should I sue? ... Haha! ... *Ugh.* Vile place.

"Oh, *you* know where my things are, do you, Maddie? ... Great stuff. Off you go then. Roger, you can help her. And when you get back, we'll have a little chat. A debrief, as it were."

"But, Mr Bourne, Mr Bourne!" The forceful nurse had found her voice. "You really shouldn't get out of bed or disconnect yourself from any of our monitors before we can all be sure you're really better, you know. This is all most irregular ... I mean to say, it's ... your apparent recovery is really – well, it's unheard of! You really mustn't do anything before... I have to notify the hospital right away ... our specialists will want to check you over and make sure..."

"No doubt," interrupted the old man, smiling at her, "but I assure you I feel perfectly well again, Nurse. And I have it on the most reliable authority that my health is fully restored. Besides, despite my great respect for the medical establishment, I've no intention of serving as its guinea pig.

315

No way. Besides, I'd only be blocking a bed that some genuinely sick person deserves much more than I do."

The young woman drew a deep breath, marshalling her arguments. But the Wingco raised a silencing hand.

"No. Listen. *Listen*;" he said. His calm voice had the undeniable ring of authority he had used to great effect in his Service years, and the nurse found herself straightening up in response to it, like a retired war-horse responding to the music of fife and drum. The old man smiled warmly at her.

"I'm discharging myself from your care – well, as soon as you've very kindly organised that food, of course - and that's all there is to it, you see. Look, I'm sure you have plenty of genuinely sick people who will be more than grateful for your excellent skills, you know? People sitting around, waiting on trollies and in corridors for you to hook them up to all these excellent machines, where they're really needed. So you won't miss me, will you?

"Tell you what, though: if it makes you feel any better, I'll sign an indemnity to protect you, the hospital, the doctors, this home - and anybody else you care to mention - from future allegations of negligence and so forth, should I fall ill again. Which I won't. But anyway. That do? ... And as a further concession I'll also make an appointment for a thorough medical with my GP in the near future. That really should be more than enough."

The Wingco paused, drew a deep breath and rolled his eyes at his grandson, who had tucked himself under his right arm. "Cripes, kid. This is tougher than unplugging a dinosaur from a tar pit," he said.

"But – but ... Mr Bourne, you had a *stroke*!" spluttered the nurse, "you were – *completely – disabled*, you know! ... I don't believe you realise just how very sick you've been. ...

316

All the scans showed it: massive and irreversible damage to your brain; *massive* ... so your apparent recovery is ... is ... well, it's ..."

"Impossible?" teased the Wingco, "I would agree, except for the fact that it's happened. So there's nothing *apparent* about it. As you can see. Besides, given that it *has* happened, by definition it isn't impossible either, is it? Ah, the joys of logic. ... So what if my recovery is due to an inexplicable event or agency – in this case rather a special one?" As he spoke the Wingco glanced round appreciatively at Nataka, who winked at him from her place in the corner of the window. "The main point, surely, is that I *have* recovered.

"Anyway, as I said, here I am, fighting fit and feeling top-notch again, thank you very much. And please believe me, I don't have the slightest intention of returning to that hospital. So that's that. ... Hey, by the way, what are we doing, still sitting in this tango lighting, for pity's sake? Let's have all the curtains wide open and let in the sunlight!"

While Ter leaped off the bed and hurried to throw open the curtains, the old man turned back to Maddie and Roger, who had been following the discussion with their mouths hanging open.

"What, are you two still here? ... Look, do me a favour and get going, would you? I want my stuff, the sooner the better. Of course, I could just wander around looking for it myself, in my fetching little Dior-designed hospital gown, so cunningly cut to exhibit my hidden assets to the entire world ... No? ... Good-oh. Modesty wins out. I'm so glad. Off you go, then.

"And as for you, Nurse, bless you for your concern, but that grub really won't organise itself, you know. But before you go, I must thank you with all my heart. I couldn't be more

317

grateful for all your care while I was disabled, and particularly for shutting everybody up when they were making all that noise just now. You'll never know how much I needed that. You're a gem. Well done, Nurse!"

After that there was nothing the nurse would not have done for this strange old man. She scurried off, determined to get him the best meal she could summon at short notice.

Chapter 21. How To Woo A Pathway Tree

"It's really hard to be serious in a tango." [cxxxiv]

The replica Fagus that had recently appeared in the fringe of woodland outside the prison for animals – er, zoo – creaked and blinked its mossy eyes. It had been roused from its daydreams by a shrill chorus of *meows* and squeaks to find an elegant little calico cat and two mongooses fidgeting at its foot. The Pathway Tree yawned and surveyed its visitors in mild astonishment.

"So you want to see Nataka the Aelfeynn Earda?" it murmured.

Chant, Lerema and Tesho froze and stared at one another in amazement. How *did* the plant know what they wanted? They hadn't even told it yet.

"This is *seriously* spooky, *Ndugu,*[cxxxv]" muttered Tesho to Lerema. The twins backed off a few steps with their fur on end (just in case, you know).

"Er... we want Nataka... don't know the other ones..." said Lerema after a confused pause. Tesho added "*Sawa...* Nataka. *That* one."

But Chant didn't retreat. Instead she reared up on her hind paws and patted the trunk of the beech tree just under its mouth-crack. "Yes, if you please, O Wise One. I see you've read our minds, which is... well, I wish *I* could do it, that's all. ... Anyway, you're absolutely right. We want to talk to Nataka about a Howler who needs to be... curl my whiskers, what's the right word? ... Rescued? ... Managed? ... Ah! I have it: *Sorted Out*," she chirruped. "And we know that *you* know where we can find her, so..."

"Time was," interrupted the tree, grumbling with a sound like the wind ruffling up the waves against a sea-cliff, "Time *was* when nobody, least of all a mere *animal*, would have dared to approach me without the appropriate ceremony, songs and seemly gifts. Yes. All that. Why, just a few startimes past, Aelfeynn Earda – she whom you call Nataka – offered me a fine tribute, one that made me feel appropriately honoured and prized, and that inspired me to keep my portals and paths available to her until further notice. Yes, indeed. That was a particularly aromatic libation."

Fagus sighed and smacked its lips, lapsing into a dreamy, contemplative silence that stretched out for what seemed an eternity to the three impatient little animals at its foot. Just as they were beginning to think that they'd made a mistake by rousing the eccentric tree and would have to find another way to reach the Protean, Fagus rustled its leaves, heaved another sigh and spoke again.

"Well, that is how it was. But, twist my roots, now here you are, three inconsequential and importunate little scraps of animal life. And you distract me from my meditation with your most tuneless squeals and caterwaulings, not to mention the fact that you fail to bring me any tribute that I can see. By rights I should simply shut my eyes and pretend you'd never bothered me at all. So, you disrespectful and cacophonous scraps of mortal flesh, tell me: why should I *not* ignore you?"

"Because, you know, Your Greatness," meowed Chant, who was a brave cat, "we didn't mean to be disrespectful. No, not at all. We had no idea you only talk to animals that bring ceremony and tribute or play you music, or things like that. Nataka never told us about that. We really don't have the slightest idea about the right protocol. We didn't even know that there *was* a protocol, before you told us. So we really can't have meant to be rude, can we? … 'Course not. But, you know, if you tell us what we should do, I'm sure we could find a way to do it. ... Couldn't we, you two?"

Her two companions rose up to the tips of their back legs and simultaneously crossed their front-paws on their breasts in a gesture so unconsciously comical that the corners of the beech tree's mouth-hole twitched, and it had to grunt and shiver a bit to mask its amusement.

"Hmm... *Hurr*... *Grunt*;" it said, startling the mongooses.

"*Oitochoi!*" Lerema hopped into the air. "Er... well, to be honest we're not really that big on *music*. In fact we're actually quite, um, *small* on music, if you follow me, O Great Big Plant With The Humungous Trunk. I'll even admit, not to beat about the bush – no offence meant – that when I try to sing, other Wanyama tend to run; you know? .... Yes. They tend to run for it like nipped lizards. Don't they, Tesho?"

Chant hissed at him. This talk of humungous stems, beating about the bush and scattering listeners with his singing didn't chime in with her idea of diplomatic discourse. But the tree's mouth had stretched into a smile. There was something strangely refreshing in meeting little animals that weren't automatically reduced to ceremonious kow-towing in its presence.

"*Kweli,*" agreed Tesho, grabbing his own tail and sucking its tip, as he always did when he was nervous. "Lerema's telling the truth. We're not at all big on music. Gymnastics are much more our line, you know – I mean, tumbles and tricks, and things. But *lakini* [cxxxvi], perhaps we could round up a few birds and get them to sing instead? ... Lerema, what d'you think, couldn't we chat up a few birds – singing ones, you know – to serenade... Whatsitsname ... Oh, yeah – The Great Lord Fagus?"

Lerema looked dubious. "Um, well ... Let's just *chunga*[cxxxvii] a minute there, *Ndugu*. What if Chant took it into her head to hunt the birds? – Chant, what if you couldn't hold back, and hunted them, you know? ... What then?"

Chant was a keen hunter, devilishly quick on her paws, and very bad at resisting temptation. Lerema knew that birds invariably triggered her hunting instinct (unless the birds were very big and scary, like owls or harpy eagles), and the canny little mongoose had an idea that the Pathway Tree wouldn't take too kindly to seeing its feathered choir shredded by a rampaging calico cat just as they were about to chant a *paean* to its greatness.

Sure enough, the tip of Chant's tail had automatically set to twitching at the thought of a flock of juicy songbirds within claws' reach. But with a jolt she realised just in time what was happening, and shook herself to snap out of it.

"Look. I *am* a cat," she meowed irritably. "I hunt. That's what I do. And when I say *hunt*, I'm not just talking about chasing creepy-crawlies, like you guys. *Sheesh*. What d'you want from me anyway, to stalk vegetables? "

At her words Fagus began to creak and shake, disturbing a jay nesting in its branches, which took to scolding. This only made the tree creak and tremble even harder.

The three animals at its foot were quite startled, before they realised from the movements of its mouth and the glitter in its eyes that it was simply chuckling.

"Heh, heh, heh," it said, "Leaf and twig, you really are quite amusing little scraps of flesh. ... Stalk vegetables, eh? Haha! Good. Clever. Yes, perhaps we should spare our feathered friends the threat of annihilation. Eh? ... Yes. Heh! Heh! Heh! In your case I *may* make an exception and consider a somewhat modified protocol. Yes. With a libation, of course. The libation is non-negotiable."

"What in the name of a batty boomslang is a *libation*?" hissed Lerema to Chant.

"It's a drink, pea-brain. For the tree. You know, a gift. The tree wants us to bring it a gift of drink," she hissed back. "Leave it to us, O Great One!" she called to Fagus, "One ceremony, coming up. You won't regret it. Come on then, you two!" [cxxxviii] The mongooses were still gazing at the enormous beech tree in fascination. Its eyes, now dancing and glinting with deep hues of green and gold, were well worth watching.

"*Sawa!*" and "*Haya, twende!*"[cxxxix] said the twins. They dropped hurriedly to all fours and darted off after the cat with their tails in the air.

"Amusing little scraps of life; very," creaked the Pathway Tree. It closed its eyes and went back to daydreaming in the sunlight.

It wasn't very long before the two mongooses and cat returned. They were not alone. All the mongoose family was there. The youngsters[cxl] were to participate in the presentation, and they had been practising all Sunclimb. Now they bounced around, chittering excitedly, under the eyes of their mothers – all except Kidole, who had already found a way to scuttle off behind Fagus when the parents weren't watching, and was snuffling and scrabbling after beetles and other creepy-crawlies around the great tree's roots. His activities sent an occasional - not entirely unpleasant - shiver up Fagus' trunk, for the tip of Kidole's nose was both moist and cold.

Chant and the twins had managed to recruit the help of a sarcastic Ghanaian Roloway monkey called Rhesus

Sardonicus (Sardo for short)[cxli]. He'd contributed a green coconut full of juice to the project (he didn't like coconut water, which explains his generosity). Sardo had also helped to distract Kelele the chimp by arguing with him about the order in which different jungle fruits ripen in the tropics while the twins sneaked into Kelele's enclosure behind his back and swiped a pair of fermenting mangoes and a large pineapple from his hoard.

After that bit of ticklish jiggery-pokery, the preparation of the libation had been plain sailing. The mongoose twins found a sharp stick and Sardo used it to dig out the soft eyes of the coconut, steadying it with his hind paws. Then, taking care not to break their skins, they kneaded each fruit against a flat stone till its insides were mushy and soft, bit a small hole into the rind of each, and squeezed its juice and mush into the coconut before plugging the holes with some leaves and shaking the nut like a maraca to mix the juices together.

Now the animals were all assembled at the foot of the tree, ready to perform their ceremony. The mongoose kittens (including Kidole, who'd been dragged tail-first from behind Fagus) were squatting and fidgeting in a row, waiting for the signal to begin their show. Hapa and Wapi had used their tails to sweep away all the small twigs and beech mast from the patch of grass on which they were going to display. Sardo had been appointed to accompany Chant, carrying the coconut when the moment came to approach the tree with the libation. He was the only one with the hands for the job ("we really should have gone into properly long fingers ages ago," commented Hapa to her sisters).

"Right, you lot, here we go then. Ready?" meowed Chant. "First things first ... *Silence,* you kittens! I've got to do my speech first, remember?"

She turned to the tree, raised one forepaw, perked her ears, tuned up her purr, and set her tail to Weave. Then she began her address in what can only be described as a caterwaul.

"O Great Fagus, Master of the Forest!" she sang.

Tain and Mether yelped at the sound of her voice. "Sounds like ten alley cats and a hyena fighting over an old carcass," whispered Wapi to Twende.

"*Squeak* Kidole *bit* me!" interrupted Jiggit's tiny voice. "*Did not!*" came Kidole's counter-squeak. "*Did!*" - "*Did not!*" – "*D-*"

"*Nyamaseni!*" [cxlii] snapped Twende.

"... *Of the Forest!* ... Any more interruptions and I'll *pounce* on whoever's responsible!" spat Chant. The infants froze.

"As I was saying ... *Ahem*! ... O Great Fagus, Master of the Forest! Pray accept our humble offerings in the spirit in which we make them ..."

At this point the calico cat, who had an inordinately high notion of her own performing skills, made a serious mistake. She paused for effect.

"*No*! - Not *yet,* you idiots!" yelped Wapi.

Too late. Yain, Tain, Tether and Mumph, mistaking Chant's dramatic pause for the end of the speech, had bounced into their opening routine, clasping one another in pairs head to tail and tummy to tummy, grabbing each other's tails in their teeth and setting off on a vertiginous series of spiralling somersaults round the space their parents had cleared at the foot of the tree.

Not one of the tumbling kittens heeded Wapi's cry. On the contrary. All keyed up and raring to go, Mether, Jiggit, Dix and Kidole squeaked excitedly and joined their cartwheeling siblings pell-mell, scrambling onto one another's backs and somersaulting off again, forming mouth-to-tail chains and rushing around in convoluted patterns, scampering up their parents' backs to their shoulders and heads before flipping off them into the arms of their siblings, all while yipping and squeaking "*hup*!"

"Better give up on the rest of your speech, Patches!" hooted Sardo. "Never mind. It was deadly boring anyway. *This* is much better!"

That tore it. The little cat had already been battling to control her temper. Not only had those infuriating mongoose brats spoilt her introduction, but now the monkey was insulting her, calling her *Patches* (how dare he?) and making fun of her beautiful speech. It was not to be borne.

Lashing her tail, her eyes wide and blazing, Chant let rip a keening, screeching hunting call, bounded into the air and pounced with her talons spread, straight at the cluster of carousing kittens ...

... ("*No!/Chunga!/Oitochoi/Saidieni/Hapana!* [cxliii]" screamed the mongoose parents, leaping towards her) ...

... Only to fetch up dangling upside-down in mid-air, yowling, spitting, twisting and scrabbling for purchase on something – *anything* - while a tearing pain seared the ultra-sensitive spot where the base of her tail joined her fluffy and much-groomed bottom.

Sardo hadn't wasted any time or energy screaming. At the precise moment when Chant launched herself into the air he'd leaped onto a conveniently low branch of the Pathway Tree, gripped it firmly with his back paws and prehensile tail, and swung himself down, head first, to intercept the little cat's tail at the height of her trajectory, snatching her bodily into the air an instant before her needle-sharp front claws could close on the tangle of cavorting mongoose babies.

And still, while all this was going on, oblivious of the carnage the monkey's lightning action had spared them, the exuberant mongoose babies never missed a beat but continued their display. You've got to hand it to them: they had terrific focus.

"*Tsk, tsk, tsk*! Temper, temper!" chattered Sardo, turning and hoisting Chant up by her tail until her muzzle was dangling upside-down, facing him. Hooting with laughter he reached out his free forepaw and tweaked her whiskers.

"Naughty, *naughty* Patches! ...*Who's* naughty? .... *You* are. Who? *You!* ... Repeat after me, you naughty pussycat: We. Don't. Pounce. On. Dancing. Babies, you wicked thing! Oh, *what* would Nataka say? Huh? Huh? ... *Hahaha!* .... *Ooh- ooh-ooh! Ah-ah-ah!*" He let out a peal of chattering laughter.

"***Yeeeoooowwwwwwllll!!!** Hssssssss!* ... Put me down, you – you – *you*...!" The calico cat screeched, slashed and scrabbled at thin air with her forepaws, all to no avail. Roloways have long limbs.

The mongoose parents were up on their hind legs, their fur on end, their tails like bottlebrushes, and their eyes wide and fiery.

"What happened? /What *was* that? /Was she going to eat our *watoto*?" [cxliv]

As one they turned and glared at the dangling cat. Their lips curled back and exposed five sets of tiny, razor sharp teeth.

And still the mongoose babies went on cavorting.

"*Oitochoi!* Look at the tree!" suddenly exclaimed Tesho. "It's working!"

"It is, it is!" replied Lerema, "Our *watoto* are doing it!"

He was absolutely right. Fagus was laughing.

Truth to tell, a very few moments into Chant's declamation the Pathway Tree had begun struggling to stay awake. But then things had swiftly become much more interesting. Its eyes had snapped wide open and its leaves and twigs begun to shiver and shake as soon as the infants launched their ill-timed interruption. But the thing to tip the venerable plant over into full-throated, uncontrollable hilarity had been Chant's foiled attempt to kill the tiny performers.

Fagus was perfectly aware that Chant's pounce and Sardo's rescue had been unrehearsed, and it was this very point that rendered the whole event so irresistible. Abandoning any pretence at dignity, the Pathway Tree collapsed into helpless laughter. This set the jay in Fagus' branches to scolding again, even as the ground trembled and roared, rocking its branches and lending an even more manic effect to the dance of the mongoose babies (who, to their credit, continued to tumble around as indefatigably as ever).

"Hahahahaha HAH! ... *Silence,* Bird!" boomed Fagus, "I can always evict you, you know! ... Hehehehahahahaha! ... Or, better still, send Chant after you! Hah! ... Pray continue, little animals, this is *most* entertaining! Heh, heh, heh! ... **HUP!**" it shouted, mimicking the mongoose babies' cries.

The ground bucked and heaved as the ear-shattering, terrifying roar of Fagus's full-bellied laughter erupted around the prancing troupe. This proved too much for the performers, who tumbled to the grass in squeaking heaps.

"Ooohhh! Hahahah! hoo, hoo, HOO, HOO, HOH, HOH!" roared the Pathway Tree. "Fear not, little ones! ... Hah! Hah! Hah! ... *hup*! ... A fine dance! Yes! .... And the ambush and rescue scene - Hahahahaha! - Perfect! ... Brilliant timing! ... Inspired! Quite inspired! ... Hohoho! ... *Hup!* A wondrous sound, that. ... Haha! One I shall certainly adopt!

"You have mightily entertained me with your unusual performance, little scraps of animal flesh. Yes, mightily," it added, catching its breath while the mongoose infants gradually regained their paws and staggered around, panting and hiccoughing.

Sardo lowered Chant to the ground because she had at last stopped squirming and trying to claw him. But he maintained a firm hold on her tail with one wiry paw, just in case. You never knew with cats.

"Could you infants repeat that roly-poly tumbling and pouncing act again for me soon, if you please?" asked Fagus, sounding more enthusiastic than it had in millennia. "You could? ... Good! Haha! ... *Excellent.* Ha. Ha. Ha! ... Hehehehe! ... *HUP!* ... Ha! ... *HUP!* ... I should like that. Exceedingly!"

Chant shook herself and tried to lick her throbbing posterior. "Well, I'll be a mangy rat, the tree actually *enjoyed* all that tomfoolery," she muttered to herself, watching Fagus as it went on chuckling to itself, "and here I was, thinking it had taste. Well, that just goes to show. Age is no guarantee of good judgement. *Sheesh.* I had such a fine speech prepared, too... all wasted. Typical."

Her fur had settled by now, and as she calmed down she began to feel sheepish.

"Er... Sardo, you can let go now, thank you. ... *Ahem.* ... And – well – thanks for – your – er – part in the performance," she said, "But *did* you have to hurt my tail so much? ... Oh, well, never mind." She was fully aware of the fact that she faced the tricky business of placating the mongoose parents. Not many animals take kindly to seeing a predator pounce at their infants. So she stretched and groomed herself to gain time while she thought furiously, searching for a way to resolve the situation.

"Of *course y*ou all know I wouldn't really have *hurt* any of your kittens, don't you?" she said at last, taking a deep breath before turning to Lerema, Tesho and their mates and purring out the words in her softest voice, "It was only – you know – a special bit of ... uh... *theatre* ... we – Sardo and I, that is – cooked up together at the very last minute – you know, to add some excitement to the entertainment. Wasn't it, Sardo? ...

"... *Ahem*!" she added into the sizzling silence full of teeth and claws and puffed up fur, "... And, well; I mean to say, I think it worked very well, don't you? It certainly amused Fagus, didn't it? ... Anyway, er, well *done*, everybody!" she concluded, hoping that she'd done enough to placate the mongooses and prevent a pitched battle.

"Oh ... Yes, of course. Absolutely," grinned Sardo, scratching himself and swishing his magnificent tail. "We wanted to spice up the show a bit. Eh, Patches? ... Haha! Not half."

"*Hsss!* Don't call me *Patches,*" snarled the calico cat.

"*Oitochoi!*" snapped Lerema, "If *that* was an act, I'd hate to have you set after me in earnest! ...Yes, you're right, it worked. But listen here, you two *wazimu*, don't think that we won't tear you into shreds if you ever do that sort of thing again, because we will!"

"*Sawa*! We *will!*" agreed Tesho. "Nobody messes with our clan. Not even a fancy cat with fancy Howler Pets. From now on, we don't want you to do anything with our *watoto* unless you ask us first. We expect you to tell us *everything* you're planning, especially if it's something like *that*, unless you want to be turned into mongoose poo. They're *our watoto*, so paws off!"

"That's right. *Our watoto*. No more messing around with them. *Sawa?* ... I nearly lost my skin!" hissed Lerema.

The other mongooses agreed vehemently, nodding and squeaking and grooming themselves fiercely. But, Chant was relieved to see, as they chattered their fur settled and their lips again covered their needle-sharp teeth.

To assure them even more thoroughly of her good intensions, the chastened calico cat now made a point of going around and giving each of the kittens a lick on the top of its head. "Nice babies," she purred, wondering what they tasted like. "Good babies. Great performance. Well done." Kidole wrinkled his little muzzle and tried to nip her tail when she turned away.

When Fagus's chuckles had finally subsided, Chant and the grinning Roloway monkey approached it for the final part of the ceremony. Sardo rested the coconut on the ground while Chant said, "Here is your libation, O great Fagus. What do you want us to do with it?"

"Oh! Yes. Let me taste a bit," replied the giant beech cautiously, "Only a bit, mind. Just to make sure it's potable. And agreeable."

The monkey lifted the coconut and dribbled a few drops of its contents into Fagus' mouth, and the assembled animals held their breaths while the tree ruminated over it. Then it said "Hmm. An interesting flavour. Unusual. Different. Nothing I've ever tasted before, of course. Not wine, certainly; but quite palatable. Something exotic about it pleases with its novelty. Yes, it is acceptable.

"But perhaps you should not waste any of it by sprinkling it around my foot, as is customary. I shall simply drink it, if you please. And..." The mossy eyes in the trunk drifted appreciatively over the assembled mongooses, "I pray you, friends, also partake of it yourselves. I have seldom been so well entertained, and in such a novel fashion. Heh - Heh! And then I shall be delighted to convey you to Aelfeynn Earda, as you request. *Hup*!"

So the huge tree drank down the majority of the fruit cocktail, and then smacked its lips and watched while Sardo made the rounds of the mongoose family and tipped a drop of fluid into the mouth of each of the kittens and their parents. Little Jiggit got some up her nose and developed hiccoughs, which made her bounce like a furry flea.

When it came to her turn, Chant sniffed suspiciously at the coconut and politely declined.

"Very wise. Coconut juice is *yuk*;" said Sardo. "Tamarind, papaya, peanuts, watermelon ... or custard apples, now. *Mmh. There's* something to chatter about. Make your fur shine, they do. Say the word, Patches, and I'll let you have a taste, next time I get some."

"Thanks, anyway. But I'd sooner have my tail squashed under that coconut of yours than eat fruit," replied Chant. "I'm a cat, remember. Er ... and – just between you and me, of course – thanks for saving us all from a real disaster there, Sardo, *and* for not letting on, afterwards. Good of you. I won't forget it. Nor will my tail, for a while;" she added ruefully. "Leto always did say I was too impetuous. He may have had a point."

For the record, Chant was as good as her word and didn't forget Sardo. The Roloway monkey and his family never again went short of their favourite fresh fruit. But I'll be a sticky tree frog if I know just how she managed to organise *that*.

Chapter 22. *The Cupid Mission*

*"What shall I call you? A fountain in a waste,
A well of water in a country dry,
Or anything that's honest and good, an eye
That makes the whole world bright."* cxlv

Paa sat up with a **yip!** and shook her head, flapping her ears.

"I could have sworn somebody spoke to me just now," she said to M'Kuu and Mond, with whom she was lounging in front of Toki's fire. "A kind of … whisper, you know … maybe an insect got into my ear?"

"Maybe. Yes, it must be. *We* didn't say anything, did we, Mond?" said M'Kuu. "Try giving your ears a really good shake, Paa. If there's something crawling and buzzing around in there, it may come out and let us look at it."

The poodle again shook her head, flapping her fluffy ears and blurring the shiny patch on her forehead. After a few moments she stopped and cocked her head.

"No; no change," she reported, "there it goes again. It's so annoying … **yelp*!* …" she lifted each back paw in turn and scratched vigorously, grumbling. *"Sticks and bones…"*

"What kind of noise is this whereof you speak, little Paa?" asked Mond, who had been lying with his huge head on his forepaws, staring into the heart of the fire and thinking of his cubs. He turned to face her. "It may be somebody is seeking to speak with you. This is a magical place, is it not? Who can tell what may be possible, in here?"

The cottage shivered and creaked around them.

"Toki seems to agree with you, Mond," said the hare. "Have a careful listen, Paa. Go on. What can you hear?"

Paa, who had started scratching and shaking her ears again, stopped and concentrated.

"It *tickles*," she complained, but then she went quiet once more.

"It's *Toki!*" she said suddenly and raised her head to gaze wide-eyed at her companions, "Toki's saying something! I didn't know it could talk to me. I mean, I'm just a dog..."

"Well, I'll be a long-eared weasel," said M'Kuu, "Toki only ever talks to Nataka – at least, usually. What does it want?"

"Hang on, it's saying something." Paa listened intently as the cottage around them shivered and creaked. Then she said, "No, seriously, Toki? ... You mean it? ... But ... but why *me*?"

After another spate of creaks and trembles, the dog spoke again. "Well, all right then, if you're sure ... but I can't promise to ... Oh ... all right ... all right, then. ... Yes, I'm going. Yes... yes, I see. Yes; *now*, right away. ... Thanks. You too."

"The little dog converses with the cottage. *C'est vraiment merveilleux;* [cxlvi] " murmured Mond, "She is special, evidently."

"Well?" prompted M'Kuu, "what's up, Paa?"

"Toki said - fluff my tail, it's difficult to believe - it's a message from Fagus. Fagus wants me to go and see it. Right away, it says. It says Nataka's busy with some Howler *matata* right now and can't be reached, so I... Yeah, I don't understand it either. But I've promised. So... Would you like to come?"

M'Kuu immediately bounced up. "I'm in," he said.

The grey wolf shivered. "Ah, no; not I," he said, "Frankly, I admit that I have fear of that… that plant prodigious. If it does not derange you too much, I prefer to remain here." He settled his head onto his forepaws again, adding, "Pray be on your guard, little Paa; that is an organism most strange. *Bonne chance.*"

The dog and hare made short work of ascending the slope to the clearing where Fagus stood smiling, its new leaves shifting and glistening in the sunlight. Sitting in front of the Pathway Tree were two wide-eyed and uncharacteristically quiet mongooses, whom Paa instantly recognised.

"It's Lerema! … and Tesho!" she yapped, bounding to meet them. "How exciting!"

"*Oitochoi! Shikamo*[cxlvii], *Rafiki!*" called Tesho as the brothers tripped over one other in their scramble to join her.

The delighted poodle introduced the hare to the newcomers, who were still recovering from the sickness, dizziness and awe of their journey through the tree's roots. Then she remembered her manners and turned to face Fagus. "Thank you, Your … Your Greatness," she said, "you know, for giving my friends a path, and for calling me."

"You need not thank me, Little One," replied the tree, which appeared uncharacteristically mellow. "No indeed, not at all. These little scraps of animal flesh have entertained me greatly. Hehehe, **hup*!* And thus I have granted them access to my pathways. But they do not know how to find Toki unaided, and I have been unable to summon Aelfeynn Earda, who appears to be otherwise occupied at present. Therefore I called for you instead, **hup*!* "

"Thank you. But ... but... Fagus, of all the animals with Nataka, I really can't work out why you'd pick me," said the poodle, "I mean, for instance M'Kuu, here..."

"Why you, you ask? Tell me, little Paa, have you not yet noticed the mark upon your brow, the one you have borne since you performed your dance with this estimable hare? I have been aware of it since it appeared. Surely you must know what it signifies! Or, shiver my twigs, is it possible that you do *not* recognise it? ... Aha. How singular! I see that you have no idea of its import. Well, well, well. Such self-forgetfulness and modesty are rare indeed. I myself have not encountered it before." And the giant tree beamed down at the little dog.

"But... please forgive me; I know I'm stupid, but ... well, I still don't understand *why*..." stammered Paa.

"Why? ... Haha! ... *Why?* ... Because the mark you bear is a sigil, little Paa, a mark of your particular gifts. And my summons to you relates to difficulties ... yes, difficulties involving a pair of Stults – the creatures you call Howlers, that is – who, I am informed, stand in urgent need of your aid. Howlers, you understand, who require – now *how* did that volatile scrap of cat-flesh express it? ... Ah, yes: rescue. Management. ... And Sorting Out ... Yes. That is it. Sorting Out.

"And it is true, is it not, that you, little Paa, have already sorted out - that is to say, *cured* - an ailing Howler of his malady? A Howler, I might add, whom you had every reason to abhor; not so? ... And yet you healed him? ... Yes. Yes, you did! Which explains the sigil. Haha! *hup*!

"And that is not all. With that sigil you have gained unto yourself a portentous name and role, *portentous*. Yes; yes, indeed. For I now name you *Elpidea* [cxlviii]: *She Who*

Understands And Heals. It is a fine title, one that has for too long lacked a worthy bearer. Hahaha! **hup*!*"

The Pathway Tree paused, ruffled its leaves and stretched its upper branches in the sunlight. Paa stood, mouth and eyes wide, and struggled to digest what she had just heard. But Fagus wasn't done yet.

"Know also, Paa Elpidea, that I foresee..." it went on, but then hesitated and seemed to reconsider, because it added hastily, "But ... er, perhaps further disclosure should await a more appropriate moment. We must not overwhelm you, must we? I can see that you are already bewildered. So it would be unwise to say more at present. **Hup*!* ... Haha! ... Yes. Let what I have said suffice for now.

"But this I *will* add: henceforth, let all those you meet accord you the honour to which the sigil on your brow entitles you, Paa Elpidea. It is decreed. **Hup*!*"

The poodle plumped down onto her haunches. Every encounter with the strange giant vegetable before her left her feeling embarrassed, out of her depth and fearful of failing in whatever vague yet massive expectation Fagus always appeared to have of her.

Pluck my fur, I wish it would remember that I'm only a dog!... There must be some mistake. What in the name of a buried bone does it think I can possibly achieve? ... I'm not magical. I'm not Nataka... I'll mess up. Oh, I wish...

But, "Trust yourself, Elpidea!" said Fagus. "You will *not* fail. Being a dog is no drawback, I assure you. A good dog is a most rare creature, combining as it does both instinct *and* heart, something that is vanishingly rare among most species of the flesh-kind. And where it is leavened by modesty and self-forgetfulness, that particular combination may yield potent magics. As we have already witnessed;

have we not? Indeed we have. *Hup*! ... Haha! But rarely. Rarely!"

With this confusing declaration the great tree clearly felt that it had said enough. It fell silent, blinked contentedly in the sunlight and smiled down on the animals at its foot.

Paa gulped. She turned to face the two mongooses, who stared back at her, tongue-tied.

"*Oitochoi!*" whispered Lerema at last, "I should have warned you. I think the tree can see what's going on in your head. It's properly spooky. So *chunga, Rafiki!*"

"You *think?*" Fagus' sudden laughter made them all jump. "Hahahaha! Yes, little mortal, you think correctly! *HUP*! Haha!"

"I ... Well, I really don't know what to say," said Paa at last, her eyes bright with anxiety. "I just – just really hope that ... that Fagus hasn't got the – the wrong dog, you know? ... I mean... well, I suppose ... no, of course I'll do my best to help, if I can.

"So ... um..." she hesitated for a moment, then went on. "Do you both feel like telling me what it's about? ... Only if you want to, of course ... and... er – if you tell me, perhaps, we could find a way to solve it, what d'you think?"

M'Kuu had been silent, listening intently to everything that was said. Now he hopped forward. "I think we should forget our uncertainty and trust the tree," he said. "It's a lot wiser than we are, and I can believe that Paa has powers and skills she herself doesn't know yet. I should know; I've danced with her, and the Dance never lies. Yes, I'd say she's really very unusual. So why don't you two tell her all about the problem? And then ... well, then we can have a proper think about it. What d'you say?"

His words were timely. Paa and the mongooses agreed to go back to the cottage for a small *indaba* about their difficulties with anyone else that cared to join in, to see what ideas might arise.

And, hoped Paa after they'd thanked the Pathway Tree and set off down the sloping path towards Toki, *with any luck Nataka will be back, so I can hand all this over to her. She'll definitely know what to do. Yes. She can take over and I'll be able to relax again. Elpidea* - me? ... *I doubt it!*

***

Toki welcomed Paa, M'Kuu and the mongooses with a jiggle and creak, and Mond surged up, his tail wagging madly as he recognised the twins that had done so much to help him escape. At that moment Brid the squirrel came bounding through the window, and for a while a joyous cacophony ensued as the visitors explained how they'd managed to win a passage from the Pathway Tree, a tale that had everybody rolling on the floor. Even Dora reeled herself in through the window (she'd been tidying her food store under the outside eaves) to discover the cause of all the hilarity.

Then, just as the twins were setting about explaining their concerns regarding their Howler Pet and her unhappy attachment, Pex came loping in at the door and Glose soared through the window looking satisfied and mellow after a good feed. So the whole business of introductions and explanations began all over again.

Glose found it very difficult to swallow the news that the Pathway Tree had summoned Paa and honoured her (*forsooth!*), not to mention that Toki had also spoken to her on its behalf. But the raven could not deny that all these things really had happened, because everybody concerned was quite adamant about what they had seen and heard. So he perched on his favourite chair-back, preened the soft feathers under his wings, peered furtively at the poodle from under his pinions, and tried to decide how he should comport himself towards her.

It was a sticky question. He was well aware that he'd been less than kind to the dog recently, arguing with her, ordering her about, calling her names and ridiculing her suggestions and behaviour; all (as Fyrd had accurately divined) because he resented the attention she'd been receiving - although he would never admit that to himself, of course. But ... *but* ...

If she *really* was something more than just a thoroughly daft, annoying, smelly, stuttering four-paws, only there in the first place because Nataka had felt sorry for her; if she *really* was something much more important than a fur-brained Nobody who got in your way, messed up your domain, slavered you with saliva when you least expected it, stole your thunder when you were trying to be particularly impressive, and was constantly and irritatingly cheerful and affectionate and friendly and accommodating (which all got *right* up his beak, for some reason) ...

To sum up: *if* she was so important, indeed, that the Pathway Tree itself had given her a new name ... and if, as M'Kuu and Pex insisted, she had met her former owner and treated him with such perfect forgiveness that, according to Toki and Fagus, she had actually *cured* him...

Claws and pinions! ... If indeed the daft, dishevelled dog had achieved all those things, then surely he, Glose, would be most unwise to continue treating her badly, regardless of how much he might resent her, wouldn't he? ... After all, who knew? If she was Special, like so many of the magical creatures he had already met, she might also be capable of sudden outbursts of arbitrary anger and revenge, mightn't she? ... Special people could be insanely unpredictable. Look at Nataka.

Besides, the raven said to himself, he could see for himself that she did have a strange, shiny mark on her forehead, the mark that Fagus had called a sigil. From his reading Glose fully appreciated the vast significance of a sigil. Besides, with the mark had come a new name, an incredibly important name that carried with it potent implications regarding her latent powers.

So thinking, Glose clicked his beak and scratched his glistening black head-feathers with one claw while he cast his mind back over all his interactions with Paa from the time of her sudden appearance inside the cottage. And now it came back to him that he *had* seen (although at the time he had discounted it as an illusion) a strange, horn-like shaft of light emerging from Paa's head – from the precise spot where the sigil now shone – when she had participated in the hare's Moon Dance. That memory could not be denied.

But w*hy*, Glose asked himself, indignantly ruffling his feathers, *why* then, in the name of all that was sane and appropriate, couldn't that blasted little – whatever she was, animal or super-animal – *behave* more like Somebody Special? It offended his sense of propriety to see the dog behave just as naturally as ever, instead of assuming more self-consciously heraldic or heroic poses, or looking down her snout at everybody and talking through it more, for example; in other words, instead of behaving more royally and with a greater air of entitlement than she was doing (and as *he* certainly would, were such a great honour conferred on him). Oh, *what* would Glose not have given to receive such an honour himself!

The frustrated, fretting bird shuffled from claw to claw on his perch and watched Paa roll on the carpet, giggling, wriggling and scratching herself just as if nothing had changed. Ah, well, clearly it would be necessary to play it safe and propitiate this strange little creature for now. Just in case. Yes. He would most likely benefit in the long run from grovelling a bit to start with. It stuck in his craw to do so, of course; but he must accept that Paa was somebody an ambitious raven should be propitiating and making up to, as opposed to alienating.

And if all this talk of sigils and special powers and whatnot should turn out to be a lot of moonshine and empty eggshells (after all, Fagus might be getting senile; Infinity knew the plant was old enough), Glose would derive great pleasure from tormenting the poodle about it afterwards. Yes. That *would* be fun. But for now...

He cleared his throat, clacked his beak and hopped down to the floor, landing a paw's length from the poodle's snuffling nose and lolling tongue.

"Er ... *hem,*" he cawed, side-hopping up to her, "may I ... may I offer my - **Arkh** ... congratulations, Paa? - Or would you prefer me to use your new title when addressing you, Honoured Elpidea?" He sketched a spread-winged obeisance, dipping his beak.

"Of course - **cough** - I've always ... believed... that you were ... *Special,* you know;" he continued, studiously ignoring the astonishment in Paa's eyes. "Which is why it has been such a ... a ... pleasure and privilege to work with you ... on the panacea, you know ... and ..."

The raven's words were interrupted by a peal of laughter. Fyrd's sleek, bullet-shaped head appeared in the doorway.

"Hahahahaha!" whistled the otter, somersaulting into the room, "Glose sucking up, is he? ... Paa more to your taste than a fat trout dinner now, Bird? ... Good one! And of course this sudden friendliness has nothing to do with what

I've just heard from Axl - you know, about Fagus's words - eh? ... Excellent!"

Fyrd uncurled sinuously, displayed his canines in a broad grin, cuffed the embarrassed raven lightly over the head with one webbed forepaw, and snatched a few walnuts from the table.

"Can't stop!" he announced, twirling a walnut on one claw, "Just thought I'd drop in to see how you all are, and explain why I haven't been around much since putting that stuff in the water for Nataka. Worked well, that; didn't it? Instantly forgetful Howlers all over the place. Grand, that was.

"But now, well. *You* know this season. I have to be about my business. The trout jumping, our pups all over the place and more trouble to mind than a burrow-full of demented water voles, and Nibblenose[cxlix] threatening to abandon the lot of us and swim away downstream if I stray too far or too long.

"Oh, and you'd best not expect to see Wurfl, either. He's up to that ugly snout of his in work, shoring up his lodge like an animal demented; says his tail and teeth warn him there's a storm headed our way in a few Suns' time. So he's all of a fury to make sure his dam stands up to it. He positively snarled at me just now, when I asked him to come with me. 'No time, no time!' What a boring rodent, so predictable during this season. He's got all his kittens and their flat-tailed lumberjack of a mother hard at it, felling young birch in the copse near the old dam. 'Keep at it! Keep at it! All teeth to the timber!' ... You know how he gets around now. You ask me, he's just showing off the young 'uns' new gnawing skills. Big deal. Our pups may not be much good at chewing wood – **yuk*!* – but then, his kits are rubbish at fishing. *Wheee!* To each his own, eh? ... Hahaha, *whoop!*"

Fyrd stayed just long enough to hear the latest news, quiz Paa on her new status, and make friends with the mongooses, who fascinated him. "You have the look of natural swimmers to me," he commented, eyeing Lerema and Tesho's slim, muscular physiques, "if you'd like to try, I can take you upriver to some fine fishing nooks one Suntime and show you how. Interested?"

"*Oitochoi!*" said Tesho, looking alarmed, "We can't swim in anything wetter than sand!"

"*Kweli,*" agreed his brother, "But if you need diggers to help you with a burrow, our paws are the best you'll get. *We* swim in sand. Just as you said, Fyrd, to each his own."

An instant later the otter had tossed the walnuts into the air with a last whistling chuckle of sheer exuberance and was darting back out of the door. "Can't stop! Nibblenose will have my tail off if I stay away too long!" he called over his glossy back as he whistled down the grassy slope. "I've still got a whole roiling of fish to catch. ... Remember, you lot, make sure somebody slips down occasionally to tell me how everything's going; all right? ... Well done, that dog, I like your new mark ... So long, Rattlebeak ... *Wheee!*"

And he was gone again, galloping across the stone river before tummy-tobogganing down the turf slope on the other side. He left everybody breathless, as if a whirlwind had rushed through the cottage.

As the noise of the otter's departure faded, a tiny rumpus of squeaks, snuffles and scuffles sounded outside, and the hedgehog's snout appeared in the doorway.

"So *there* you are at last, Miba!" chirruped Brid, hopping to the door to greet his friend. "I wondered where you'd got to! ... So much news..."

He got no further.

Line astern behind Miba, three tiny hedge-hoglets hove into view. Their diminutive bodies were covered in minute rubbery bristles, and the smallest of the hoglets was no larger than one of the walnuts Fyrd had abandoned on the floor. It was keeping up with its larger siblings by clamping its muzzle onto the tail of its slightly more substantial brother and half-sliding, half-trotting along at the tail-end of the procession.

"Miba ... are those ... *babies*?" breathed the squirrel, "I mean ... *your* babies?"

"Who else's?" responded the hedgehog, turning back to shepherd them over Toki's threshold, "Tytus the Baron's, maybe?"

The piglets stumbled over the doorsill and instantly curled into quivering balls of bristle on the floor. They might easily have been mistaken for chestnut burrs.

"There, there, there now, Tich; Tick; Seed," crooned Miba, nudging them with her nose, "uncurl, already. Don't be afraid. Remember what I told you, nobody here's going to hurt you. Easy, now."

"But... but... but... you never told me you were ... you know ... *female*," stuttered Brid, "I didn't even know you were... were... making babies..."

"You never asked," chuckled the hedgehog. "Anyway, I'd have thought it was obvious. I *was* getting fat. That wasn't all wind, you know." She raised her snout and looked him over. "What does it matter, anyway? You going to get all weird on me now, is that it? ... Want to stop being friends, just because I'm a mum? ... Sheesh. *You*'ve got kids, too. Have I ever complained?"

"No ... no, 'course not ... 'Course we're still friends ..." Brid combed his tail, eyes wide, "But ... what if they don't like me?"

"Oh, they'll love you, never fear," said the hedgehog, "Look."

The hedge-piglet called Seed had uncurled and made a beeline for the warmth and softness of Brid's underbelly. She was burrowing into his fur and uttering little questing noises. Her brothers followed her.

"*Ouch!* – **Eek*!* ... That tickles ... what're they doing? What do they *want?*" yelped the squirrel, rearing onto his hind paws and trying to back away.

"Relax, they're only hungry," laughed Miba, "Fat lot they'll get from you, though. Eh?" She lay down on the cottage floor next to the wolf, exposed her tummy and raised her voice. "Oy, you dozy lot! Over here ... come on, then!"

The infants extricated themselves from Brid's fur, turned and trundled towards their mother's voice. Undisturbed by the laughter and comments of the animals that clustered around to watch them, they latched on and settled down to feed.

"So *that's* how they do it," muttered Glose, shaking his feathers and turning away. "Messy lot, mammals. Why can't they just stuff grubs and worms down their fledglings' throats, like normal folk? Beats me."

"This sight brings to me even greater nostalgia for my family," said Mond, lowering his head to sniff at the infants. "I must find a way to return to my home."

"*Ach*, just go home, already. *Do* it, you great soft dog," Miba cuffed Mond's snout and bared her tiny fangs in a friendly grin. "You know? ... Whatever it takes, mate. Your piglets need you."

As usual, nobody noticed Tytus the Baron's silent arrival and landing on the windowsill until he spread his wings and hooted. Glose jumped and cursed.

"*Salvete!* [cl]... I bring a message for Paa from Nataka," he announced. "Actually, strictly speaking it's *four* messages. Feel free to call me Hermes[cli] if you wish. They are: *good idea; get on with it; follow your feeling;* and *trust yourself.* She said you'd understand.

"I flew over to that horrible stone nest-mountain to check what was happening, and found her watching an *indaba* - actually more of a *matata* - between a clutch of Howlers," he added by way of explanation. "*You'd* disappeared, Glose. Hungry, were you? ... I thought so."

"**Arkh*!* I suppose *you* never get hungry?" complained the raven, "I suppose I should be prepared to starve just because her *lah-di-dah*-ship might want to send messages, eh? I'm not her ..."

"Crimp my feathers, they're a noisy lot, though; almost as noisy as a raven," interrupted the Baron, not in the least discomposed. "The ones I found with Nataka were so busy quarrelling that I'm willing to wager all my pinions they wouldn't even have noticed me if I'd been visible. Howlers; **tsk*.* No idea of decorum. I wonder why she's taken up with them. And, I might add, from the way her eyes looked, she seemed to be getting far too involved for my liking. We all know how she gets when she spends too much time with those Howlers; don't we, Toki?"

The owl paused and ruffled his snowy feathers. A little groan from Toki suggested that the cottage agreed with him.

"Well, anyway. All that apart, Paa, has the message been received and understood, then?" added Tytus, turning his round eyes to face the poodle. "Yes? ... Good. Oh, and I should relax, if I were you. If our wise old friend trusts you to do something for her, I'm sure you have nothing to worry about."

The owl blinked, spread his downy pinions and turned a bright amber gaze onto the sky outside the window. "Beautiful Sunhigh, perfect for a nap. *Valete, omnes!* [clii]"

And the square of light where he had perched was empty again.

"Say what you like; that bird's nothing short of spooky," grouched Glose, hopping back onto his favourite perch, "you'll never convince me his behaviour's normal. And pretentious, too. *Hermes,* indeed."

Ah, bones and whiskers, now I'm for it.

Paa fought the urge to run and hide. She shook herself, drew a deep breath and nudged the mongoose twins, who had forgotten all about their mission in their fascinated contemplation of the hedgehog family.

"Well, Lerema and Tesho," she said, "It seems that Nataka really does want me to do this ... whatever it is. Would you like to tell me all about it? I only hope I can help. Anyway, I'll do my best."

***

Anthony rose from behind his desk with a broad smile on his face and extended a hand to Bryony, who jumped up and grasped it.

"I'm delighted that you've accepted my offer, Bry," he said. "I'm sure we'll work excellently together, and I'm very excited. Particularly in view of the fact that Geoff's decided to walk out on us today. I'd have been in a bit of a pickle if you'd turned down my offer, to be honest."

"Thanks, Tony," Behind the freckles, Bryony's face was pink. "I'll try to live up to your faith in me. Still can't get over Geoff just up and leaving like that, though."

"Yeah; well," sighed Tony, "It's been on the cards for some time now, I reckon. He hasn't been too happy with us, has he? And after that last Wardens' meeting, well..."

They both burst out laughing at the memory of the great coffee fiasco, and then shared a rueful look.

"So... he'd clearly been brooding on the riot act I read him that day," Tony went on, "It *was* firm, I'm afraid. So today he storms into my office, slaps down a letter of resignation and says he's leaving right away. I reckon it's best just to let him go. Of course I'll give him his pay in lieu of notice; poor fellow'll need it. And I hope he finally finds something he really enjoys doing."

"Ah, poor blighter," said Bryony. "It *was* hilarious, though. Still can't work out why he got his knickers into such a twist, can you? That was some meeting, all right. ... And Marcie, bless her..." They both laughed again.

"I'll show you her letter of complaint about Geoff," said Tony, sobering up. "It's quite a piece of work. Hardly surprising, really, after that soaking he gave her. I managed to calm her down and even got him to apologise - very ungraciously, of course! - But I'll be grateful if you keep an eye on her, make sure she doesn't decide to leave too. She's an excellent warden and I'd hate to lose her."

"Righto, Tone; no problem," said Bryony, "I'll do that."

"Great, thanks. And while I'm on the topic of staffing, I've got an idea. What d'you think about promoting Jim Bell to Warden of Mammals - I mean, combining your and Geoff's vacant positions under him? Could he cope with that, in your opinion?"

"Oh! ... Oh, blimey, *yes*. He'd do a great job!" exclaimed Bryony, then stopped and flushed. "But... but would you mind making the offer without me around? ... Uh, I mean ... coming into it? ... Er ..." she faltered.

"Don't worry, Bry," Tony's expression was understanding. "It's difficult, isn't it, when one's feelings are involved? ... Are you worried that he'd take it amiss if he thought you'd had anything to do with the offer?"

Bryony nodded, grateful that she didn't have to explain. If Jim were to hear that she'd been asked for her opinion about the promotion he might misinterpret her motives, and who knew how he'd react then? She didn't want him to feel embarrassed or beholden to her, particularly after that painful little scene outside the mongoose enclosure. Since then, neither of them had been comfortable in each other's company. The easy familiarity and banter of their earlier relationship had disappeared, and now they could hardly meet each other's eyes when their paths crossed.

"Yeah, well." Bryony flushed even more. "Sorry about that."

"Nothing to apologise for, lass;" said Tony. "Happens to us all, sooner or later. Unless we're malfunctioning in some way, of course. Tell you what, you go out there and nab the idiot. We men can be quite blind to what's right in front of us unless our noses are rubbed in it. Best thing that could happen to him, somebody like you."

A little later, Bryony emerged from Anthony's office and slowly walked away, kicking a pebble down the gravel path that led to the Small Animals section of the zoo.

It had been both an embarrassment and a relief to discover that everybody seemed to be aware of the way she felt about Jim Bell, and to find in Tony and his wife Fran (who had come in with tea and biscuits, and stayed to join the conversation) an empathetic and encouraging audience for her sorrows. Now, if only she hadn't totally messed up her chances with Jim…

She cursed herself for a fool. She should have shut up, kept it light when he'd wittered on about that (blasted) woman at the hospital, told him that he was absolutely right to be pessimistic because no self-respecting female could possibly look at him twice, and so on. He clearly had all the self-esteem of a bottom feeder in a pool of sludge, so she shouldn't have been surprised that he'd reacted like a poked rattlesnake when she challenged him to think more highly of himself. Fat lot of good her attempts to help him had done. She should have laughed at him, mocked him and … made him feel even worse. *Damn.*

I hate hormones! she thought. *Blasted things. They just mess with our heads. Maybe I should have my ovaries removed. Make life a lot easier… Or maybe I should just hook up with women from now on. They're less hung up on this kind of thing; much more likely to think straight. But … no, impossible. I just don't butter my bread on that side. Face it, Bry. In spite of Fran and Tony's encouraging words, I reckon I'm doomed to remain heterosexual – and lonely – forever.*

A small, furry grey body flashed past Bryony from behind, disrupting her thoughts. It pelted down the pathway ahead of her with its brindled grey and black tail erect. It took her a couple of seconds of sheer surprise to register that it was a mongoose.

A mongoose, outside its compound … A *mongoose*!

"Oy! You! ... Stop!" she yelled, breaking into a run after the fleeing animal.

Twit! As if calling will make the little beggar stop … Gosh, I mustn't lose him! Hot dog, but the little villain can run…

The brindled tail was now some 20 yards in front of her, its owner loping along and glancing back occasionally, for all the world as if it wanted to lead her somewhere. Suddenly it dodged off the path, swerved and disappeared around a tall, dense clump of ornamental pampas grass that had not yet begun to sprout its first feathery flower heads. Bryony sprang after it, panting –

("Wait'll I lay my hands on you, you little …!" she gasped, starting to laugh despite herself. "I'll flippin' well skin you alive; see if I don't!")

- And was just in time to catch sight of the tail whisking around the clump of pampas as a *second* mongoose came pelting round the plant in the opposite direction, heading straight towards her. With a little squeak it screeched to a halt just out of reach, and reared up onto its hind legs. Bryony could have sworn that the pointed face, quivering nose and bright eyes bore a look more of mischief than of fear.

She lunged forwards and made a grab for it, but it pirouetted on its hind legs like an ice-skater and bounded away, back in the direction it had come.

"*Damn!*" she exclaimed, cast caution to the winds and launched herself forward in a tackle-dive with both arms outstretched. "*OOF!*" The dive knocked most of the wind out of her, but even so she flailed her hands round the base of the pampas, hoping to capture some part – *any* part – of the escapee. Then she heaved herself up onto her hands and knees, and crawled round the grass more carefully, trying not to wheeze too loudly…

… And stopped dead with her nose just a few inches from the muzzle of a beautiful, cream-coloured poodle that was standing directly before her.

In her jaws the dog had firm hold of the tail of the mongoose Bryony had just tried to catch. The animal's soft, golden-brown eyes gazed beatifically at her, and her luxurious tail and rump were wind-milling so energetically that she could barely stay on her paws without toppling over. Bryony caught sight of a patch of silver paint some idiot had splashed onto the animal's forehead, but otherwise she appeared to be in fine condition.

But where had she come from?

Before Bryony could move or utter a sound, two long, khaki-clad legs appeared from behind the pampas and Jim Bell strode up, looking flushed and excited. In his arms he was holding the mongoose she had been chasing to begin with. He stopped and took in the strange tableau of Bryony on all fours in front of the dog. Then he broke into excited speech.

"Did you *see* that?" he exclaimed, "I mean, this dog – I swear she's only caught *this* mongoose and given it to me. Honest! Crazy, eh? … It came belting past me just now –

over *there* – near their compound, you know? … So of course I gave chase … and … well … it streaked over here, and I was chasing it round this – this pampas, you know? … And then – listen to this; it's unbelievable – *then,* this dog just … well, she just turned up, you know? … Scooped up the mongoose in her mouth and carted it over to me. Just like that! I mean it, she literally handed it over to me!

"And then off she dashes again, in this direction … to *here,* I mean, just now … so, naturally I followed her, and here *you* are. *And* it looks like she's caught another one. How crazy is that? … I mean, I've *never* …

"Oh, crikey, look, *look* … She's only doing it again!"

Sure enough, the cream-coloured poodle had planted one paw on the tail of the mongoose, pinning it to the ground, then deftly transferred her jaws to pick up the little animal by the scruff of its neck. As the nonplussed keepers watched, she approached Bryony with her quarry dangling quiescently from her jaws. Bryony scrambled up to a kneeling position in time to receive the little animal into her hands, and examined it. It was quite unscathed.

"Unbelievable," breathed Bryony, staring wide-eyed from the mongoose to the dog, "un-be-bloody-*lievable*! I only chased that one – the one you're holding, Jim – down the path just now. The cheeky little rat came belting up and overtook me from behind, going hell for leather in this direction. I ran after it as fast as I could, of course, but I just couldn't keep up. I swear I thought I'd lost him when he dodged round this pampas. Great that *you* got him, though; well done!"

"But I'm *telling* you, it wasn't me at all. This dog did it all … I couldn't believe my eyes," exclaimed Jim. "She some kind of trained rescue dog, d'you think? … I mean…"

"Ah, *look* at them, Jim!" interrupted Bryony, who was so relieved by the capture that she was only half-listening, "Just look at the little scoundrels. You've no idea. They've been leading me a right old dance for ages, escaping from their compound all the time. I could put them into a pie, I swear. Mongoose pie. And what's even more annoying, I *still* haven't figured out how they're doing it.

"But blow me down, now they're not even trying to get away, are they? ... What's that all about?"

She lifted the mongoose lying quiescently in her hands and brought its snout level with her eyes.

"What're you little horrors up to, then?" She scolded lovingly, scratching its ear. The sharp-faced animal half-closed its eyes and chirrupped. "And where are all the rest of your family, for pity's sake? How *are* you all doing it, huh? Tell me, you furry Pimpernel, what's with all this *Stalag Nine* shenanigans, anyway? "

"Clever little beasts, mongooses," observed Jim, who seemed to have forgotten all about being awkward. It's impossible to be inhibited around somebody for whom you've been chasing escaped animals. He turned his captive over onto its back and scratched its belly. It crooned, tucked up its hind-legs and began to suck the tip of its own tail.

Both wardens burst out laughing.

"You're a little beauty, aren't you?" said Jim to the animal in his arms, "quite the charmer, even though you're a crook. Oh yes, you are. You *know* you are. Running rings round us like that. Yeah, I could easily ... *Hey!* ...What the...?"

All this time the cream-coloured animal-capturing dog had been sitting and watching their faces with eyes that looked disconcertingly intelligent. But she had suddenly uttered a muffled *wuff!*, taken hold of one leg of Jim's trousers with her teeth, and begun to tug him towards Bryony, who lurched to her feet, still clutching her prize.

"What's she doing?" demanded Jim, "... *Oy*, dog! Mind you don't tear my trousers. *I* don't need to be captured, you know. I'm not an escapee..."

Paa (tugging away): *Little do you know. Curl my whiskers, but these Howlers are slow on the uptake. Good work, by the way, Friends.*

Lerema and Tesho (blinking innocently up at their captors): Sawa, Rafiki. *Keep it up.*

"...Oh, right, I get it. You want the two animals to be together, is that it?" hazarded Jim, and obliged the dog by shuffling forwards. "Just don't tear my trousers, all right? They're nearly new."

The poodle now turned to Bryony, reared up, and licked her hand.

"Oh! Did you see that?" said the young woman, staring down at the dog's head, "I thought ... er ... no, never mind; must have been a trick of the light or something..."

She bent down and reached out her free hand to stroke the soft, dense curls on the dog's brow, gazing down at the mark on her forehead. "What d'you make of this, Jim? ... Look, this mark here. Is that paint, d'you think?"

Jim bent down to inspect the dog's head.

"Hm. Doesn't look like paint to me," he mused. "...But I don't know what else it can be. I mean, I've never heard of such markings happening naturally; have you? ... I reckon it's unlikely to be some kind of mutation. ... Um. Let's have a closer look. … Pretty much pure silver, isn't it? I've never come across that before … Hang on; hold still, doggie, let's see if this – whatever it is – goes all the way down to your skin..."

He put out his hand to part the glistening curls on the animal's forehead, and his fingers accidentally encountered Bryony's hand.

Both the keepers gasped and straightened back upright, their eyes snapping wide.

For an instant the strange, shiny patch on the dog's head had sparkled like a tiny rainbow, and at the same moment an exhilarating, terrifying, electrical sensation had coursed through them both, a feeling of delight and revelation so intense as to be practically unbearable.

Their eyes locked. Suddenly it felt impossible to keep their hearts from bounding in their chests, to breathe normally, or to look away from one other. Had the two little hostages in their arms wanted to get away then, they could easily have done so. They had been entirely forgotten in the maelstrom of emotions that coursed through their captors. But for some inexplicable reason neither mongoose moved a muscle.

Paa: *Well? … Caught on yet? … Or, dock my whiskers and claws, do I have to do all the work here? … Oh, all right, then.*

Lerema: *Keep it up,* Rafiki. *They're Howlers, you know. Slow as frostbitten worms.*

Tesho: Kweli. *Not like us Wanyama at all. But they'll get there, sooner or later.*

The poodle *wooffed* again. She rose onto her hind paws and her rose-coloured tongue flicked out of her mouth to lick both the keepers' hands, jolting them again with what felt like an electrical charge.

Then it seemed to Jim and Bryony that she lost patience, because she let fly a series of short, sharp barks before seizing the grubby fingers of Bryony's free hand in her jaws and tugging them over till they encountered Jim's large, work-hardened hand.

Paa: *Look, you dumb Howlers, I can't make it any clearer. Over to you. Get to it...*

Speechless, the two young people gazed down into the dog's eyes, which shone back up into their own, bright as pools of molten gold. Then they raised their faces to gaze at one other. There was a long pause.

Paa: *C'mon, c'mon,* c'mon! *Time's a-wasting! ... Honestly, how do the crazy creatures ever actually make puppies, at this rate?*

"Bry ..." breathed Jim through a dry throat, noticing for the first time the subtle colorations in her eyes, and wondering why he had never seen just how winsome and lovable were her freckles and snub nose and wide mouth.

"Bry... I ... I've been..."

"Ssshhh," interrupted Bryony. "I know."

Paa: *Whoa... Curl my whiskers; I do believe the female Howler's got it at last.*

Tesho: *You* did *it!*

Lerema: *It's working, it's working! Well done,* Rafiki!

Paa: *Thanks, lads. Took some doing. You were great.*

Couldn't have done it without you.

Lerema: *Brilliant plan,* Rafiki!

Tesho: *Excellent chase. And -* Oitochoi! - *Just look at the two* wazimu Howlers *now!*

Lerema: *Hooray!*

Paa: *At last. *Phew*, that's a relief. Just stick with them a while longer, lads. All right? Make sure they're properly hooked up. ... Well, I'll be getting home. Goodbye, then; be safe, see you soon...*

Tesho: Kwaheri! [cliii]

Lerema: *Safe journey,* Rafiki!

Paa (quietly): *Suck a dry bone, I've no idea why it worked. Sheer luck, I expect.*

Later, after the two wardens had safely locked the strays back into the mongoose compound (which those reprobates immediately abandoned to rejoin their mates and kittens); after they had found their way to the shade of a massive spreading beech in a particularly secluded part of the woodland fringing the zoo; after they had caressed and whispered and chuckled and wondered, exploring the new world they were creating between them...

As they lay in one another's arms and contemplated the dappled sunlight slanting down through the fresh green leaves above them, it occurred to the two young people to wonder what had become of that extraordinary poodle. She seemed to have vanished into thin air. One moment she'd been there; the next...

"Where did she go?" wondered Jim, "If she's a stray I'll take her like a shot, and make *such* a fuss of her for the rest of her life. She brought us together, didn't she? That was a clever dog. Almost uncanny."

"I think," said Bryony, fiddling with one of Jim's ears, "*I* think we may never see her again. I *think* - and don't laugh, promise? All this business is testing my scepticism to the full as it is - that dog may have been an angel, our guardian angel. Don't you?"

"An angel? ... Looked substantial enough to me," Jim grabbed Bryony's hand and kissed it. "Do angels need to be fed and groomed and walked? *Mmh.* I could happily live with that kind of angel."

("Welcome back to my Pathways, Paa Elpidea, Healer of Sorrows," sang Fagus to the mote of silver and gold whisking homeward through its labyrinth. "Welcome back indeed!")

Chapter 23. Explosion

"Thou little valiant, great in villainy!
Thou ever strong upon the stronger side!" [cliv]

"Argh, I'm bushed," complained the Wingco. "We're never going to resolve this argument, no matter how long it goes on."

He sighed and turned to his grandson's stepfather. "Roger, look. You must agree that I've said everything I can. And so have you. Yes? We've been through all our arguments over and over again. In fact we've repeated ourselves so often I'm sick of it. This has all just degenerated into a completely useless and circular wrangling circus. And to be honest, the longer we go on bickering at one another, the clearer it is to me that you and I will *never* agree on the fundamentals. So that's it. There just isn't any point in going on with it. So I'm calling a halt.

"Just let me emphasise one last time before I go that nothing you say will alter my decision. It's final, all right? You'll simply *have* to accept that your plan to use my life insurance for your own private speculations won't wash. I'm not allowing it. I'm going to make sure right away that when I die, Ter alone will get the benefit of my life insurance, with or without the bonus. And I'll also make darned sure there's a strong, unbiased board of trustees in place to secure it for him, if he's still under-age when that happens.

"And as for you, Maddie, my dear, I'm sorry, but this time I won't involve you at all, because you're simply too soft-hearted. Aren't you? ... I can't risk you having to deal with any kind of tactic that Roger - or anybody else, for that matter - may deploy to get their hands on the money once I'm dead. Which will continue to be a risk if I keep you as either a trustee or a beneficiary of the insurance payout on Ter's behalf. No hard feelings though, Dearest. You do understand, don't you?"

"Of course I do, Wingco, dear;" the old man's daughter-in-law tucked her hand under his arm and squeezed. "Actually, I'm relieved. I'd much rather have nothing to do with that insurance at all. You're taking a weight off my mind. Thank you."

Roger uttered a noise between a snort, a snarl and a groan.

"You don't know what you're doing!" He snapped. "That money's *important*! ... Look, unless I can come up with the funds to cover my ... my..."

"Your *debts*?" the Wingco pounced. "Spit it out. You're already in debt on what you thought you could get out of Ter's legacy. Am I right?"

"Yes, yes, *yes*. All right! ... So I'm in debt, OK?" Roger's face was puce. "But how was I to know you'd cut up so rough? ... I was just going to ... to *borrow* ... the money to make more. I mean, no big deal, right? ... But here's the thing. I have to pay it back or there'll be trouble. Look..."

He leaned forward again and stared into the Wingco's eyes with all the urgency he could muster. "You don't know these people. The ones I'm in debt to, I mean. They're not – well, they're not pukka bankers, if you get my drift. They're... uhh... well – they won't take no for an answer, and they don't negotiate, if you get my meaning. And... let's put it this way: if they don't get their money, there's no knowing what they'll... I mean, I won't be able to guarantee the safety..."

He faltered at the expression on the old man's face.

"Are you telling me now that you've actually endangered yourself – and the rest of us - with all this business? Is *that* what you're saying?" The Wingco's voice was icy. "Well, you'll just have to find a way to honour your debt when it comes due *without* using Ter's money, that's all. Good grief, d'you really think I'd give in to this kind of blackmail?

"Look, Roger, by now you really must realise that it would be entirely unacceptable to use the insurance money for any other purpose than to secure the future of my grandson, even if that other purpose were less morally repulsive than the one you have in mind. I hope you do! ... Please tell me you understand *that*, at least. If you do, I can still respect you a bit. ... You *do* get that, don't you?"

The old man paused and examined the SF's face carefully, hoping to catch even the slightest sign of remorse or comprehension in it. But all he saw were tightly set lips and eyes dark with frustration, anger, resentment, and just a hint of fear. The man appeared entirely incapable of making the emotional leap to empathy, or to say or do anything more than sit glaring at the Wingco and Maddie with his arms and legs tightly crossed and his lips gradually curling away from his teeth in a snarl that reminded the Wingco of a hyena at bay.

The Wingco sighed again, and stretched his arms and legs. "Oh, Lord. Well. That's that, then. I can't change a mind set in stone," he said. "A thousand pities, but there it is.

"Well, I'm done. I'm going home. This discussion is over."

He turned to his daughter-in-law and grandchild, who had both been sitting close to him, having moved as far away from the other man as they could. "Come on, Gang. Let's get out of here," he said. "All set? Got everything?"

There were empty plates on the little table in front of them from the meal Ter and the Wingco had eaten while the Wingco revealed all that he had discovered about Roger's plans for his insurance pay-out, as recounted to him by the still-invisible Nataka.

At first Maddie had been incredulous, refusing to believe what she was hearing. Then she had become tearful and, finally, outraged.

For his part, Roger had exploded more than once. To begin with, he denied with all the vehemence he could muster that he had already begun to invest in arms against the promise of the Wingco's life insurance pay-out with its gold-plated bonus; arms that had been bought from distinctly shady organisations and were being traded on to different warring factions in the Middle East (a much more gradual process). However, to acquire the arms in the first place, he had needed liquid funds. And those he had borrowed from a consortium that specialised in such lending against the promise of a substantial, interest-laden repayment, for which he had been counting on gaining access to the Wingco's life insurance pay-out.

To be fair, Roger couldn't really continue to pretend otherwise, given all the evidence - letters, emails and texts - Nataka had presented to the Wingco.

Where did he get those? wondered the frustrated entrepreneur. *Has the sneaky old bastard had an investigator on my tail all along? ... Has he been going through my stuff? I bet he's been going through my stuff. Curse him!*

Confronted with the evidence, Roger had changed his story. Yes, he finally admitted, he had been dealing in arms. But only with the best possible motive: to secure a comfortable life for Maddie and the boy – oh, and naturally, he added almost as an afterthought, for himself as well. Then he'd offered a justification for his conduct that he considered unanswerable, summoning for it the bullish, hectoring voice that generally worked wonders with his business contacts and colleagues.

"What does it matter *who* gets those arms or who sells them, anyway?" he snapped, "It's stupid to be squeamish about all that bleeding-heart stuff! This is the way the world *works*, people. Get used to it. Enter the twenty-first century, already! You're either *in* the winning game or you're not. You'll never get on if you don't!

"The point *is*, anybody who wants to buy arms will get them, regardless. Isn't it? It makes no difference *who* provides them, in the end, does it? So why not take advantage ourselves, and make good money? If *I* didn't do it, somebody else *would.* So why shouldn't I – er, I mean *we* – benefit from it, then?"

He kept returning to this argument over and over again. He seemed genuinely unable to comprehend why it should outrage them so much, and was desperate to win over Maddie at least.

Now, as he saw them preparing to leave, he decided that he must try again to win his wife over to his point of view. He leaned forward and gazed into her eyes, determined to have another shot at convincing her.

"Listen Maddie; *listen* to me. You get it, don't you? At least the money will do *us* good, don't you see? ... No matter *where* it comes from. Right? ... So it's arms. So what's the big deal?"

As he spoke he tried to take her hands. But she snatched them away with a look of despair and disgust on her face that infuriated him even more.

And in that instant *something* - a mountain of pure fury - towered inside the invisible Nataka, who was still sitting in the corner of the window.

An iron claw clapped down on Roger's arm, heaved him out of his chair and spun him round.

"THIS!"

The word hit Roger's ears on a deafening, roaring, hissing, bellowing wave that shook his skull and rattled his teeth. His outrage at being manhandled congealed into uncomprehending horror as he caught a glimpse – for the briefest moment – of a gigantic pair of scaled, grey-and-green crocodile jaws lined with yellow fangs in a mayonnaise gullet that reeked of decayed fish - jaws that crashed together mere millimetres from his face.

– But surely this had just been an illusion –

Because instead/and then/somehow, bewilderingly, he was crouching on the floor of a burning building - or what had been a building and was now a chaos of broken beds, tangled, tattered plastic curtains, collapsed ceilings and walls, shattered bodies, tubing and glass - and some kind of iron shackle, clamped on the back of his neck, was holding him down, forcing him to stay where he was, instead of running away in search of shelter, as every part of his body was screaming for him to do. He was coughing and gagging in the dense clouds of yellow, grey and black dust, fumes and smoke that billowed around him and filthed his carefully pressed suit and shoes with a smell that nauseated, raw, burning, corrosive, bloody: a stench of blood and cordite and piss and vomit and shit and burning rubber and flesh and tar…

He clamped his hands over his ears to shut out the cacophony of helicopters thundering overhead, of masonry falling amid the intermittent, deafening, crunching, thumping detonations of bombs gradually fading in the distance, whose noise almost drowned out the desperate cries of a few dishevelled, dust-covered, frantically working figures he glimpsed through the smoke; figures that scrambled like ungainly, damaged spiders amid the shambles of broken masonry, dragging one another out from under stones and bricks; straightening limbs; staunching and bandaging wounds; hauling other dusty, supine bodies into the open on stretchers hastily improvised from splintered doors and tables and bed-frames ... figures that bellowed and cursed and called for help ...

And, worst of all, filling the occasional lulls between the crashes, roars, thumps and blasts, thin yet piercing, mind-numbing and unremitting, he heard the screams of wounded children, men and women; the terrified, hopeless, animal sounds of minds and bodies at the limits of their physical and spiritual endurance.

Something warm spread in his groin, trickled down the legs of his trousers, soaked into his socks and puddled around the expensive, dust-covered Italian shoes over which he was crouching. His heart seemed determined to burst out of his chest. His head and ears pounded with it. Surely his brain must burst from that *noise* and *stench*...

"What? ... WHAT? ... *WHAT?*"

Was that really *his* voice screaming hysterically through a throat both tight and raw, barely audible in all the noise?

"WELCOME TO SYRIA!"

The words were a rolling, crashing thunder that rattled through Roger's bones and threatened to liquefy his organs. As they sounded, *something* forced his head to turn and see who had spoken them. With a jolt he recognised the obnoxious black medic with those disturbing eyes that had been so insolent to him at the hospital some days before. She was standing upright behind him (but where had she come from? How could she possibly be there?) and what he had mistaken for some sort of shackle clamping the back of his neck and immobilising him were, he suddenly realised, the fingers of one of that repulsive young woman's hands gripping him and holding him down. But how could *that* be? How could she possibly be so strong that he didn't even dare think of trying to break free?

The eyes she now turned on him were two blood-red vortices.

"Pay attention!" roared the (what *was* she?) in a voice that made his teeth ache. "This morning an insurgent with a hand-held rocket launcher shot a missile from a nearby building into territory occupied by opposing forces, forces that are vastly superior to his. That act provoked the usual reprisal, during which a number of cluster bombs were dropped. One of those bombs has just destroyed this building you're in, a field hospital run and staffed by a neutral medical charity.

"So where do *you* come into this? I'll tell you. That rocket launcher passed through *your* hands a few months ago as part of a substantial consignment of weapons you acquired and sold on to the insurgents, all through illegal channels. That transaction earned you a tidy dividend, which is now safely hidden in your off-shore Cayman Islands account, even though you still haven't paid off one penny of the massive loan you secured to buy those weapons in the first place... and which, of course, is also why you've been so intent on robbing your stepson of his inheritance."

She paused and glared at him, her face vivid with contempt and condemnation.

"Look around you. This is what you've achieved. This is the outcome of your speculation. *You* put that weapon into this arena, fuelling the slaughter. Tell me: ARE you proud of what you've achieved? Look at the consequences of your activities, and then dare to tell me you still feel it's acceptable to promote such killing. Go on, then; tell me:

"ARE YOU PROUD?"

"For ... for Chrissake! How did you ... *do* that? ... How did I g-*get* here? ... What are you d-*doing*?"

His voice didn't seem to be working properly. Every word he spoke emerged as a stuttering whine, a cross between a croak and a whisper. He cleared his throat and tried again, summoning what he hoped would be a tone of authoritative outrage.

"What - what is this, some kind of trick? ... How *dare* you? ... Look, you – whoever you are - whatever you're d-doing, I demand..."

Again the stutter; the croak. He gulped and fell silent.

"You've wet yourself," The young woman's voice was the sound of a dead weight of metal dragged over rock. The menace in it made his skin crawl. Her smouldering eyes never left his face. He had the horrifying impression that if he so much as blinked he might fall into them and be immolated.

"You're crouching in your own urine in the middle of a bombed-out field hospital in Syria, getting a first-hand opportunity to enjoy the rewards of your own commercial activities. Different, isn't it, to experience the effects of your own acts at first hand? ... Oh no, don't tell me you aren't enjoying yourself! After all, as I said, this mayhem is as much your handiwork as anybody else's! You worked long and hard for it! I repeat, **ARE YOU PROUD OF YOURSELF?"**

Roger was dumb.

The terrifying creature waited for an answer, but then grew impatient at his silence and roared again, in that voice that was a thunderbolt crashing into him, so shocking that he wet himself all over again.

"Well? No answer, Scum? ... None at all?"

"You... you... you! ... who *are* you?" he gasped.

"But of course," the black girl ignored his question, her face implacable and her voice still like the grating of a tumbril, "if *you* didn't do it, somebody else would; isn't that right? Isn't that what you said? This kind of killing would still go on. Horrifying weapons would still be sold, and innocent people would still die. *And* there's money to be made from it; *money!*

"So let me ask *you* the question you threw at your long-suffering family. Who cares about the loss of a few lives, of a few doctors and aid workers and innocent civilians and medical supplies, compared with the fantastic income you can realise from this kind of trade, eh? Think of the *money*! What are a few lives, by comparison with your bank balance, your *tax-free* bank balance?

"*That* was your argument; wasn't it? That was your excuse for contributing to the horror. Why not grab a share of the pie for yourself, seeing that innocent people are going to suffer and die, regardless? ... Oh, a brilliant argument, that. If you can't beat 'em, join 'em!

"And you also asked something else. You asked *what's the big deal,* didn't you, Scum? ... Come on."

Her grip on the back of his neck tightened. She hauled him to his feet and shoved him, stumbling and whimpering, through the dust and débris to where a small, strangely twisted bundle of rags showed under a drift of plywood, plaster and loose bricks.

"Pick him up. He's bleeding to death. We have to get him out *now*!" snapped the nurse, shoving Roger over till his face was inches from what he suddenly realised was a small boy lying half-covered in rubble. There was a gaping hole where the child's left inner thigh and groin should have been; a hole out of which the arterial blood pulsed, startlingly bright against the muted, dusty colours of the bombed building.

The gorge rose in his throat. He twisted himself to one side and vomited.

"I ... I *can't*," he gasped, "I won't ... you – you can't make me..."

"You can't? ... You won't? You're beneath contempt."

The young woman let go of his neck and shoved him to one side. She bent over, shifted the débris and lifted the child into her arms in two swift movements. Then she turned away, to where dim light filtering through the dense smoke and dust revealed what remained of a doorway with a splintered frame in an unstable brick wall.

"*Follow*, Scum!"

Although he longed for the strength and courage to pick up a brick and hit his tormentor over the head with it *right then*, while her back was turned, Roger knew he could only do precisely as she ordered. Try as he might, his limbs refused to obey any other instruction. He might have been a marionette. Seething with horror and resentment, he stumbled in her wake as she worked her way out of the room, picking her way past the collapsed lintel and smashed frame of the broken doorway into the scarcely brighter light of a shattered courtyard littered with débris. There she hurried to the nearest piece of relatively level ground, heaved a toppled stone table upright with one hand while cradling the child with her other arm (*Good Lord, she's STRONG... How can she be so strong? ... I wouldn't stand a chance if I tried to fight my way out...*) and lowered her burden onto it. Then she bent over it, and her hands moved swiftly and carefully, uncovering and cleaning the wound. Her back was turned to him and her body shielded the toddler from view.

Roger hung back, tortured by fear and indecision. He couldn't bear to approach; he didn't dare try to escape. He just stood there. Perhaps, if he stayed very quiet, she would forget him.

He could make out that now one of his tormentor's hands was resting on the child's head and the other on his stomach, and that she was speaking softly in a language he did not understand. The child seemed conscious and aware; his eyes were gazing into her face. Roger realised he was desperate for the boy to live, because otherwise ... but he couldn't bear to imagine what the woman might do to him.

Then she stopped talking and moving, and instead simply hung over the body on the table. She was so still that she seemed turned to stone. But of a sudden she shuddered and straightened up with a jerk. Roger caught a glimpse of her profile: tears were pouring unchecked from eyes suddenly black as twin pits. They seemed to suck the light out of everything they rested on.

Please don't let her look at me with those eyes, he prayed to a god he had never believed in. *They'll kill me... I won't be able to stand it ... I don't want to die ... please...*

He shuddered with relief when she turned back to the body on the table, hiding her appalling face from view. But his relief didn't last long.

"*Changed*," moaned the woman, and it seemed to Roger that the ground under his feet shifted in response to the agony in her voice, a voice like a whirlpool groaning inside a cavern. "Changed. I was too late. Oh, little one, why did you have to go so quickly? Couldn't you have waited for me a little? Why did you have to leave so soon? Why did you have to go so far that I could only watch, but do nothing to stop you? ...You, *you* deserved to live, if any of these mortals did!"

Roger breathed fast, trying to still his thumping heart. Of course; he had it at last. The damned woman was insane. Mad as a – a – *hatter* was too mild. She had to be an escapee from an asylum. But how had she managed this massive con, making him believe all this? Surely none of this was *real*, was it? Had she fed him some kind of drug, maybe? Whatever it was, he tried to reassure himself, he was going to make a killing when he sued her.

"Toki, my heart, my *heart!*" the woman raised her head and howled like a hyena in agony. The ground rocked under Roger's feet to the sound, and he staggered and fell onto all fours, grazing his hands. "*Toki!* Do you hear me? Why must I feel this? How can anybody see and feel *this*, and continue sane?"

That was it, all right. She was totally crazy. *Mad as bat shit*, he thought. He repeated it under his breath. *Mad as bat shit.* It had to be the only explanation for her behaviour. And yet, despite the contempt he tried to summon with the words, his heart refused to stop pounding. He had never known such terror before. He'd had no idea one *could* feel so frightened. A tiny detached portion of his mind wondered briefly whether his heart might simply burst with it.

The woman slumped over again, her shoulders heaving, and hung sobbing over the child for what felt like an eternity to the man behind her. But at last she drew a few hoarse breaths, dragged both her forearms over her eyes, and straightened up.

"Farewell, Little Sapiens. Take your journey in peace," she whispered, reaching out to draw down the lids over the blank eyes. "I failed you. I came too late. You should have lived long enough to find joy and fulfil your promise." She drew a shuddering sigh. "But rest now, rare little mortal. Rest."

After another silence the woman stretched one hand behind her back and beckoned to Roger. The grimy man was again compelled to approach till he was standing beside her. He struggled to turn his eyes from the sight before him, but the adamantine will that held him in thrall locked his eyes open and directed them onto the dusty, bloodstained figure on the table, compelling him to take in every detail: the torn and stained clothing, fingernails and knees; the bruising on the young face that had already assumed an incongruous sternness in death; the dust that clogged the tightly curling black eyelashes and hair, and powdered the sunken, once-plump cheeks and freckles, forlorn talismans of a brief sunlit infancy; the fly-beset blood congealing and darkening around the puckered baby mouth and shrunken lower belly.

The gorge rose in his throat again.

"Study your work, Scum," the nurse's voice, again: a steel blade, sharpening on stone. "Study it closely. So what's the big deal? A life, innocent, barely launched. Gone. A child like countless others, snuffed out in a struggle for power that had nothing to do with him, and that had already destroyed his family. A life rich with promise and potential, erased from this planet, this Dimension, for the sake of your and other criminals' greed. *This* life.

"*That's* the big deal, Scum. That. Look at him and know him. His name was Hassan. A few days ago, before they were killed, he told his family that he wanted to be a doctor. He'd been running around in this hospital, young as he was, carrying bandages and holding hands, comforting everybody: those who'd been wounded and who were dying, and those who were grieving for their dead. He found his vocation in this place, and received his father's approval for it before losing him, too. This child, Hassan, held his father's hands and comforted him as he died.

"But he didn't cry any longer, as he'd done when his mother and sisters were killed. He'd already learnt that all his tears and prayers wouldn't bring them back. So instead he went back to helping wherever he could: carrying supplies and water; mopping floors; cleaning up blood and vomit and excrement; washing dirty linen; holding hands; offering consolation; comforting other orphaned children.

"That's what he did, Scum. He was just a few of your years old, but he did all that. Despite his youth and suffering, he was great. And if he'd lived he would have been even greater. He'd have saved lives, for no other reason than that they *were* lives. He'd have done it without ever wondering what was in it for him. Unlike you. *Unlike you.*"

Roger shook with resentment and outrage. Nobody had ever spoken to him with such contempt before, let alone forced him to submit to the nauseating humiliation of confronting his own greed in the face of such selflessness and generosity in a mere child. He had nowhere to hide from the contrast, and it was unbearable.

"By *Christ,* I won't put up with this any longer!" he shouted suddenly, finding some courage in the outrage to which he'd been stung at the woman's words. "There're laws! I've got rights! I'll have you for this, you bloody *bitch!* ... I don't know *how* you're doing it, but I'll have you for ... for kidnap ... distress ... mental torture ... personal injury ... see if I don't! ... Just you wait; I'll clean you *out!* ... When I'm through with you, you'll wish ... you'll ..."

His brief tirade stuttered into silence. The young woman had turned her horrifying, tear-streaked face to him at last. He gazed, mesmerised and appalled, into the two lightless pits, inside which lurked the unspeakable menace of that briefly-glimpsed crocodile.

The eyes advanced on him, widening and yawning into an all-consuming chasm.

Roger's bladder and bowels loosened again, adding the stench of yet another voiding to his nightmare. "No. no, no, no! ... *This isn't real, it isn't real, it's a con, it's a con!"* he gabbled to himself , fighting to resist the tide of nausea, horror and oblivion that swept out of the pit to engulf him.

"You won't remember any of this, more's the pity," the loathed, grating voice of the – monster? – woman? – hallucination? – sounded through his failing consciousness, "but *I* will, Scum. I'll remember that you showed no remorse for the evil you've done or pity for the lives your greed has destroyed, for murders you have committed by proxy; that the only concern you felt was for yourself.

"Oh, yes. I *will* remember, Scum. FOREVER!"

***

The Wingco surged to his feet.

"What's the big deal? *Seriously*? You can actually *ask* that? ... Does this really mean that you still don't understand, that you're not just deliberately ignoring the truth? ... What's the big deal in doling out death for profit -

not to protect your loved ones, not even to defend your country, but simply for money? ... Oh, my stars! Roger, if you can't understand just how outrageous - and *evil* - I find that question, we can really have nothing more to say to one another, ever again!"

Disorientated and confused, Roger ran his hands over his face and tried to collect his thoughts. What *had* been his last words, and why had they infuriated the old man so much? ... Why did he feel so dislocated, so distanced, from everything that had just been said in this room? ... Hadn't something else just happened, hadn't he been somewhere else (insane as that sounded even to him)? ... What had happened to him, just now? Why did he feel that a huge hole had suddenly been dug in his immediate memory? ... And why did the back of his neck feel bruised and tender, as if it had been clamped in a vice?

He frowned, struggling to make sense of the situation. Yes; there was a tiny wisp of remembrance there, dissipating even as he tried to capture it, like the very last tendrils of morning mist that vanish into the warming air after a cold autumn night, and leave no trace of their passing. Yet he could have sworn that in that moment he had felt ... seen ... dreamed? ... *Something*, something huge and horrible and disgusting and terrifying and humiliating, and... and...

But whatever it might have been, the experience was lost.

He was still sitting in his armchair in the ugly green room at the nursing home, staring up at the outraged old man, who stood with his arms around his daughter-in-law and grandson and gazed back down at *him*, Roger, with the expression people generally reserve for something they've picked up on the soles of their shoes during country walks.

"You really are *beyond the pale*," the old man's voice shook. "You're not even going to bother, are you? ... That's it, of course. You really don't care enough even to try to understand. Oh, ye gods, ye gods ... Well, so be it. That's it. I've got nothing more to say to you, nothing at all!"

And on those words, everybody - the Wingco, Maddie, and the boy – turned and left the room without a backward glance.

"What *is* the big deal?" Roger asked the empty room, "I'm only trying to make some money!"

***

Outside the nursing home Ter turned to Nataka, who had left the room with them and who was still invisible to his mother.

"Where are you going now?" he asked her, taking advantage of a short consultation between his mother and the Wingco, "I mean, if you haven't got anywhere else to go you could come home with us, you know. I'd like that... I'd ... well; I'd really like you to stay with us. I could introduce you to my mum, and... and – well, I'd really like you to be with us." His eyes shone.

Nataka gazed down at him, surprised at the odd lurch she felt in her midriff at his words. The Howler infant was fond of her. How strange it was to receive the affection of such a creature. And how much stranger to feel a reciprocal fondness kindle inside her heart in return. In the past she had liked and enjoyed the company of many Howlers, but she had never felt love for them. And now, twice in one Suntime, she had encountered this strange emotion: first with Hassan, the child she had been unable to save and whose memory tore at her mind, and now with this young creature who stood gazing up at her so confidingly and warmly. Contemplating him, she experienced a resurgence of the fury against his stepfather that had overwhelmed her before.

"Er, Nataka ... Wha - what's happening to your *eyes*?" faltered Ter, stepping backwards. Nataka's eyes were again darker than the inside of an unlit cave. But she forced herself to smile and laid a hand on his shoulder.

"I'm sorry, Ter. I can't join you right now," she breathed deeply, fighting to control the anger rising within her throat and chest like a surge of lava in a roused volcano. "I'm ... well, I'm not very safe to be around at the moment. Sorry. I've got to... got to get rid of some stuff - straighten myself out - first, you know? ... But don't worry. I promise you'll see me again. ... Actually, I've got an idea. Listen."

She leaned down and spoke into his ear. "If you need me, all you have to do is raise your voice and call. I'll hear you, wherever I am, and come right away. All right? But only if you *really* need me. Now I must go, before ... before it's too late."

And she vanished.

Chapter 24. *Love And Its Consequences*

"... for there is nothing either good or bad but thinking makes it so..." [clv]

"I should have *killed* the scum! Why didn't I just *kill* him?"

Nataka the Crocodile prowled, roaring, around the cottage floor.

Her scaled tail and razor-sharp talons had reduced most of the furniture to matchwood. The cauldron dangled sideways, suspended by a single chain from its twisted arm, the other two having been snapped off. The woodpile lay scattered across the floor, its logs splintered and gouged, and every time Nataka stumbled over one of them in her rampage she hissed, snapped it up in her jaws and tossed it into the air to land with a crash on furniture or broken crockery, causing yet more damage. Every shelf the demented crocodile had been able to reach had been destroyed and its burden of delicate vials, pots, foodstuffs and glassware smashed, trampled and scattered. Shards of glittering glass, crystal and glazed earthenware littered the floor and table, which listed dangerously on three legs. Every surface was slippery with spilt potions, unguents, oils and powders, and the air thick with a sickly sweet-and-bitter cocktail of fumes and scents that had escaped from their smashed containers. Countless varicoloured powders and smokes hung and swirled in the disturbed air, detonating and hissing as they met and mingled before drifting gradually to the floor in strange, light-distorting patterns and layers. The shafts of light from the windows and doorway reflected and refracted around the cottage, splintered into bizarre colours and shadows and sparks. Toki's window was still largely intact, but its wooden door had not fared so well. It was splintered and gouged, and dangled drunkenly from a single twisted hinge, half-blocking the entrance to the cottage.

Mond's sensitive ears had detected Nataka's roaring

approach and scented the strangeness of her when she was still a fair distance from the cottage. Uttering a whimpering snarl he had instantly bolted out of the window with his hackles on end and bushy tail clamped up between his hind legs. M'Kuu and Pex, who had been dozing alongside him in the warmth of the firelight, instantly bounded out behind him. Dora had scuttled into the thatched underside of Toki's roof, where she lay still, curled into a tight ball. Miba the hedgehog and Brid the squirrel had left the cottage some time before with Miba's hoglets trailing behind them, and were already ensconced under the yew hedge in an abandoned rabbit scraping, catching up with each other's news. The rumpus of the approaching crocodile froze them all into cowering, wide-eyed silence.

Axl had wandered up the slope to the Pathway Tree to wait for Paa, who was still away on her mission of mercy for the mongooses. Lately the fallow deer had come to feel ill at ease if he was separated from the dog for too long. Deer-like, he never stopped to question the feeling but simply acted in line with it. At Nataka's approach he had cocked his ears, head and liquid eyes in the direction of the commotion before fleeing in great bounds up the rest of the slope and under the branches of the great beech tree, where he became like a statue. He found Fagus awake, quivering and muttering to itself.

"Oh, no, no, *no*; this is not good. Not good at all!" fretted the beech, "this is perilous. Aelfeynn Earda has found her emotions at last, but not in a good way; no, not in a good way. This is too sudden, too painful for her. And I? I am impotent to intervene, to reach out to her while she remains in the grip of her new feelings. Her spirit is shut to me, as it is to the Gatekeeper Toki. What can be done? We teeter on the verge of a disaster … Ah, little Dancing Deer, this is perilous! *This* is what my dream forewarned. Alas, alas, *why* did we never discuss my dream? I have been beguiled and forgetful, even as she strayed unwittingly into danger, such danger! ... Oh, I have failed her..." The tree shuddered again, every leaf trembling. "Do not leave me, Dancing Deer; Stay close, close by me," it begged.

Axl approached the tree until his warm flank was resting against the smooth trunk next to its eyes. He could feel the swirling agitation inside the plant, which shook like a pine forest in the path of an avalanche, and deliberately stilled every muscle of his own body, allowing his mind to become a limpid pool, registering without resistance every sound and sensation it encountered. As he did so, his heart slowed, his breathing deepened, and he entered the waking dream every Startime grazer can summon at will to preserve its energy while yet remaining alert and aware of everything that moves around it.

After Axl had rested some time like this, immobile, calm and unquestioning, Fagus drew a shuddering breath. "Thank you, little Dancing Deer," it said, its voice like the swish and murmur of the tide ebbing away from a shingled shoreline, "I feel no shame in admitting to you, who are so warm and comforting, that, little Mortal creature though you be, you have eased my fear with your presence. I pray you, bide by me a while longer until Paa Elpidea returns. She is late returning to my paths, but she will come. Yes; she will come, and not an instant too soon!"

Inside Nataka's sanctuary Glose alone remained, everyone else having bolted. Like Mond and his companions he had been drowsing with his head under his wing when the din of the approaching crocodile roused him. His first response had been annoyance. So Nataka was in a bad mood? That didn't mean she had the right to disrupt everybody's nap like this! She'd just have to be chivvied out of it with a bracing homily. And when it came to bracing homilies, *he* was the only one of her companions who knew how to deliver them. Everyone else was too mild and wishy-washy for the job, in his opinion. So he stayed put, rolling a few trenchant phrases around in his head while he waited.

"Get out, Glose!" cried M'Kuu as he fled, "Get *out*! ... She'll have you! She's out of control!"

"**Arkh**! nonsense," scoffed the raven. "It's only Nataka in one of her tizzies. Not the first I've ever seen. And she won't break her own *no hunting* rule, no matter what. So she's upset, (just as I warned her she would be if she got too involved with those Howlers); so what? **Tsk, tsk**, the silly imp. *Keep your temper,* I've told her more than once. *That temper of yours is going to get us all into trouble one day.* And I've also warned her about Howlers, in so many words. *Keep your distance from those crazy Howlers. You know you always let them get up your beak*, I've said. Oh yes, I've warned her. But would she listen? 'Course not. I ask you, why have an adviser if you won't take his advice? ... In any case, I know her better than anybody else. Even if she's absolutely crazy she'll never harm *me*." He preened a wing.

"Harm you? ... *Parbleu,* she will veritably *kill* you, you bird demented!" urged Mond, who had caught sight of the creature Nataka had become an instant before he and his companions scrambled out of sight under a low-hanging yew. "This ... *thing* ... is no longer the Nataka we know. I implore you, little bird black, be not a hero! ... Our Wise One cannot still be wise if she 'as assumed that form. I 'ave never seen such a creature before, but assuredly she will not be reasonable. *Au contraire* ^{clvi}, I know, my nose and my stomach know, that the beast she 'as become must be entirely *un*reasonable!"

"Rubbish. You're exaggerating," cawed Glose, but even so he was beginning to feel rather less sure of himself. The noise made by the approaching creature was such as to make even the most courageous raven reconsider his convictions.

For some time Toki had been immobile and silent; so silent that it had felt practically lifeless. But now it shook and trembled, rocking everything inside it. A pained moan resonated through its fabric. In its eaves Dora curled into an even tighter ball.

"*Arkh* ... Claws and pinions, perhaps the wolf has a point. She does seem rather out of sorts," muttered Glose, feeling his beak go dry. He hesitated for a moment, then flapped up to perch on one of the beams in Toki's eaves (*just in case. No harm in making sure*).

And then the huge, green- and grey-scaled reptile was upon them, devastating as a fanged hurricane.

Nataka the Crocodile was so furious that she could barely speak, so the only way she found to vent her outrage, grief and frustration was through a spate of wholesale, mind-numbing destruction, all accompanied by a sound that was no longer anything like singing so much as the hoarse, screaming roar of an infuriated, anguished monster.

Halfway through the destruction, the monster managed to articulate her feelings in a single cry:

"I should have *killed* the scum! Why didn't I just *kill* him?"

The cottage trembled and groaned deeply in reply but said nothing more, even though Nataka's rampage threatened to bring it tumbling down around her ears. To Glose, cowering in the eaves, where he could not help squawking and flinching every time a precious flask shattered or scroll tore under the beast's claws, it seemed that even Toki had abandoned all hope of soothing the demented creature Nataka had become.

"*Gaahk*! This hiding around and waiting for her to come to her senses just *won't do*!" he rasped at last, stung into

385

outrage by seeing one of his favourite chests of scrolls reduced to splinters and shreds. "This *can't* be allowed to continue! Who does she think she is, anyway? How dare she trash our treasures like that? She's behaving like a spoilt brat! ... Beak up, Glose, it's only Nataka, after all. She mustn't be allowed to get away with such outrageous behaviour, especially after all her lectures to the rest of us about *no hunting* and *tolerance*, and ... and... Sheer hypocrisy, if you ask me! If she is, we'll *never* be able to control her. We'll be making a rod for our own backs. *Somebody's got* to stand up to her. So come on, Bird: up and challenge her; earn your daily grub. Crushed eggshells and rotten nests, you're her *mentor*, after all!" [clvii]

So the raven behaved in the bravest – and stupidest – way he had ever done in a long life full of brave and stupid behaviour: he swooped down to perch on the back of the single remaining intact chair, summoned as much sarcasm as he could into his (very dry) throat, and addressed the crocodile that was still bellowing around on the cottage floor, smashing everything she could reach.

"*Caw*! Well, pluck my pinions, stuff me with straw and call me a cushion!" he rasped as loudly as he could, "Is *this* how you demonstrate your famous philosophy of tolerance, Nataka? ... So much for all those homilies you've made us endure over countless Suntimes and Startimes! In the end you're no better than the worst of those disgusting Howlers you keep going on about, are you? ... No, you're not. Something goes wrong; somebody annoys or upsets you; you can't somehow, magically, turn things the way you want them to go, and what d'you do? ... Oh, of course; *silly* me. It's simple really, isn't it? You just Transform into a smelly, disgusting, dirty great beast (and what kind of a beast *is* that, anyway? Nothing self-respecting, I'll warrant), and go about, trashing everything and terrifying innocent Wanyama, don't you? ... Yes. *That's* what you do. Well, all I can say is, *well done,* Nataka, you great Immortal spirit. Well *done!* A fantastic role-model you are, I *don't* think!"

"**AAAARGH!!! ROARRRRRRR!!!**"

The crocodile reared up, roaring, and snapped at the raven with jaws wide enough to gulp down a decent-sized goat. Her finger-long yellow fangs crashed together, splintering the chair-back on which Glose had been perching while he harangued her. Screeching, he only *just* got away by bounding vertically into the air, his wings a blur, and leaving a good number of tail feathers stuck between Nataka's fangs.

Again the beast reared onto her back legs to snap after the escaping bird; but she overreached herself, lost her balance and toppled over her own tail, slamming down onto her ridged, scaly back. But with a convulsive twist and wriggle of her muscular tail she instantly righted herself again, hissing, and surged back up onto her hind claws, using her tail as a prop. She snapped wildly after the shocked and disorientated raven, who was fluttering randomly around the cottage, struggling to maintain height. At one point he flew into a cloud of greenish haze, which detonated with a *crack*, briefly turning him into a giant thistledown seed that bobbed around on the vortices generated by Nataka's rampage. There was another *crack* and Glose regained his form in time to peer with horror into the monstrous yellow gullet yawning just a wing's span beneath him, and espy the crest of viciously curving horns that had begun to sprout around the beast's jaws and brow.

"**Skreeeek**!! *Shame* on you!" Glose flapped hysterically around, so beside himself with outrage and fear that a blob of guano splattered down onto the scaly nose of his assailant. "*Now* look what you've done! Picking on somebody much smaller than you! How *dare* you? ... You've *injured* me, you great bully! ... You've *shamed* me - *me!* ... How *dare* you hunt me? ... I'll... I'll... **Aaaahhhhkkk*!*"

The demented crocodile's forelegs were lengthening and thickening into two tightly scaled, green and red arms, and her forepaws into muscular, long-fingered hands that terminated in lethally sharp talons. Simultaneously, her rear paws and claws stretched, metamorphosing into the legs of a Howler. The rough-scaled crocodile tail lengthened, smoothed and curled into a sinuous pythonesque tail and her snout sharpened and elongated to accommodate the additional rows of yellowing, stinking fangs springing up inside it. The colour of her gullet changed from a creamy mayonnaise to a burning red, while her demented eyes widened and tilted, glaring hungrily through the thicket of thorny scales that had sprouted around them. The emerging chimaera reminded the horrified raven of some illustrations of dragons he had once encountered in an ancient scroll.

The creature - part-crocodile, part-human, part-dragon – began to swell, her bulk filling the cottage. Again she reared up, raised one gigantic hand and snatched at the screeching raven, who again only just managed to evade her swiping talons.

*** DESIST AND DEPART INSTANTLY, PRESUMPTUOUS BIRD!! ***

A thunderous voice, one that Glose had never heard before, rocked the cottage. The spider in its eaves dashed out onto the roof, abseiled to the ground and scuttled away through the grass, and the Creature into which Nataka had Transformed froze just long enough for the traumatised, bedraggled raven to flap out through the smashed doorway and into the open air, where he blundered into a nearby aspen and perched, gasping and trembling and not quite daring to believe that he was still alive.

Inside the cottage, silence.

The deformed Beast sprawled, panting, on the floor. A forked red tongue flicked in and out through the blunt, lipless mouth at the end of her elongated snout, tasting the dusty air. Her tail lashed with each rasping breath she drew, sweeping the débris inside Toki into even greater disorder. Tendrils of sulphurous smoke issued from her nostrils and her head swept rapidly from side to side with a demented, distracted air.

gradually, as time passed and no further challenges arose, the violent heaving of the monster's flanks slowed and the stertorous breathing in the gigantic lungs softened and eased. The smoke stopped curling out of her nostrils and her eyelids drooped. At last, the Beast heaved a groaning sigh, turned her head and gazed around her, seeing the damage she had wreaked.

When finally she spoke her voice was raw, emerging on the ebb tide of her anger. The words came haltingly, hampered and distorted by her reptilian tongue and palate.

"T-Toki?" croaked Nataka. "Ithsss that ... you? ... What'thss ... h-happened ... happening ... to me?"

The cottage creaked a question, and the chimaera crouching on the floor replied, hesitantly to begin with, but ever more articulately as her tongue shrank and her voice grew less rough and faltering: about her recent confrontation with the Howler; about how she had terrified him with an experience of the horrors arising from his actions; and about her outrage at realising that despite witnessing most terrible pain and suffering he had remained impervious to any other emotion apart from his concern for himself. Throughout her account Toki remained silent, but Nataka knew that it heard and absorbed every word.

"I - I don't know what thiss iss," she moaned at last, in a voice that was almost normal again, although she still tended to hiss. "I mean, in the passt I've seen other Howlers behave even worse than he did, often and often. You know I have, Toki. Over and over again. But, but ... I've never felt like *thiss* before, and ... I don't know ... it all sssuddenly became too much to bear...

"It all began with Paa... No – with that dance... That dance ... No – *no*, that'sss not it either. It *was* Paa! Yess ... *Paa* sstarted me feeling things I hadn't felt before, that day I saw her lying on the sstone river. I jusst *had* to do sssomething for her then. For the firsst time, jussst for a moment, I felt... I felt real pity. And... and..."

She drew a shuddering breath.

"And I couldn't resist punishing that disgussting Howler for all the ssuffering he'd laid on her. I did it out of anger for the pain he had caused her, Toki; *anger*. Do you realisse what that meansssss?"

As she spoke, Nataka's voice lost its sibilance and her speech became more fluent.

"But even then, that was... well, if I'm honest, it was also a lot of fun," she said, "Making that disgusting old Howler suffer for what he'd done to Paa. It made me laugh. Whereas now ... well, now they – the feelings – have ... well, they've taken over. And they're controlling me. I don't know how to stop them. I've never felt this before – this sadness, and this – this fury. I want to kill; I want to *punish*... and at the same time I feel that my heart is – it's broken...

"I can't stop thinking about the little boy, Toki; about what he suffered before he died. And it's made me realise the pain all those others have suffered like him - *are* suffering like him - in the past; right now; all the time. It's unbearable! How can anybody bear that? ... And it's just going to go on and on and on, isn't it? ... Just a sea of ... of anguish... And the worst thing of all is the thought that all *I* ever did before was just – well - just *watch* it – Oh, Toki! – and *laugh* at it... or get annoyed at the stupidity of those blasted Howlers, those *Stults* with their idiotic excuses for doing horrible things to one another, when all they really want, if they're honest, is to get something out of it for themselves.

"But mostly, honestly, I was simply resentful about the *irritation* all their grief made me feel because it drowned out my own music and made it difficult for me to *think*, you know?

"Oh, Toki, Toki! I never did anything else! That's what's driving me crazy now, because now, well, *now* it's all coming home to me. And I'm going mad, realising just how *wrong* this place is, and how wrong *I've* been!

"But *why* is this happening to me? And how can I stand it? ... How *will* I stand it?"

The Creature sank down, buried her head in her scaly forearms, and wept. At length she raised her shrinking snout, and spoke again, sounding bewildered and fearful.

"I mean it, Toki. I could have destroyed that Howler," she said. "I could have squashed him like a cockroach! Infinity alone knows, because *I* don't, why I didn't simply wipe him out; what stopped me from crushing him. ... And you know that just now I wanted to *eat* Glose, just to shut him up once and for all. With all my heart, I wanted to kill that idiotic, screeching, nagging bird. And yet *he's* been a faithful friend to me for moons and moons! It's ludicrous, isn't it, that I wanted to kill *him*? ... But I swear to you, the only reason he's still alive right now is because I couldn't catch him. Oh, Infinity, that thought makes me want to shrink away... That's ... that's horrifying!

"Toki, please help me, *please* tell me at last. What *is* this? What's going on? ... I don't know how to handle this ... this ... whatever's happening to me! ... What can I *do*?"

While she spoke her tail had been shrinking, the scales smoothing out, and the spikes that had haloed her head disappearing. She dwindled and darkened, until all that remained amid the débris was the dishevelled black girl, whose tears carved two dark runnels down her dust-paled cheeks.

After a pause the cottage spoke.

"So. Here it is, then; the moment we have awaited for so long," it whispered.

Nataka raised her head. Her mouth and eyes opened wide. Toki rarely expressed itself other than with creaks and movements.

"This is an earnest of your growth and maturation, Nataka Aelfeynn Earda, Child Spirit. Now not only do you see what is ill in the world, but you show signs of desiring to remedy it. No longer are you moved to act solely because the sadness you encounter in others is an annoyance. *Now,* finally, you feel and share the pain and sorrow of Mortals.

"Gone are the days of your untrammelled playfulness, when everything that occurred served only as material for you to observe, play with and enjoy - or punish and revile - at no cost to yourself. Now its consequences touch you; move you. Yes, you are maturing."

There was hope and sadness, infinite sadness, in the voice.

"At last you begin to know Love, Child Spirit. Yet I fear that even now, after so much time has elapsed, the lesson comes upon you too soon. You are not yet spiritually ripe enough to embrace this new experience without great conflict and danger. But, premature or not, here it is, and you must strive to contain it.

"You must lean in to bear this new burden of Love with all its consequences, Aelfeynn Earda. You must shoulder the weight of suffering that is the price you pay for this precious new deepening of your emotions, for only with such effort will you grow. ... But be warned."

As Toki spoke a face began to coalesce out of the cottage wall, a face at once earthly and entirely alien; ancient yet unlined; with a high brow and gentle lips; with a strange light glowing in its brow; and with eyes bottomless as Death, and just as full as Death of both peril and solace.

"Now, for the first time, you become truly dangerous, Nataka Aelfeynn Earda," it said. "You have discovered anger, outrage and vengefulness, the companions of self-forgetfulness and compassion; companions that may overwhelm and destroy all that Love may achieve, if you do not regulate them. As you well know, for you have destroyed before.

"This, then, is your time of greatest danger. Controlled, your new-found feelings put you on the threshold of untold personal reward and liberation. Uncontrolled, they bring with them the seeds of a destruction that can barely be imagined."

Toki paused, gazed into the eyes of the Protean, and sighed. "I warn you again, Child Spirit, you who are so ancient in your knowledge and actions yet so very young in your emotions," it said, "strive with all the might you can summon to master your new feelings, lest they master *you*, and bring everything to ruin."

Toki Emerges

Chapter 25. *The Lesson*

> *"... O hang the head,*
> *Impetuous child with the tremendous brain,*
> *O weep, child, weep, O weep away the stain..."* clviii

Paa bounded down the hillside with Axl at her side. The sun was dipping away towards Sunsleep and the lengthening shadows it cast were tinting the spaces beneath the trees and hedgerows. A song thrush perching in a towering chestnut tree had launched its *paean* into the slanting light of Sunsink, every note shivering and cascading through the still air. It seemed to the poodle racing down the slope that all the woodland paused to listen.

Then she had reached the hedge surrounding Toki's grounds and burst through it, forgetting all about the thrush. Axl stopped short outside the cottage as the dog bounded in through the ruined doorway.

"Your Honour! Your Honour!" Paa reared onto her hind paws and began kiss every part of Nataka her pink tongue could reach. "Fagus told me you were upset, so I *raced* home. Yes! ... And when I arrived, Axl said a monster was attacking you and Toki ... and ... Oh – oh, dear! I'm too late to help you, aren't I? You *have* been attacked! Oh, those cowards! ... Oh, why wasn't I here to defend you?"

As Paa spoke, the fallow deer peeped round the doorframe, to check that she was safe. His eyes widened at the havoc inside the cottage and he hastily backed out again.

"Oh, Your Honour, I'm so sorry I didn't get back sooner! But those dumb Howlers you sent me to help with their mating took ages to get the message. We all - Lerema, Tesho and I - tried hard to hurry them up, but they're so *dumb,* you know? They nearly drove me crazy. And ... but.... Oh, bother, never mind, why am I telling you all this anyway? Who cares why it took so long? The thing is that

395

it *did* take a long time. And so I couldn't get back before. Bother, bother, *bother*! ... But why isn't anybody looking after you? Where *is* everybody? ... Who hurt you? Who upset you? .... Oh, how you must have suffered! ... I *wish* I could have got home sooner! ... Can I help? What can I do?"

"Hush, hush," Nataka stroked the agitated poodle and forced a smile through her tears. "You're here now. Never mind anything else. You're here. Yes. Thanks for coming home, little Paa; thank you..." Her voice broke.

Paa pulled back and drew a deep breath, wondering and concerned, but determined to help put things right. She wanted to see Nataka smile again; nothing else mattered.

"Whatever hurt you, *whoever* hurt you, we'll deal with them together, good and proper!" she said. "Yes, we will! I'm not leaving your side for a moment from now on, Your Honour. I promise. And as soon as you tell me who attacked you and made such a horrible mess of Toki, I'll show them *exactly* what a fierce dog can do." She snarled, displaying her fangs. "Who was it? Tell me! I'll teach them a lesson they'll never forget. I'll take them apart!"

"You'll have to take *me* apart then, little Paa," Nataka hiccoughed, laughing despite herself. "I made all this mess myself. Nobody else had anything to do with it. I trashed the place. Poor Toki, what a nightmare..." Her voice broke again.

"*You?*" Paa gulped and cocked her head. But the look on Nataka's face was so woebegone that the poodle decided not to ask any questions. "Ah, um," she said at last. "I understand..." A sneeze shook her, flapping her ears. "No. I don't understand," she admitted. "But that doesn't matter. I'm sure you must have had a good reason for it. You always have a good reason for everything you do. And –"

She sneezed again, "we'll just have to clean this mess up again, that's all. This dust ... *arrghmff!*... No harm done..."

A little cloud of glittering blue powder drifted down and landed on Paa's nose. She sneezed again twice in rapid succession, and a nosegay of star-shaped flowers sprang up on her muzzle and faded again as suddenly as it had appeared, leaving behind a sprinkling of pollen that provoked yet another spate of sneezing.

Toki chuckled, and Paa spun round at the sound to confront the face she hadn't noticed in her absorption with Nataka. Her hackles rose. "Who's *that*?" she demanded, baring her fangs, just in case.

"What? ... Oh, that... er, that's Toki," said Nataka

"Welcome back, Paa Elpidea," the unearthly eyes fastened on the dog, who stopped snarling, covered her fangs and licked her chops instead; the eyes were making her feel a bit giddy. "You have been dearly missed."

"*You're* Toki? ... Oh!" The poodle tested the air, trying but failing to gain a scent from the apparition. She plumped down onto her curly bottom and scratched an ear. "Er ... why do you pretend to be a cottage?"

"It's complicated," said Toki, "But you may find it useful to think of me as Nataka's guardian and gatekeeper. I take the form of a cottage because I find this the best way to protect her and her friends."

Paa cocked her head. "But... but why does she need a guardian? ... And ... a gatekeeper? ... What gate? *I* don't see a gate..."

As she spoke a wisp of pink smoke landed on her rump and sprouted into a little thicket of silvery twigs festooned with lilac bubbles and with iridescent, diaphanously finned floating fish.

"Ah. Those are important questions. Nobody has asked them before." Toki paused while Paa twisted her head round to gaze at the rapidly dwindling apparition on her back, and then went on. "Nataka was sent to this Dimension to complete her ... I shall call it her *education*, for want of a better word, Paa Elpidea; lessons it was decided she would most readily learn here, on this planet, in this Reality. I was tasked with watching over her and guarding the passage between the Dimensions. Do you see?"

"No, not really, sorry;" answered Paa. "Lessons? As far as I'm concerned, Her Honour's perfect. So I don't understand why she needs to learn any lessons. I've seen her change things, and disguise things, and rescue people who were in trouble. And she makes us laugh and keeps us safe, and gets really, *really* annoyed when somebody does something nasty, which isn't only natural, it's also ... well, it's *honourable*. Isn't it? So, I mean, how could she be any better? How can she need to learn anything else? ... She's perfect already!" She reared up and licked Nataka's face again.

"Oh, Paa," groaned Nataka, holding the loyal dog close, "You give me too much credit. Ask me why I do all those things; go on. Toki knows."

"I don't understand. What do you mean? You do all those things because you *can*, and because you *care*, Your Honour. Don't you?"

Nataka tugged gently at Paa's ears. "No, Paa. I never do anything because I really care... at least I *didn't,* before I met you. When I met you something happened to me. Before that, honestly, I just did all those things because I wanted to have fun. And other people being sad irritated me and prevented me from enjoying myself. D'you see? It was easier to interfere, and stop them from feeling unhappy, than to have to put up with the annoyance of their emotions. I either interfered or avoided them altogether... and of course, with very few exceptions, I also despised them. For a long time.

"But then you came along - or better said, you collapsed on the stone river outside our garden. And there you were, in pain and upset and desperate to die. Your suffering roused something inside me I'd never felt before. Up to then, I'd had no idea what it meant to love anybody or anything; not properly. But suddenly there you were, looking so sad and silly, covered in the ridiculous decorations your disgusting Howler had forced on you, and ... well, *everything* began to change. I felt it as soon as I saw you. I knew that you were important to me. That's the main reason I rescued you. I was quite selfish, really.

"And yet, at the same time as wanting to learn the things you were beginning to teach me with your amazing, loving behaviour, I was scared ... No, not scared; *terrified*. And now I know why, little Paa. And now I think I should have been even more afraid of you than I was."

"But why? ... Why?" whimpered the poodle, "why should you have been afraid of me? I was just a stupid pink-painted, wrecked old dog with an idiotic name and an even more idiotic master. Curl my whiskers, I was half-mad with pain and despair when I saw you, and all I wanted to do was die. I meant it. I only wanted you to kill me. D'you remember? I *knew* you were special, I *knew* you could help me, and I *really* wanted to die. You could have done that. I didn't want anything else. You'd have been doing me a favour!

"But instead you gave me a second chance and made life wonderful for me. And that's because you're *good*, don't you see? ... Besides, you're so powerful. I could never ever hurt you, even if I wanted to - which I don't, because I loved and worshipped you right away. I could never do anything to hurt you – or anybody else! So why be afraid of me?"

"But that's just it, little Paa, don't you see?" urged Nataka, gazing into the bewildered eyes of the poodle, "it was what you asked for in the first place that made everything else happen. If you'd asked me to punish the Howler who was torturing you, I would have done it quite happily. In fact I did it anyway, even though you never asked ask me to. And if you'd asked me to cure you, I'd have done that, too. But in that case I wouldn't really have cared about anything apart from getting rid of the whole annoyance of it, *and* getting rid of you too, because you'd have been just like everybody else, only looking out for yourself.

"But, see, you didn't even *think* about getting any kind of revenge on your torturer, did you? It never even crossed your mind, although you told me that you hated him. All you begged me for was to help you die. I was quite willing to kill him for you, but you were shocked at the idea. You said you couldn't make that choice for him – for *him* – a Howler that had tortured you! And then you said sorry, you *apologised*, to me! ... That floored me.

"*That's* what changed everything, don't you see? I found myself wanting to be able to care for others like you; to love them – or at least to respect their right to be alive, whether they deserved it or not... but I didn't know how. And I'd never felt that way before. Oh, of course I'd read and heard all about it, but it had always struck me as another form of Howler stupidity, to be honest. And yes, I've *liked* plenty of people, too. But real *love* hadn't happened to me. So I never realised just how painful it is, this love, the kind that doesn't want anything for itself but instead longs to be the best for someone else - for everyone else - until *you* showed me. Before then, I simply had no idea.

"But, oh, Paa, it's so hard! It's unbearable! Until I can find a way to care for everybody around me, regardless of whether I think they *deserve* it or not, until I can get past even thinking about whether they deserve it, I can never be genuinely loving, can I? And yet that's all I want, now.

"And worst of all, now that I've discovered this blasted love thing in my own narrow, selfish way, I also can't stop myself from getting so furious when I see innocent people suffer that I simply lose control. *Now* I could destroy everything in this Dimension, just to punish the Howlers who hurt others – which is most of them, of course – for all the harm they do all the time to so many innocent lives, not just to Wanyama but to one another, too, just because they're so greedy and selfish and stupid and unfair and bigoted and… and … and… "

Nataka's speech had been growing more and more vehement and rapid. Now she unclenched her hands and caught her breath, her eyes widening as she realised how close she had come to losing control again. She struggled to slow and deepen her breaths, to suppress the fury her own words had rekindled within her. Toki and Paa watched in consternation, afraid to speak.

After a while, during which the colour of her eyes faded back from red to a sombre blue, she spoke again.

"Do you remember the dream Fagus had, Paa, the one it spoke about after I roused it? *It* knew. It knew I could be a monster. Fagus's pathways traverse and contain so many times, dimensions and probabilities that all its dreams must be taken seriously, because we don't know where – or when – they may come from. Often they predict things that haven't happened yet. And Fagus did particularly want to talk to me about this one dream in which it had seen me as a beast devouring the earth. Do you remember? … But like a fool I never gave it a chance; I never made a point of going back and having a talk with it, because I was so wrapped up in the moment, in messing around with the Mond *shauri* and the Old Biddy and Rav'n business ... and, of course, with that *matata* of the ageing Sap and his grandson Ter, which is what's finally driven me *wazimu*.

"Yes, Fagus's dream should have warned me. You see, I've done it before, long ago. I destroyed a whole civilization because I despised it. *That* time, I was in total control of my emotions, and so I limited the destruction to just one culture. But I certainly annihilated them, oh yes. I coldly and deliberately trashed a whole population of Howlers, and ripped up their lairs and nests, because they were being so destructive to one another that I was sick of constantly being annoyed by their emotions. They had really nasty habits, that lot: cutting each other's stomachs open as sacrifice to some idiotic sun god they'd invented; practising slavery; raping, torturing and killing one another, not to mention any Wanyama they could find... Their behaviour was contemptible. And besides, the disturbance from the suffering they were causing one another had become intolerable. It bit and tore at my concentration and peace of mind, and overwhelmed my songs whenever I tried to sing ... It was like getting sucked and chewed to death by a swarm of starving but toothless piranhas, if you can imagine such a thing.

"So one Suntime, when their idiocy and cruelty had escalated beyond anything they'd ever achieved before, I suddenly had enough. I was absolutely fed up. And so I deliberately Transformed into a monster and wiped them out, simply to get a bit of peace, and because it satisfied me to see them go through what they'd been dishing out to one another, and all the other species around them, for such a long time. Yes, I did it; and what's more, I didn't bother to make their destruction easy or painless. I gave them all a taste of their own cruelty. And the *satisfaction* of it! Tremendous.

"Oh, please don't look so shocked, Paa! I warned you, didn't I? I'm not at all good or kind. I wiped out those Howlers without a second's thought, *and* I enjoyed it. Yes, and felt relieved and amused afterwards, too. So have I finally convinced you? That wasn't the behaviour of a *good* person, was it? … Was it?"

The poodle sat silent and stunned while Nataka glared at her with a mixture of resentment, shame and defiance on her face.

"And that, Aelfeynn Earda, was when I was instructed to block your way home; to detain you in this Dimension indefinitely," said Toki. "It was then that the decision was taken: until you had learnt to love truly, without anger or judgement; until you had genuinely mastered yourself and could no longer pose a danger to any other creature, you were to remain here, in this Reality, with myself as your guardian and sentinel. After all, your powers are such that, unshackled, they would be – they *are* – potentially devastating to any Dimension you occupy. So this is the arena in which you must finally attain a sufficient level of maturity and self-denial to win your own release from it."

A soft sigh escaped the shadowy lips. "I confess that I grow weary for a sight of realms beyond this; for my own kind; for a re-opening of the Ways we used to traverse … simply, for the freedom to pass between Dimensions again, Child Spirit," it said. "But until we can be assured that your new-found capacity for love is leavened with true moderation and patience in your actions, the Way must still be barred to us both. You must remain here, and I with you; both of us unable to enter the great Change that will release us from this Reality."

"Yes," grieved Nataka. "I know. I understand that properly, at last. And I also know that now things have become so much worse than before. I could easily inflict it all – all that violence – again, except that *this* time I might not be able to stop myself from destroying everything, as I did before. That time, I stopped short of annihilating everything and everybody, because I could still stand apart from myself. But now I've lost control. And the irony is that if I did it again, I would actually be doing it out of love and the desire to avenge somebody's undeserved suffering, rather than from impatience and contempt.

"But it wouldn't make any difference *why* I did it, would it? Motives are ultimately irrelevant. Destruction is destruction, regardless of its motive. Lives are destroyed, whatever the reason; innocent lives. People are wiped out that don't deserve to die; people full of potential who shouldn't have passed through their final Change so soon, and who can never be recovered once they're gone. People like that wonderful little Sapiens, the one who died this Sunclimb, despite all my skills.

"*That's* the terrible truth. Revenge is useless. But until I met you, Paa, I never really appreciated it. And even now, even realising it, I'm still imperfect. I can't *not* revenge. D'you see now? That's why I feared you. And that's why you're all wrong about me. I'm not at all honourable, I'm selfish. Except that *now* I feel the suffering of every one of those individual Howlers or Wanyama out there as if it were happening to *me*. And it's driving me crazy. I can't bear it. I don't know how not to hurt people in return. I don't know how to let it all happen and *not* get violent. Ah, Toki, what an appalling paradox; the one lesson I had to learn has made me worse than ever!"

Nataka groaned and buried her face in her hands. "I nearly killed poor old Glose just now, Paa;" she mumbled into her palms, "Imagine: that poor daft, harmless raven. I actually wanted to *eat* him."

Neither Paa nor Nataka noticed the flash of pure amusement that rippled across Toki's face and fled again, like the brief ruffling wave on a field of ripe corn when a warm breeze blows over it.

"But why do you have to be dangerous?" asked the dog, "why does your love have to go with anger? Isn't there any other way you could feel?"

"What do *you* do, Paa Elpidea, when you are upset and angry?" asked Toki.

"Er… um… I don't know," said the poodle, "I just, sort of … I … I don't know…" she stuttered to a halt.

"Let me be more specific. What did you do with that old Howler when you cured him?" persisted the Sentinel, "why did you not simply leave him to the suffering Nataka had laid on him as punishment for torturing you?"

"Oh, *that* … I'm not sure what I did, exactly," the poodle licked her nose for a moment, thinking. "I suppose I just couldn't see what good it would do to let that stupid old Howler go on feeling miserable. It didn't make any sense. Besides, he'd been doing all that talking, you know? Telling me how he felt and why he'd done the things he did. And then, while he was yapping and whining away, I realised that he really believed he'd been doing a good job for me with all that stupid painting and curling and bathing and training and shows. He'd never *meant* to be nasty. He just *was* nasty – and stupid, of course… and then he said that he wasn't sure he *had* been good, after all. He was asking questions about himself. I never expected that.

"I suppose I realised that he'd never thought it through properly, at least not until I saw him again at the gate, you know? *Then,* he seemed to click at last that he *had* made me unhappy. He even wanted to apologise. He was breaking his heart because he thought I was dead and so he couldn't say sorry. Sorry! … To *me!*

"So in a strange way he really did love me all along, didn't he? – in his own selfish, mean way. So maybe his… his… thinking? … loving? wasn't big or deep or open enough for him to find another way to treat me – I mean, in a less demanding, more generous way, you know? – without expecting anything back.

"So I thought, what's the point, anyway? … It wasn't as if letting him go on being miserable and sick would change anything he'd done to me, was it? … And besides, being furious with him was really hard work. It made *me* feel miserable. Like being covered in fleas. It kept me from enjoying all the sounds and smells and colours going on around me. I mean, you know, none – not one tiny bit – of all that suffering made any sense or was any use. To anybody. So I … um… well, I just decided to let it go.

"And then I thought he might feel a bit comforted if I licked his hand, you know? Make him feel better. Calm him down. So, well, that's all I did. I just went up and licked his hand to make him feel a bit better. It really wasn't such a big deal. And to be honest, I'm still not sure *how* it could have made any difference, you know? Just licking his hand. That's fair flummoxing, that is.

"But curl my whiskers, did he *stink*. Just like rotten fish. Poor old Howler. Pex was absolutely right. Good thing I didn't have to do it more than once." The poodle wrinkled her nose, remembering, and then began to scratch herself vigorously. "Thinking about fleas makes me itch," she observed to nobody in particular.

"And there, out of the mouth of this innocent, you have your answer, Nataka Aelfeynn Earda," Toki's unearthly face beamed down at the little dog (whose tail was beginning to sprout cockerel feathers, another cloud of magic dust having drifted down onto it).

"Forgiveness. Forgiveness is the magic Paa Elpidea exercises, such forgiveness as can only occur when one understands another's pain and seeks to heal it. *There* is your lesson, Child Spirit. *That* is what you need to learn."

"Really? Is that it? I had no idea. Are you sure?" The dog scratched herself a bit harder. "Sounds too grand for me," she said. The cockerel tail wilted off her rump.

"Of course! There is yet another, quite crucial, final element," exclaimed Toki. "Not only does Paa Elpidea bestow unconditional love and forgiveness on those around her, but she does so in a state of absolute self-forgetfulness. Look at her, Nataka -" The poodle was gazing cross-eyed at Toki through a magical bubble of lighter-than-air potion that had escaped from a smashed flask and drifted in front of her nose, shrinking her muzzle and enlarging her eyes. "Look! She is the epitome of unselfconsciousness. She has no inkling of her own goodness, because she has never questioned its need. She is a true innocent.

"Yes, there you have it, Child Spirit: forgiveness, unconditional love, *and* self-forgetfulness. Attain those three states, grapple them to you, and you need never fear again!"

"All right, old friend. I get your point. But *how* do I do it, exactly?" demanded Nataka. "It's not just a matter of *wanting* to do it, you know. How do I overcome my own nature and reactions? I'm not Paa and never can be, however much I may long for it!"

Paa's expression at the idea that Nataka might desire to be like her set Toki off into peals of laughter. Again the floor rocked under the poodle's paws and the precariously balanced piles of débris that had once been furniture, crockery, books, scrolls and utensils shivered, tumbled and cascaded together into fresh, teetering drifts and ridges on the cottage floor. Dusts and fumes that had settled out to the floor rose again, as the fine silt on the bottom of a calm brook is disturbed into tiny clouds by the flicking tail of a passing trout. Paa winced as a flurry of multicoloured detonations and flashes marked the meetings of various mismatched concoctions. She whimpered, flopped down with her tail well tucked between her legs, and buried her muzzle beneath her forepaws. *Make yourself small. Make yourself ever so small.*

After a little while the commotion eased, so the poodle ventured to peep out again, and caught her breath at the oceanic joy she espied lurking behind Toki's eyes, like a deep reservoir of water behind a dam on the point of bursting and cascading in irresistible torrents over everything in its path. She simply *had* to smile in return, and her tail began to wag at … at what, exactly? She didn't know; but for some reason it didn't matter. The only thing that *did* matter was that the cottage was joyous, and its joy infectious. Suddenly life felt awash with hope and potential again; she cared for nothing else.

As Toki's bell-like laughter rang around the clearing, accompanied by Paa's excited yapping and a sudden chortle from Nataka, the Wanyama that had fled before the Beast began to trickle back to the cottage from their various hiding places. One by one, they crept into the haven and picked through the rubble, moving tentatively and unobtrusively, scenting the air and poised to fly or scuttle away again at the slightest sign of renewed peril.

And right at the very end, after everybody else had assembled, Glose fluttered down from his perch in the aspen, crouched on the windowsill, and peered nervously into the cottage, his legs tensed and wings braced to bounce him back out into the open. He had been struggling to set his scrambled feathers to rights, but no amount of preening could disguise his sorry state; too much of his plumage was missing, torn or bent into angles that made flight ungainly and difficult. Nataka turned her head and beckoned to him, and the contrition in her face encouraged him to flutter onto her shoulder, where he laid his head against her cheek.

"Oh, my poor Glose, look at you; you're all messed up," crooned Nataka. "Did I hurt you, poor Glose? I'm *so* sorry, forgive me!" She murmured a little tune under her breath and ran one index finger the length of the raven's body, leaving him glossy and whole again, then she caressed his head and neck. "We *have* been going at one another recently, haven't we, my poor old bird? We really must both try to be a bit kinder to one another from now on, agreed? … You know, you *were* brave just now, you foolhardy thing." Glose shut his eyes and uttered a soft caw.

"Yes, yes, *yes*; that's all very well," M'Kuu thumped the floor with a back leg. "But look at our lair, everybody! Just *look* at it. It's a thumping disgrace, is what it is. Before we settle down all sweet and loving to an *indaba* or feast, Boss, we really must tidy up. I want my woodpile back!" As he spoke, there was a particularly loud ****pop****, and in the centre of a silvery haze trembled a luminous ostrich egg with floppy ears where the hare had been.

"Oh-oh! Nobody make any omelettes till M'Kuu's back, please," said Nataka.

Chapter 26. Roger makes some calls

"How strange it is that though some god hath devised cures for mortals against the venom of reptiles, no man ever yet hath discovered aught to cure a woman's venom." [clix]

Roger's day wasn't getting any better.

By the time he'd pulled himself together after the row with the Wingco and made his way out of the nursing home (after fielding the querulous nurse and a hefty bill at their Reception), the Wingco and his family had hailed a taxi and left. Roger bared his teeth in a humourless grin as he threaded his way between a variety of parked vehicles to his own car (a fine BMW, that; the latest model; no *schmutter* for him; no *Sir*), settled into the driving seat with his mobile phone in hand, and (swallowing a rather sick-tasting lump in his throat) began to try to work out a way to fill the gaping hole that had been delved in his shady trading deal by the Wingco's recovery.

He started by phoning his trading partners and creditors. But he found the business of explaining that his assured pay-out was jeopardised - and then trying to placate what had suddenly turned into a pack of seriously disgruntled creditors - much more difficult than he'd feared. He tried various ways of getting them to grasp why the return of the money he owed them had suddenly become so problematic, contrary to all his previous assurances. But to no avail. His hands grew clammy as the phone call progressed and the tone of the conversation deteriorated.

No, that conversation had been far from ideal. There had been some (to his mind entirely inappropriate and unnecessarily threatening) talk on the part of Gabriel, the soft-voiced, Armani-clad thug with angelic features who spoke on behalf of the loose consortium of 'businessmen' Roger had been dealing with; talk about other, more painful ways of extracting their loan repayment; talk that did not rule out what Gabriel euphemistically called "a terminal solution".

By this time, Roger's hands were no longer the only clammy portion of his anatomy. When he finally managed to extricate himself from the phone conversation with a scant promise of a limited grace period from Gabriel in which to work out an acceptable payment plan, his heart was racing and he urgently the toilet. So he scurried back to the nursing home and hurried into the Gents', avoiding eyes. While he relieved himself he went over his dilemma once again.

He didn't waste much time on the idea of simply reneging on his debt; the consequences of doing that would have been dire. Those people weren't the types you played fast and loose with if you wanted to keep your health. There was nothing for it; he would have to find adequate funds quickly enough to pre-empt any drastic action to which his suddenly very unpleasant creditors might resort. But *how* could he do that? How many people did he know who would willingly loan him a substantial sum to tide him over while he pursued another solution for funding his questionable enterprise without comprehensively wiping out the funds he had managed to salt away in his Cayman Islands account?

Cursing under his breath, Roger exited the nursing home again and instantly stumbled on the front steps. He had switched to the contacts directory on his mobile and begun to trawl through his list of business acquaintances and friends, and wasn't minding his feet. But that search was a waste of time. Nobody on his list of contacts was suitable. No: the people he most often frequented in the course of his legitimate day-to-day business activities were most emphatically not the types to leap into any deal, let alone such a legally dodgy one, without first securing a whole fortress of cast-iron guarantees through exhaustive due diligence research. These City frequenters conducted their larceny on a much more sophisticated level, one that involved much subtle twisting and 'spinning' of the rules. They never got their hands dirty. They lacked Roger's rather more relaxed and gung-ho approach to shady trading. Besides, even supposing that one of those contacts might be persuaded to invest in his illegal enterprise, the minute they caught the scent of the slightest risk (as would be unavoidable), they'd pull out of the arrangement again more quickly than a scat exiting a gastroenteritic heifer.

Roger unlocked his car and settled into the driver's seat. He turned off his phone, then sat with his hands on the steering wheel and stared unseeingly at the ugly façade of the nursing home while he contemplated his dilemma. Bitterness and resentment grew inside him. Why *had* that old bastard had to get better like that, anyway, just when everything had been going so well? What had he (Roger) ever done to deserve it? It wasn't fair! The way things were going, he'd find himself back where he'd been before, without a penny to show for all his hard work, his carefully saved dividends squandered to pay off a bunch of cut-throat hoodlums for the arms they'd supplied. *This* wasn't how it was supposed to go! Why didn't anything ever work for him? ... And so on. For a while he wallowed in self-pity.

In the end all he could think of was to phone his sister right away, even before he went on to the next urgent activity (which featured the consumption of copious alcoholic drinks). But even having made that decision, he carried on sitting and mulling over his grievances for a while longer. What stuck in his craw was that he *knew* the old man had been at death's door. All the docs had said so. If he (Roger) hadn't intervened and kept the old bastard alive, he'd have died on the day of the stroke. So what *had* happened? What had changed that? No matter how hard he tried, he couldn't figure out just *how* the old man could have recovered so fully from one moment to the next, coming back from what really was as good as being dead (and right where Roger had wanted him) to bouncing around, totally healthy and fit again. And now the old bastard looked as if he'd live on forever ... in fact, the way things were going, he'd probably even outlive him (Roger) ... particularly if Gabriel had anything to do with it.

It was all so unfair, so entirely unfair! There was no doubt, after everything he'd said during their row, that the old man wasn't going to waste any time changing his will. He'd said so. And once he cut Maddie out of it altogether this would be total disaster for Roger's plans. As long as the will remained unaltered, he might *just* have a chance – a tiny chance – of pulling the chestnuts out of the fire. If he worked hard to propitiate that miserable woman and win his way back into her favour, that was. But *this* way, if the old man altered his will? ... This way meant curtains, or penury, which as far as he was concerned would be just as bad, if not worse, than curtains. People would know he'd been taken to the cleaners by an old man and a gang of crooks; that he'd royally cocked up a huge, illegal deal. Such stories always got out, and as soon as it did he'd be pilloried. He wouldn't be able to show his face among his business colleagues; he'd become a laughing stock. He'd be disgraced... *Christ!* It didn't bear thinking about.

A handsome grey cat with deep green eyes emerged from behind some potted shrubs and began a leisurely stroll through the car park, stopping every so often to sniff a tyre or bumper.

At last, sick of grinding over the same thoughts again and again, Roger picked up his mobile and called his sister. He could try to prise some financial support out of her, at least. Even a bit of money might yet stave off disaster. He'd have to go about it carefully, though; she was tighter than a fish's sphincter, and *that* was watertight. Old cow; she had much more money than she needed, in his opinion. And if she was so willing to waste it on her stupid church, surely she could give *him* some of it. He was her brother, after all. *And* she hadn't contributed anything towards his parents' upkeep in the last years of their lives, or indeed to the ridiculous expense of their funerals. She owed him, and she knew it.

While the phone rang he composed himself, throttling back any sense of shame and pumping up his sense of entitlement by way of preparing for the conversation.

"I hope you're calling to apologise!" snapped Ida before he could say a word.

Roger ground his teeth and tried to inject surprise into his voice. "What for? Why should I apologise? *I* haven't done anything to you…"

But this was a red rag. The bull charged and away they went, squabbling as usual.

"Oh, you haven't? Is that what you think? You've only sided with her against me, that's all!"

"Ida, I haven't sided with anybody. I didn't want you to leave. I asked you to stay. But you decided to storm out, and …"

"Well, you didn't come with me, did you? You could have! I'm your sister … but no. You had to stay with that snooty, selfish bitch who thinks she's so much better than us, and with her brat of a son, not to mention the old man, who should be in his grave by now – who *would* be in his grave, if it weren't for you spending goodness knows how much to keep him alive. I really can't understand you. Why are you *doing* that, anyway? That kind of care costs money, you know! Why not let him die, and cash in? … And anyway, they should be grateful to you - *and* me – for everything we're doing for them!

"And *then* she throws me out of the room, and you decide to stay with her! Outrageous! Never a thought about how *I* might be feeling, of course. And now, I suppose, she's still refusing to talk to you. Is that it? Crawling to me for sympathy, are you? Or is it cash you're after, as usual?"

This was much closer to the bone than Roger liked. He could feel his blood pressure mount. What *was* it with women, anyway? Why did they insist on standing on their own dignity all the time? *He* hadn't insulted Ida, had he? But just because he hadn't wanted to alienate his stupid, wishy-washy – and suddenly awkward - wife, he hadn't been able to slap her down as hard as he'd wanted. And now Ida was getting her knickers in a twist about it. Stupid cow!

Roger clenched the phone and fought for calm. It was important to keep his voice mild; there was no good to be gained from alienating the woman.

The grey tomcat had noticed movement inside Roger's car. It pricked up its ears and approached, looking intrigued. Roger watched it absently, imagining just where he'd plug it with a BB or air gun if he had one to hand (*right there: between the green eyes: *Splat*...*), then turned his attention back to Ida, who was still rattling away, recounting decades' worth of ancient grievances. He waited until she stopped to draw a breath, and leaped in.

"Look, Ida. *Listen.* I phoned you because I want your advice. All right? You're my sister and I've got a proper problem here. Something happened after you left. Something that's... that's ... well let's just say that I'm really scuppered by it. And I can't figure out how or why it all happened. So I thought I'd tell you about it, and ... well anyway, can I please just talk now, without you jumping down my throat every five words -"

He got no further.

"Oh, that's *nice*. That's very nice. Jumping down your throat. Every five words!" interrupted Ida, her voice rising. "How *dare* you? I ..."

"Look, can you please try not to make it all about *you,* for once? I just want your advice, OK? I need your help!" snapped Roger, but Ida was well away on a familiar litany, ranting as if she were standing in a pulpit.

The grey tomcat seemed to be attracted to the sound of Roger's voice. It gathered itself and leaped, landing on the bonnet of his car with a solid **thud**. Roger wound down his window, shot out his right arm and gesticulated wildly to shoo it away. His actions seemed to interest the cat even more, because its green eyes narrowed and focused. To Roger's annoyance it hunkered down on the bonnet, wound its ample tail around its paws, and settled down to track Roger's increasingly agitated movements with its eyes and head. The tip of its tail began to twitch.

"Next you'll be reminding me again that you had to pay for Mother's and Father's funerals, I'll bet! Just to make out I'm..."

"That's nonsense! *You're* the one that keeps raising the topic. I never say anything about it. So if you have a guilty conscience, just keep it to ..."

"Guilty conscience? See? You're mentioning it *again*! You're *always* doing that!"

Ida paused to catch breath, and Roger again snatched at the opportunity to make himself heard.

"Ida. ... Ida. ... *Ida*! Listen. *Listen,* Ida. Let's forget all about that. You listening? ... Let's start again. I'm calling because something really weird happened just after you left. So. D'you want to hear about it or not?"

He stopped and waited, listening to his sister mouth-breathing at the other end. Ida couldn't resist mysteries or anything that sounded even vaguely like gossip. Would she hang up?

After a pause she sighed noisily and answered, managing to inject a lifetime's worth of grudge and resentment into her words. "Oh, go on, then, if you must. Tell me. What's happened *now*?"

At last. Roger forgot about the cat on the bonnet of his car and launched into an account of his argument with the unaccountably revived Wingco, letting his right hand settle on the frame of the car window with the fingers resting on the outside of the windscreen. As he spoke, his forefinger tapped the glass, following the cadence of his own voice.

The twitching of the grey tomcat's tail-tip escalated. It began to switch from side to side, then to lash as it watched the fascinating movements of the blunt, carefully manicured fingers on the windscreen. The animal tensed, shifted its weight to its hind-paws, raised its rump, narrowed its eyes, flexed its back legs and shoulders, extended its neck and lowered its head, never looking away from the twitching fingers.

"... I mean, how impossible is *that*? ... Have you ever heard of such a thing? *You* saw the state of that old sod this afternoon, Ida. Nearly pegging it, right? ... So you tell me. How could he suddenly, just like that, be fit as a flea again? ... And *then* we had the most god-awful row. He said he knows all about my private financial affairs, and told me that he's going to change his will so I can't ...

"*AAAAAAAaaargh!* ... *BLOODY CAT!*"

417

Rav'n (for it was he) had pounced, catching three of Roger's digits between his claws and fangs in what he considered one of his finest tackles. He was going to enjoy this game. But instead of playing along with him after all that inviting foreplay, the Howler in the smelly whizz thing screamed, shook his hand violently and then snatched it away, cuffing his muzzle as he did so, and earning a couple of deep lacerations in return.

Rav'n hissed, screeched like a demented banshee puncturing a bagpipe, and sprang off the car with all his fur on end.

"*Howlers*!" he spat as he dashed away, his tail lashing. "One moment they invites yeh ter play, then they scares yeh outta yer pelt. Suck a toad! Hissin' mad, the lot of 'em." He went on yammering into his whiskers for some time, and only stopped after he'd found a sunny spot under a magnolia and settled down to groom himself. "Still, that *wuz* a grea' tackle," he consoled himself, "one uf me best."

Roger dug around in his trouser pockets with his left hand, searching for something to use as a bandage. In the end he found a rumpled but largely clean tissue and folded it into a thin strip, which he wrapped around his lacerated fingers. He had to make a fist to hold the makeshift bandage in place. Then he noticed the bloody splatters on his shirtfront and cuff. *Could* life get more awful than this?

It was only when he caught sight of his mobile phone lying on the passenger seat where he had dropped it, that he remembered his sister. He snatched it up and put it to his ear. "Hello, Ida? ... Ida? ... Sorry about that. You wouldn't *believe* what just..." he gabbled in a rush, before realising that he was talking to thin air. The line was dead. Ida had hung up. And when he tried to call her number back there was no reply.

Roger let go of the phone and slumped over the steering wheel with his forehead on his hands. He shut his eyes - but snapped them open again in an instant, shocked by the image of a gaping crocodile gullet that had flashed before them, making him want the toilet again. *What was that?*

This was it. He would have to do something, anything, to stop the Wingco. Fast. He didn't have much time.

He picked up his mobile, opened it and removed the chip. Then he fumbled his wallet out of his breast pocket, extracted another chip from it and slotted that one into the phone. A number appeared on the screen. He clicked on it and waited.

"Talk."

"Gabriel -"

"*Don't* use that name." The voice was gentle, full of resonances suggesting a childhood spent in church choirs.

"Sorry, I forgot… Uhh… I want you to deliver a package for me. Urgently," said Roger. He began to sweat again.

"Will that take care of our business?" asked the gentle voice.

"Yes," said Roger. "But to work it's got to be today or not at all." And he explained, fighting to keep his voice level.

When he stopped talking there was a brief silence. Then:

"Done. Lose the phone," said the church choir voice, and cut the line without waiting for a reply.

Roger sat for a while, turning over the device in his good hand. Then he dropped it onto the passenger seat and started his car.

Well, he'd done his best, he said to himself, trying to ignore the taste of bile rising in his throat. The miserable, pig-headed old man hadn't left him any other choice. What happened next would be on *him*. If only he'd *listened*.

The vision of a crocodile's wide-open jaws flashed before his eyes again, and a voice in his ear said, *"SCUM"*.

Nonsense! It's nonsense. Just ignore it, he exhorted himself. But even so he began to sweat again.

Chapter 27. The Beast

"An eye for an eye, and a tooth for a tooth..." [clx].

The doorbell rang just as the family was thinking of rising from the table. The sandwiches at the nursing home had not even scratched the surface of the Wingco's and Ter's hunger, so they had stopped at a rather good takeaway on their way home and loaded up with ("definitely nutritious!") fish and chips, southern fried chicken legs and wings, and juicy pickled gherkins. They didn't often indulge in junk food, so this treat slid down very well, accompanied by one of Maddie's famous salads of mixed leaves, sunflower seeds, cheese and apples in a tangy lemon and honey dressing. And with it they drank lashings of good strong tea, military-style, compliments of the old man. For a little while there had been no room for talk as they concentrated on the serious business of filling up.

There finally came a point when even Ter leaned back, sighed with satisfaction, and admitted in a Pooh Bear voice that he was *stuffed*, making everybody laugh. The family was in that state of hilarity you reach when a very difficult and emotionally taxing situation has ended and all you want to do is collapse into a comfortable chair with a hot drink and a good book or television programme, and forget the outside world for a while.

"Murphy's Law," groaned the Wingco. He levered himself off his chair and turned towards the passage that led to the front door. "Probably Jehovah's Witnesses. Never mind, I'll see 'em off. And if it's Roger ... well, you'll just have to stop your ears, gang. Sorry, Maddie. There'll be no more Mister Nice Guy from me."

And then the phone rang.

"Just ignore it," called the Wingco over his shoulder as he walked away. "If it's important they'll call back. Let's deal with one thing at a time."

The phone carried on ringing for a few more beats. Then it stopped.

"Better check who it is, first, Wingco," called Maddie after him. A shiver had suddenly run up her spine. "Ask for credentials, OK? ... Oh - and put the chain on before you open the door."

"What're you worried about, Love? Somebody after you? My, but you're popular," chuckled the old man. "The secret lives and loves of Maddie Bourne." But he stopped and put the chain on, then peered into the peephole in the front door. Better safe than sorry.

On the doorstep stood a slim, lithe man of middling years in an expensively tailored grey suit. He had golden hair, angelic features enhanced by a sprinkling of laughter lines around eyes of such a startlingly light blue that at first sight they appeared colourless, and a smile that invited your wholehearted trust. He was carrying a briefcase in his left hand and a raincoat draped over his right forearm, hiding his hand.

The angelic stranger clearly had great patience, too. He didn't fidget or look around while he waited for a response to his summons. In fact, he never moved a muscle, apart from his smiling lips, which broadened a touch as he heard the chain go on inside.

"Probably a travelling salesman of some sort," said the Wingco to himself. As if he had heard the words, the man on the doorstep put down the briefcase and dug inside his right breast pocket with his left hand. He pulled out an ID card and held it up to the peephole. When he spoke his voice was mellifluous.

"Wing Commander Bourne?" he called through the closed door, "I know you're at home, Sir. Allow me to introduce myself. I'm ..."

But the Wingco stepped back. Something about the man didn't stack up. Just to start with, it was a sunny day and there really was no need to carry a raincoat around. The old man tended to notice such things.

The house phone rang again. There was an urgency about the repeated ringing that made Ter's scalp prickle. "I'm answering it, Mum," he said, and picked up the receiver. "Hello?"

Then he gasped and nearly dropped the phone. Roger had begun to shout the minute he answered the phone.

"Boy! ... BOY! Don't say anything, just listen. You don't have much time. Listen to me! get out of there! Grab your Granddad and mother and get OUT of there, you hear? You're all in danger! ... *Listen* to me! Where's your grandfather?"

"The Wingco's just answering the door," Ter's eyes were wide. Maddie gave a little cry of annoyance and snatched the phone from his hand.

"That's *enough*, Roger!" she snapped, cutting through his expostulations, "The Wingco *told* you, it's over. It's OVER. For me too. So don't try to call us ag..."

"Shut up and LISTEN, for Chrissake!" screamed her husband. "Don't let the old man open that door! Just get away, get right away, get OUT! Go out the back and run! Run to a neighbour or – or he'll *kill*..."

423

"Who? ... WHO? What *are* you talking about, Roger?"

"The MAN! The man standing at your door right NOW, you stupid bitch! He's a *killer*! Why else d'you think I'm calling? ... Just get *away,* d'you hear? ... I'm on my ..."

"*Mum*! Don't let the Wingco open the door, Mum!" whispered Ter, grabbing Maddie's arm. "Hold him off as long as you can. Tell the Wingco to hold him off. Bar the door ..."

His mother gasped, dropped the phone and scuttled down the passageway towards the front door, where the old man still stood, tugging at his lower lip and thinking. "Don't open it, Wingco; *don't* ..." she panted.

As his mother ran out, Ter snatched up a copper-bottomed frying pan and a carving knife from the draining board. He slid open the French window that gave onto their back garden, and hurried round the side of the house and onto the lawn that fringed it, keeping off the gravel path that led to the front of his home. As he ran, he remembered to breathe like a hunting fox by extending his tongue and panting through his open mouth in swift, silent breaths.

If only the Wingco wouldn't unlock the door...

But a second later, when he was halfway up the side of the house, Ter heard two shots, immediately followed by his mother's screams and a shout from his grandfather. There was no point in being stealthy any longer. He dropped the frying pan and broke into a headlong run, dashing full tilt round the house in time to see a smiling man in a spotless suit lift one polished shoe to kick down the front door. He'd been shooting at it to destroy the lock. In his right hand he held a large, ivory-handled gun. Ter didn't stop to think, but followed his first instinct, which was to draw the man's attention away from the door.

"NO!.... *No!* Leave them alone!" he yelled as he raced towards the man. And then, remembering her promise, he raised his voice even more. "Nataka! ... Nataka! **HELP**! I need you! ... **NATAKAAAAAAAAA**!"

The man with the gun lowered his foot and turned to face the boy pelting straight towards him, holding a kitchen knife with its blade pointing straight at his chest. He noted with some admiration that even though the child was sobbing, the hand clutching the knife was rock-steady and the blazing blue eyes glaring unflinchingly into his own.

The beautiful man's smile broadened. He raised his gun, aimed carefully, and squeezed the trigger.

Ter gasped once as a single bullet took him in the chest, directly under his breastbone. He somersaulted backwards like a downed rabbit, shook briefly, and then lay still, face down in the driveway. [clxi]

Behind the splintered, shattered door Maddie screamed again. The Wingco cried out as he wrestled with the lock, which had been warped by the bullets. "Ter! ... *Ter*! What are you *doing*? ... What are you *thinking?* ... TER! ... Listen, you - whoever you are - don't shoot! ... **JUST WAIT**, all right? Wait! Don't shoot! ... I'm coming out…" His voice broke.

Roger Court's BMW juddered to a halt on the gravel driveway. The door flew open and Roger half-fell out of it, calling. "Gabriel! For pity's sake, *don't shoot,* Gabriel … I've changed my mind, you hear? …. I've changed my mind! …We can work it out some other way… just don't – don't shoot…"

Then he caught sight of Ter lying on the driveway, and both his hands flew to his mouth. "Oh *God,* Gabriel ... Oh God oh God oh *God*... What have you done? What have you *done?* I didn't... I didn't mean ... I didn't..." his whispers faded. He swayed with his hands over his mouth, his eyes wide and horrified.

The gunman's smile broadened. He didn't bother to answer. Instead, he turned and contemplated the little figure lying face down at his feet. A dark stain had begun to spread from under it, staining the gravel. The knife Ter had carried lay some distance away from his slightly grubby, outflung hand. Gabriel noticed that its fingernails were chewed: a worrier, he'd been.

"Brave kid," Gabriel's tone would have graced a prayer meeting. He moved one foot to avoid the blood spreading towards his expensive shoe, put down his case beside the front door steps and carefully draped the raincoat over it. "Pity," he added. "He had guts."

Then, "The kid's down, Wing Commander," he called through the door, his tone helpful and informative; the voice of a waiter recommending a dish. He paused, flicked a mote of dust off his expensive suit and listened with an indulgent smile to the fumbling noise of the old man trying to break out of his mangled door. He was enjoying himself. This was the easiest day's work had in a long time; like shooting fish in a barrel, this.

"The kid didn't *have* to die, you know, Wing Commander," he added, "*he* wasn't my target. So why send him out? ... Want to know what I think? I think you're a coward. *I* think -"

But we will never know what he thought, because at that moment Nataka struck.

Sheathed in a hurricane of blood, brimstone and fire, and more devastating than a summer storm at sea, a thunder-and-banshee-voiced monster with claws of ice and adamant surrounded and engulfed the assassin, stopping his thoughts forever.

Roger Court slammed to his knees on the driveway, his hands still clamped over his mouth to stifle his screams. With Nataka's arrival every excruciating moment of the nightmare he had endured in Syria had come flooding back to him.

Maddie and the Wingco finally got the splintered door open and stumbled out in time to witness Gabriel's dismemberment by a monster they could barely discern through the vast, howling, twisting vortex-distortion wrought on the air by Nataka's song of fury, grief and retribution, at the heart of which the assassin hung suspended, rotating like a leaf in a whirlpool.

The brief glimpses they caught of the demon defied clear description: a darkly gleaming nightmare of fangs within fangs and claws sprouting claws; hissing, clashing, sulphurous scales and eyes lethal as lasers; a horror that simultaneously wrung its victim like a teacloth, plucked the flesh from his limbs as if they were the carcase of a boiled chicken, and alternately stretched and crushed his body like a lump of soft clay.

The man still lived, even as his bones, sinews and joints snapped and tore, and his eyes and tongue bulged and burst under the unbearable forces wrought on them by the demon in the vortex. Nataka made sure of that. In her demented outrage she refused to grant him one second's respite from his pain, much less the boon of a swift ending. He still lived; the occasional thin, tearing, wordless screams that broke through the apocalyptic song of the demon bore testimony that he still lived. And he went on living, conscious and aware, throughout the long moments of exquisite agony Nataka inflicted on him, granting him no quarter as she slowly, ever so slowly, tortured him to death.

Gabriel's gun had fallen from his hand as Nataka attacked. It lay on the gravel, reduced to a shapeless lump of molten metal that bubbled like molasses on a hot plate. Smoking chunks of scorched ivory, all that remained of its fancy handle, tainted the air with the reek of burnt fur. And the expensive case and coat no longer existed at all, having instantly been reduced to a fine ash.

Maddie stood frozen to the doorstep, unable to tear her eyes from the scene before her. But the Wingco had spared not one glance for the horrific execution or for his retching, sobbing son-in-law. He was already at Ter's side, cradling his small body and struggling to staunch the blood that poured from the single hole in his chest.

"An *ambulance*! Call an ambulance, Maddie! ... Roger!" he shouted, furious. "For Chrissake, come *on*! We need an *ambulance*! ... And then – and then something to bind him ... and water, lots of water ... with sugar... and salt ... D'you hear? ... Now, Maddie! NOW!"

***

Ter's call had shattered the peace of the cottage, making everybody's fur stand on end yet again and the hedgehog family curl up more tightly than ever before. Nataka had let rip a howl that shook Toki from chimneypot to cellar, swept out of the window and disappeared, a thunderbolt inside a black cloud with molten eyes and gleaming fangs.

Toki's face looked shocked for an instant, then it turned to the poodle.

"Go with her, Paa Elpidea!" it cried. "Follow her. Help her, lest we lose her forever!"

"But... but... *how*?" stammered Paa. "I'm a *dog,* Toki! I can't keep up with... with... *that,* whatever it is ... Besides, I don't even know where she's going..."

A shaft of white light shot out of Toki's eyes and touched the shining patch on Paa's forehead. "Be now what you have always been, Paa Elpidea," it ordered. "Know yourself at last! Follow Nataka, I say; help her. And fear nothing; you already command all the powers you will need. We have no time for explanations. For the sake of Infinity, *Go!*"

And she was outside and half-flying, half galloping across a blurred succession of stone rivers, fields and woodlands until she came upon a small cluster of Howler dwellings not far from the river, and knew without thinking which was the one she sought. She no longer questioned how all this could be happening; Toki's words and touch had banished every doubt from her mind, and it was easy to discern Nataka's path - a dark, lightning-streaked trail before her in the air - and to race down it like a winged bloodhound, tracking the Protean.

When she arrived, Nataka's vengeance was complete. Gabriel was dead, and Nataka's song of destruction had given way to a sinister, rumbling, low-pitched threnody pulsing with grief and fury, a sound that weakened knees and lurched entrails as it reduced the gravelled driveway beneath the assassin's mangled remains into a viscous, stygian whirlpool of mud and tar. Gurgling and hiccoughing like a blocked drain, the whirlpool began to suck down the grisly tangle of bones and tissue, all that remained of the elegantly dressed psychopath.

The monstrous creature composed of sulphurous smoke and scales, flame and blood that had emerged from the vortex now swayed, fulminating and snarling as it gazed into the horrific whirlpool. As the last scraps of the dead killer disappeared from sight with an obscene gurgling, belching noise, Nataka the Beast raised her head and stared at the dead child in the Wingco's arms. Again her rumbling, moaning song of anguish and fury flooded through the senses of all who heard it.

And now Nataka's horned snout turned and her burning eyes lighted on the retching, sobbing figure on the gravel before his car. The monster lurched to within striking distance of the trembling man and raised a scaled, spiked, bloodstained talon, from which a steaming shred of Gabriel's viscera still dangled.

"Please, please, please ... *please*..." whispered the distraught man and stretched out his arms. "I'm sorry ... I'm so sorry... I didn't want the boy to die... I swear ... or the – the Wingco ... not really... I swear it! ... Oh, *please* believe me... As soon as I - I'd called him – Gabriel .... I changed my mind... I wanted to stop him, I ... I tried to stop him; I tried to call him back; I *did* ... but he wouldn't answer his phone ... And then – and then I started to see - to see *you* ... *there* – with that baby, that other one ... and I remembered ... I remembered everything you showed me... And – and I rushed over here to warn them ... I *tried* to warn them, I swear I did ... I – I phoned to warn them! ... Too late ... Oh, God, too late ..."

He stopped and sobbed, fighting to breathe. Nataka never moved; but she did not lower her talon either. Roger drew a shuddering breath, and went on.

"But... Ok – OK, yes, honestly ... I admit it, for a while, before ... I ... I was just – just ... God, I mean, I was just... *crazy* for a while... When the Wingco recovered ... and then when we argued... I was desperate ... Oh – oh yes, I *know* I was wrong! ... But I never meant to – to hurt him, not really, not until ...

"No, no... I mean I *did*, sorry ... Yes, I admit it! I do, I confess it. I made a mistake, I didn't *think* ... but I only wanted to *scare* him, honestly! ... I was afraid ... afraid of what *they* would do... But I swear, I *swear* I didn't want any of this ... *this* ... to happen – not to the boy ... he's only a kid! ... Oh God! ... Yes, you're right; I'm a bastard. I know I'm a bastard, but I'm not a killer ... and especially not a child killer ... I swear it! I could never kill anybody, really ... I was only crazy, for a while ... But then, but then I wanted to stop it. I'd have done *anything* to stop it! ... Oh, Please... *please* ... You must believe me..."

Roger Court buried his face in his hands and collapsed, face down and sobbing, onto the driveway. "Please, please, *please...* I only needed – no – I *wanted* – the money... I know I was wrong, but ... I swear, I didn't want to hurt him ... the boy ... Oh, *please* ..."

And at last, through sobs that shook his whole frame, he begged, "Please forgive me ... forgive me... forgive me..."

The beast towering over the trembling, shuddering figure snarled. Her reeking talons clenched and unclenched to the heaving of her flanks. Deep, brimstone-tainted breaths rumbled and rasped in and out of her nostrils, so close above his crouching head and back that he could feel his hair and clothes begin to scorch. She snarled again, drew a juddering breath, spread her talons and opened wide her jaws.

"***A death for a death,***" rasped Nataka.

And then a shaft of pearl and gold landed over the top of the huddled man, straddled his body with long, elegant legs and levelled its delicate, spun-crystal horn to face the monster towering above him.

Roger Court's eyes were screwed shut. He crouched, certain of his own imminent annihilation. Instead, the fiery, stinking breath of the infuriated Beast eased as if a barrier had risen before it, and a soft voice spoke.

"Stop, Your Honour; stop. *Stop*, I beg you. You know this is wrong. He has begged you for forgiveness. You heard him. He's just confessed, and asked you to forgive him. And you have to do it, Your Honour. You know you do.

"Forgive him, and let it go, Your Honour. Please. You know this is wrong. This isn't the way. It'll do no good. It won't change anything. Let it go, and let him go. I beg you."

It was a low, gentle voice; a voice heard more in the mind; a voice so soft that for an instant Roger wondered that he should be able to hear it at all over the dark thunder of Nataka's song. But he forgot to wonder in the rush of gratitude he felt at what it said.

"Let it go, for your own sake, I beg you," repeated the voice, "before it destroys you. Oh, Your Honour, you are too precious. You *must* set yourself free."

"Let it *go*?" Nataka's thunderous eyes never moved from the cowering figure on the ground. Her voice rose, and with it the threnody of her outrage and grief escalated in pitch and intensity. "Let it go? ... The boy is **dead**!" Her voice broke on the word. As she spoke, her long, scaled tail lashed from side to side and one clawed talon gouged the earth, scattering gravel and mud, while the bones and entrails of every mortal present resonated to her fury and anguish.

"Ter is **DEAD**, Paa! ... On the orders of this... this ... **worm** ... by **his** admission ... Because of HIS **GREED**!

"And you say *let it go*? No, I cannot let it go. I **WILL NOT** let it go, not again! This, *this* is **unforgivable!**"

The monster lurched forward, and bellowed again.

"I warn you, Paa. Stand back. **Stand back**, I say, or be destroyed with him!"

Roger Court felt the creature standing over him rock and tremble before the beast's rage. But still his fragile protector held her ground, her glittering horn level and golden eyes steady, hopeful and loving as she gazed into the twin furnaces that were the demented Protean's eyes.

"And yet you know you really, *really* must let it go, Your Honour," she urged again, her voice still low and humble. "If you don't ... if you just destroy him - *and* yourself, as Toki and Fagus have already warned you ... if you don't forgive this Howler but tear him apart instead, *you'll* be lost. Yes, you will. You know you will. The Beast inside you, this Beast you are now, this very one you've been desperate to stop yourself from becoming ... well, *it* will win, Your Honour. Won't it? It'll beat you. And then you'll be trapped forever.

"And – and even if you go ahead and kill this Howler, and allow your fury to destroy everything else; if you sacrifice yourself for the Sap child you love ... Oh, Your Honour, don't you see? You still won't change anything. You still won't be able to bring him back, will you? Your revenge can't rescue the child!"

As the gentle voice continued to speak and the beast still held back despite the fragility of the creature that had so unexpectedly leapt to his defence, Roger held his breath, barely daring to hope for a reprieve.

Now the voice of his advocate paused for a long moment, then added as if testing a new thought, "So ... so, Your Honour, why not try something else? You're so powerful, why not try what you can do with Love, instead?"

"Why not indeed, Nataka Aelfeynn Earda?" suddenly asked a third voice: a deep voice, rich with patience, humour, suffering and hope.

Chapter 28. Thresholds

Though inland far we be,
Our souls have sight of that immortal sea
Which brought us hither,
Can in a moment travel thither,
And see the children sport upon the shore,
And hear the mighty waters rolling evermore." [clxii]

Startled, Paa and the Beast turned to face the tall figure that had materialised beside them. As it spoke, the wild, sweet refrain that had accompanied its last appearance among them rose and swelled, overcoming Nataka's throbbing song of rage. Paa realised that the tune was emerging from a set of simple reed pipes that dangled from a strap slung across the newcomer's massive shoulder.

"*You ... you're* the magical dancer!" she exclaimed, "*You* joined M'Kuu and Axl and me that night! ... Oh, I'm so *glad* you're here! ... But ... but where did you come from?"

"Do you not know me, Paa Elpidea?" urged the splendid figure. Cloven hooves rang on the gravel of the driveway as the muscular, densely furred legs and gleaming torso strode closer. "What, not though I have sheltered you, lent you the speed of the wind, and held long speech with you and Aelfeynn Earda just a short while ago?"

And at last, as she gazed into the wise, sceptical, benevolent eyes and the strange light scintillating on the broad brow beneath the densely clustered locks and sweeping ram's horns, Paa understood.

"Ohhh..." she breathed, "You're *Toki*! I never realised. You're so – so magical! But... but I didn't know that you could – you know – do what Nataka does, change and..."

"Why," smiled Toki-as-Pan, "I would be a poor Protean indeed were I unable to change at need, as Nataka does. I seldom choose to employ my powers to their full extent, and I resist Transforming myself as swiftly and as frequently as she does; but that is purely a matter of taste and preference. I have always been slow to act, unlike her. And this is why I sent you on before me, Paa Elpidea, while I prepared to follow."

"Oh! I had no idea. I thought I was on my own. Oh, this *is* a relief. Thank you, Toki. I was so afraid that I'd fail. And I think that I *have* failed, you know. I'm so sorry – and so glad you're here," said Paa. "Yes, I've failed. I've let you both down. I really, *really* don't know how to persuade Her Honour to change her mind. She's still desperately upset, as you can see, and I really don't know what to do. We both need your help."

"My dear Paa," responded the magnificent figure, its voice grave, "I am the one that should apologise. And I owe you a debt of thanks and explanation. Despite the fact that I was quite sure of your courage, and didn't doubt for an instant that you already have all the skills you need to face any challenge, I should not have burdened you so suddenly by asking you to face this situation unsupported, without preparation.

"But believe me, nobody could have achieved a better outcome. You have held poor Nataka back from unleashing all her destructive force, as she would have done, had you not intervened. Oh no, you have not failed. You have prevented her from sliding into irrecoverable disaster. Look: Nataka is still here. She is not lost yet. And, most importantly of all, she has not struck again. Thanks to you."

Now Toki turned to face Nataka, who had retreated a few steps at its arrival, but continued to glare down at the cowering human in their midst.

"Nataka," it said, "Think. Think, Nataka. You know all too

well that with every additional moment you indulge your fury, you jeopardise not only yourself but countless others, many of whom are dear to you. Remember my warning, Aelfeynn Earda, and do not allow your passion for vengeance to overwhelm you.

"With every capitulation to the Beast within you, with every moment you indulge it, you render a return to your true self more parlous. And yet, despite knowing this, in your fury and despair you insist on clinging to the Beast; yes, even to the point of threatening with death this brave, blameless creature, your dearest friend and ally, whose only desire it to help you save yourself.

"So ask yourself, as Paa already has, what will your fury avail you? What good can it achieve? What good can *you* achieve by destroying those that offend you? Can wanton destruction ease your pain or restore your lost loves to you? … Indeed, what good can such destruction *ever* achieve? Oh, Child Spirit, you know the time is more than ripe for you to practise wisdom as well as Skill. You know you must abandon *this* at last!"

Toki reached and laid its large, supple hand on the hideous brow of the monster. "What can it gain you, in lives recovered or happiness restored, to remain a Beast and destroy those who should be beneath your contempt, let alone your hatred? … Come, Nataka Aelfeynn Earda! Preserve and moderate your emotions. Anger and vengeance have availed you nothing. I urge you, listen to our luminous little ally at last, and try what Love may do instead.

"It is time for you to return, Nataka Aelfeynn Earda, old friend. You are dearly missed. Return to us."

The Beast shuddered, clawed the earth, lifted her bloodstained muzzle and howled her anguish to the sky.

Then she fell silent and her great horned head sank to her chitin-plated chest. Her flanks shuddered and heaved with sobs.

But Toki tugged impatiently at the spiked horns. "Come; up. *Up*, Nataka! Turn away from this flawed mortal -" it nodded towards the cowering man, "- at last, and help us *now*. Before it is too late. As for that -" it pointed to the swirling maelstrom that had swallowed Gabriel's remains, "- *that* must not remain. Be rid of it."

Nataka raised her head and grunted, lifting a claw. A sound like pebbles falling down a well sped across her talons on a streak of blue and grey. It vanished into the grinding, sucking whirlpool of mud, gravel and tar beside her. And as suddenly as the vortex had appeared it vanished again, leaving behind it no sign that it had ever existed, save for a slight bowl-shaped indentation in the gravelled driveway.

"Good. And now, would you also do something about *that*?" Toki pointed to the shattered front door. Again Nataka grunted. For an instant a sound rang out that reminded Paa of a busy carpenter's shop. The shards and splinters of the broken door rose, straightened, assembled and welded themselves back together ... and in the space of a few breaths the intact wooden door was again in place.

"Good," said Toki. "And now we must hurry."

For an instant Nataka the Beast stood and swayed, staring at the door. Then she turned and lumbered after Toki without casting another look at Roger. Paa exhaled a breath she hadn't realised she was holding, stepped carefully over and away from the figure she had been straddling, and followed.

The Wingco raised his tear-stained face and gazed without interest at the bizarre trio approaching him where he sat, cradling the lifeless body of his grandson. Maddie lay on the ground beside him with her arms around her fallen child and her face buried on his chest. She wept in the helpless, hopeless way a mother grieves whose child has been torn from her.

"Come. We cannot stay. Time is sliding by," urged Toki again, because Paa was lingering and whimpering softly, desperate to console the bereaved Howlers. "We must not linger, much as we may long to. If we are to do any good, any at all – and I warn you that we may not – you will have to focus all your concentration, songs and path-finding skills, Aelfeynn Earda, and your love and compassion, Elpidea. We have no time to indulge in tears."

"But – but where are we going?" asked Paa, bewildered and inclined to resent being dragged away from the grieving Howlers.

"We are going on a hunt, Paa; a difficult hunt. And we must go *now*. Fagus will appear at any moment. I summoned it with my song when I arrived," replied the Pan figure with a swift, slightly impatient smile. And indeed, as it spoke, the familiar shape of the giant beech surged up in the middle of the driveway and shook itself like a dog emerging from a pond, dislodging and scattering pebbles and gravel around it.

"Well met, Toki, old friend," it said, in a voice both alert and expectant, "this *is* a rare summons. And, I might add, to a remarkably ugly place, at that (**hup!**). Why have I been called?"

"You already know our need, Fagus," said Toki, "We seek a pathway to your thresholds. Urgently. Will you accommodate us, for old fellowship's sake?"

"Well, now. It *is* most irregular to be petitioned without a libation," responded Fagus. Its moss green eyes roved speculatively over the figures on the ground. "But where there is urgency, and where innocent blood is involved, as I see is the case here, I am willing to waive my usual terms (*hup*)! Who seeks to enter? Be warned, I never admit Stults."

"I wish to enter, if you please, Your Lordship," said Paa, who had begun to suspect what Toki was trying to do. "With Her Honour, of course. ... Oh, you already look *so* much better, Your Honour!" The Protean's appearance was changing back to the young woman that had befriended Ter and the Wingco; only the scaled tail and a disconcerting crown of thorns and horns still marred her appearance, although these also were rapidly shrinking away.

"We three will all enter, with your permission," confirmed Toki. Fagus smiled and opened to admit them.

"But what's going to happen to *them* while we're away?" fretted Paa, looking over her shoulder at the trio on the ground and at the more distant figure of Roger Court, who was still crouching on the gravel. He appeared too terrified to move.

"They know nothing of this," replied the Pan figure, "Time does not pass for them. Come, Paa. Do not linger! We have great need of haste."

"Oh, my whiskers and claws, Toki's frozen Time," whispered Paa to herself, and jumped through the hole in the tree.

***

The labyrinth through which they now sped was even more intricate and bewildering than the one Paa had traversed on her journeys to and from the Prison for Wanyama. It was not long before she lost all sense of direction, if such a term can even be applied to the time-and-space-transcending routes that unfolded in response to Nataka's urgent singing.

Often – Paa could not say how often, but *often* – they paused at thresholds into strange spaces and chambers, openings onto new dimensions and the verges of whirlpools that resembled nothing so much as vortices leading into oblivion, all of them rifts Nataka summoned into existence with her voice. At each halt, the two Proteans would lean and quest forwards, seeking some sign that they were on the right path. Often they changed direction, veering upwards; downwards; laterally and in spirals that felt to the bewildered poodle that they must somehow be swallowing themselves, turning themselves inside out and upside-down... But always they moved on again, frustrated in their search.

They met and passed countless phantoms; lights; snatches of speech and song; the sough of wind sighing through leaves and of waves gnawing at sandy beaches or falling back frothing from their onslaught on cliffs of slate or chalk or granite; they sped past the plaintive cries of gulls flocking over deserted promontories and atolls, the muffled, melancholy tolling of bells in various deserted and teeming stone nests and burrows, and the cry of birds over deserted mountaintops and forests ...

Until at length, quite by chance, after traversing a weary waste of desert and thorn in which the very rocks seemed to gape at their passage, they stumbled upon an opening in the ground through which emerged the intermingled sounds of children playing and calling in a ghostly schoolyard.

Nataka dropped onto all fours, as though the Beast in her were emerging again. She craned her neck and turned her head from side to side, peering intently. Then she shook herself impatiently and turned to Paa.

"I need your nose, Paa. Did you catch the scent of that boy we left behind when we entered Fagus? ... Do you remember his odour?" She laid a hand on Paa's head and the poodle felt it tremble. "Oh, please say you know it," she whispered, "please!"

Paa drew a deep breath, shut her mind to every other sensation, and rifled through her most recent scent memories. After a pause, during which she could feel the tension mount in her companions, she nodded, hesitantly. "Yes ... yes, I think so, Your Honour," she said, "I think... no, I *know*. Yes. I remember his scent."

"*Oh!*" the word emerged on a burst of expelled air. Nataka threw one arm around Paa, drew her close, and kissed her. "Oh, Paa Elpidea, you *are* wisely named! I couldn't bear to lose him too, he trusted me so much ... Is he here? Can you sense him here?"

But then, before Paa could reply, the Protean burst into tears. She had recognised Hassan, the young Syrian, amid the floating and drifting shadows of the many children crowding that dim schoolyard. He was sitting cross-legged at the centre of a circle of infant wraiths, chanting a soft Arabic counting song and holding up his fingers in various patterns as he did so. Young spirits clustered around him, mesmerised by his song. They gazed with translucent eyes and mouths wide, leaning in towards the little figure that sat singing so calmly and sweetly in their midst.

Nataka trembled and yearned towards the wraith of the little Arab boy. But Toki, which had been silent ever since entering the Pathway Tree, laid a hand on her shoulder. "Painful as it is, you must not be distracted, Nataka. Although I know that you are desperate to recover this life, for him we have arrived too late. And if we linger here any longer we shall also lose the life of the young Sapiens whose body lies on the ground outside Fagus at this moment. ... Look -" it added, "the child departs."

The figure of the little boy had begun to flake away at the edges, peeling off in shimmering flecks and drifting away like leaves dropping from an autumn tree. But, unlike leaves, these flakes did not settle to the ground. Instead they rose, whirling, and dispersed around the dwindling shape in increasingly transparent patterns, their glitter growing fainter and fainter until at last they vanished. Paa also observed with awe that, instead of appearing disconcerted at his own dissolution, the shrinking, ghostly child turned his shining eyes and gentle smile to his infant companions, reached out to them, and moved his lips.

"This was a rare Sapiens indeed," said Toki. "Even now he is consoling the other little ones, encouraging them to accompany him and not to fear this final step in their Transformation. ... But we must not – we *cannot* – stay. Come, Nataka, let him go. We still have to find the one you call Ter. For if once *this* begins to happen to him, there will be nothing more we can do."

So, with a final glance at the rapidly dissipating form of the boy she could not save, Nataka swallowed her sobs and turned to the poodle. "Is the other one here? Can you sense him?" she asked again.

But try as she might, Paa could catch no scent of him. So they sped on with greater urgency, past opening after opening, scene after scene; until at length, just as the exhausted poodle began to despair of ever detecting the elusive scent of the child, there - on the threshold of yet another opening into a dimension teeming with small ghostlike forms - she caught it at last, faint at first, but quite unmistakeable: the spirit-scent of Ter.

"He's here!" she exclaimed and bounded forward, her fatigue forgotten. "He's here, Your Honour, I'm sure of it!"

And so they found him at last: a forlorn little figure standing alone, halfway down what appeared to be a long, gently sloping beach of sand and shells, and staring about him with a bewildered expression at the wraiths of other children that materialised at the head of the beach and then wandered around, stooped to finger the sand and shells or stretched out on its glittering, silvery surface under a bright, pale sky festooned with high ribbons of cloud.

Translucent seabirds swung and dipped in that sky, calling faintly, while shimmering butterflies formed fluttering patterns in the air over the incongruously dark sea of indigo and purple that lay beneath the bright dome of sky like an inverted nightscape, its depths teeming with the light of innumerable drowned stars in unrecognisable constellations. The slowest sea-swell lifted its tenebrous waters up and down the sandy beach in oily, whispering tongues that trailed lacy ribbons of bubbles onto the shore, where they lay and glowed for a few moments before sinking back into the sand.

Every spirit wandering the beach in apparently random patterns invariably gravitated towards the water, apparently unable to resist the lure of its dark, star-laden depths. One after another, those who had been there longest and whose random movements had led them to the very verge where the dark water washed the sand and shells in whispers, waded slowly but without hesitation through its furling, lacy wavelets and out into the glowing darkness, becoming ever more transparent and smoky as they distanced themselves from the sand and immersed themselves in the water. At last, all that remained where each child had disappeared beneath the surface was a faint, silvery mist that hung briefly over the surface of the drowned star-field before it also vanished.

Ter's face bore the stunned expression of one who has been translated too suddenly by violent death. He had not yet begun to fade, nor had he voluntarily moved down the slope towards the water; but even though he was immobile, still the beach was carrying him gradually down its slope like a gentle conveyor belt, bringing him ever closer to the water that whispered and called, claiming every soul that saw it.

Yet Ter was seemingly unaware of what was happening to him. He stood helpless, gazing with absolute incomprehension and bewilderment around him at the wraiths that processed slowly and randomly down the beach and towards the water.

"Ter!" cried Nataka, "Oh, *Ter*!" Her eyes had been dark with grief, but now they flashed to a gold so bright, they seemed to cast a gilded path onto the sand between her and the boy. At the sound of her voice his head jerked up, his eyes widened, and he surged towards her, his arms outstretched.

"Nataka! Nataka!" he panted. "I ... I don't know what's going on ... I called you ... there's a man in front of our house... a man ... Oh, Nataka! He's going to *kill* them! He's going to kill the Wingco and my mum! We've *got* to save them! ... That's why I called you ... while I... I... I was ... running..."

His voice faltered, slowed and stopped. With a puzzled expression he looked around him again, then down at his own hands. "I had a knife ... I was... charging... and – and then..." he added haltingly, "I - I don't know what happened... What happened, Nataka? ... Where are they? Where am I? ... What am I doing here? ... Why ..."

But even as he spoke, he turned his head to gaze at the sea behind him; and as he did, a vagueness grew in his eyes.

"That water…" he murmured after a long moment, "that water… I've got to… to…" his voice became distant, absorbed.

He turned like a somnambulist and took a slow step down the slope of the beach. He seemed to have altogether forgotten Nataka and her companions.

"Ter?" said Nataka, reaching out to him, "Where are you going? We've got to get back to the Wingco. We've got to go *right now*, before it's too late. Come with me!"

"But … *ohh,* wait … I know where I am, now … this is my favourite place," murmured the boy dreamily, slipping away from her grasp, "I - actually, I don't want to go anywhere else. This is where I used to come with the Wingco… and my Dad… when I was little. Before … you know. … We used to sail here. Yes. His boat … his boat'll be here too … *He's* here, too. Look…"

As he said those words, the cove and the headlands around the bay subtly shifted in response. A small, single-masted sailboat with a triangular sail appeared on the skyline, sailed over the horizon and approached the beach with its sail spread, heading towards a jetty that now hung out over the inky water, complete with stanchions, ropes and half-submerged, barnacle-encrusted fenders dangling off its sides. A few small dinghies also materialised; moored alongside the jetty, they rose and fell to the gentle swell of the waves.

The boat swept towards the jetty as if driven by a following breeze – a breeze that stirred nothing else, for the sea remained smooth and oily, and the mists rose from it and dissipated, as before. In the boat sat two shadowy figures, and now one of them raised an arm and beckoned to Ter, who raised his hand in response, then turned resolutely and walked towards the jetty with quickened steps.

"Ah, of course. The boy's memory of a place where he was idyllically happy in life is generating everything we see here," said Toki. "It is his longing for happiness that animates this seeming Reality. This is his reconstruction of the place where he was happiest in life; of Perfection: a safe, unthreatening threshold from which to enter his final Change and dissolution. Just as the child Hassan's embodiment of Perfection was an intact schoolyard teeming with busy, laughing children, from which *he* was able to depart with contentment, without fear.

"Nataka, if you wish to retrieve him, the child must *not* go any further. Understand me: on no account must he touch the water. If he does, he will be lost. We will be powerless to retrieve him. Stop him, Nataka; turn him back! I cannot intervene, for he shares no bond of love with me!"

Nataka didn't pause to question her mentor. She raced down the beach to intercept Ter, who was still walking steadily towards the jetty. "*No!*" she said sharply as she seized his arm. "Don't go! Look away from the water, Ter; look away. Look at *me*! Listen, if you go down there, you'll…"

"But… look, they're already waiting for me," protested the child, pulling away from her, his eyes fixed on the little sailboat, "He's here, the Wingco … and my dad … I can't keep them waiting, I've got to go…"

"No… no! This isn't him, this isn't the Wingco," urged Nataka. She stepped down-slope to stand between Ter and the water. "This is an *illusion*, Ter! A – a dream, *your* dream. That's all this is. It isn't real. But if you come with me now, I can take you back to the real Wingco, who's waiting for you. Yes, Ter. He and your mother *are* waiting for you, but not here!"

But still Ter walked on, pulling her with him as he advanced

447

down the beach towards the dark, star-laden water, where the sailboat had landed and now lay, secured against the jetty. One of the dark figures inside it had risen to its feet and stood, steadying itself with one hand on the mast.

"Charon," muttered Toki, "Charon - for this soul." [clxiii] It laid its broad hand on Paa's head. "Paa Elpidea, we need you again!" its voice was urgent, "Nataka cannot turn the boy, and neither can I. Be what you truly are again, my gentle one. You alone can do this. Save the boy. Save him before he is lost forever. You have heard: he must *not* touch the water; it is Oblivion. *Save him!*"

Paa's brow flared, sending a shaft of energy through her, painful in its intensity. And once more she was speeding towards the jetty, so swiftly that she had the momentary illusion of being immobile, the only static thing in all that scene, while everything else – the sand, rocks, wraiths and shells – rushed towards and past her as she raced to reach the child.

Ter had grown ever more transparent, till now, as he approached the very verge of the shore of dark water with its jetty, his figure could barely be made out against the waves and sky.

"Come, Ter," called the shadowy figures on the bobbing, translucent boat, "We're waiting. Come along!"

"No! *No!*" sobbed Nataka. But her clutching hands lost their grip and passed through his vanishing body, and she stumbled down onto the sand.

"*Now,* Elpidea!" cried Toki.

Reaching the jetty, Ter lifted one foot onto the first step. His eyes were fixed on the figures in the sailboat, so he did not notice until it was too late that as soon as he stepped onto it, the jetty and everything else – the bobbing dinghies, the fenders, the sailboat; *everything* – vanished, leaving only the dark, oily swell of water before and beneath him. Gasping, suddenly terrified, he flung out his arms in a vain attempt to stop his dysbalanced body from toppling into the dark, dark depths, from which a starlit wave curled lazily up to meet him.

But even as he fell, in the instant before his plunging foot encountered the water, Paa bounded forward with her head down and neck outstretched - and touched his outflung hand with the sparkling tip of her horn.

A rainbow flashed between them.

And now the child hung suspended over the dark water, halted in his fall by the rainbow bursting from Paa's brow.

Soundlessly and unhesitatingly, the vaporous figure turned away from the sea at last, flowed unhesitatingly into the rainbow, and disappeared.

Paa's body pulsed and glowed. She stood for an instant, swaying and catching her breath. Then she shook herself, drew a deep breath, and burped.

"Whoa. Just like eating too much all at once," she said. "Come on then, little Sapiens. High time we were getting back, don't you think? ... Definitely. *Twende*." [clxiv]

Chapter 29. Restoration

"If paradoxes bother you, that betrays your deep desire for absolutes." clxv

"I've lived too long."

The Wingco's voice was husky, spent. Something had fled from his eyes, leaving behind it a hopeless emptiness Maddie had never seen before, even on the dreadful day they had received the news that an improvised explosive device had destroyed their beloved John. *Then*, there had been grief, impotent rage and indescribable suffering, yes; but not the look of desolation and capitulation in his every expression, movement and word she saw now; a look that constricted her already broken heart within her.

She knew what it meant. Quite simply, the old man was giving up. He had lost his last remaining reason for continuing to fight, and to live. The only remnant left to him of his treasured son had been the grandson for whose future and well-being the tough old warrior had been willing to battle on, suppressing his own sorrow. But now that Ter was gone, torn away so arbitrarily, the old man was like the broken shield, a fallen soldier.

"Oh, Wingco... oh, Papa..." she sobbed, but could find no other words. He turned to her, aware of her again.

"I should have chosen death," he said dully, letting his tongue articulate his thoughts. "I had a choice, you see... She gave me a choice, and I – I chose to live. But ... I should have chosen death. Maddie, I should have chosen death. A body can only take so much; a mind can only take so much before - before failing. And I'm failing. I've failed all my life."

He raised his voice.

"Oh Nataka, why? Why did you tempt me, poison me with hope? ... I shouldn't have listened to you! I should have chosen death!

"I couldn't even keep them safe. Why should I live? ... I couldn't even protect them. And it's all my fault, anyway. *My* fault. If I hadn't been in the military, John wouldn't have joined up... Ter would have a proper father today. *You* would be safe and happy today, Maddie. ... You wouldn't have had to find some- somebody else instead. You would have had a loving, protective husband today, somebody who would never – *never* – have done anything to put you in such danger!

"And now our boy, our darling boy..."

His voice broke. He slumped down with his head on the breast of the child in his arms, who might have been asleep had it not been for the wine-dark stain that obscured the print on his favourite grey T shirt. It was the image of a confused-looking robot. A speech bubble emerging from it held the words "***Think? I wish I could!***" Ter had saved his pocket money to buy it in a size too large for him because he'd wanted to wear it forever.

Maddie still could find no words. She sat with one arm across the old man's shoulders and the other around the body of her dead son, oblivious of the bloodstains on her face and hands and of the tears rolling unchecked down her cheeks. She stared dully, without interest or comprehension, at the gigantic beech tree that had inexplicably appeared in front of her home. After this day of repeated reversals, she was so emotionally spent that she no longer felt able to summon any surprise at whatever might happen next.

Some distance away, she registered without emotion, her flawed, selfish, pathetic husband continued to kneel on the gravel. She shut her eyes against this reminder of the worst mistake she had ever made, dismissed him from her mind, and abandoned herself to her desolation.

And so it was that she missed the moment when the trunk of the great tree before her cracked open and three figures that might have come out of a myth leaped out.

As they emerged, "Again you must do this alone, Paa Elpidea," said Toki. "Nataka and I will Disappear. But we shall still be here, beside you."

Maddie opened her eyes at the sound of hooves on the gravel. What she saw instantly dispelled her lassitude. Without taking her eyes off the approaching figure, she shook the old man urgently. "Look! ... *Look*!" she whispered. The Wingco raised his head - and gaped.

Paa stopped, a bit taken aback.

Why do they look so shocked? ... Oh, of course. Silly me. My horn.

Don't be afraid, she said. *I know I look weird with this silly thing sticking out of my head. It is rather a pain, to be honest. I'm always afraid it'll get tangled up in things or accidentally stab somebody. Not good. But if you can forget that part of it, it's quite useful.*

Um... Mind if I come closer? ... Now, let's see, how do I do this...

"Is it ... is it *real*?" whispered the Howler female, whose eyes, Paa observed, seemed to be taking up most of her face, "I thought they only existed in legends. ... Or am I seeing things? ... Wingco, am I going mad? ... Can you see it too?"

Real? Of course I'm real. Since when do poodles only exist in legends? replied Paa. *There are lots of us around. ... Now you'd best make a bit of room for me. I don't know how this works, but let's have a go anyway. I can tell you one thing: he really,* really *wants to get out again. And I don't blame him. I'd like him out, too. ... Er ... look, can I get* really *close, please? It seems to be a matter of – of touching, you see.*

"Yes, I can see it too. Let it come closer, Maddie," whispered the old man, adding to Paa's surprise. "It seems to want to come closer. I don't think it wants to hurt us, do you? Look at it. It's beautiful. It looks gentle. Let it come closer." The female Howler had put out her hand as if she wanted to prevent Paa from approaching, and now the old Howler reached out and gently pressed it down.

Beautiful? scoffed Paa, stepping forward. *Then she hesitated. Er, well, perhaps I am, for a poodle. Hmm. I never thought of that. Come to think of it, I did win some prizes in my time. ... Good; that's much better. I can get closer; thanks. Mind my horn, now. I don't want to skewer you.*

Then she had to stop talking because at last she had advanced to within touching distance. And besides, the urgency and pressure building up inside her made conversation difficult. She paid no further attention to anything anybody said, but lowered her head and focused all her thoughts and energy. She had to make sure the tip of her horn touched the precise spot on the child's body that was leaking blood into his outer wrappings – touched, but did not enter. It was a tricky operation.

Here we are at last, little Sapiens. Time to disembark.

"Wingco, truly, is that really, I mean *really* ... a – a *unicorn?*" whispered Maddie.

"I - I think so," he replied, "*Oh!* ... What's it doing with its horn?"

"I mustn't try to touch it, then," said Maddie with a small sobbing laugh, "in case it disappears..."

The unicorn's golden eyes blazed. Her body, tail and mane lit up, scintillating like a diamond in a patch of sunlight. Then she shuddered, and what looked like a bolt of lightning sped down her horn and disappeared into the wound in the boy's chest.

Paa heaved a huge sigh and collapsed back onto her haunches. *Ahh! That's better*, she breathed. *That's more like it. Fair takes it out of you, that does. I need a nap.*

She raised a hind leg to scratch her ear, only to find a hoof attached to it. So she sat and looked at it in a bemused sort of way.

But the two Howlers were no longer paying any attention to her. The boy lying in the Wingco's arms had moaned, stirred, and was now trying to sit up. His mother uttered a little shriek and started to cry again as she stroked his face and hair and hands, and "Your wound!" gasped the old man, lifting the boy's bloodstained shirt, "I can't find your *wound* ... and what's happened to the bullet?"

"Oh Ter, darling, darling!" sobbed Maddie, "You're all right, you're all right! ... But how could you ... what *made* you do something like that? Why *did* you have to run into danger like that? You almost got yourself killed!"

"He *was* killed," the Wingco sounded agitated. He stroked and massaged Ter's limbs. "He *was*! If it weren't for this unicorn..."

*Unicorn? – I'm a **unicorn**?* Paa's mouth dropped open. *Ohhh... so that's why I've got hooves. Sneaky one, Toki.*

Ah no, Paa Elpidea; this is none of my doing, replied the Protean. *This is simply what you are; your true nature. This is the source of all your powers. Did you really not know that? ... Singular.*

But the boy didn't say anything. Instead he turned to Paa and spread his arms wide. The unicorn stepped delicately forward until her shimmering head was resting on his shoulder, and let him embrace her.

Feel free to scratch my ears; I like that, she suggested hopefully. *But mind that horn, everybody. It's dangerous. And annoying. Put an eye out just like that.*

... Er, Toki? She added, *how long do I have to stay like this? ... I mean, I can't even scratch myself properly.*

"What happened? How did this *happen?*" insisted the Howler female, sobbing again.

Well, actually, Nataka and Toki did all the real work. I just sniffed him out to start with, and then collected him - you know? - And carried him back till he could get back into himself again, said Paa. *Not such a big d-"*

"This amazing creature did it, obviously," replied the Wingco in hushed tones, interrupting Paa. "I don't know *what*, exactly; but I think there must be some kind of power in its horn..."

But I've just told you. I only carried... Hey? Hello? ... Can you hear me? ... Whiskers and claws, am I talking to myself here?

455

Paa reversed, reared her head and stared at the two Howlers. They didn't reply, so she turned to the child. *Can't they hear me?* she demanded.

Ter gave a little chuckle and stroked her silky mane. *They can hear you, but they can't understand what you're saying,* he replied. *All they can hear is you making little whickering noises, like a horse or deer. They don't even know you're talking to them. And to be honest, I'm not sure why I understand you. D'you think it's because of Nataka? ... Or maybe because you carried me...*

Oh... OH! ... You... you saved my life! he added, his eyes suddenly round. *I... I would have...*

Forget about it. I would; advised Paa hurriedly. The little Sapiens had turned a very strange green colour. She didn't like it at all. *You're back now, that's all that matters. And look, your Howlers want to make a fuss of you. I'd let them.*

Then she turned and looked at the lonely figure kneeling on the driveway. She released herself gently from the boy's embrace and approached the man, stopping before him.

"Your Honour?" she called, "What about ..."

Nataka the Harpy Eagle materialised beside her and stood with her wings and crest spread, glaring down at the hapless Roger Court, who stared wordlessly back at the apparition through reddened, hopeless, terrified eyes.

"Um, Your Honour," ventured Paa, "Your look ...it's a bit ... a bit scary, you know? You're frightening him. Perhaps, if you adopted a different Transformation ..."

The Harpy Eagle turned her fierce eyes on Paa. "Why? He deserves to be frightened!" The words were talons scraping across a slab of slate. "It's the least he deserves!"

"He *is* frightened, Your Honour. He's terrified, look. Almost out of his wits," urged Paa. "*Please*, Your Honour, if you could just stop for just a moment and think how it must feel to be him ... how he must have felt, to – to do all the things he did... how he must have suffered – must still be suffering, you know? ... Perhaps you could also..."

"What? Do what? Kiss him?" demanded Nataka, her voice rising.

"No, Your Honour. Something much harder than that, sorry ..." Paa drew a deep breath. "Forgive him. You know? ... If you can just say *Yes: he's nasty, he's made people suffer, he's been disgusting; but I don't really know him. I don't really understand what made him the way he is*... well, if you could do that, then maybe you could also – you know, pity him. Forgive him. You know?"

The Harpy Eagle uttered a derisory screech. But then she stopped herself. Her sharp eyes stared into the face of the Howler kneeling before her, and Paa saw a gradual softness enter them. She screeched again, tossed her crested head, shook her wings ... and was again the black girl, who bent forwards, knitted her brow, and studied the man before her.

Then she turned and looked into Paa's eyes, and a smile eased the stern lines of her face. "All right. You win," she said, "Yes. If they forgive him, I will, too." She turned back to Roger Court. "You: *up!*" she said, "up, on your feet. You need to go and talk to *them*." She tilted her chin at the Wingco, Maddie and Ter, who had been watching her in silence. "If they can forgive you, so can I. Go on!"

"No ... no, he doesn't have to come any closer," said Ter hurriedly, standing up, "My stepfather and I ... we never liked each other... but I didn't behave all that well either. It must have been hard for him. I'm sorry..."

"What? *You're* sorry? ... *You* didn't try to kill him!" interrupted Nataka, her eyes sharpening again. "Don't apologise to him, Ter! The question is, can you *forgive* him?"

"We all make bad choices occasionally," the Wingco rose to his feet and helped Maddie to hers. "All of us. How would we look, if we were caught behaving at our worst? How might we behave or look to others? ... No, goodness knows, I'm no angel. I can't pretend to be superior to anybody else.

"And besides, to be fair, Roger did try to stop that – that man – from doing what he did. I heard him. We both heard him, didn't we, Maddie? He tried to stop that – that maniac. He regretted what he'd started, before ... before everything happened to Ter. Yes, I can forgive him. I do forgive him."

"And I," said Maddie, clinging to the old man's arm. She had struggled to assimilate Nataka's sudden apparition and Transformation from a harpy eagle to the black girl, but was heroically following her menfolk's lead. If they trusted this strange creature, she would, too.

"I forgive him," she said. "I didn't think I ever could, but... well, you're right, Wingco. He *did* try to stop that – that ... and besides, there was a time when I loved him. Although..." she turned her head away to hide the tears rising in her eyes, "although maybe I didn't love him enough, compared to – to John... and it all disappeared again a long time ago. Perhaps I was always comparing him to your dad, Ter; noticing everything he wasn't, compared to him. And that wasn't fair. That must have been so hard to live with. I'm sorry for that.

"Anyway," she shook herself impatiently and stared directly into her husband's eyes as she spoke, with only a slight tremor in her voice to show what it cost her. "I forgive you,

Roger Court. Even though I'll be divorcing you, and can never love you again. But I do forgive you. My darling boy's safe, and that's all that matters. And I've decided that from now on I never ever want to feel guilty and upset and disappointed and furious with you – *and* myself – again because of the way I let you and Ida treat my son and father; never. It's too hard. It isn't fair on them, and they don't deserve it.

"So it's over. I'm ending it completely. Right now. And the first step is to say I forgive, you, Roger Court. And I hope you can forgive me too. And now please go away. Forever. Thank you." She turned to her son and father-in-law, and heaved a deep sigh. "There."

"Oh, I forgive you too," said Ter immediately. He smiled. "If it hadn't been for you, I don't think I'd ever have found Nataka and her amazing friends. Yes, I owe you that, and … well, it's wonderful. Oh, I'm too happy; I can't be upset! … So, yes, I forgive you – *and* thank you, too – Mr Court. Shake hands?" He strode up and held out his right hand to the kneeling man, who gazed at it dully but did not lift his own to take it.

Nataka had listened intently as the others spoke. Her eyes were more thoughtful than Paa had ever seen them. As she listened, the stern lines in her face gradually smoothed and disappeared. She contemplated the man, who appeared unable even to raise his eyes, let alone his hand, to the boy. And at last she comprehended his plight.

"And I;" her voice was soft, "I forgive you too. Freely. They've forgiven you because they feel sorry for you. Just like Paa. And now I understand why. Nobody can act as you did or become what you are without having suffered - and probably too much – from a lifetime of crazy Howler ideas and behaviour. Yes, you poor Howler, you've been through enough. You need never fear me again, ever. I give you my word. Be at peace."

She bent down and laid the palm of one hand on his forehead. "I forgive you. Be at peace," she repeated, and breathed a silvery mist into his face.

There was a sudden peal of thunder, a tremendous flash of light, and –

In the lengthening golden light of the setting sun that gilded a verdant, flower-starred lawn before a quaint little woodland cottage, the air and ground around Nataka, Paa, the startled boy, his mother and grandfather exploded into a cacophony of song and chatter and calling as a host of animals burst into view and converged on the small group clustered in the shade of the spreading beech. A magnificent grey timber wolf and a large buck hare bounded out of the cottage; a white deer trotted out from under the shadows of a yew hedge; a beaver and a hedgehog herding three tiny piglets snuffled up, accompanied by a red squirrel that flicked its tail and scampered up the tree; a downy barn owl and a huge raven flew out of the cottage window to perch on Nataka's shoulders. There was a riot of jostling, calling, chattering, whistling, bellowing and barking as the creatures cried out to one another that Nataka had returned, and strove to come close enough to touch, kiss and lick her where she stood with Paa and her companions.

Of the kneeling Howler they had forgiven there was no sign.

In the sky a chorus of skylarks, blackbirds, nightingales, tits, robins and the first wheeling flock of returning swallows and swifts burst into song. A hovering kestrel skirled its haunting cry before plummeting down to land on one of the pale deer's horns. And a grumpy looking badger emerged from the woodland undergrowth behind the cottage, sniffed and stared sh ort-sightedly at the scene, and then grunted and ducked away again. A fox, its mate, and their clutch of tumbling cubs loped out of the forest and headed straight for the unicorn, who called out excitedly to them. From down-slope a whistling, chuckling otter rolled into the clearing, having galloped all the way from his holt beside the river to join the fun.

And that was not all. Before the eyes of the nonplussed Sapiens, the great beech tree gaped wide and released a small calico cat, a family of mongooses, a handsome grey tomcat and an even more handsome Roloway monkey to join the gathering. The wolf greeted the new arrivals with joyous whimpers and barks, wind-milling his tail. From the eaves of the cottage descended a huge orb-web spider on a strand of silk that swung lightly in the breeze.

"*This* is sumfink like!" called the grey cat, bounding up to Nataka, "Wher've yeh bin and what've yeh bin up to, Nat, old girl? That place ain't much fun wivout yer to shake it up, like!"

Dumbfounded, Ter and his family gaped around at the swarming Wanyama.

"What's happening? What's all this about? Where have you lot all come from?" exclaimed Paa, swivelling her head from side to side. "What's the matter? What's going on? What's happened? *What*? ..."

Nataka laughed aloud. "It's Toki! Toki's brought us all home, Paa! And – look – it's a cottage again," she added, "Oh, Toki, this is wonderful!"

A great booming voice rang out, silencing the assembled animals.

"Hear me now, Paa Elpidea, She Who Understands and Heals!" cried Fagus, "And witness my words, you Saps, privileged to join our gathering and understand our words – the first in the history of your kind ever to look upon us or to enter the domain of Nataka Aelfeynn Earda!"

("I think the tree means us," whispered Ter to his grandfather, "*We're* the Saps. I wonder what it means.")

"I say, hear me, Paa Elpidea! The mighty Toki and I have summoned to your side – *hup* * yes! – We have called to your side all our companions and friends, to bear witness to the honours being bestowed on you. *HUP!*

"Before them do I solemnly and rejoicingly declare that you have fulfilled the promise I espied in you when first we met; a promise that has led our beloved Awakener and Friend of many names, Nataka Aelfeynn Earda, and her wise companion, Toki *Tane Papatuanuku*,[clxvi] Lord of Forests, Birds, and Worlds Separated, Gatekeeper between Dimensions, Mentor to Nataka Aelfeynn Earda and Guardian of the Keys to Other Realities (alas, for the sake of brevity, I can enumerate a mere fraction of the full count of its names and powers; *hup*!)

"Where was I? ... Ah. Yes.

"Here and now I say to you, Paa Elpidea, that it is your promise, your realised promise, that has fulfilled our dearest desire: that is, the liberation of Nataka Aelfeynn Earda from her emotional thrall and from the great peril under which all of Dunia lay while she remained in its thrall. In turn, her liberation restores both to her and to her Mentor Toki the Freedom of All The Worlds There Are; that is to say, of All The Dimensions Existing in this our Multiverse; theirs once again to wander at will, without let or hindrance. *Hup*!

"And this liberation of our most beloved friends and of all we hold dear is solely attributable to you, Paa Elpidea, who have come into your true nature, Magical Unicorn, epitome of purity and Love, whom now I also name *Rangi*[clxvii], Bearer of the Light of Rainbows, and *Roho la Dunia*[clxviii], Heart of the Earth!

"But the full tale of your deeds is not yet told, Paa Elpidea, Rangi, Roho la Dunia, soul of kindness! Not only have you, with your forgiveness and love, banished the Beast that lay within Nataka Aelfeynn Earda, and in so doing liberated two precious Immortal spirits from their earthly bondage, but you have also saved lives, Roho la Dunia! For you have healed a Stult that had done you wrong, intervened to unite two estranged Stults in bonds of love and mating, and restored to this Dimension and into his truncated life the lost spirit of a Sap child unjustly slain, reuniting him with himself and with his kin. Truly you wield the Light That Heals and Recovers, Rangi, Roho la Dunia!

"Therefore I say, let all who hear me, be they winged, finned, clawed, crawling, slithering or swimming, horned, thorned or leaf-bedecked, honour you!

"Praise her with me, all you gathered in this place!

"**Praise with great praise and honour with full throats the mighty, modest saviour spirit that is Paa Elpidea, Rangi, Roho la Dunia!**"

And as the clearing, woodland, earth and sky around the little cottage rang with the acclamations of all those present, the booming roar of the great beech tree and Nataka's clarion song of delight soared above all the others, shaking foliage and setting the ground to dancing. Butterflies, dragonflies and bees pirouetted, buzzed and fluttered through the honey-scented air, their wings glittering in the lengthening golden light-and-shade of Sunsink. And from the cottage, which had risen to its sturdy, trunk-like legs and was performing a surprisingly agile jig along with the hare, the fox and the deer, there arose again the wild, sweet refrain Paa had first heard on the night she danced with M'Kuu and Axl in the silver-rose light of the full Strawberry Moon. But now it was accompanied by a full-throated instrument that was unknown to the Wanyama, and that sounded to Ter, the Wingco and Maddie like a vast organ playing music so entrancing, it could only be descending from the spheres.

"Now *that's* what I call a paean, Patches!" Laughing, Sardo the Roloway Monkey tweaked the calico cat by her tail. "*There's* a speech, if you like!"

"Don't call me *Patches!*" spat Chant, and bounded off to talk to the wolf.

At first Ter, his grandfather and mother had stood silent, bewildered and nervous amid the cavorting, celebrating animals. But they were rapidly caught up and swept along in the tide of enthusiasm and delight that greeted the giant beech tree's words, and joined wholeheartedly in the applause at the end of its speech.

"Hear, Hear! Three cheers for Paa! Rangi! Roho la Dunia! ... *Hooray* for my saviour!" cried Ter and threw his arms around the unicorn's neck. Nataka turned and studied Ter for an instant, a tiny frown creasing her forehead. Then she snapped her fingers and sang a single note. The dark stain vanished from the front of the boy's shirt, leaving no trace of his recent ordeal. At the same moment, the stains of his wound also vanished from the clothing and limbs of Maddie and the Wingco.

But amidst all the celebration, Paa stood wide-eyed, silent and abashed, pawing the turf with one glittering hoof. *Curl my whiskers, I feel like a fraud. I didn't do any of it by myself. I couldn't have done anything without the others.*

"Er – um, excuse me, Your Honour," she whispered to Nataka, "Please don't be offended, but ... but I never expected any of this – I mean, all this praise ... and the names, and..."

"Listen, Paa, I've already told you: you're special. Just accept it, because it's true... *and* you're Immortal now, too!" said Nataka joyously, "This is your reward. You're a unicorn, and Immortal. In fact, you're a *god* now. You need never feel afraid again. Nobody can hurt you. Nobody can even *touch* you, unless you want them to. You can have whatever you want, do anything you want, and go anywhere you like. All you need do is desire it. And believe me, you deserve it all. Isn't it splendid? Aren't you excited?"

Paa hung her glowing head and studied the rainbow shafting off her diamond hooves.

"*Do* I have to do all that, Your Honour?" she asked, "I mean, if you want a hero or a new god, does it *have* to be me? ... Couldn't I give it to – oh, I don't know, Glose, maybe? – instead, and go back to just being plain old Paa again? ... I'm simply not cut out for this kind of thing. Honestly. For a start, I couldn't bear to live forever, and have to watch everybody I loved die and disappear. I really don't know how *you* manage it, Your Honour ... no offence meant ..."

"*Is* that really what you want?" asked Nataka, gazing intently into the gold and pearl eyes of the unicorn.

"It's all I've *ever* wanted, Your Honour," insisted Paa earnestly, "a family to love - and to love me; a garden where I can roll on the grass in the sunlight and play with my friends... Oh – and a good fire I can lie in front of, with a bone to gnaw when my teeth itch; you know? ... And, sometime, who knows, perhaps some puppies who will stay

with me until they want to move on, but not before. ...
That's what I really want. That's what I long for. In fact, I
can't think of anything else I could possibly want."

At the look in Nataka's face she hung her head again. "I'm
really, *really* sorry to disappoint you again, Your Honour,
but it's true," she said. "I know I'm stupid. I suppose if I
really *am* a god, as you say, I must be a very backward one,
don't you think? I..."

Her eyes widened as Nataka burst into peals of laughter.
"No; I mean it; I *do*, Your Honour," she urged. "I just don't
seem to have any of the qualities or interests I'd need to do a
proper job of being a god. You know, wanting sparkly
things, and gifts and fame and people singing and
worshipping me ... all the things gods like. Such things just
don't interest me. There must be something very wrong
with me, I think. And - well... Oh, fidget and scratch, Your
Honour, you *know* I'd be rubbish at it!"

"You - a backward god? That's priceless! ... Well, if those
really *are* the only things you want, you odd, self-effacing
little thing, of course you have the right, and the power, to
take them," replied Nataka, still laughing. "You're not
obliged to go for all the extras, you know. Nobody can tell
you what you must or mustn't do. The important thing is,
from now on you won't ever have to ask for anything you
want. You have the power to get it. So, if you *honestly*
prefer to be a poodle, you can turn back into one - although,
believe me, you're also great as a unicorn. And if all you
want really is a fire and a bone and some puppies... well, go
for it!

"But between you and me, I earnestly urge you not to give
Glose any of your godlike skills. He wouldn't know how to
handle that kind of power. He's quite different from you,
you know: stuffed full of ambition, conceit and scroll
learning, but without any genuine wisdom or modesty. He'd

turn into a tyrant in short order, and end up making everybody miserable, including himself. Take my word for it, dearest godling, he'd really mess up.

"However, I can only advise you, even about that. You're in charge now. So that decision's up to you, too. Obviously. At least I won't have to clean up the mess if you *do* decide to turn Glose into a tyrant, thank Infinity!" She laughed again, doubling over with her hands on her knees.

Then she hiccoughed once or twice and straightened up again. "Oh, I needed that laugh," she said, wiping her eyes. "I feel so much better. ... But seriously: from now on you don't have to ask me or anybody else for permission or approval, Paa. Whatever you want you can get for yourself and keep for as long as you want. Best of all, if ever you change your mind and want to be or do something else, even to be immortal again – yes, even that – well, you'll have the power to do that, too. You're entirely *free* at last, dearest, dearest Paa. So by all means follow your heart's desire. And I shall do exactly the same!"

"As will I," cried Toki the cottage, dancing in the slanting sunlight and shooting sparks out of its crooked chimney, "I also shall follow my heart's desire. For which I thank *you*, Paa Elpidea, my liberator!"

Chapter 30. *And So It Goes*

*"And shall I ask at the day's end once more
What beauty is, and what I can have meant
By happiness?"* clxix

*"But yet I know, where'er I go,
That there hath passed away a glory from the earth.
... Whither is fled the visionary gleam?
Where is it now, the glory and the dream?"*clxx

As the sun dipped beneath the horizon and the first stars began to pop out, the celebrating Wanyama in the clearing settled down into little groups and clusters to preen, groom, gossip and snooze, according to their several natures. Those familiar with the ways of the magical cottage emerged from it carrying fruit, vegetables, meat and water, which they distributed with the willing help of Ter, Maddie and the Wingco.

Paa had long since abandoned her unicorn identity for her familiar, comfortable dog shape. Tail wagging and tongue lolling, the relieved poodle accompanied the Saps as they wandered from group to group of the gathered creatures, squatted down and listened to their talk, fondled the tiny hedge-piglets and the velvety ears of the hare, questioned the giant tree and stroked assorted ruffs, feathers and muzzles. Every so often the poodle would lift her muzzle and give Ter a tickly wet kiss, to which he responded with giggles and caresses. They had also enjoyed a prolonged romp around the garden with Pex and Axl. The Wanyama had instantly and unreservedly welcomed the little family into their circle. Nataka had marked them for her own, after all; and none of her woodland companions even thought to question her endorsement.

At last Toki called Nataka to its side. "This has been glorious," it said. "We have had great cause to celebrate, and done it justice. But now the time comes to draw our celebrations to a close. And, dearest Nataka, we shall also have to bid farewell to your new friends, who have proved themselves true Sapiens, rare and praiseworthy.

"I see that you understand me. If you love them, you must surely agree with me that they cannot in all mercy be permitted to retain any memory of what has happened over this past Suntime, lest it mar their happiness in the seasons to come. The infant in particular has undergone a profound trauma, one of which it would be nothing short of cruelty to leave him any memory. And indeed, the very joy he is presently feeling would prove a serious obstacle to his return to a normal Sap life. So, for his sake as well as for that of his family, we must be strong and release him to his own life; a life that will not be hampered by any risk of further intervention on our part."

"But I *love* the boy," yearned Nataka. "If I've finally understood what it means to love, I owe it to Ter as much as to Paa and Hassan, the Sap infant I couldn't rescue. And as for the Wingco and Ter's mother … Oh, Toki, they're very good too, aren't they? She's gentle, quite unlike most of her kind, and he's so brave and caring and decent. Besides, they're cheerful and helpful, *and* everybody's accepted them, even Fagus. You can see that, can't you? All the Wanyama love them. Look, Mond is even asking Ter to help with his grooming!

"Oh Toki, they could be so happy with us, couldn't they? … And as for me, now that I finally know how it feels to love, how can I bear to make them forget all this - me - us, again?"

"You know you can, and must," replied Toki. "If they remain as we have made them, we cannot always be present to care for them; and who knows what might befall them then? If you were to make a cage for them with your love, how would that serve them? Think of the consequences. If they spoke of what they know to others of their kind, how would they be received? ... Remember what befell Socrates; Archimedes; Copernicus! [clxxi]

"We both know too well what cruelties so many of that bizarre, contradictory species are capable of perpetrating on any of their number they consider *different*. That is a dreadful word! These gentle, well-intentioned Sapiens would be ridiculed, ostracised, persecuted and dismissed as insane. Do you truly wish to condemn them to such a fate?

"No. Surely you cannot be so cruel, merely to satisfy your own need for their affection, no matter how new-found it may be, Nataka Aelfeynn Earda. These Sapiens *must* be allowed to live their own lives; good lives, grounded in their own good natures.

"Liberate them from this dream into which you have led them, and let them go their ways. They are safe now, thanks to you and our gentle Paa. They will live full and happy lives, again thanks to you both. Release them, knowing that when their time comes to depart this Dimension you may, if you wish, greet them once more, and guide them through their final Change."

"Oh Toki, Toki..." Nataka choked. "Why must we lose those we love? Why must we suffer such pain?"

Paa had joined them while Toki spoke, and now she gazed sorrowfully up at the beloved face of the Protean. "I wish I could take it away from you, Your Honour," she said.

"That is the price of Love, Aelfeynn Earda," said Toki, "Pain for love: a harsh lesson we all have to learn. Every creature, mortal or immortal, must lose those it loves, sooner or later. That is our doom. Only water, stones and other lifeless things never suffer the pain of separation. Oh, my poor friend, I can no longer call you Child Spirit, now that you know this feeling!

"Come; you are strong. Do what you know is right. While these Sapiens are happy and peaceful, full of health and hope, release them. Give them the greatest gift at your disposal: absolute liberty from us, a gift only true Love can confer.

"Everything you need for your task is awaiting you inside."

So Nataka entered the fully restored cottage with Paa at her side. A vial of the same glowing Forgetfulness potion she had prepared for the Mond rescue was standing on the table beside an earthenware jug of cold, clear spring water. Had it really been just a small finger-count of Suns ago that she had used it to make the Howlers forget Mond, and revelled at the outcome? It felt to the grieving Protean, as she leaned her fingers on the tabletop and contemplating the items on it, that aeons had passed since that first adventure.

She picked up the vial, removed its stopper and tilted it over the jug. A drop of potion, glowing like a moonstone, formed on the lip of the vial and hung trembling for an instant. Then it fell with a tiny 'plink' into the water, which brightened briefly in response. Twice more Nataka dispensed a drop of the precious fluid into the water before she re-sealed the vial and put it away on a high shelf. She turned back to the table, picked up a long-handled wooden spoon, and began to hum a soft tune that sounded like the first chirpings of a distant dawn chorus while she stirred the contents of the jug. Gradually the potion began to shimmer, and then it emitted a brief, pearly glow that lit up the smoky, swirling liquid.

Nataka heaved a deep sigh, laid the spoon to one side, and poured the contents of the jug into a small flagon, which she corked.

"Well, Paa, it's ready;" she said. "As soon as Ter and his family drink this, everything - the Wingco's illness; Glose; you and I; the attack on Ter; Toki's appearance; the rescue; our journey through Fagus ... oh dear, even this celebration - literally *everything* to do with us will be wiped out of their memories. They'll blink their eyes, and then wake up again to continue with their lives as if they'd never met us. Their minds won't retain a trace of us. We'll never have existed for them.

"But before we do that, I'm determined to let them spend every instant of this last Startime with their new friends, even though they won't remember any of it afterwards. I want them to experience that brief joy, at least." She raised her voice. "Do you hear, Toki? I'm giving them that, at least." Toki smiled but did not reply.

Nataka laid a hand on the poodle's fluffy head. "Will you come with me, Paa?" she asked, "I don't want to …to steal their memories on my own. I just can't do it. I'm such a coward!"

Paa raised her muzzle and licked the hand. "Of course I will. You know I will, Your Honour," she said.

They emerged to a tranquil scene. Many of the Wanyama had wandered back to their lairs, burrows and nests, but the most familiar of Nataka's companions were still gathered on the lawn. Mond and the fox family were circling and stretching, preparing to salute the setting moon; Tytus the Baron was on a low bush, at the centre of a circle of Wanyama he was enthralling with an account of Nataka's wolf rescue; Hapa, Wapi, Twende, Miba and Brid (who had fetched his mate and infants down from their drey in the branches of the tree) were comparing babies and swapping parenting anecdotes while their young lay snoozing around them. Fyrd, Chant, Rav'n and the male mongooses were engaged in some kind of competitive game that involved showing off their different digging and clawing techniques. Sardo the Roloway monkey was bounding around in Fagus's branches and paying the gratified tree such extravagant compliments about its growth and beauty that it giggled, shivered and swayed like a sapling.

The three Saps were reclining at ease on the lawn, talking together in low voices and smiling as they watched the creatures around them. "It's like the Garden of Eden," [clxxii] confided Maddie, "except that there's no serpent around to spoil it. It all feels too good to be true. I haven't felt this happy since before your dear father died, Ter. Tell me again how Nataka cured the Wingco. I still can't quite believe it. That really *was* a miracle, wasn't it? ... I wish I could have seen it!"

Axl and M'Kuu had been watching the door of the cottage, and bounded up to meet Paa the instant it opened. Glose, who had been perching on Toki's roof ridge, sunk in uncharacteristic thought, flapped down onto Nataka's shoulder.

"What now, Boss?" asked M'Kuu, "The Howlers look all in. They need sleep. Odd creatures, really; imagine them wanting to hunker down just when we're getting to the best part of Startime. Well anyway, where d'you want to settle them? I can lend the little one my form on the woodpile if he doesn't mind curling up tight, but what about the other two?"

"Thanks, M'Kuu, please don't worry; you don't need to do anything," said Nataka, "I'll be guiding the Howlers back to their own lair soon. It's all organised."

And, "Paa, Glose, please come with me when I go," she added in a whisper only the poodle and bird could hear.

"*Arkh!* Nataka," cawed the raven, "what ails you? Why are you so sad?"

"Oh, Glose," grieved the Protean, "I hate to say goodbye!"

***

And then, more quickly than Paa or Nataka could have imagined, it was over. As if a shutter had been drawn from the sky, the first rays of Sunwake were scuttling over the horizon towards them, revealing a lightening, breezy sky with the treetops toppling against its high, scudding clouds.

Chant and the other Wanyama from the zoo had left with the first fading of the stars, after bidding a prolonged farewell to the Proteans and their friends. Rav'n had remembered with a surge of catty pleasure the warm cot awaiting him and the fine meal his new Howler Pet Gertrude would prepare, and jumped into the giant beech tree with them (however reformed he may be, an alley cat is never too full for another meal). Skald and the Baron had long since flown away on business of their own.

Miba shepherded her brood back to their safe rabbit scraping under the hedge, where they curled up to sleep Suntime away; and Pex, Brid and Fyrd slipped away with their families while Mond and M'Kuu retired into Toki to rest, leaving behind only Axl to settle under the trees of the forest. As the Wanyama drifted away to their various lairs, Nataka's garden began to feel oddly silent and depleted, particularly after the departure of the mongoose family.

The Saps had embraced each Nyama as it departed, and now they too were ready to return home, accompanied by Nataka, Glose and Paa. Ter paused and looked back before passing through the rusty gate that opened onto the stone river. "See you later, Toki ... and you too, Fagus," he called, waving. "I can't wait! ... Thanks for everything! ... Bye for now!"

The Saps were all too fatigued to notice that for some reason their every step covered a good dozen of their Howler yards, so very little time elapsed before they found themselves back on the gravelled driveway before their house.

Every trace of the previous Suntime's occurrences had vanished. Roger had departed the scene long before, whisked away in a stinking whizz thing with demented flashing eyes and a banshee call, which the Howlers called an *ambulance*. He was gabbling incoherently about things none of his attendants and helpers could understand, and they didn't trust him to look after himself. His grim-faced sister had appeared in another stinking whizz-thing with a sign on it, paid its driver and helped to push Roger into the ambulance, before getting into his car and taking it away. She wasn't very good at directing those particular objects, and her departure had featured a number of juddering false starts accompanied by clashing, groaning complaints from the car's insides. The bowl-shaped depression down which the mangled assassin had disappeared was still there, of course; but it was too shallow for anybody to notice it.

In the rapidly lightening sky a single lark rose, singing, over the grassy meadow that sloped down to the river behind the Wingco's home. Its song bounced around the sky like tiny sparkling glass beads tumbled in a beaker. Ter stared up and laughed aloud. Despite his exhaustion he began to talk about all the adventures he and the Wingco would enjoy alongside Nataka and her friends. "We'll have such *fun* together!" he exclaimed, drawing breath. "Let's start today. Can we start today, Nataka?"

"Oh, darling," his mother's voice was both indulgent and long-suffering, "You've still got most of the Easter holiday ahead of you, you know. What's the hurry? You've been through so much, you really need a good long rest first, if you're not to get sick. So it's bed for you, my lad, before you even think of doing anything else. I'm sure Nataka agrees with me; don't you, Nataka? And, tell you what, I won't even mind if you sleep away the whole of today. Same for me and the Wingco."

"But..."

"Now then; no *buts,* young man," said the Wingco, "Mum's orders, you know. Sacrosanct. She's absolutely right. Bed. Sleep. After that we'll see what's what. It'll all still be here, waiting for you, when you wake up. Come along now: we're home and safe at last, and I for one am ready to go horizontal. It isn't every day you're saved from death *and* meet magical creatures all at the same time, my boy, and even if your adventures haven't knocked *you* out, I'm bushed. I need a good long kip before I do anything else."

Ter heaved a blissful sigh. "Yes," he said, "Yes. It *will* all still be here when I wake up, won't it? Oh, I can hardly believe it. I keep wanting to pinch myself... Oh, it'll be *such* fun! I'm *so* happy I found you, Nataka and Glose - and you, Paa..." on an impulse he bent down and embraced the poodle. "I don't know how I can ever show you what I feel... but... but I'll be your friend *forever.* OK? Forever. I can't ever pay you back for saving me, but I'll do everything else, everything I possibly can to make you happy. I promise. As long as I live, I won't forget that you saved my life. And I *can* pay you back a little bit, by playing lots and lots and LOTS of games with you. I *love* you!"

Paa licked the boy's face. "I love you too, and I'll never forget you either, little Sapiens," she assured him, "not for as long as I live. I promise."

"Before you go in," said Nataka as Ter straightened up from embracing Paa, "We have one last ritual to complete together. Whenever we say goodbye to new-found friends, we share a final drink with them before our first parting. Call it a – a libation – of thankfulness, you know?"

"One for the road," the old man smiled. "Now that's what I call civilised. Sorry, I should have thought of it myself. Where are my manners? Come on in then, everybody; let's brew up."

"Oh no. I meant that *we* give *you* a special drink," explained the Protean. "Look, I've brought it along in this flask, specially prepared. All we need is something to drink it out of…"

"Not another word," interjected Maddie. "Key, Wingco? … Thanks. I'll be right back!" She hurried into the house and returned within a few moments, carrying a tray on which she had arranged four glass tumblers and two small bowls ("for Paa and Glose, you know," she explained, looking a bit pink).

Nataka crooked her fingers, beckoned and sang a single note. The tray lifted off Maddie's hands, floated to where the black girl was standing, and hovered before her.

"*Whoa*!" breathed Ter. "How cool is *that*…"

His mother and grandfather watched open-mouthed as Nataka drew the cork from the flask and dropped a measure of its opalescent contents into each container on the hovering tray. "Guests go first," she said.

Three tumblers floated off the tray to hover before Ter, the Wingco and Maddie, who reached out and took one each.

"Now, this bit is done all together. You repeat the words I say, and then drink together. And then we follow. Ready? … Here goes: *To long lives; good lives; great happiness; and may the Sun light all your ways.*" Her eyes glowed.

"To long lives; good lives; great happiness; and may the Sun light all your ways," echoed the old man and the woman in hushed tones, arrested by the solemnity in the Protean's face. But Ter gazed into her eyes, his own suddenly wide and troubled. He clutched his tumbler, but did not raise it to his lips.

"You ... Nataka? ... I feel... that sounds like something you say before – before leaving forever..." a shadow grew behind his eyes and his voice caught. "I - I'm not sure why, but... Oh, Nataka, you're *not* going away forever, are you? I *will* see you again, won't I? ... Won't I?"

"You *will* see me again," said Nataka, and if her voice shook a little, only Paa noticed it. "I promise."

The boy sighed and raised his tumbler. "All right... all right, then;" he said, "But remember, Nataka, you've *promised*." He took a deep breath. "To long lives; good lives; great happiness; and may the Sun light all your ways!" he said.

His grandfather and mother had waited for him to complete the words, and now they lifted their cups to their lips when he did, and all three drank together.

While the cups were still at their lips, Nataka raised one slim finger and chanted a single shimmering note that emerged on a soft mist, spread and hung in the glow of the rising Sun, and mingled with the liquid song of the rising lark.

She and her companions Vanished into the song.

The tray, four goblets and two bowls winked out. They reappeared in the dark kitchen, standing back on the shelves whence Maddie had taken them.

The notes cascading from the lark reached a climax. Having sung its heart out as it rose, the little bird crested in its flight like a surfer riding an invisible wave that is about to topple and roll to shore, tucked in its wings and tipped over, falling silently and swiftly back into the long grasses of the meadow.

Ter blinked, rubbed his eyes, yawned and looked up at the Wingco, whose face bore the expression of one who is struggling to hold on to the elusive tendrils of a vanishing memory. "I feel so *tired*," said the child, "And …oh, I had *such* a dream last night! … But I can't remember it now. Maybe that's why I'm so tired. Can dreams do that to you? I bet I could sleep for a week."

"So could I," agreed the old man, "And I must have had a fantastic dream too, Ter … I do wish I could remember it. … Ah well; that's the way of dreams. They vanish. Perhaps it's all just part of the spring. This season gets into your bones and brain. How about you, Maddie? You tired, too?"

"Yes, I am," replied the young woman. She seemed particularly fragile that morning, as if for a while her skin had become transparent, exposing her nerves to the world.

The Wingco put his arm around her shoulder and drew her to him. It was natural, he reflected; she had a right to feel fragile. Breaking up with Roger hadn't been easy, and *that* had happened just the day before, after a long argument about Ter's inheritance. Thank goodness *that* painful, unpleasant business was finally over. Roger really had been the limit; but even so, it had been hard to give him his marching orders, particularly for somebody as gentle and kind-hearted as Maddie. She might well want to talk it over sometime; but the Wingco was determined not to broach the topic with her unless and until she raised it first. The thing to do now was to support and give her as much space as she needed to work the whole thing out of her system in her own good time. They'd weathered much worse together.

As if she had heard his thoughts, Maddie leaned her head on his shoulder and smiled up at him. "I'll be all right," she said, "I'll be fine; don't worry about me. And that was a great idea, Wingco, bringing us both out to hear the first lark sing. It was lovely.

"But now I really do think we should all copy that bird and dive back into bed for more sleep, don't you? And after we've had a good long rest, just for a treat, I'll organise breakfast in bed for us all. Waffles, I think. And honey."

"Maple syrup!" said Ter.

"All right. Maple syrup. And fresh fruit juice. And scrambled eggs with ham and mushrooms. How does that sound? ... Thought so. Come along then, the men-folk; quick march!"

***

"I noticed that you didn't tell the little Howler *when* he would see you again, Nataka;" cawed Glose as the Protean, the poodle and the raven made their way back to the cottage. "Good move."

Paa trotted close to Nataka and licked her hand. "You told him the truth, Your Honour," she said. "He *will* see you again, after a long and happy life. You always keep your promises."

Neither of them commented on the fact that Nataka's cheeks were slick with her tears.

Chapter 31. **Home at last**

"How canst thou part sadness and melancholy, my tender juvenal?" clxxiii

"Dearest Paa, are you *sure* you don't want to join us?" asked Nataka the silver wolf. She was preparing to guide Mond home to his pack, and the look in her iridescent eyes told Paa she would not be staying around for very long after that. Nataka was burning to revisit old haunts and explore new ones in all the Dimensions and Realities that had been barred to her for so long. But she also longed to have at her side the quiet, self-effacing Nyama whose magic had released her and Toki from their banishment. Paa licked a paw and listened, but did not know how to reply.

"If you came with us, we could show you such places, such things; wonderful things," urged the Protean, "we could reward you with adventures and sights you can't imagine. Aren't you tempted even a little bit?" She leaned down and gazed into the loving eyes of the poodle, and repeated, "Not even a little?"

They were all gathered together in the shade of Fagus, which still kept its place inside Nataka's compound and looked happy to stay there indefinitely. Along with the owl and the raven, Axl, M'Kuu and Pex were sitting alongside Paa, listening quietly, while Mond paced and prowled around, bracing himself for a return to the labyrinth inside the great Pathway Tree. Before them all loomed a parting of the ways and momentous changes to familiar, well-established routines and activities. It was not surprising that with their anticipation they were also all feeling a little sad and apprehensive.

"*Arkh*!" said Glose, "*I'll* come with you, Nataka. *I'll* never leave you, wherever you go!"

"And you are very, very welcome, Glose;" said Nataka, "I've got so used to you that I don't think I could cope without you, now. So I'm really grateful. ... But what about *you*, Paa?" she added, turning back to the poodle, "Won't you come too?"

"*Caw*, yes, please join us, Paa," added the raven, fluttering down onto her back and gently tweaking one of her furry ears, "I like you *very* much, now, you know. I've got used to you. Please don't let my earlier ... awkwardness ... put you off coming with us. We'll have so much fun together!"

"Oh, Glose; Your Honour," said the poodle, "You know I love and admire you both more than I can say. And if I were going to travel, I wouldn't want to go with anybody else. But ...but I simply couldn't cope with all that – the moving from place to place, and constant changes and celebrations and adventures, I mean. I just wouldn't be able to deal with it... or at least, not right away. Would you really mind terribly if I stayed here quietly instead, and found myself a new home and family? ... Perhaps later I may get to feel less strange and alien inside this new ... skin? ... identity? ... you've all given me. Who knows? But honestly, right now the thought of doing all the things you say just fills me with ... well, with fear. I'm so sorry to disappoint you, Your Honour. I don't mean to offend either of you. I'm such a coward. Can you forgive me?"

"Revered and beloved Paa Elpidea; Rangi; Roho la Dunia, do you not wish to rove the Dimensions, as your godhood entitles you to?" Fagus chimed in, "Your qualities are much prized, and not merely on Dunia. And your great skill in working wonders with your kindness is a gift beyond compare! You would be celebrated wherever you appeared, you know. It is a surprise to me that you should not wish to enjoy such rewards. But be that as it may. Can you answer me this, you reluctant godling: even if you should choose not to travel with Nataka Aelfeynn Earda, will you at least avail yourself of all the magics that are at your disposal here, on Dunia, even as a dog? *hup*!"

Paa turned to face the tree, reared up onto her hind legs and braced her front paws on its trunk, getting as close as she could to the deep, mossy eyes. "I really, really, *really* love you too, Fagus," she said, her tail wagging and her eyes bright. "But if I start doing that, how many more complicated and scary names will you give me? I've been trying to escape that kind of thing all my life!"

The Pathway tree chuckled appreciatively.

"I promise not to confer any further title or label on you until *you* want me to, my self-effacing little friend," it replied. "Indeed, your words remind me that I would be wrong to attempt anything else. The secret of your powers lies in your modesty and self-forgetfulness. I shall not – nay, I *cannot* – attempt to obstruct or alter you, *hup!*

"But know this, Paa Elpidea: you will always be that which you have become. You cannot unmake yourself. Inside you, you know there sleeps the unicorn capable of great deeds. She emerges even while you remain a poodle, allowing you to forgive, cherish and heal. And there will be times when you know that your powers are needed, and desire to employ them for the benefit of others. At those times, you may wish to be the Unicorn again, even if only briefly. Therefore, hear the vow I now make: When such times arise – as arise they will - I shall be at your disposal, whether it be for a short season, a Startime, or forever. Henceforth, my ways remain open to you and to yours in perpetuity. I shall never require a libation or ceremony to accommodate you. I say again: all my paths and Dimensions are yours, to enter as a dog or unicorn, or as anything else you choose to become. You need but ask. This I swear."

The poodle wagged her fluffy tail and kissed the tree repeatedly, unable to summon the words to express her gratitude. And the great beech tree's leaves shivered with pleasure at her caresses.

"I agree. This is not goodbye, dear friend," now spoke Toki, "Fagus is correct; you are what you are, and your choices are sacrosanct. Like Fagus, I place myself at your disposal. With me you will always have a home, as well as all the tools, materials and advice you may need to work any magics you wish. You need only come or call to me. I shall always be present for you, my beloved liberator. This I swear."

"But... but, claws and whiskers, how *can* you promise that, Toki?" Paa plumped down onto her haunches and gaped at the cottage. "You're going away too, just like Her Honour, aren't you? You're not trapped here any longer! So how can you promise to be here for me all the time, as well? *How?*" She scratched her ear. "No. It beats me. I don't understand."

"Ah. That." The Protean chuckled. "I see the time has come for more explanation. I have been perfecting a useful new Transformation, Paa Elpidea. It occurred to me after Nataka showed me how she can simultaneously adopt two entirely different appearances. Such a very clever device, it captivated me. So I adopted the idea and practised by myself, to the point where, now, I can both *be* different manifestations and *occupy* different dimensions and spaces, simultaneously. I am greatly relieved, because this new skill resolves the one aspect of my existence on Dunia I would have been deeply sorry to abandon: my physical presence and guise.

"It was only when, through your intervention, I was faced with the sudden prospect of complete freedom that I realised how much I had come to treasure my role as a shelter for other lives. There is something profoundly heartening about the act of safeguarding little animals, knowing they can move and live inside me, warm and protected. It reduces the essential loneliness and isolation every Immortal must feel. And I did not – *do* not – wish to relinquish it. Nor shall I have to, now. Henceforward, even when I travel away into other spaces and worlds, I shall always also remain a cottage, Paa Elpidea; a haven for you and other Wanyama to use whenever you wish or need me."

"*Ohhh!*" breathed Paa, "Oh, I see! When you danced with us, and when you came to Ter's rescue with us, you were doing that, weren't you? Claws and whiskers, that's amazing! It explains everything! … Did *you* know, Your Honour?"

"No, Paa; I didn't. I'm amazed. Sneaky, Toki; very sneaky," Nataka reached up and patting the lintel over the cottage door, "…but so generous and ingenious, too; just like you. I'm impressed!"

M'Kuu thumped the ground with a back paw and Axl bucked, delighted that they would still be able to shelter inside the Immortal that stood before them, glowing in the sunlight and puffing rainbow-coloured rings out of its chimney. In its eaves, Dora the spider clapped four of her eight legs together and then scurried about, galvanised into weaving a magnificent new web to celebrate the preservation of her home.

"Oh Toki, I'm *so* grateful!" The poodle's tail was wagging fit to fly off her rump. "Just think of all the Wanyama who will be able to shelter with you! I've been awfully worried about them, you know; but I didn't want to say anything, in case it made you feel bad. You've done so much for us already!" Then she turned to Nataka, "Oh, Your Honour, this *is* perfect, isn't it? Now, even if I don't come with you,

I'll always be able to find out what you're doing from Toki, which is the next best thing. Isn't it? Please say you forgive me for not wanting to come with you, please!"

Nataka stooped and kissed the dog on her sparkling forehead. "Of course I understand. I don't have to forgive you, dearest godling," she said. "I have no right to expect you to abandon your nature and your home, just because I want you at my side. I'm still selfish, aren't I? Well, I've just got to learn to take no for an answer occasionally, and this is a good place to start. You've already done so much for me, after all. You've got every right to lead your life as *you* want to.

"Be happy, Paa, with my thanks and goodwill. Find yourself a loving home, and be happy. And think of me from time to time, until we meet again."

***

And then there were just Paa, Axl, M'Kuu and Tytus the Baron on the grass outside the cottage, which looked as if it wanted a nap, and Fagus, which sat smiling and turning its leaves to catch the sunlight as it half-listened to their conversation.

Everyone else had departed. Nataka the silver wolf had vanished into the tree some time before with Mond trotting behind her, anxiously panting, while she sang a path to his home forest. Glose had left with her, clinging to her back and keeping up a running commentary in his grating voice until, craving a bit of silence, Nataka bound his bill with a temporary *muzzle* charm.

"Well..." Paa suddenly felt lonely and awkward. "I'd better get going. Don't forget me, M'Kuu and Axl and Tytus, promise? I love you all so much. Please don't forget me!

I'll miss you all awfully..." She went around, kissing each Nyama and fighting the urge to whimper.

"I won't forget you because I won't need to," said M'Kuu. "I'm coming with you to find your new home, Paa. Did you think I'd let you do that on your own? And when I know where you're going, I'll be coming back to see you often and often, because you and I are one, joined in the Dance. We're more than merely friends, you know. You're the strangest dog I've ever met, and I want to stay in your life. You're not getting rid of me that easily."

"And I," whickered the quiet deer, touching noses with the poodle, "I too am one with you. I too follow you."

"And I," hooted the Baron, fluttering down to perch on one of Axl's antlers, "I also shall come with you, Paa. And I will return to you frequently. I could never just fly away and forget you. You are Nataka's friend and saviour, and I love you as much as I love her."

"So you see, you are not alone. Wherever you go, we will all accompany you, and see you safe. And afterwards, even if we are obliged to separate occasionally to pursue our own affairs, you can be sure that we will always return to you.

"And just like Toki and Fagus, I don't doubt for a moment that you, Paa, *you* will return here to us as well. Over and over. You know you will. The Dance and Toki and all of us who love and need you will draw you back. Yes, you will return. It's in your nature. You're loyal; you don't forget your friends. This place is your domain. It is the rock on which your Siren sits and sings to you, and you will never be able to deny her! [clxxiv] ... Come, friends; we should set out. Sunhigh is already behind us."

Fagus smiled a wide smile as it opened to admit them. And so they passed into its shadows one by one: the owl, the deer, the hare and the poodle.

And then there was nobody left in the clearing with the cottage and the gigantic beech tree, apart from a busy orb web spider, who hummed contentedly to herself as she worked.

***

The glorious Easter weather had drawn record numbers of visitors to the zoo, and its wardens, keepers and managers had had their hands full all day, policing, clearing up after litterbugs, restoring lost children to careless parents, fishing mobile phones and cameras out of pelicans' and ostriches' crops ... all the rumpus, in short, that attends that most noisy and exhausting of phenomena: humans on holiday.

When it was all over for the day and the zoo gates secured behind the last departing stragglers, Bryony and Jim stumbled as much as walked back to their little cottage inside its grounds. They had nothing more in mind than a quiet evening and a long sleep. The crazy jamboree would all be starting up again on the next day, and they needed their rest.

After the usual good-natured tussle to be the first under the shower and wash off the aromas of all the creatures they had tended during the day, they ate their supper of minestrone and warm crusty rolls sitting on the sofa in front of a brisk little fire that set the shadows to dancing in their comfortable, un-fussy living room. The clear spring skies they were enjoying made the nights chilly, and on such nights, nothing was more soothing to tired limbs than a friendly, chattering fire.

Their eyes were getting heavy – to tell the truth, Jim was already more than half asleep, sprawling with his long legs stretched out and almost in the embers – and the only thing that had kept them from going to bed was the effort of standing up, when of a sudden they were roused by the sound of barking outside.

"Wha'?" mumbled Jim, struggling to sit up, "Did you invite anybody round, Bry? ... Anybody with a dog?"

"No, 'course I didn't;" said Bryony on a yawn. She rose, knuckled her eyes, and slouched to the window that overlooked their front porch. As she drew back the curtain and peered out, she added, "I'm not a masochist, you know. Whoever it is, they'll just have to turn right round and go away again. I don't care if it's the Queen. I'm too knackered to..."

Then her voice changed. "*Hello*...Oh, my goodness..."

"What's up?" Jim raised his head.

"Oh! ... Jim, JIM... look, look! ... She's back!"

Jim joined Bryony at the window. "Well, I'll be..." he whistled.

Sitting on the lawn before the cottage and staring straight at them with her luminous golden eyes was the poodle. There was no mistaking her; the moonlight glinted off the distinctive silvery patch she wore above her eyes.

And, behind her, the young couple caught a glimpse of two shapes that looked very like a white deer and a large hare. But they couldn't be sure, because in an instant the two figures had slipped away and melted into the shadows under the honeysuckle and wisteria hedge that surrounded the cottage. Besides, Bryony and Jim were distracted by a huge barn owl that swept by close to their window, called once, and then disappeared.

The poodle rose to her paws, stretched, and shook herself vigorously. Then she trotted onto the porch, sat down on her haunches facing the front door, and barked again.

So Jim opened the door.

THE END

EPILOGUE

"...And so to bed." [clxxv]

I don't know about you, but I can't stand loose ends. You know what I mean: coming to the end of a story and not knowing what happened to everybody, particularly if I've started to care for any of them, merely because the person telling the story's stopped telling it.

So anyway, feel free to skip this bit if you're the kind of person who doesn't need everything neatly wrapped up, or if you've had enough and are satisfied with what you've read.

On the other hand, if you're like me and want to tie off all those loose ends (always bearing in mind, of course that nothing ever really has a proper ending – as I hope you've realised by now – and, by the same token, that there's never a real beginning to it, either. Or is there? ... Is there?) ... Er. Where was I?

... Oh; OK. Sorry. No more badgering. Instead, here are the questions I imagine you may wish to clear up (if you're like me), with their answers (and if you don't like them, feel free to make up your own). And if you want any more answers, drop me a line.

Right: Here goes.

* What happened to Mond?

As you know, the timber wolf took Miba's advice to heart and went home immediately after the great festival in Toki's garden. Although he was still nervous about once again facing the labyrinthine journey through Fagus, he gritted his fangs, thought of his cubs, mate and hunting companions, and stuck close behind Nataka while she sang the way with the chattering raven bouncing around on her back. His hackles were up all the way, but he managed to keep his head as she guided him through one of the finest root networks Fagus had ever grown in response to her songs. It took a full Startime of high-speed travel before they finally fell out of the Beech tree onto the pine-needled floor of a scented virgin forest of conifer trees. They were greeted by the crisp light of the Sun shining on patches of snow that still lingered in the hollows and humps between stands of pine, larch and spruce.

"Oh, Nataka, *ma parfaite amie immortelle!*" [clxxvi] The wolf bounded out of Fagus, whimpering with excitement. "You and this tree *magnifique* 'ave brought me 'ome – 'ome to those I love, those I feared I should never again see! …" He was just about to settle into a long oration in praise of his guides when he stopped dead and lifted his muzzle, quivering in every limb. He had picked up the scent of his pack and (to Nataka's relief and Glose's annoyance) lost all interest in further rhetoric. Instead he stretched his neck, filled his lungs, and called to his pack-mates: a full-throated howl that shook the lingering snow off the branches around him.

We shall leave him there, with his mate and cubs racing to greet him more rapturously than I can ever hope to describe. Nataka and Glose slipped away again, knowing that such reunions are sacred and not to be intruded on without very good reason, even by Immortals.

… Oh, and of course Mond and his pack and family spent many long seasons thereafter living very full, very contented lives, hunting and playing in their virgin woodlands and tundra. In due course, as a natural consequence of his many adventures and great wisdom regarding the wider world and the strange ways of Howlers, Mond succeeded to the leadership of the pack, which he still rules and protects both wisely and fiercely. In particular, he makes sure that *everybody* from cub to grey-muzzle knows all there is to know about the strange, evil traps Howlers might prepare for them. None of his pack has ever fallen into one of *those* again. Now that's what I call great leadership. Plenty of Howler leaders could learn a thing or two from him.

* What became of all the other Wanyama that had been Nataka's companions, after she left?

With the exception of Tytus the Baron, Axl and M'Kuu (about whom you already know), the majority of the Wanyama went back to their normal lives, returning to Toki whenever the mood seized them:

* Pex and Ala are excellent parents, having raised numerous litters of cubs and taught them to avoid the (so-called '*banned*') fox-hunting Howlers that still crash around during the colder seasons of the year, making life miserable for all decent Wanyama. Pex returns regularly to the cottage to renew his friendship with Dora's offspring, touch muzzles with Paa whenever she's there, and catch up on the local gossip.

* Fyrd, his hardworking mate Nibblenose and their many descendants are steadily populating the banks of the river and its tributaries, swimming and hunting as they go. They will never lose their playfulness and delight in everything they encounter.

* Wurfl the beaver and his vast extended family are also spreading ever more widely into the waterways around the great river. Where they are allowed to get on with their work undisturbed, they accomplish much good with their dams, which prevent flooding on the lower reaches of the river during the wet seasons, and also provide lots of interesting and varied wetland habitat for other Wanyama and plants. And of course, by thinning out the woodland around their homes they also encourage new and vigorous tree growth.

* Brid and his family continue to flourish in the branches of Fagus. He is a still great friends with Miba, taking in his stride the succession of tiny, rubber-prickled infants she produces and rears every season. For her part, Miba treasures Brid's undemanding friendship. She never shows any inclination to find other friends among her own kind, or to settle down with one or other of the fathers of her babies. In her opinion, female hogs are more boring than empty snail-shells, only interested in discussing who has the biggest babies or their encounters with slug pellets, while the males are even worse, being monosyllabic and greedy, only useful for making hedge-hoglets. Once they've fulfilled that single function (and it's a good thing they seem to enjoy their role, all things considered), the further away they stay from Miba, the better she likes it. Well, there you have it. It's the way of her species. Her babies never fare any the worse for being fatherless.

* Dora the orb-web spider has long since passed through her final Change and is no doubt enjoying a Dimension crammed with fat flies. Her many descendants can be found in every garden and woodland that hasn't been poisoned by Howlers' villainous concoctions of pesticides and herbicides. On dewy mornings, the sun shining through the complex, perfectly balanced webs of these brilliant weavers festoons every tree, shrub and clump of grass with sparkling magic. No wonder the eight-legged artists hold a special place in Nataka's and Toki's hearts.

* Scrumpy the badger has had a difficult time of it for a number of seasons, what with a particularly obnoxious obsession on the part of Howlers who have invaded huge tracts of land all over the place, call it their own and stock it with domestic animals, especially cattle. They keep trying to kill him and his relatives off, keen to blame his kind for any disease they find in their over-bred and overcrowded domestic Wanyama. But the canny old badger is still alive,

and continues to be worse tempered than a cow with a burr up her... her... (I'll leave you to guess what). He receives regular renewals of Nataka's chilblain potion whenever the turn of the seasons requires it (every time Nataka returns to this Dimension she makes sure to replenish the stock of potion), so his chilblains are kept well under control.

* Skald and Nifl worked hard, rearing their three hatchlings all through the Seasons of the Dancing Hare and the first Moons of the Dragonflies and Gnats. Everything went excellently until the youngsters started to fly. Then one of them, hovering over a stone river and scanning the verges for small Wanyama, was caught in the downdraft generated by a huge, snarling, howling and stinking whizz-thing that roared by on the stone river below. He struggled hard to fight the pull of the draft and maintain altitude, but didn't manage to get away (the turbulent stench produced by the flatulent whizz-thing surely contributed to this failure; besides, his muscles were still developing, and they tired quickly). The poor young bird panicked, plummeted down and was crushed under the murderous monster's whirling paws. There was nothing anybody could have done about it. But despite their heartbreak, brave as they always have been, Skald and Nifl continued to care for their remaining two fledglings, who passed unscathed through the perilous first stages of their early flying careers and are now rearing their own broods. Nifl is a particularly caring (actually, frankly, an interfering) grandmother, constantly telling the overworked parents how they *should* be doing things, and boring everybody with tales of the Great Egg Evacuation during what she calls the Saga of the Moaning Mond.

* The Mongooses are all in fine shape. They continue to run rings around the zoo staff, who still haven't the faintest inkling of the full extent of their activities and shenanigans. Kidole has grown into such an excellent escapologist that not even his parents can match his tricks. The mongooses have a paw in every mischief going, and frequently dive

through Fagus to visit Toki in Chissadove. Fagus is so besotted with them that they can do no wrong as far as it is concerned. In fact, the Pathway Tree would cheerfully drop a branch for them. They repay it with ever more exciting and hilarious performances and antics.

* Rav'n the (erstwhile) alley cat enjoyed a long and happy succession of seasons with his Pet Gertrude, who finally twigged that he would *never* accept a bath. That was a happy moment for him. And when she moved on to her well-deserved final Change, he adopted another equally malleable Howler to care for him, using the Lap Skills Nataka had shown him. Every so often he wanders out into the night air and touches noses with his Wanyama friends, stepping into Fagus as you or I would onto an escalator, without a second thought. He still has a few Seasons left in him, and he's enjoying them to the full.

* Sardo the Roloway monkey and Kelele the Chimp still argue about the correct order of maturation of tropical fruit. Sardo likes to rile the irascible old primate at every opportunity, teasing him about his lack of a tail, and so on. He'll never change.

* Chant aged into a venerable cat. She receded from public life, preferring to stay close to her Pets' home and drive them crazy with her demands and airs. But they loved her dearly. After all, she had survived well over 100 Seasons in that particular incarnation, a fabulous age for a feline, and they reckoned she was entitled to a few foibles. She attributed her longevity to her own excellent self-husbandry (she'd never was given to modesty). She liked to claim that she "put the *purr* into *perfect*", and from their behaviour, her Pets clearly agreed with her.

As the Moons drifted past, she spent more and more time lying on her favourite table inside her glassed-in shelter, watching the birds dip and swing around the garden and keeping a weather eye open for next door's intrusive ginger cat. The birds seemed to have a lot of fun, surfing on the breezes, squabbling and comparing travel plans as the Season of Bird Flight approached.

One Sunwake, a buzzard plummeted down onto the lawn directly in front of where Chant was curled inside her shelter, straight onto the fat hindquarters of a woodpigeon that had been waddling around, pecking at the young clover-heads. The outraged pigeon only just managed to escape from under the talons of its would-be killer and whiffle away with a clump of down missing from its rear end. The frustrated raptor's fierce eyes glared around the garden, and for an instant it locked eyes with Chant lying wide-eyed behind the glass, before it bounced vertically back into the air and thundered away. Chant spent the rest of that Suntime thinking about the fire in its eyes and the noise of its wings. They reminded her of Nataka.

At last there came a Sunclimb when she opened her eyes to find that she could no longer climb or jump. Her legs felt wobbly, and her appetite seemed to have abandoned her without saying goodbye. The Howler who poked and prodded Wanyama paid her a visit and confirmed what she could have told him without all the poking and prodding: she was ill, very ill. And even to Chant, who really had firmly believed in her own immortality, it was clear that at long last her current incarnation was drawing to its close and her tired old body preparing to rest. Well, she consoled herself, it had been a long and exciting life, even the bits she hadn't enjoyed so much.

Her main Pet, the female who had bonded with her when she was a kitten and who now lived a long way away, came to visit Chant, who by now spent all her time resting in her cot. This Pet had always understood her better than any other Howler and didn't bother her with unwanted noise. She sat with her for a long time, didn't talk too much, and stroked her exactly where she liked to be stroked. *Mmh,* mused the little cat, *this special attention from my Main Pet confirms that my time's running out. Ah well. It's gratifying to know that she still worships me as I deserve. Leto's right: no matter what, such things will never disappear.*

Chant's very last Startime came in the Season of Fire and Fruit, under a full Moon. She made one last effort and went round to Paa's Pets' garden, where she watched the poodle, hare and deer dance in the cool silvery light, and then spent some moments bidding them farewell. When eventually she returned to her bed, she wasn't entirely surprised to find her Damp Pet waiting for her. The Pet stayed with her through the rest of that Startime, offering her water and nibbles, and stroking her whenever she moved. But Chant only wanted to be left alone. She snarled at her Pet to go away and stop fussing, but as usual the dumb, damp creature caught the wrong end of the ball of string, because she only worried and fidgeted even more. It was annoying.

At length, despite everything the Damp Pet did with her ministrations to prevent it, the little cat managed to fall into a fitful doze. She dreamed that she had abandoned her aching body and was flying over a vast, restlessly moving ocean full of stars.

On the following Sunhigh she was finally able to rest, lulled by the same magical potion that had smoothed the path to her littermate Leto's ultimate Change.

At last, she purred to herself. *But where in the name of a blunt claw has Leto got to? I'd have thought he'd turn up, at least. Useless mog. Never trust marmalade toms.*

Her thoughts grew muzzy and her purr faded. She drifted away on a tide of well-being, trying to ignore the sobs of her Damp Pet.

She couldn't tell how much later she came round again, feeling light and young, and looked about her. Her Pets were still grieving over what had once been her living shell, so it hadn't been very long. And beside them sat the shade of Leto, weaving his magnificent tail.

You took your time, she said. *Tell me, how do I stop our Pets from crying? It's almost as if they're sorry that I've stopped suffering.*

Can't be done, said Leto. *I tried it; remember? Didn't work for long. They'll just have to get over it on their own. And don't be so sniffy. You were just as bad as them.*

... So. Are you ready?

Yes. Tell you what, though, next time I fancy flying. I don't suppose there's any chance I could be a bird, for a change - you know, a big, fierce bird that nobody messes with? I'd like that. I'd come back and give that blasted cat next door a proper fright, for a start.

Hmm. I'm not sure. Leto ran a snowy forepaw over one ear. *We could ask, I suppose. But are you sure? What if you end up having to eat fruit or seeds or worms all your life?*

Good point. I hadn't thought of that, said Chant. *I'll think about it. Let's go.*

And they left.

* Leto's camellia blooms sweetly every Season of the Dancing Hare, keeping his memory alive for all who loved him. There are times when Anthony or Fran catch a glimpse of a shadow of a hint of an amber tail and four soft white socks strolling across the lawn… but that may just be next door's tomcat, who, as I said, is a pest. Who knows? I like to think that it's Leto. Just as I like to fancy that the dappled, multi-patterned, elegant little shade that occasionally wanders at his side is the spirit of Chant, back to sniff the blooms on the memorial rose adorning her own resting place. She *may* have got her wish and become a buzzard or fish eagle or some other terrifying raptor in her next life, of course; but even so, surely the Shade that retains the memory of her previous life will wander through her old haunts, if it wanders at all. There's no harm in being optimistic.

* What about Fagus?

As previous notes make clear, Fagus continues to enjoy its Immortality and powers to the full. And no, if you're a Howler you'll never find it, search as you might. Sorry about that. You're just the wrong species. But one day, when *your* Big Change is upon you, who knows? You may find that Fagus agrees to be the portal through which you step into your next adventure. It all depends on how you treat the Wanyama around you.

* What happened to the other Howlers?

*The Busybody never forgot the 'miracle' cure he'd received from Paa's tongue. He took to religion and became more and more involved in organising fundraising events and competitions for the church he attended - which, coincidentally, was the exact same one frequented by Ida Court.

* Ida didn't take at all kindly to having the old Busybody gate-crash what she had come to consider *her* church, and steal the limelight with his money-making activities. There ensued the inevitable confrontation between them, which ended with the majority of the congregation (who had become increasingly fed up with Ida's bullying and rants) siding with the Busybody and reading her the riot act. Poor

old Ida felt dreadfully betrayed by them all, so she abandoned that congregation and tried her hand at colonising another, smaller one instead. But though it was small, this congregation was also fierce and its leader not somebody to be browbeaten by anybody, so she didn't make much headway. Of course, she also had to spend a lot of time looking after her brother Roger, who never fully recovered from his confrontations with Nataka the Beast. All of this rather curtailed her hegemonistic tendencies. She blamed Roger for it, naturally.

* For his part, Roger, who had moved in with Ida after he lost his job, was largely oblivious of her resentment and wouldn't have given a flying frog if he *had* known about it. He wasn't destitute because he still remembered how to draw on all that lovely money he'd salted away in his Cayman account (though Ida never heard about it). But he didn't do much apart from spending the rest of his rather short life going to seed. He smoked too much tobacco, drank too much fermented fruit-and-grain-juice, and ate all the worst food he could lay his hands on, while hanging around pubs and parks, trying to convince anybody who'd listen that he'd come face to face with a *bona fide* demon. The more he hammered on about it, of course, the less anybody believed him, even though he was telling the strict truth in all sincerity for the first time in his life. Now *there's* a paradox for you. Told you most Howlers were *kichaa*.

* The Howler consortium that had loaned Roger money in the hope that they would make a huge profit from his misappropriation of the Wingco's insurance never managed to work out what exactly had happened to Gabriel, their beautiful, psychopathic colleague and handy assassin. In the end they decided that he had absconded with whatever fabulous sum of money they believed Roger had managed to raise and paid over to avoid getting *nyoroshered*. So they stopped searching for Roger and started looking for Gabriel instead, planning ever-more sophisticated ways of torturing

him when they finally caught him. For all I know they're still looking.

* The Wingco, Maddie and Ter lived long, full and joyous lives, just as Nataka's parting toast had proposed. Maddie never remarried; she'd had enough of *that* adventure. Instead she poured all her love and warmth into Ter and the Wingco, who repaid her with their steadfast love and support. Their home was delightful, a place full of celebration and laughter. The Wingco lived on long enough to celebrate Ter's graduation as a veterinary surgeon and see him marry and pursue a stellar career in his chosen profession.

* Ter worked hard, published widely and became a lot richer than he'd ever expected. He seemed to have a way with animals. They took to him, accepted his ministrations, and even appeared to communicate with him. He had an uncanny ability to spot their ailments, almost before they occurred. And all his life he felt particularly drawn to dogs and ravens.

One day, when he was himself a husband and father, Ter took his mother and young family (two girls, one boy) and their mother to a zoo south of the great estuary, outside the sphere of his own operations (he was living in the Lake District). The zoo was well run, and the animals contented and healthy, which delighted him. He also enjoyed a very illuminating and friendly conversation with the zoo's Head Warden, a cheerful woman called Bryony Bell (her predecessor Anthony had retired some years before, and was volunteering in a rescue centre for animals. Talk about a busman's holiday). Ter's family left him to his shop talk and went to sit outside a terraced café that had been built near the small mammals' enclosure, where they licked soft ices and laughed at the antics of a pair of importunate mongooses that had escaped from their enclosure and were trying to wheedle treats from the visitors.

After leaving the Head Warden's office, Ter walked out to join his family. As he approached where they were sitting, he was astounded to see a beautiful, cream-coloured poodle trot up to the mongooses cavorting around the tables, quietly pick up first one and then the other of them by the scruff of its neck and dump it onto her own back with a casual, practised swing of the muzzle, and then stroll back down the path up which Ter was approaching. The little creatures on her back appeared unharmed; indeed, they were obviously quite accustomed to their treatment.

As the cream-coloured dog approached him, Ter noticed a strange mark - a curiously shimmering patch of silver - on her forehead, directly above her eyes. Something stirred inside him. He stopped dead, gazing, astounded at the surge of recognition and regret – yes – and of nostalgia – evoked by the sight.

The poodle locked eyes with him. She came on steadily, stopped a couple of feet of where he was standing, and settled onto her haunches (the mongooses adjusted easily; still comfortably seated on her back, they dug their little paws in her fur and nestled against her back like a pair of infant marmosets). Then the dog lifted her muzzle, opened her pink mouth and *smiled*. Her honey-gold eyes glowed strangely, and for an instant the shiny patch on her brow seemed to sparkle like a tiny rainbow.

Ter caught his breath. "I know you," he whispered despite himself, "I don't know how, but … but I *know* you…"

I know you.

It seemed to Ter that a gentle voice murmured inside his head. The poodle's smile widened; her rosy tongue came out and licked her nose.

"But - How? ... Where? ... How do I know you?"

You know how. You know where.

"But we've never met before!"

We've met before.

"Ah! I see you've met our special warden," said a voice behind Ter. He looked up, startled. Bryony had approached from behind and was standing beside him, smiling down at the poodle. She bent over and fondled the dog's ears, then the two mongooses.

"She's our treasure, Doctor Bourne," said the Head Warden, "forever rescuing and rounding up naughty creatures - like *these* two - for us." She indicated the mongooses. "And she's an absolute God-send with sick animals: cares for them, supports them, keeps them warm, alerts us to changes... you name it. And just by being with them, she seems to make them better. She's saved us any number of lives – *and* vet bills. I've no idea how she does it, mind you. Lovely, isn't she?"

"She's amazing," said Ter. "That mark on her forehead...?"

"Yes; odd, isn't it? Everybody comments on it. My husband Jim and I haven't been able to work out *what* it is, or how she got it; and believe me, we've done plenty of digging. All useless. It goes down all the way to her skin, believe it or not. It won't come out either. So it must be congenital, though we really don't understand how *that* might be. And what's more, none of her puppies has ever had anything like it. But we're not about to mess with it, particularly as it doesn't seem to be harming her. She's had it ... oh, ever since she came into our lives, a good fifteen years ago, now."

Something stirred inside Ter again. Fifteen years. Why did *that* feel so significant? And, more strangely still, the poodle looked to be in the prime of her life, even though she had to be immensely old, for a dog. It was all strange and illogical, and yet it felt so eerily familiar...

"You'll have to tell me all about that, one day," he said lightly, smiling at the tall, rangy woman beside him. Though she was a good decade older than he and her curly hair peppered with grey, Bryony looked as fit as a teenager. "I'm always fascinated by anything out of the ordinary."

"Happy to! You and your family are very welcome to come by sometime and meet our gang. Here..." she fished a business card out of her back jeans pocket and handed it to him, "I forgot to give you one of these, just now. Do give us a bell next time you're in these parts, and let's get together. Please do. Jim and the kids'll be delighted to meet you. We've read all your publications, Doctor. You're by way of being a bit of a celebrity with us. In fact, you've inspired one of our lads; he wants to study veterinary medicine."

"Thank you... thank you; I will. That's a promise," Ter bent down to the poodle and gazed into her eyes. "I shall see *you* again too," he said, "I want – I *need* – to understand this. ... Yes, I'll definitely see you again. I promise."

As he spoke, another shiver ran through him, and he caught a flash of an image in his mind's eye: of his own arms wrapped around the soft neck of a cream-coloured poodle – no, a unicorn – no, a poodle; a poodle that sparkled with warmth and reassurance and delight; of early morning light in a sky full of driving clouds, against which the trees toppled and tumbled; of the liquid song of a lark that rose and rose and rose ... and of a promise ...

"I promise," he whispered again, doubting whether there

would be a reply, not daring to hope it would come.

It came.

I promise.

"Oh, good Lord!" Ter gasped under his breath and bolted straight upright, stunned by the feeling surging in him again. Was he losing his mind? He turned hastily to the Head Warden, who was still standing quietly by, watching him. "Well… well, Mrs Bell … I - I'd better go. But I'll definitely contact you," he said, wanting nothing more now than to get away and examine what was happening to him.

"Don't worry, Doctor," said the woman. Her smile was understanding. "There's nothing wrong with you. She has that effect on a few people. Tell you what - and you're welcome to think I'm nuts - she even told me her name, when she first came along and adopted us. I'm sure of it. I wanted to call her *Angel* - long story; I won't bore you with it now - but she made it quite clear she wasn't having any of it. Instead, somehow - I'm not sure how, but *somehow* - she got across to us what she likes to be called. Didn't you, you little old despot? … And a weird name it is, too. Her name is Paa."

Paa, Paa, Paa! echoed the voice in his head. The poodle lifted her muzzle and gave a cheerful *wuff*.

"Paa!" This time it was as if the sky turned inside out while the ground heaved under his feet and briefly dissolved into a well of deep, dark water crowded with stars. And inside his head *Paa, Elpidea, Roho la Dunia!* boomed a second unfamiliar, familiar voice full of laughter and green energy.

Ter staggered. But then he regained his balance and, not daring to look at either of them again, hurried off down the path, away from the smiling woman and the cream-coloured dog with her little passengers.

"Oh, Paa," sighed Bryony, "I do hope you haven't chased him away forever with your – what *is* that thing you do, voodoo? ... Anyway, I hope you haven't scared him away with it. I like him. I hope he comes back."

(Okay. I know this is jumping the gun, but ... Oh, what the hell. This is my story, and I'll tell you if I want to.)

Many years later, after a full and fruitful life, Ter found himself walking down a familiar beach of sand and shells towards a jetty that hung out over a dark sea teeming with stars in strange constellations that shimmered under a pale blue sky full of hovering butterflies and the cries of seabirds. Soon a sailboat with his parents and the Wingco in it would arrive to fetch him away, and he didn't want to keep them waiting.

And as he approached the jetty, he saw the figure of a dark, beautiful, instantly familiar woman whose endlessly variable eyes glittered like iridescent pebbles bathed in a rushing mountain stream.

And beside her, glowing like a beacon, Paa: Paa the poodle; Paa the unicorn; Paa who, many years before, had snatched him back from the brink of an untimely dissolution. Her eyes were sparkling, her unicorn's horn a shaft of rainbow-hued diamond light aiming straight at him. She was whimpering with excitement, her body wriggling with joy and affection, and her tail wagging so quickly and enthusiastically that all he could see of it was a creamy blur as she surged towards him over the glittering sand.

And at last he remembered.

* **What did Nataka and Toki do?**

Well, both the Proteans started off by bouncing around a whole plethora of Dimensions like giddy schoolchildren at the beginning of their long holidays. They dived through portal after portal into every Reality they could find, renewed old friendships, started any number of fresh ones, wallowed in water-worlds, danced in the storms of gas giants and tornado-dimensions, and teased humourless gurus and self-obsessed artistes (note the *e* in that word) on countless planets, each one of which considered itself totally, *totally* unique in the most predictable way… until at last they decided that what they really needed was a long rest from all their holidays. So they rested up for a while. They've got into the habit of popping back to Dunia every so often, just to potter about and see how the mad old planet is getting on.

* Nataka still goes everywhere. And wherever she goes, Glose accompanies her. His love for her is as strong as hers for him. She wouldn't know what to do without his infuriating, argumentative, clever company. And the raven will continue her companion for as many seasons as he likes, because Nataka has rewarded him for his loyalty with the gift of Immortality. And so, although he's many, many Seasons old now, he will never weaken or slow up. And he isn't fazed by any of the Dimensions and Realities through which Nataka whisks him, however bizarre it may be. He always finds something to deride and something to eat. He's got it made.

* Because Toki has mastered the art of being in two places as two entirely different manifestations simultaneously, it's having the time of its… life? … immortality? … omnipresence? (Ach; you know what I mean). Regardless of whether it's off somewhere participating in a Harvest or Spring celebration as Pan or Bacchus or Shiva, or wafting through the air as a self-willed dirigible on a cloud-world, or participating in fire sculpting competitions with the

Incendiary Demons of the Nether Dimension of Inx, it continues to be the cosy, ever-flexible and accommodating cottage on our Dunia to which all Wanyama seeking sanctuary, a good meal, warmth and companionship can turn whenever they want. It faithfully inhabits the same dishevelled plot, which is still under a special magical influence preventing the majority of Howlers from paying any attention to it - or, if they do pay attention, from seeing anything more than a rubble- and litter-strewn patch of derelict ground with a stagnant pond, where a pile of bricks that once were part of a terrace of council houses moulder into decay amid the nettles, wild celery, columbine, goose-grass, Honesty and cow parsley mercifully blanketing ancient drifts of the rubbish countless passing Howlers used to dump over the creaking, rusty iron gate.

All that said, let me to leave you with a friendly warning.

If it should ever come to pass that you're travelling through a sleepy little hamlet called Chissadove, which lies a short rook's flight away from a town called Chissaperchè in the borough of Addov'vai somewhere in the West Country not far from Hereford; *and*, because you haven't been paying attention to your navigation *or* the wind has suddenly veered from the south to the north-west *or* there's a double Z in the month *or* you've been dreaming of dancing with unicorns and hares under a strawberry moon (*or* any combination of the above), you end up walking down a narrow, rather poorly maintained stone river with crumbling edges and the odd pot-hole, a road that winds a bit ditzily between the foot of a wooded hill with footpaths and riding paths on one hand and a meadow sloping down to a great river that glints on the horizon on the other ... (Crikey. That took some writing. Worse than the kind of sentence you get in ponderous Victorian novels, that. Hang on a tick, I've got to catch my breath) ...

Right.

If, I say, finding yourself there, you happen to notice a particularly shabby little patch of waste ground surrounded by an overgrown yew hedge in which a rusty iron gate creaks when you touch it, and there's a mosquito-breeding pool in one corner (which will be well hidden under the weeds and rushes, so keep a sharp eye out), and there's a pile of crumbling bricks and mortar in one corner of this weed-infested plot that may once have been a terrace of three ugly council houses (no guarantees that you will, mind you; very few Howlers do. But you'll stand a better chance of doing so if there's a child accompanying you) ...

And if, then, you start to feel an unaccountable tingly sensation between your shoulder blades, together with the sudden, irrational impression that if you were to drop a sweet-wrapper over that rusty iron gate into that messy dump on the other side you might, just *might* find yourself Transformed into a cockroach ...

Well, all I can say is, don't drop that sweet paper. OK? Just don't.

If you know what's good for you.

Farewell!

*** *REALLY* THE END ***

A Note From the Author

"The sole duty and justification for art is social criticism" [clxxvii]

I'm permitting myself the luxury of presenting a few words on this story, ones I trust will interest those who've read and enjoyed it (even in bits).

I've been told that this tale is difficult to categorise in a variety of ways, the chief ones being:
  (1) Its target audience (friends have asked me more than once just whom I wrote it for);
  (2) Its main purpose (is it to entertain; teach; satirise; complain; level a sneaky moral lesson at its unsuspecting audience; other?)
  (3) 'Voice' (this keeps chopping and changing. One minute it's young, cheeky, subversive and colloquial; the next it becomes long-winded and explanatory. At others it's unashamedly romantic and lyrical. So what's all *that* about, anyway?)

Without such clarification, I understand, it must surely struggle to find an audience, because folk like to know what a book contains *before* they open it. They want sneak previews. They don't like buying cats in bags. They're dead set against surprises. And so forth.

Well, I've got to throw up my hands on all points. I admit that when I first started to write this tale I had very little idea about its true nature and/or intentions. What I *do* know is that once the initial idea for the story presented itself, there was no way I could make it go away again. It demanded that I shelve all other activities to follow it - and, I might add, was nothing short of despotic in that respect.

Believe it or not, this whole thing *began* as a short story. But, as I say, it took over. It grew and grew and, like every true despot, would nag away at me so insistently whenever I stopped working on it for a while to focus on other things that I simply *had* to go back to it and carry on.

Not only did this tale hag-ride me, it also began to develop in ways I hadn't foreseen at all, the main one being that a whole lot of new characters arose, multiplying the themes and ideas I'd started with. And each of those characters demanded to be written in a specific way and with its own 'voice' – which, I suppose, addresses *that* particular question.

There were times when I had the slightly crazed impression that I wasn't so much creating a tale as unwrapping it to find many of my greatest resentments, fears, loves and hopes for the world and life in general lurking inside the various layers of narrative. All I did was record what every character in it said and did as accurately and truly as I could, hoping against hope that sooner or later it would all come together and make sense.

And then, one day, it happened. The tale was told, each sub-plot and participant complete and in its place within what had somehow (but *how*?) turned into a coherent account. Everybody that had plagued me to write about him or her barely said goodbye before unceremoniously jumping ship. Nothing disturbed my nights, compelling me to keep writing, any longer. It was done.

(Good grief, all this comes across as tooth-gratingly pretentious, doesn't it? I'm sorry! But, what the heck, I'll let it stand, because it reflects precisely how I felt).

Come to think of it, I suppose this is also why I never actually paused to ask myself any sensible, hard-nosed questions like: "For whom am I writing this, anyway? Kids? Adults? ... Just who will want to read this?" Or: "Am I tailoring the language to my target audience?" (Target audience? Good grief! I was hanging on to the tail of a bizarre chimaera, a many-faced beast that was infantile at some moments, ironic, bitter and humourless at others, with a veritable menagerie of participants in it, and each one demanding language that fitted with it. Who's got time to think of *target audiences* while all that's going on?) ... Yes, I confess that I was most unprofessional about it all. I did no more than write down the tale as it presented itself, and try to make it as grammatical and comprehensible as I could.

But one thing I *was* sure of: I wanted at least one other person to read my story. I wanted an audience, even if only of one person. It never crossed my mind to keep it private. What use *is* a story, anyway, if nobody else hears or reads it? ... Yes; despite not knowing how to define that strange thing, my *Target Audience*, I don't buy into the pretentious claims of some people that they really only ever write for themselves and that they never imagine a pair of eyes and a brain not their own reading their words and interpreting, feeling and responding to them in his or her own unique way. As far as I'm concerned, every story *needs* an audience because it's the co-creation that occurs at the moment of its reception that either kicks it into existence or kills it stone dead (just like music, or the visual arts, or even a building. Seriously, what earthly use is an *empty* house?) ... Until that participation happens, then, the tale might as well be a series of indecipherable tracks a crab leaves in a patch of sand.

So all through the years during which I charted the mad doings of my characters, a reader - a curious, critical, clever reader full of laughter and scepticism and questions - was the imaginary companion of my labours. S/he sat at my elbow, read over my shoulder and poked me in the ribs when anything didn't ring true, forcing me to rewrite it again and again until it felt and sounded right. That imaginary reader became part of the story and still figures in it at this very moment. That reader is YOU, whoever you are, reading this. Thank you!

And for your sake, my Reader, one of the very few genuine 'executive' decisions I took about halfway through the writing of this story was to add notes and appendices, hoping the information they contained would prove amusing as well as useful, pre-empting and resolving potential questions or difficulties with any of the more obscure references or bits of foreign language that cropped up. Because, between you and me, yet another thing I can abide even less than the pretence of 'not wanting an audience' is the Smart-Alec author that burdens his/her (otherwise absolutely excellent) accounts with arcane references, oblique hints and mottoes in languages s/he apparently assumes we should *all* master, regardless of our education, interests or backgrounds. The subtext of such a tactic, surely, is, "If you can't understand this stuff, why not? Why are you, ignoramus that you are, even presuming to read my story? You don't deserve to understand it!" etc. Now *that's* pretentious, if you like).

... Well, let that rest. What really matters is my hope that the additional guidance proves useful. Still and all, it needn't be considered essential reading. Anybody who enjoys working things out for him/herself is cordially invited to ignore it.

So this was the outcome: a tale I still struggle to categorise, but which I hope will amuse and move and, maybe, also prove thought-provoking. I call it a fantasy because of the fantastical elements in it. At times it could be what literary critics call an Apologue because it's told from the perspective of non-human animals, but you may consider it a bit too satirical to qualify for that title. Besides, it has other sides: polemical; addressing a number of human and animal rights issues close to my heart; bitter; ridiculous; brutal; sad; romantic; optimistic; occasionally unapologetically sentimental ... and, hopefully, also funny.

And yes, it starts off looking like one thing and grows into something else. Whatever *that* may be, all that I can say is that what I had in mind as I wrote was an audience of the young at heart, of any age from the mid-teens upwards, who enjoy stories that are somewhat 'out of left field' and zany, and who have a fair amount of thoughtfulness, scepticism and social criticism in their make-up. And if anybody, having read it, feels like passing on his/her thoughts as to its true nature or wants to categorise my work for me once and for all, I'll be *delighted*. I mean it.

But none of the above is as important as my hope that you you've enjoyed the story, despite the fact it starts off bearing all the hallmarks of a simple children's yarn when actually (I hope and trust you agree) it really is anything but.

Thanks for reading!

Signed: **Leo K Daniel** [clxxviii]
At: **Nataka's Chissadove Sanctuary,**
Addov'vai Valley
In: **The Season of Bird Flight in the Howler Year 2018**

***

APPENDIX 1

List of Characters (in alphabetical order)

The Magical Creatures

Fagus: The Beech Pathway Tree

Nataka: Protean imp/sprite/elemental/deity

[*Some of her other names:*
Hexe (German) / **Witch** / **Nihtgenga, Galdricge, Aglaecwif** (fiend) (Saxon)/ **Stregina** (little witch) (Italian) / **Dryas** (tree spirit) / **Erynie** ('fury'/conscience), **Gaia** (land, earth) (Greek) / **Oma Gembe** (witch doctor) / **Orisha** (m/f/ godling/god of many things - Yoruba) / **Aelfeynn** (elf kind - Britonic)/ **Earda** (Saxon) / **Siva** (Hindu) / **Erce** (Celtic) / **Rhea** (Greek) / **Demeter** (Greek) / **Prithvi** (Hindu) / **Dhara** (Hindu) / **Emesh-Enten** (Sumeria)/ **Enki** (Sumeria) / **Fjörgyn** (Earth - Norse) / **Geb; Peri** (Egyptian) / **Yōllōtl** ('heart', 'interior' -Aztec) / **Tudi, Houtu** (earth, soil - Chinese) / **Veles** (earth, waters, forests, the underworld - Cyrillic) / **Voltumna, Veltha** (Etruscan - N Italy) / **Alignak** (lunar god; god of weather, water, tides, earthquakes, eclipses - Inuit) / **Amurru, Martu** (Shepherd, storm-god - Akkadian & Sumerian) / **Atum, Atem, Tem** (Creator and Finisher - Egypt) / **Daikokuten** (God of darkness, god of five cereals- Japan) / **Tane** (god of forests and birds), **Papa** (world), / **Sumugan** (god of river plains and cattle) (Sumerian) / **Ten Ten-Vilu** (god/goddess of earth and fertility - Chilota mythology, S Chile) ... (*That'll do. Ed.*)]

Toki Tane Papatuanuku Nataka's home

The Wanyama (Animals)

Ala: Vixen, Pex's mate
Aryadnodondra (Dora): Orb web spider
Brid: Red Squirrel
Chant: Calico Tortoiseshell/Tabby Cat, Tony and Fran's owner - Zoo

Fyrd: Otter
Glose: Raven
Kelele: Grumpy Chimp - Zoo
Kidole, Yain, Tain, Tether, Mether, Mumph, Dix, Jiggit: Mongoose kittens - Zoo
Lerema & Tesho: Banded Mongoose brothers - Zoo
Leto: Ginger-white Tom Cat, Littermate of Chant and owner of Tony and Fran - Zoo
Miba: Hedgehog
M'Kuu: Hare
Mondrian des Forêts (Mond): Canadian Timber Wolf - Zoo
Nifl: Skald's mate
Nibblenose: Fyrd's mate
Paa, Rangi, Roho la Dunia: Poodle *(formerly* Tarquiana Trichitina Tantamount III, 'Trixie Snuffles' for short*)*
Pex: Fox
Rav'n (Rav'nous): Alley Cat – Sunny Shores Nursing Home
Rhesus Sardonicus (Sardo): Roloway Monkey - Zoo
Scrumpy: Badger *(AKA* Scrépfftmch»ffftnyommenm – ScrabbleMunching)
Skald: Windhover
The Toffee Emperor *(RIP)*: Gertrude's defunct Persian cat – Sunny Shores Nursing Home
Tich, Tick & Seed: Miba's babies (hedgehoglets)
Tülku Dux *(RIP)*: Tibetan Siamese Cat: Guru & Leto's mentor - late of Lhasa Monastery, Tibet
Tytus The Baron: Barn Owl
Wapi, Hapa & Twende: Banded Mongooses, mates of Lerema and Tesho - Zoo
Wurfl: Beaver

The Howlers

Anthony: Chant's Pet; Director and Head Warden - Zoo
Bryony: Chief Warden, Small Mammals - Zoo
The Busybody: Paa's former owner

Fran: Anthony's mate, Chant's Damp Pet - Zoo
Gabriel: Arms dealer, negotiator and assassin
Geoff, Malcolm, Marcie: Wardens - Zoo
Jim Bell: Assistant Keeper - Zoo
Gertrude: Resident - Sunny Shores Nursing Home
Ida Court: Ter's step-aunt
John Bourne *(RIP)*: Ter's deceased father
The Humorous Ginger Driver: Employee - Sunny Shores Nursing Home
The Lumpy Do-Gooder: Employee - Sunny Shores Nursing Home
Maddie Court-Bourne: Ter's mother
Roger Court (The SF): Ter's stepfather
Terence Bourne (Ter): Schoolboy
Wing Commander Carl Bourne (The Wingco): Ter's grandfather
The Wishy-Washy Do-Gooder: Employee - Sunny Shores Nursing Home

APPENDIX 2

Alternative Names For Howlers

Sap, short for '**Sapiens**' (Latin for 'wise'): a label the vain species has conferred on itself. Very few individual Howlers deserve that label, even though most of them may be quite clever in all sorts of ways (which isn't the same thing as *wisdom* at all, of course). Wanyama will only use that label to refer to a Howler they *really* respect.

Ganda Tupu (pronounced 'GAHndah Toopoo'): is of African origin and means '**empty rind/shell**'. This name reflects the idea among many Wanyama that the reason most Howlers are so unpredictable and inconsistent – probably crazy, in fact – must be that they're all surface and no content - that is, empty inside, like a hollow coconut shell. That would also account for all their hullabaloo. An empty drum always makes the loudest noise.

Stults is short for '**Stultifera**', the word for 'fools' in Latin, an extinct Howler tongue. Nataka began using this label after she ran across a rather surprising German Sap called Sebastian Brandt, whose brilliant and hugely popular work "*Das Narrenschiff*" ("*The Ship of Fools*"), originally published in Germany in the Howler Calendar Year of 1494, anatomised the different varieties of foolishness he observed among Howlers His work was quickly translated into Latin under the title "*Navis Stultifera*". In 1509 it appeared in English.

Stone eaters arose from the observation that the vast majority of Howlers appear obsessed with digging up, consuming and changing stone, and then burdening their surroundings with all the different artefacts, structures and tools they can derive from it: stone rivers; stone nests and burrows (some of them in complexes that can take up whole forests' worth of space); stone-derived equipment to enhance their powers; stone hippo-like monsters to float on waters or to dive under them; strange roaring and stinking stone-derived whizz things, driven by pungent stone juice, to run around on their stone rivers and crush any Wanyama that can't get out of their way quickly enough… The list is endless.

To keep things simple, the term most commonly used in this chronicle is **Howlers**, with one of the other variations only appearing if it's genuinely warranted.

APPENDIX 3

(a) The Seasons (temperate areas)

Roaring Wolf – January, February, early March
Dancing Hare – Late March, May
Dragonflies and Gnats – June, July, early August
Fire and Fruit – Early August to early September
Bird Flight – Late September, October
Sleeping Bear – November, December

(b) Times of day and night

Sunwake (dawn)
Sunclimb (morning)
Sunhigh (noon)
Sunsink (afternoon)
Sunsleep (dusk)
Wolflight (twilight)
Batlight (deep night)

Suntime (day-time: includes Sunwake, Sunclimb, Sunhigh, Sunsink and Sunsleep)
Startime (night-time: includes Wolflight and Batlight)
Moon (~ 1 Howler Month / 28 Howler Days): the time taken for the moon to go through a whole cycle from full to full

*

© 2018 Dani F Kaye / Leo K Daniel
All Rights Reserved

NOTES & REFERENCES

[i] **Dunia:** kiSwahili for 'Earth' (pronounced **Doo -NEE-ah**)
[ii] T. S. Eliot, 'The Waste Land: The Burial Of The Dead' (1922)

[iii] Howlers call them **mobile phones.**
[iv] For the sake of clarity, **Appendix 3** contains a list of how the common Wanyama seasons relate to the Howler-designated ones in temperate regions. Howlers arbitrarily divide their seasons into periods based on the faces of the Moon, which they call months **(NB**: regional variations for the Wanyama calendar aren't given, otherwise we'd be here forever). (G)
[v] These names are pronounced with a hard 'Ch' to sound as follows: **Kissaperk-eh, Kissadov-eh**. It's said that some particularly disoriented shipwrecked Italian Howlers founded them back when they still floated around attacking one another with old-fashioned weapons like cannonballs and swords. If you ever hear anybody mention 'Kiss a dove' or 'Kiss a perch' (Howlers are particularly good at mangling foreign words), you'll know you can't be far from the Addov'vai valley.
[vi] For the record, Nataka went everywhere; there was no part of the planet she hadn't explored.
[vii] You won't go very far wrong if you think of them as the Animal equivalent of Japanese Knotweed.

[viii] All Wanyama are capable of silent communication. Howlers used to have the same skill, but they got so used to employing noises instead of feelings, smells and movements to transmit their thoughts that they've pretty much forgotten how to do it by now.

[ix] The singular of **Wanyama.**
[x] Howlers make you do such-like daft tricks at their so-called 'shows' and 'gymkhanas'.
[xi] **Showing** is what Howlers call taking people around and displaying them at different doggy or catty or horsy or piggy (etc) gatherings – see Footnote 18 - hoping they'll win prizes (which aren't even good to eat).

[xii] (This is a much –altered and abbreviated version of a powerful and ancient sub-Saharan curse, too obscure and obscene to be translated in polite society.)

[xiii] *("Good grief, that's a dorky smile you've given me," she'd said. "And since when have I ever worn clothes like that?" Leo had sniggered. "Oh, you know; we can't scandalise the neighbours too much by painting you naked. I've joggled the apple cart quite enough with some of my anatomy drawings, not to mention with one or two of my personal affairs, don't you think?")*
[xiv] *Which, as you already know from* Appendix 2, *is short for* **Sapiens** *('Wise'), don't you? 'Course you do. (T)*
[xv] *In actual fact his true name was* **Scrépfftmch!»ffftnyommenm**, *which is a magnificent badger name with a long history that reflects the moment when a badger's sharp claws uncover a particularly edible worm or root or fruit and his fangs bite into it. No translation can do it justice, though* **Scrabble!mmmffSnortMunching** *comes closer than most. However, in view of the fact that most folk can't pronounce it properly, let alone remember it, we're calling him Scrumpy for short.*
[xvi] *Tom Stoppard: 'Rosencrantz and Guildenstern are Dead'.*
[xvii] *Tom Stoppard: "Rosencrantz and Guildenstern are Dead"*
[xviii] *M'Kuu means 'leader' in KiSwahili (pronounced* **Mmh-Coo**)
[xix] **Maine Coon cats** *come equipped with all sorts of attractive long- or short-haired coats, are intelligent and playful, and love to swim. Nataka could have been any kind of cat, of course; but she liked being as big and impressive as possible, on principle. Her favourite Maine Coon Transformation, which she was wearing when Glose found her, was more like a combination of silver-black- marked MC cat and snow leopard. She was about the same size as a well-grown Springer Spaniel, and you can take my word for it that* nobody *messed with her.*
[xx] **Sunsink**: = *Afternoon. Nataka and her friends have their own terms for the times of day and night. See* **Appendix 3**.

[xxi] **Thomas Culpeper** *was a 17th Century Howler botanist, herbalist, astrologer and self-styled physician, whose writings are still published today. His ideas on the* **Humours** *are particularly amusing and entirely incorrect, but a number of his herbal remedies can occasionally be useful, provided that one takes them with a pinch of salt (pardon the pun). I recommend his* **'Herbal'** *for its entertainment value. (N)*

[xxii] ***Ad hominem fallacies*** *are errors in argument that involve attacking the person who is making a point rather than the logic of the point itself. There. Don't say I never teach you anything. (G)*
[xxiii] *Nataka knew all about the years, months and periods used in Howler calendars, of course, having sat alongside many astronomers, earth scientists and philosophers over the long period of her stay on this planet. For any Howler reading this, **A Moon** equals the time that passes from one full moon to the next. There are currently some 13 Moons in a Howler Calendar Year (there were more in the past); so 30 million Moons are roughly equivalent to 2.5 million Howler Years before the Present (if we take into account the progressively decelerating spin of the planet, as Nataka did). This coincides with the first appearance on the earth of the genus Homo, from which all Howlers are descended.*
[xxiv] *Tom Stoppard: "Rosencrantz and Guildenstern are Dead"*

[xxv] *Antoine-Laurent de Lavoisier was a particularly clear-minded French Sap who lived in the 1800s and was involved in many scientifically revolutionary developments that paved the way for modern Chemistry, Biology and Physics. One of his many great achievements was to demonstrate that, unless you remove bits of it, the mass of an object or element never changes, regardless of whether it alters its shape, temperature, appearance or size. Exciting, huh? He also did everybody a great favour by exploding the moronic myth of Phlogiston. Needless to say and true to form, a bunch of bloodthirsty, imbecilic Howlers murdered him for being too clever by half. QED.*
[xxvi] *Um. More about that later...*
[xxvii] *Friedrich Nietzsche*
[xxviii] *Wendell Berry*
[xxix] *Not that Nataka needed to eat, of course. Which made it even more enjoyable.*
[xxx] *Thus spake the Most Enlightened Siamese Guru Tülku Dux in times of yore from his gilded cushion in the windswept Tibetan fastness of Lhasa. And he should have known, because for Season after Season he kept a whole army of Tibetan Howler monks dancing to his every meow.*

[xxxi] *Mond's full name was **Mondrian des Forêts,** which if you say it quickly sounds like this: **Mondriawhdayforay**. So it's not really surprising the animals couldn't pronounce it, let alone remember*

it.

[xxxii] *For every sensible person apart from Howlers, the only logical and acceptable reason for killing anybody else (though preferably not somebody belonging to your own species) is because your survival depends on it. So if you kill somebody because you have to eat them or feed your young, that isn't Murder but Survival. And if you kill someone else to avoid being killed by them yourself, or to protect your pack or family from them, that doesn't count as Murder either. And even killing because you need to wear the coat of your prey to keep warm counts as Survival, although only Howlers do that. But if you simply kill somebody else for fun, to show off, to use them for decoration, or because they're a nuisance you could avoid some other way, those are not Survival matters and therefore the killing qualifies as Murder. Furthermore, once somebody's dead, whatever the cause, what's the point of wasting all that meat unless it's actually unsafe for some reason? You might as well Change it into yourself by eating it. It's really all very logical and moral.*

[xxxiii] *"I **can** do it! ... And I promise I won't spill anything either"*

[xxxiv] *Tytus the Baron, 'Fifty Howler Paradoxes'*

[xxxv] *"No... I still understand nothing; nothing; nothing ... Alas! Name of a name, what kind of wolf is this, then? ... No, no, no. This must definitely be another nightmare... Does not have the air (appearance) of being normal, this animal... Is it possibly a demon? Am I therefore dead and do I find myself in some kind of hell?... It is unbearable, this..."*

[xxxvi] **Midas** *was a mythical Howler king who got his wish to turn everything he touched to gold. Which he very quickly regretted when he realised that he was doomed to starve to death surrounded by golden food and drink. Well, duhhh! (T)*

[xxxvii] **Ulysses**, *also called Odysseus, was a Greek Howler hero of the Trojan War (he was responsible for that nifty trick involving the wooden horse) who spent ten years struggling to get home after the fall of Troy because he angered a Howler god or two. The story of his adventures has been told in many ways by lots of writers, but none of them beats the original legend as told by Homer in the **Odyssey**. (T)*

[xxxviii] *"By the blue"*

[xxxix] *Euripides: 'Helen'*

[xl] *Pronounced **Keh-leh-leh**, ironically enough this name means 'noise' in kiSwahili.*

[xli] *The mongooses hailed from East Africa. They had been living in the zoo for some time; long enough to organise a sophisticated secret escape route out of their enclosure, which they left regularly for adventures around the zoo and in the surrounding countryside. The Howler keepers had no idea that the mongooses only returned to the cage because they enjoyed the plentiful free food and the way Howler visitors cooed over them. They had hidden their numerous squirming kittens in a very comfortable, sandy burrow on the northern bank of a brook some distance from the zoo; a place where they could chase their tails, take dust baths and teach their young to hunt beetles (and the occasional lizard or viper) in peace. The bank was a regular suntrap during the warm seasons, ideal for burrowing. Bryony, their Howler warden, was repeatedly flummoxed to find that as soon as a mongoose kitten was born it disappeared again. Some keepers had even begun to wonder whether the adult animals might be systematically killing and eating their own infants. Nothing could have been further from the truth, of course; but the Howlers weren't to know that. The mongooses' names are pronounced **Leh-reh-mah**, **Teh-shoh**, **Wah-pee**, **Hah-Paa** and **Twen-deh**.*

[xlii] *KiSwahili: "**matter/business**" (pronounced **shah-ooh-ree**).*

[xliii] *This is an exclamation in kiTurkana. It pretty much means "blow me down!" or "Good Lord!" or "Curl me up!" It bursts out of Tesho and Lerema whenever they're particularly delighted, shocked, excited or surprised. It's pronounced gutturally: **Oy-toh-ghoy**.*

[xliv] *Nyama: the singular of Wanyama (**Nyah-mah**)*

[xlv] *(She was referring to pegs next to a desk.)*

[xlvi] *"Just like that!" and "No problem!" The brothers tend to break into different African languages when they're excited for any reason. These two phrases are in kiSwahili (pronounced **Namnah he-oh** too and **Billah shah-ooh-ree**).*

[xlvii] *An indaba (pronounced **in-dah-bah**) is kiSwahili for a meeting or conference.*

[xlviii] *KiSwahili for "Right /Good/Correct!" (Pronounced **sah-wah**)*

[xlix] *It was their river's immensely wide estuary, deep and subject to*

sudden squalls and storms.
[l] *He sure knew his classics, did Tytus. (See Shakespeare's 'King Lear' if your taste runs to extreme storm scenes).*

[li] *Robin Hobb: 'The Liveship Trader Series, Vol. 2: The Mad Ship'.*
[lii] *Margery Allingham, 'The Tiger In The Smoke'.*
[liii] ***Angelica archangelica** (also called **A. officinalis**) is a beautiful, aromatic herb that grows both domestically and in the wild in most temperate regions. Its name reflects an early Christian Howler legend that it was revealed to them by an angel who said it could cure the Bubonic Plague (it can't). Others say that its name comes from an early myth that it blooms on the feast day of the Archangel Michael (the first angel created by their god). But don't let all this fool you into thinking that the herb wasn't known, loved and used long before Howlers contracted Christianity. Every part can be employed: for medicines; confections and sweets; teas and dyes. A woodland variety, **A. sylvestris** has purple streaks and hairy stems. Every nest should have some. (G)*

[liv] ***Sir Isaac Newton** (1642 – 1727) really was a brainy Howler; so brainy that he deserves to be called a Sapiens. In fact, he is quite rightly considered* the *genius of his era. He was both a mathematician and physicist and, among lots of other achievements, demonstrated that white light is made up of all the colours of the spectrum (a property of their wavelengths), which annoyed any number of his fellow-scientists. He also discovered and named Gravity (which annoyed them even more). And to cap it all, he knew how to bear a grudge without letting it spoil his digestion, which takes some doing. This* really *drove everybody crazy. Howlers loathe successful people with good digestions.*
[lv] *Charles Kingsley, 'The Water Babies'.*
[lvi] *This was Brid's first season as a mate and father. He was inordinately proud of his new status and doing a fine job at it, although he still hadn't shed all his own infantile habits.*

[lvii] *They call it **Space-time** and are busy searching for examples of it in the universe using incredibly expensive equipment, when they could simply look under their own feet - that is, if Fagus were visible to them, of course. Tough breaks.*

527

[lviii] *Please don't go thinking that there's only one Pathway Tree. Other species of super-organism like Fagus exist all over the world, even if they may not crop up in this story (pardon the pun). This also is a good reason why Howlers really shouldn't **ever** chop down ancient and venerable specimens, just in case they happen to destroy a visible Pathway Tree).*

[lix] *A **wolf length is** a measure of distance. Opinions as to exactly what it means vary from place to place and have given rise to some rather heated disputes. In our part of the world it's based on the average length of a full-grown male wolf from the tip of his nose to the end of his extended tail. In the Nordic areas the measure is based on the stride of a running wolf, while in northern America it's based on the distance of one step taken by a walking or tracking wolf... and so on. So it's not really surprising that people frequently fall out about it, particularly when something important is being organised or discussed, like a hunt or the distance to a lair or carcass.*

[lx] *The Cat Guru Tülku Dux (he of Tibetan fame) claimed that the only Howler he had ever met who came anywhere near spotting the breathing of a tree was the Enlightened One whom other Howlers called **Gautama Buddha** (definitely a Sap, that one) and that it took **him** more than 600 Moons to achieve the feat. That, according to Tülku Dux, is the reason the Buddha sat under a Banyan tree without moving for such a long time.*

[lxi] *These ancient Saxon names mean **Creature That Goes At Night, Goblin, Evil Spirit, Enchantress, Fiend, Magic/Witch Woman**, etc.*

[lxii] *Frank Herbert, 'Dune'.*

[lxiii] *Iain M Banks, 'Against A Dark Background'*

[lxiv] *"How did you know?" in kiSwahili (pronounced **oomeh jooah nahm-nah-gah-nee?**)*

[lxv] *"There are more things in heaven and on earth, Horatio, than are dreamed of in your philosophy." (Shakespeare, 'Hamlet'; Act I Scene IV) ... Ah, the Divine Shakespeare. Now **there's** A bona fide Sapiens! (T)*

[lxvi] *"Useless/broken"; it can also be used to mean "rotten";*

kiSwahili (pronounced **boo-reh**)
lxvii *"Empty rinds"; kiSwahili (pronounced **wah-gahn-dah toopoo**)*
lxviii *"Insane"; kiSwahili (**Wah-zee-mooh**)*
lxix *Another word for "insane" or "mad"; kiSwahili (**Kee-ChAah**)*

lxx *"Friend", kiSwahili (**rah-fee-kee**)*
lxxi *Jane Austen, 'Pride And Prejudice'*
lxxii *Oddly enough, very few Howlers have ever worked out that in actual fact* they *are the pets of any animal that chooses to adopt them, and not the other way round.*

lxxiii *Having spent a long time in the Swiss Alps at one point in her career, Nataka occasionally resorts to the Helvetian vernacular when she's startled. This phrase means "Damn it, and again!" in Schwiizertuetsch, a still-surviving precursor of modern German (pronounced **Fair-dAHMMt - noh-mOW!** with the accent on the second syllable of each word).*
lxxiv *It's a great language for imprecations, Cat. Take my word for it.*

lxxv *French: "**A clap of thunder**"*
lxxvi *Don't ask.*

lxxvii **"Then stepped forth One, in appearance like the starry night."** *Friedrich Schiller, 'Die Räuber' ('The Robbers')*
lxxviii *What Howlers call a **window**, of course.*
lxxix *Shut up! (kiSwahili) (**Nyah-mah-seh-neeh**)*
lxxx *That white stone stuff is called **concrete** and sets as hard as the Howlers' horrible stone rivers. So it isn't surprising that the otter and beaver were stymied.*
lxxxi *"First you will come to the Sirens who enchant all who come near them. If any one unwarily draws in too close and hears the singing of the Sirens, his wife and children will never welcome him home again, for they sit in a green field and warble him to death with the sweetness of their song." (Homer, Odyssey Book XII, translated by Samuel Butler)*
lxxxii *Euripides, 'The Trojan Women'*
lxxxiii *Expletives deleted. There were lots of them.*
lxxxiv *Euripides, 'Ion'*
lxxxv *French: **Love at first sight** (literally, 'lightning strike')*
lxxxvi *This is a common and extensively demonstrated psychological phenomenon called the* halo effect. *Beauty is mistaken for*

529

goodness and truth, and biases individuals in favour of good-looking individuals. So if you ever have to fight a legal dispute with anybody, make sure to hire a gorgeous lawyer.

[lxxxvii] ***Potz Donner!*** *= 'Pop Thunder!' – another exclamation in vernacular Schwiizertuetsch. Pronounce it exactly as it's written, and enjoy.*

[lxxxviii] *'Working out' is what modern Howlers – usually adult ones – call going into special nests and caves to spend time doing completely unproductive things like heaving oddly-shaped objects about or jumping around on weird artefacts that don't take them anywhere, instead of hunting or foraging or planting or constructing things. It's a particularly confusing term because most of this activity doesn't happen outside at all. So why don't they call it 'working in' instead? (G)*

[lxxxix] *Latin:* ***'A healthy mind in a healthy body'.*** *This brilliant motto appears in the work of the satirical Roman poet Juvenal (2nd Century AD). Smart, those Roman Saps… well, OK, maybe not so smart, considering that they got such a kick from chopping one another into fish food for sport. (T)*

[xc] *She was spot on. The rather clever Sap cardiologists* ***Friedman and Rosenman*** *(1974) conducted an entertaining and informative (if ethically rather questionable) long-term study that involved deliberately annoying different Howlers to see how they reacted, categorising their reactions into personality types, and then tracking the medical conditions they developed over time. They found a link between the Choleric (A) personality type and a heightened risk of heart disease. Later studies have consistently supported the proposal that health is closely related to temperament, as well as to the manner in which different Howlers respond to stress. Which is all rather a feather in the cap of our old mate Juvenal.*

[xci] *T. S. Eliot, 'The Cocktail Party'*

[xcii] *Euripides, 'Andromache'*

[xciii] *His real name was Carl Bourne. But, because long ago he'd been a Wing Commander in the British Fleet Air Arm, everybody called him The Wingco.*

[xciv] ***Mickey Free*** *(b. 1848 or 1851; d. 1913 or 1915), whose real name was Felix Telles, was an Apache Indian scout and bounty hunter on the American frontier. He was kidnapped by Apaches as a child and raised as one of them, and he became a warrior when*

he was still a child, before going on to serve as a scout at Fort Verde between December 1874 and May 1878. (And yes: this is historical fact, not fiction. As most of these notes are. Go ahead; look it up if you want. (G)
[xcv] *Helmuth von Moltke (19th Century German Field Marshall)*
[xcvi] **Le Mans** *is a* kichaa *stone river in France, constructed to fetch up where it began without going anywhere. Howlers with a passion for racing one another in Stinking Whizz Things roar round it over and over and over again, for the whole of one Suntime and one Startime. The first* wazimu *Howler to get to the finish line wins an inedible prize. This is considered great entertainment and a fine test of Howler strength and endurance and so forth. But all they really achieve with this mindless roaring around is noise, unnecessary poisoning of the atmosphere, and occasional injury or death. (G)*
[xcvii] *You simply can't go chasing cats up stairs without cheering up, no matter how miserable you may feel.*

[xcviii] *Elspeth Huxley, "The Mottled Lizard"*
[xcix] *This part of Ter's account took a lot of explaining because Rav'n simply couldn't wrap his furry brain around the idea of a church, let alone Hell, vicars, pulpits and so on, and asked dozens of questions in his efforts to figure it all out. Ter got into quite a tangle trying to tackle all his questions, till in the end Nataka had to tell the grey cat to shut up, otherwise the story would never get finished.*
[c] *Which is all right, because killing to eat is survival, remember? ... Yeah. 'Course you do.*
[ci] **Fitina** *= underhand dealings, manipulations or shenanigans. Yet another good kiSwahili term (pronounced:* **Fee-tEE-nah,** *keeping the vowels short and sharp.*
[cii] *Not that it makes any difference to this story, of course, but it just so happens that at that very moment a goose taking a short cut through a graveyard to her favourite pond waddled over the precise empty plot that the old codger would end up occupying, having spent a few more seasons peacefully vegetating among the Sunny Shores antimacassars, bingo sessions and daytime telly.*

[ciii] *Elspeth Huxley, 'The Mottled Lizard'*
[civ] *Howlers of a certain mentality are obsessed with the 'purity' of a person's blood, and may even get to using bits of dead material*

to prove who had sex with whom, and so forth, till one of their owners (whom they always confuse for pets) were born. They call these bits of useless parchment **pedigrees**, and never seem to remember the uncomfortable truth that folk with the purest pedigrees, regardless of whether they're Howlers or Wanyama, are also much more likely than anybody else to inherit all sorts of nasty medical disorders from their narrowly selected breeding. In fact there's nothing better for an animal's fitness than diversity, with lots and lots of different breeds getting together and making puppies. What Howlers call 'mutts' or 'mongrels' are the fittest of all dogs. Calls the bluff on all this 'racial purity' nonsense too many of them use as an excuse to torment one another, doesn't it?

[cv] *Yet another Howler fantasy, these 'miracles' and 'angels'. I suggest you look them up; they're quite amusing. (N)*

[cvi] *George Bernard Shaw: "Heartbreak House"*

[cvii] *Tytus is being pedantic. He says that* tendencies *and* instincts *are pretty much the same thing. I don't give one of his hoots. This is* my *monograph.*

[cviii] *Unless you have the good fortune to enjoy it,* Contentment *is very difficult to imagine or name, let alone to achieve. Most Howlers struggle with it. They've chopped down and flayed countless trees and Wanyama, and turned them into parchment on which to pour out their thoughts about how to catch it. They would do better if they just watched any Nyama simply going about its life without fussing about whether it's really happy or fulfilled, or other suchlike guff. If they did, they might just realise that the more you chase after Contentment, the less likely you are to capture it.*

[cix] *Better tell them what a Halcyon is. I'll wager not one in a thousand of your readers will know. (T).* You *do it then, Squash-Mush. I can't be bothered (G). Manners, Tar-Face. *Ahem*: The Halcyon was a mythical bird that, many Howlers believed, nested on the ocean and had the magical power to calm storms and promote perfect weather. (T)*

[cx] *Let me hasten to assure you, lest you be entirely disheartened, that not all the writing Howlers do on their parchments and other materials* is *useless. There are great thinkers and scholars in their number, as Nataka has already shown. She calls them Saps. And many of their best thoughts have also been recorded. That this same species, capable of such greatness and wisdom, mainly consists of selfish, thoughtless, destructive and worthless*

individuals only deepens the whole conundrum for us Wanyama.

[cxi] *Howlers don't lay eggs (T.) Tough. I categorically refuse even to contemplate the messy alternative (G.)*

[cxii] *I myself have never seen this 'packet' so many Howlers talk about. I surmise that it's some kind of special egg that can only be laid under very specific circumstances.*

[cxiii] **Funerals:** *the rituals Howlers use after one of them dies. Believe it or not, these involve either burning or burying the person who's dead, after shovelling him or her into a solid wooden cage. None of which I understand, because they're* dead, *right? It's not as if they would be able to escape or anything, is it? So why the solid cage? Why the burning or burying? ... Well anyway. Addled as it sounds, you'll just have to take my word for it that they dispose of their dead like that, wasting plenty of valuable nutrition in the process. The only species to benefit from such behaviour are worms and plants. I ask you, how illogical is that? What in the name of a tattered nest are they trying to achieve with it?*

[cxiv] *This* manhood *is yet another Howler artefact I've never managed to catch sight of, despite much painstaking research. Nataka says it's got something to do with a Howler's notions of virility or sexual potency, which I take to mean the size of their genitals... And this in turn suggests, does it not, that the size of a Howler's genitals may be related to that mythical 'packet' I've already mentioned. But is it? Constructive insights are invited.*

[cxv] *Glose has clearly been scrabbling through my Bowlby again. I thought* there were fresh claw marks all over my books. (N) *Hardly surprising. John Bowlby's ground-breaking* **Attachment Theory,** *which began with his discussion of maternal deprivation in the Howler Year 1953, is still the most authoritative study of the influence of parenting styles on a fledgling's overall development *preen*. (G)*

[cxvi] *All this is mere speculation. You can't* know *any of it (T). Actually, Mr Smarty-Claws, I had it from Nataka, who looked into his mind for me. So nuhh. One more comment like that, and you can write this thing yourself (G.) Cool it, minions (N.)*

[cxvii] **Arms** *are the things Howlers use to hurt and kill one another. They're noisy, sharp and can kill at a distance or close up. Not only that, they tend to be very noisy. And wherever they are they*

terrify the Wanyama. They also cost a lot of money. Howlers love them, (unless they happen to be the ones getting hurt and killed by them, of course). **Arms deals** involve spending and receiving money to buy arms or to make them for someone else. It's one of Howlers' favourite games, second only to the various **wars** (games in which they use their arms). Unlike normal people, Howlers hardly ever rely on their own claws, beaks or fangs to do their killing and maiming.
[cxviii] *You've been eavesdropping again. Naughty. (T).* Not eavesdropping; data gathering. (G)
[cxix] *Leave me out of this. (T).*
[cxx] The Howlers and other animals in the various nest complexes on which the results of Roger's efforts landed certainly would not have agreed with his definition of successful. Incidentally, have you noticed how nobody who isn't a Howler ever gets mentioned when that lot try to work out who has been benefited and who has been hurt in one of their kichaa wars?

[cxxi] *I must confess that this account makes me feel rather sorry for that poor Howler. He strikes me as having suffered deeply throughout his fledgling season, which is why he was compelled to make others suffer in turn. He knew no other way. Like Orestes, whose mother murdered his father Agamemnon and who then destroyed her. He was damaged, too. (T).* Well, you're welcome to your feelings, Owl. As far as I'm concerned he was about as kind and loving as a scalded scorpion. (G.)
[cxxii] **Sigh*. If you don't know about these things I'm afraid you'll have to pay attention, because this is seriously boring but important. I'll try to keep it simple.* An **insurance policy** is a complicated bit of parchment on which Howlers write the promises made by everybody involved about how much money, and how often, one of them must pay to another Howler (or group of Howlers) to guarantee that if s/he dies or has an accident or any other problem suddenly comes up, the Howlers who've been collecting money from them will give them back a sum of money to help. This is called a **payout.** You with me so far? Good.
Most things can be insured. For instance, one Howler, a musician by trade, had his claws insured in case he couldn't use them to play music any longer. Another Howler who danced, had her tail-end insured, not because it produced particularly fertile guano or anything useful like that, but because she was afraid that

it would become wrinkled and baggy, and then everybody would stop giving her money for wagging it at them (which other Howlers enjoyed. They liked to watch her wagging her tail end. I'll just leave that thought here for you to digest). And lots of Howlers pay to insure their own lives, so that when they die, their nest-mates will receive money. (I know; it sounds impossible; but if you just begin with the premise that all Howlers are kichaa, it becomes a bit easier to understand. Told you, didn't I? Everything in Howler life revolves around money.) So anyway: if you have one of those policies, the longer you keep putting money into it and don't claim any back, the bigger the final payout becomes.

cxxiii A good kiSwahili slang word, this. It means 'blatted' or 'messed up' or 'taken apart', or indeed, something rather more rude (pronounced **Nyoh – roh – shuh'd**).

cxxiv Forget it. I'm not going to explain this one. You're on your own.

cxxv ... Or this.

cxxvi Guess what. *Snigger*. (Tytus and M'Kuu say I'm being mean; but I'm fed up with writing all these blasted notes about idiotic Howler money blabla. And besides, I don't see either of them *doing it*. (G).

cxxvii On one occasion, when I was sitting in a convenient tree listening to him, I heard the Wingco call this money his nest-egg. But don't be fooled by that term: there was no nest and no egg. I looked very carefully. All I ever saw was the Wingco showing Maddie a piece of parchment with writing on it. This is yet another example of the misleading way Howlers talk to one another. No wonder so many of them are half out of their wits with confusion and annoyance.

cxxviii I thought you'd like to see how Glose writes, so I've left his signature unaltered. (Ed.)

cxxix R. D. Laing

cxxx *"True"* (pronounced **Kweh – lee**)

cxxxi **Kidole** is one of Lerema and Hapa's kittens. He's a mischievous little tike, sticking his nose and paws everywhere he shouldn't. Hence his name, which means 'finger' in kiSwahili (pronounced **keeh-doh-leh**).

cxxxii Another name for Howler: 'empty rind' in kiSwahili (see

Appendix 2)
cxxxiii *W. Shakespeare, 'Hamlet'*
cxxxiv *Laurie Hernandez*
cxxxv *'Brother' (pronounced **ndoo-goo**)*
cxxxvi *'But' in – yes, you've guessed it – kiSwahili. (And yes, I know it's a redundant word, but you'd be surprised at how many people combine the English and kiSwahili words to make this phrase. (Pronounced **lah-kee-nee**).*
cxxxvii *This means 'watch out' or 'be careful'. (Pronounced **choong-gah**). I'm sure you'll have grasped by now that kiSwahili always involves straightforward phonetic spelling and pronunciation. Yes?... No?... Yes? (Aw, come on!)*

cxxxviii *From all of this you've obviously gathered that, after a few Sun- and Startimes of grieving, Chant had come to terms with the loss of her littermate Leto and reverted to her normal behaviour, which can best be described as a combination of bullying and cajoling. The iron claw in the velvet paw, if you like. All of which, of course, her Howler Pets Anthony and Fran knew all too well.*
cxxxix *"All right, let's go!" (pronounced '**Hi-yah, twen – deh**')*
cxl *Kidole's siblings were called **Yain, Tain, Tether, Mether, Mumph, Jiggit** and **Dix**.*
cxli *Sardo's name is misleading and a bit of a joke, of course, since Roloways aren't Rhesus monkeys. But he rather enjoys it. His motto is 'Let confusion thrive!'*
cxlii *"Shut up!"* **(Nyah – mah – seh - nih)**
cxliii *"Help! / No!" (**Sah-eeh-dee-eh-nee!/ Hah-pah-nah!**). ... You know the rest already.*

cxliv *"Children"* **(Wah-toh-toh)**
cxlv *Edwin Muir, "The Confirmation'*
cxlvi *"It's truly marvellous"*

cxlvii *Shikamo : "Greetings" in kiSambaa:* **(Ssh-kahm-oh)**
cxlviii *This Greek name is pronounced **Ell – pee – THÉH - ah** (with the stress on the third syllable and a very soft 'th'). It's the female variant of the male 'Elpidios' (**Ell - pee – thee – oss**).*
cxlix *This was Fyrd's nickname for his extremely efficient mate. Alas, her true name is not recorded.*
cl *"Greetings!" (Latin)*
cli *Hermes was the messenger of the gods in Greek mythology (his*

*Roman counterpart was Mercury). Yeah, that's right. Those all-powerful, immortal entities who, Tytus tells me, could shake the planet, make lightning and storms and plagues, start wars, send droughts and winter… in short, who could pretty comprehensively mess up life on the planet, needed a **messenger** to pass information to one another. Go figure. (G). That'll do. (N).*

clii *"Farewell, everybody!" (Latin)*
cliii *Kwaheri! = Good bye!* **(Kwah – heh- ree)**

cliv *William Shakespeare, 'King John'*
clv *William Shakespeare, 'Hamlet'*
clvi *'On the contrary'*
clvii *We mustn't be too hard on Glose. He really did believe that he was Nataka's mentor, poor deluded feather -brain. (T) Oy! (G)*
clviii *W. H. Auden, 'Anthem for St Cecilia's Day'*
clix *Euripides, 'Andromache'*

clx *Code of Hammurabi.*
clxi *What, did you honestly believe that a little boy armed only with a knife could have overcome a professional assassin with a gun? Seriously? ... Oh,* come on!
clxii *William Wordsworth, 'Ode: Intimations of Immortality from Recollections of Early Childhood'*

clxiii *Sap myths of Ancient Greece tell of* **Charon**, *the boatman who ferried the souls of those who had died across the rivers* Styx *and* Acheron *to* Hades, *the domain of the Dead. The two rivers encircled and separated it from the realm of the Living. (T)*
clxiv *Which, as I'm sure you remember, means "**let's go**" in kiSwahili.*

clxv *Frank Herbert, 'Dune'*
clxvi *Maori: 'Worlds Separated' (pronounced* **Papa-too-ah-noo-koo**)
clxvii *Maori: 'Rainbow' (pronounced* **Rahn-ghee**). *It's a fascinating coincidence that this exact same word also means 'Colour' in kiSwahili.*
clxviii *KiSwahili: 'Heart of the World' (Pronounced* **Rho-hoh lah Doo–NEE- ah**)
clxix *Edward Thomas, 'The Glory'*

clxx William Wordsworth, 'Ode: Intimations of Immortality from Recollections of Early Childhood'
clxxi **Archimedes of Syracuse** *(c 287-212 BC)was a thoroughgoing genius, whose contributions to mathematics and physics are recognised to this day. But just because he failed to get out of the way of a Roman soldier invading Syracuse (look, he was very busy studying a formula he'd sketched in the sand and really couldn't have been expected to pay any attention to such trivia as an invasion), a Roman soldier killed him out of hand. Just like that. Nice, not.* **Nicolaus Copernicus** *(1473-1543) dared to think independently from the Catholic Church (a particularly powerful Howler sect, still going strong today), proposing that* Dunia *revolves around the Sun, instead of vice-versa (the Heliocentric Model). The church leaders condemned his work as heretical because it contradicted and undermined their arrogant assertion that Howlers and the planet on which they lived had been created by their god to be the centre of the universe (forsooth!) Luckily, Copernicus had already entered his final Change when they did that; otherwise they'd have ceremoniously and reverently tortured and burnt him to death for daring to think clearly. (N)*
clxxii **The Garden of Eden:** *For that particular bit of far-fetched Howler fantasy you'll have to consult a huge collection of fairy stories they call The Bible. But you'll need plenty of stamina; it takes a LOT of wading through.*
clxxiii William Shakespeare, 'Love's Labour's Lost'
clxxiv *Good ole Baron. Still making with the classical references. (N)*
clxxv Samuel Pepys, 'Diaries'.
clxxvi *My perfect immortal friend!*
clxxvii Tom Stoppard, 'Travesties'
clxxviii *Goes on a bit, doesn't he? (Ed)*

*

© 2018 Dani F Kaye / Leo K Daniel
All Rights Reserved

Printed in Great Britain
by Amazon